THE STAFF

Ron Samul

First Edition Winter 2019

Book Cover Designed by Cynthia Samul

ISBN 978-0-578-40680-0

A Divine Image
Cruelty has a Human Heart,
And Jealousy a Human Face;
Terror the Human Form Divine,
And Secrecy the Human Dress.

The Human Dress is forged Iron,
The Human Form is fiery Forged,
The Human Face a Furnace seal'd,
The Human Heart its hungry Gorge.

William Blake

Cain's scarred and stitched forehead had finally stopped bleeding. In a state of oblivion, his young face and his empty mind concealed the crime. Four men gathered over his unconscious body. The last few shafts of afternoon sunlight faded from his head and chest as dusk drew on. The musty rooms of the doctor's cottage smelled of camphor and rotting cloth. A few blood-stained stitching needles and some tattered muslin were tossed between burnt matches and a Bible on the table next to the bed. Spots of blood on muslin spilled off the table - decoration for a room filled with worried faces.

Reverend Conrad and three council members — Emmit, Langston, and Jarod — stood over Cain like they were in solemn prayer. Then, they spoke softly in worried whispers. Each council member had a distinct political voice. Some spoke out for the better of the village and their lives. They read the law and administered it to the letter. Others used their voice to leverage whatever they could snatch up. They saw the law in a distortion of personal advantages and manipulative possibilities. These men used the council for the better part of self-indulgence. Over the last twenty years, the law and the collection of the tax money had caused a simmering rift in the council between the corrupt council men and the village conscious. And now, this darkness. Murder. It was on the faces of the councilors, some concerned, some afraid, and some just angry.

Dr. Keller, an old tired looking fellow came in checking the gloomy faces of the village statesmen. They had stopped their debate to give the doctor their undivided attention. The doctor was a man of firm mental dexterity. He was brilliant at curing sickness with pastes and elixirs, quelling fever with ice and boiling water; infection wrapped with tight, wet bandages; but village life had taken a physical toll on him. His bony frame was stiff and brittle like a dead, fallen branch ready to snap. He constantly rubbed his arthritic elbow and arm, rubbing away the aching pain. The human body was meant to degenerate and he accepted his decline with a stern pride. The sad fact was that no one was in a position to take over when the doctor couldn't carry on. He had no apprentice or children to pass on his medical knowledge, and it weighed heavily on the minds of the villagers. They were predisposed to dwindle and fail.

Dr. Keller looked grimly at the body on the bed, seeing beyond the battered flesh and into the heart of this dark matter of murder.

Emmit, the council leader, stood in disbelief. It had happened so quickly — suddenly. He waited nervously for the doctor's report. Dr. Keller took off his glasses and rubbed his bloodshot eyes. The doctor forced the words from his rough throat, "He is not dead. He will live."

Emmit fiddled with the cuffs on his jacket. The fabric

was wearing out where the elbows bent around his thick, bulging arms. He was a bull of a man with a dim stately air, and strength that came from his bulk. He jerked up his head and said, "The council must meet."

Langston, a skinny man with a nose that resembled a beak, sighed. His hollow black eyes and balding head made him seem like he was waiting for something miserable to strike him down. The liver spots on his forehead seemed to grow little by little, month by month. His hunched over posture was permanent.

"A lottery, Emmit. If he wakes, we must have someone chosen and prepared," Langston said.

Emmit agreed; it was the way of the village. Jarod, a bit younger, feared the lottery. He had a daughter at home. He looked at the body on the bed and turned his mouth down in disgust. "He cannot survive. It won't be proper if he lives. It would mean a life sentence. Something must be done. We must stop this."

Emmit looked at him accusingly, "No harm will come to this man. We must follow the law. While no one can forgive this murderer, we cannot condemn him to death. No one actually saw this man commit murder. It would be wrong to hang him with such doubt. If he lives — then he must be judged by our laws."

"And he lives," Dr. Keller added.

The Reverend nodded in somber agreement. "We don't even know his origin. Did he come from the heavens, or from the teeth of a darker place?"

Emmit grew agitated.

Jarod tightened his lips, "You wouldn't know what it's

like to go through the lottery. You do not have a daughter with her name in the barrel." He glared to the Reverend, "God help us all."

The Reverend nodded and whispered, "God will help us all."

Jarod stormed out of the room, slamming the door behind him.

Emmit and Langston didn't react to Jarod's temper. "Let us know when he wakes, Dr. Keller."

The seagulls swooped down from the rooftops, crying out and searching for their last meal before dark. They circled the vast courtyard and the rickety piers. All the village fishing boats were tied up, while the ocean surged and rocked them gently back and forth into evening slumber. The sound of ropes rubbing against cleats sounded out as the current pushed and pulled at the hulls. Fishermen stowed their gear and hurried to get home to dinner and a warm hearth. The open ocean chilled their bones. Their sails were furled and their small catches were already sold for meager wages or in wrapped bundles to take home.

Old Kavner, the oldest fisherman in the village, walked across the open market area paved in cobblestones. This was the only paved place in the entire village and because of that fact, it was considered the center of the hamlet. The courtyard was surrounded by warehouse sheds, the blacksmith's shop, the cobbler's stall, and wooden cradles for wintering the fleet. The vast courtyard had seen years of festivals and holiday celebrations. The old fisherman had a sharp memory and often told stories that fell on the deaf ears of the younger generations. He remembered setting foot upon the cobblestone landing for the first time — afraid for his life. To most of the people in the village, that was all ancient history. And like his age, his memories extended over a vast amount of time, smoothing over the pain like tumbled rocks upon the shore.

The old fisherman walked to the top of the wooden steps that were attached to the front of a warehouse. He pushed open the door and stepped inside. In the dark room of the small supply shop, a woman sat running thread through a piece of cloth.

"Sophia, where is everyone?" the fisherman greeted her. "It's like winter has come and everyone is huddled in their homes. I wanted to see your father."

Raising her head to the old man, her auburn hair fell around her face, "He is at the meeting hall. Tonight they are gathering, the fate of the assassin must be advanced."

"Your father knew James Colberton well — they served on the council together. They were like brothers. His murder is a terrible loss."

"Yes, they were close friends," Sophia said. "He has been with Mrs. Colberton all day. They are all at the council meeting now."

"Do you think it will come to a lottery?" he said knowing the clandestine nature of the word. Sophia looked at the clock.

"Perhaps."

"Why don't you go and see what is being decided. I'll mind the store for a while," he said adamantly. She noticed

5

the sun had faded outside of her window.

"Very well, I shall return as soon as someone is chosen," she rose and plucked her cape from a hook by the door. "I won't be long," she said hurrying out.

The old man smiled, "I will be here."

As an unmarried woman, Sophia worried about the lottery and being selected as warden. Like a snowstorm ached his joints days before it came, Old Kavner could feel the ache of desperate times ahead. He settled into a chair near the fire and whistled a worried tune to pass the time.

The church stood on the outskirts of the village atop the hill. It faced to the east where the wind often came sweeping down from the mountains. The great mountain range isolated this small hamlet from the rest of the world, like God had folded up the earth with a pinch of the fingers, making passage back impassible.

The church overlooked the mountain range as a spire of worship on the edge of the world. Next to it was a cemetery where all the village dead were buried — craggy field stones marking each grave. Everyone had a hand in the upkeep of the church. It was their united cause. Everyone worked in some way to preserve the church — keeping the white clapboard facade free from the tarnishing of wear and weather. Attached to the church was a large hall where the village convened every week for council meetings. It was also the concert hall and the banquet room. The cavernous meeting hall made praying to God seem secondary to the villagers desire to gather and socialize.

This meeting, however, was different. Most of the village assembled inside the hall. Eight members of the council sat behind a large table made by the woodcrafters as a gift for the dedication of the hall years ago. They sat waiting for the villagers to settle into the rows of stiff straight benches. Stern faces loomed down over the crowd. The widow, Mrs. Colberton, sat in the front, her face streaked with tears.

At most of the council meetings things were discussed that seemed of little relevance to all. Grievances were brought up that concerned just a handful of people, so not everyone needed to attend. Villagers would settle land disputes or small claims of missing property. Every property transaction, dispute, or change went through the council, and their decision was final —right or wrong. On the end of the council bench was an empty seat, where James Colberton use to sit. His absence was noticed by all. Now, with eight council members, it would be difficult to preside and govern without deadlock votes.

The meeting began with three sharp blows of a gavel. Emmit stood and waited for everyone to quiet down. Only a few times had the entire village gathered in Emmit's fifty-six years. It made him uneasy to be in judgment of every one, all at once. Because of the lottery, the hall was filled to over flowing. He brought up his large hands that shuffled the debts and voucher-notes all day in his office. He gazed down at the table and waited until it was silent. Nervous women sat in desperate worry, waiting for word of the lottery.

"Because of the nature of this meeting, we have most of

the village here. I would suggest we get this over with quickly so we don't have to crowd into this hall all night," he said with a deep, booming voice.

In the back, Sophia slipped in quietly and sat down on the nearest bench. She took off her cape and laid it across her lap. Out of breath, she asked the people around her what she had missed.

Emmit paused and looked around him, not just at the faces, but at the large posts that rose above the crowd, holding up the open rafter roof above. He didn't want to look at a particular face. He began.

"Before we get to the matter at hand — I would like to mention the absence of James Colberton who was murdered yesterday. May he rest in peace."

Everyone sighed an "amen" and looked down to the stone floor.

"We are here to discuss the crime that has occurred of which we all know. But for the minutes of this council, I shall recount the current situation."

Everyone listened pensively as a piece of paper was handed to him.

"Yesterday morning in the hour of seven o'clock, on September eighth, 1819, a man came to this village and sought out Sir James Colberton. This man entered Colberton's home and cut his throat. After murdering Colberton, he fled on foot, back to the pier. When Alice Colberton found her husband dead, she ran out and saw the fleeing stranger. Alice Colberton rushed down the street chasing her husband's assassin. With the help of eight fishermen, they managed to wrestle him down and flog him with sticks and rocks. We believe his plan was to escape by way of a fishing boat."

Emmit paused to ponder the situation rather than reading from his parchment as he had done earlier — alone in his office. Holding the village upon his every word, using a pensive pause was part of his public theatrical presence.

"According to Dr. Keller, this man who we have named Cain, will survive his thrashing. He will be judged upon as guilty."

The mumble of the crowd seemed to imply that he deserved what was coming. They spoke quietly. The killer's sentence of lynching was apparent.

"However, we will not hang this man for his crime," he proclaimed. The silence lingered for a moment, then a clamor of confusion roared from the crowd.

Jarod stood and asked everyone to be calm. His face was worried. The crowd was riotous. Emmit allowed Jarod to speak, "We cannot hang this man! There is doubt in his case. He had no weapon, and nobody saw him actually commit the crime."

A man from the village rose and yelled, "He is a stranger to everyone in the village — he had to be the killer. He is not one of us; he doesn't follow our laws."

"Then banish him, and be done with talk of a lottery," said a farmer.

A woman rose, "There must be a lottery! If one must serve, then we all must serve."

The meeting was getting unruly.

Emmit rose while Jarod sat down, "Enough! There must be a lottery. His punishment is like any crime. The law is

written for us to follow and so we shall! We can't succumb
to the same heinous act of murder with more killing. We
have had eleven previous wardens take custody of the
condemned. All of the condemned were reformed, released
from their wardens, and went on with their lives. We know
who the criminals were; we know who the wardens were.
They have served with the will of God and sacrificed for
Him in the name of everyone else in this village. We know
of their sacrifice. But, understand that this man has been
accused of murder and his sentence is like none we have
faced before. The warden, as written, shall take custody of
this condemned man for his entire sentence — a life
sentence."

The villagers all broke out into a riot of questions and
gasps. How could they protect their eligible daughters and
widowed mothers from this lottery? The magnitude of this
lifelong purgatory that this lottery would inflict was hard for
anyone to bear. It would be worse than the crime, worse
than the criminal's existence, because of the purely random
chance of ruining a family. To be placed into this
guardianship was the end of freedom. Tonight, one life
would change forever.

Emmit continued, "This is the first life-time sentence we
have imposed upon a criminal. But we must not break our
own laws to suit this one criminal. We mustn't let all the
wardens of the past be tossed aside while we abolish our
system. We compel this criminal to realize that his crime
will be the punishment of others, for a prolonged period of
time. This is how it is written and this is how it will be
viewed in the eyes of this council. Hillmond Wenner is

present to consult the chosen and prepare her to receive the staff."

Langston brought out the barrel. He opened the lid and placed it on the table next to Emmit.

Emmit spoke without his stoic rhetoric, "For the minutes, this lottery will be held to select the warden of Cain, the named assassin. The selected warden will acknowledge the task set before her and uphold the duties that she is selected to enforce the laws established by this village and its charter. Those failing to do so will face a penalty to be determined by this council — no less than beating, no more than death."

He reached into the barrel and pulled out a tile card. He knew not to wait, but he paused to read the name to himself. It was desperately quiet.

"The name is Taska Valimar."

Sighs filled the room.

The shifting of people searching for the chosen filled the hall with a low murmur.

Taska Valimar rose from her seat in the rear of the hall. The villagers regarded her with pity and sadness. Deep within Taska's being, she tried to recall her faith, her honor and composure that was ripped out of her with a sudden sweep of one man's voice. Taska Valimar stood and looked to Emmit on the podium and tried to comprehend her service to God, her eyes blank with abandonment.

Every woman in the village was told serving as warden to the condemned was a very noble and honorable act. Most of the women who served prior to this tragic crime served for a few years. Some worked through their time without incident, while others took it very hard. Everyone made it through; however, no one ever had to face a life sentence. Taska Valimar was twenty-three years old and unmarried. She was considered eligible for the lottery like the other one hundred twelve women of the village. The charter, created by the original council, stated that warden take possession of a criminal and use him as a servant or slave. While the men worked in the fields or on the fishing fleet, the women in the village could use the prisoners to help them in their domestic routines, labor, or any other hardship they could imagine. At age eighteen, Taska Valimar was taught about her potential duties as a warden along with other girls her age. It was the highest honor to fulfill. The staff master, Hillmond Wenner, taught the girls of control and defense against the prisoners. After serving a term with a prisoner, it was common to celebrate a warden's freedom. In a public ceremony before the council, the staff was presented to the warden with great honor. These were people who served with a vision of the future, knowing that after seven years, eight years, and the longest-term, eleven years, there would be a better life to live. But for Taska Valimar, she faced the end of her life, without affirmation, all for the sake of an unknown criminal.

After the meeting, Taska had to listen to condolences from villagers she didn't know. She was consoled by her close friend Sophia, but it didn't matter — her life changed forever. Hillmond Wenner, the staff administrator took Taska aside and consulted with her about her duty — but

Taska heard little of what was said. When she tried to convince herself that her selection at the lottery would somehow be justified before God, she was always brought back to the horror of this civil matrimony. She returned to her small house alone. She sat weeping next to the fireplace. She tried to pray and ask God for a sign, but nothing came to her. She asked for answers and wept for a few hours, finding it difficult to pray through her tears. Just when she felt like she could overcome her emotions and go on, she would snap and the great anxiety of her plight would pour over her like ocean waves pounding at her soul.

Jarod knocked on her door. She managed to wipe away the tears and compose herself. It was unusual for anyone to come to her remote cottage. Everyone knew where Taska Valimar lived, but no one came, with the exception of Sophia. It didn't bother her to live in the blurry world of her mind away from the entire civilized world. Isolation was a tranquil escape. She liked to think of distant thoughts and reflect upon words and ideas that came to her while she did her chores. Village life made her uneasy. Social mannerisms and constant gossip of the village brought on an unknown misery, cluttering her thoughts. Everyone in the village spoke to her through an invisible curtain that no villager came out from behind. They would say a pleasant greeting or speak briefly to her, but they would never allow Taska into their intimacies, into their problems or their secrets. Taska stayed away from the village. Alone, she could manage her gardens and her small field. Alone she could take in wood, cook, and see the world clearly. If she needed something, she could always walk into the village.

Taska was thin and possessed a natural beauty that was construed as brazen and wicked. Everything she knew about being a woman was an emulation of how she recalled her childhood memories of her missing mother. Taska had pitch black hair, eyes a rich, warm brown and a slender, courtly face, like that of an illustrated angel from the church Bible depicting a spirit floating into heaven. Her skin was smooth and flushed with color. Her build was strong and healthy from cutting wood, hauling water, and hand-plowing her garden.

Jarod knocked a second time. This made her angry, "Why can't I be left alone?"

She stood, lifted the hem of her dress from the floor and went to the door. A cold fear came across her chest and up through her neck as she turned the door latch. Each motion, each pondered thought, each spoken word, brought her unwanted prisoner closer.

The door fell open and Jarod waited impatiently. His eyes were dim and his face turned down to his dirt-covered boots. His horse was tied to a nearby fence post. He was alone. She let the door fall open and he followed her in.

"Miss Valimar, I have been asked to come and speak to you. I know it is late, but these matters need to be dealt with quickly. The council would like to explain a few things. I suppose there are things that are not ... publicly known."

He walked to the table where Taska ate her meals and worked at her sewing. Jarod's eyes moved around her cottage and stopped at her pressed rose in a frame on the wall. He moved closer to look at it. He was a tall, bony man who smelled of sweat and wood shavings all the time. His gray hair was always mixed up in a fray of tangles and twists. His legs bowed outward from the knee to the ankle.

Her patience was wearing thin, "What is it Jarod?"

"No warden has ever received a sentence for life. This man must be condemned for life. I realize this is a great burden, but the council wants to make it perfectly clear to you, that... after a certain period, what might seem appropriate, should the condemned become accidentally... injured beyond the repair of the doctor... no questions will be asked."

Taska glared at him quickly, "You are suggesting... "

"No, I am not suggesting anything. It is something to be understood, between the council and the warden."

She nodded. That was all she could do. She wasn't going to be honored for serving as warden, but as executioner. She tried to imagine killing someone a few weeks after she had known them. The horror of such a scheme illuminated a darkness never before explored in her heart. Killing a stranger out of rage or impulse was killing. Killing a man that she took care of, spoke with, and even tried to understand – that would be murder.

"Who sent you to explain all this, Jarod?"

"Emmit and Langston discussed it after the lottery, in Emmit's office. For you to spend your entire life with a killer, it is not fair," he said. He was almost pleading.

"It is the law. It is written in the charter."

He didn't want to argue with her, "I will come in the morning with the staff and the belt. It is hard for you to see what is happening in the village — you are out here all alone. But, it is a sad and desperate time. It could have been my daughter... it could have been anyone."

Taska waved him off. Behind his mask of pity and regret remained a dignity and happiness that his daughter was spared. Jarod thought he could conceal it, but it was just under the skin, and in his voice — too confident to really care and just a bit too loud. Jarod left the cottage, mounted his horse and trotted off into the woods.

Taska walked out to the stoop to breathe some of the fresh evening air. Sophia approached on foot.

Without words, she walked up the steps and embraced Taska. All they could do was sit in silence. The trees swished and moved their branches in the stiff north wind. Soon, the autumn leaves would carpet the road leading into the village. The cold was coming.

Meanwhile, Philip Lazarous was attending the all-night wake for James Colberton. The funeral procession would start at daybreak. It was tradition in the village to sit up all night with the deceased to assure that evil spirits didn't defile the corpse. Reverend Conrad tried desperately, for years, to convince the village that this all-night vigil was unnecessary, but he couldn't break them from the pagan beliefs. A crew of young men had been out to the cemetery, picking at the hard and rocky ground to make way for the coffin. Perhaps it was the wilderness and the mountains that proffered this fear of evil. Or, perhaps, it was rooted under the cobblestones in the heart of the village.

James Colberton was laid out in a rough square pine box. He was dressed in his Sunday clothes, cleaned and posed into his final resting place like a statue.

The open casket was in the middle of the cottage surrounded by sobbing family, consoling friends, and curious villagers. Philip Lazarous, Sophia's father was there, sitting with Alice Colberton, an older woman hunched over in a mourning dress of silver satin thread and a veil of lace. Her grief was desperate.

James and Alice Colberton had two children, a boy who worked on the fishing fleet, and a daughter, Katherine, who was among the names in the barrel during the lottery. She had been spared the greatest irony of having her father's killer bound to them forever.

Alice Colberton confided in Philip as a friend and a member of the village council. Her face was blotted from crying and her voice quivered. She looked to the floor to avoid the pain of seeing her husband's face in the mitered and planed pine box.

"I was with James when he took his last breath. That killer opened his stomach with a knife — then his neck. The blood stains are under the casket... still defiling the floor. He loved us all so much. He wanted you to have his papers and his books... if you want them."

Philip took her hand and whispered, "There will be time for that. Emmit will preside over his last testament... I will take you to him and be sure you are treated fairly."

"Would Emmit take advantage of someone like me, with her husband's blood still damp on the floor?" she said gathering up strength.

"I cannot say. It might help to have someone with you," he said. "I will miss your husband."

Alice Colberton nodded, "Take his papers and things before we see Emmit. Then I know they are safe with you."

Philip nodded. He stood, "Excuse me."

He left Alice consoling her daughter.

Passing by the coffin, Philip paused to look at James Colberton one more time before they buried him in the morning. Why would a stranger make his way to this village, for no other reason than to kill James Colberton? The Annual Visit brought men into the village every year to collect the taxes and count the villagers, but this killer had no boat, no horses, or anything. Who killed James Colberton? Who was this man among them now?

Outside, a few people were milling about, talking about the tragedy. Down the road, Philip could see the lights on inside Dr. Keller's cottage. The silhouettes of Emmit, Langston and Jarod moved around the door, smoking their pipes and glancing up the street. They would never come to the wake in Alice Colberton's house. They were not welcome. It was that simple. Their perspectives on the council were harsh and often self-serving, while James and Philip opposed the subtle tyranny of these men. There was a division between what was right in the village and the dark and off-handed schemes of Emmit and Langston. It was the balance of the council for almost fifteen years. Now the balance had shifted in their favor. Philip grew weary and tired. Emmit and Langston were down there with the killer waiting. Philip weighed his feelings and decided to go up to the church and pray for his dead friend.

The next morning, the sun broke over the sea casting a golden light over the village. Everything was still and quiet. James Colberton's funeral procession was leaving in a somber, silent parade heading out toward the church and the cemetery beyond. The golden morning light illuminated the village sending down hope and salvation for the soul of the dead.

It was in that same hour that Cain opened his eyes and stirred on the small cot in the doctor's cottage. He tried to focus on something in the room, a lantern, alive with light, flickering at the wick. Nothing made sense to him. The sleeping watchman was motionless in light slumber, slouched down in the chair next to him. Cain couldn't remember. He tried to lift his body up on his arms to look around, but he couldn't gather the strength. His hands were cut and scraped, his palms were raw.

Cain moved and stretched his body, waking the watchman. The watchmen peered at Cain through blurry, tired eyes. He leaned forward and looked closely. He gasped with surprise.

He hurried to fetch the doctor. Cain looked up to the ceiling trying to remember something. He searched for a reference or meaning to the world. Nothing came to him. He searched his mind for something to remember, trying to recall any piece, fragment or splinter of his being, but it was all shrouded. It was just what he felt at that moment, sharp pain on his face and head. Cuts, bruises, littered his head and neck. His arms bruised and throbbing.

Dr. Keller returned with the watchman. He looked Cain over. He examined his eyes and checked his pulse. He didn't speak a word to the suspected killer. The doctor ordered the watchman, "Go wake Emmit and Jarod."

The doctor gazed at Cain's beaten face with pity. Death would have been gentle in its deliverance.

"Is there pain, anywhere?" he asked. Cain watched the doctor's wrinkled mouth and his worn down teeth as he spoke.

"Where am I?" he said and looked toward the lamp's pleasing glow.

"You'll have to wait. Pain, anywhere?" he said softly, but Cain didn't answer. The doctor left him alone and locked the door.

The doctor sat out on the stoop of his cottage when Emmit and Jarod hurried down the lane. They worried over the doctor's absent gaze. Emmit showed a distrustful look on his face, "Is he up?"

"He is up, asking questions."

"Our questions will come first, Keller."

Jarod stopped and thought for a moment, "Did he confess?"

Dr. Keller shook his head, "He is having trouble remembering."

"Perhaps I should see him alone. Stay with the doctor, Jarod. I will call you in a few moments. Perhaps he will blurt something out if I speak to him intimately."

Jarod agreed and stepped back.

Emmit went through the cottage with the doctor who unlocked the door and let the council member in. Emmit stepped in to confront the killer. His face twitched with anger.

Cain sat on the edge of the bed, his head bent toward his lap, the pain throbbing and wearing him down. He looked up at Emmit's face, then brought his eyes back to his lap. Nothing registered in Cain's mind. His entire life was in a fog of amnesia.

"I suppose you have something to say for your actions," Emmit said with his hand still on the door latch. Cain watched him and rubbed his stomach. Nothing sparked recollection or understanding in his mind.

"Where am I?"

"You are in the doctor's cottage."

"Who are you?"

"You shouldn't be asking the questions. What was the reason for the murder of James Colberton?"

"Who?"

Emmit turned his eyes to the lantern and the Bible that lay on the table, "Don't try to dupe me, just answer the questions. God has condemned you already, your guilt is known publicly."

Cain felt the dull pain of his injuries wave over him. His knee was sore and his forehead seemed to throb more and more, "I have no answers for your questions."

Emmit sighed, "Who put you up to this? How did you know James Colberton and why did you kill him?"

"I cannot remember anything - everything is lost in a dream."

Emmit nodded, "Where did you come from?"

"I don't know."

"What is your mother's name?"

The killer shook his head. Nothing emerged from

recollections of the world.

He studied Cain for a moment. Was he telling the truth? Emmit opened the door and called Jarod and Dr. Keller to come in.

Emmit spoke quietly to the doctor, "Do you think he knows what has happened?"

Studying Cain and his swollen face through the open door, the doctor shook his head, "He took sharp blows to his head. Those scars show it. He may have lost his memory. It is a phenomenon known as amnesia — a complete loss of memory. A beating like he took will do that."

Emmit examined the dents and scars on Cain's brow, "Regardless, you have been condemned of killing James Colberton two days ago. Therefore you have been sentenced accordingly."

Cain shook his head, "I don't know you, sir, or a James Colberton. Where am I and who are you?"

Jarod turned away in frustration, "If this man can't remember the horror that he has cast upon this town, then we are the condemned, and he is free of guilt! He may as well be set free! He knows nothing of guilt!"

He left the room and marched out of the cottage.

Emmit and Dr. Keller walked out into the other room leaving Cain alone. Emmit spoke softly, "What should I believe?"

Dr. Keller pushed his glasses up against his forehead, "Consult the Reverend. You should call the council to confer on the issue. Jarod's anger is justified. Resolve this now, don't hesitate."

Emmit nodded and glared to the door where the

watchman remained posted.

"You better inform Taska Valimar that he is awake, and fetch Hillmond Wenner. She must administer the staff today."

The watchman walked out into the breaking dawn on his errand. The quiet moment of golden light and complete stillness had passed into bright rays of sun, streaking through the trees across the lane — leading out of town.

Taska woke that morning with focus and composure. She needed busy work to get her through the day. She tried to see herself and her cottage as if nothing happened at all, believing that the council meeting and the lottery the night before was merely a nightmare. She tried to calm herself down. She whispered, "Nothing has changed, only my perceptions, nothing more."

Taska began planning out each chore in her day and how long it would take her. She thought about the market and the extra food supplies that she would need for winter and perhaps another mouth.

She began getting the cottage in order and brewed some hot water and herbs for tea. Beneath her chores and everyday work, fear would be buried close to her heart, far from the surface of her appearance. She couldn't break down and fall apart. The sound of her shoes across the wooden floor made her realize she needed to sweep the cottage. Suddenly, Taska's eyes fell upon Sophia's bonnet. She must have forgotten it last night when she came to comfort Taska.

She realized with one sudden shudder of fear that her

nightmare was a reality. It all fell apart.

Later in the morning, as the church bells tolled six o'clock, Taska shut the door of her cottage and began walking to the market. The sun had risen and the trees were golden in the early autumn morning. The damp dirt road seemed firm under her step. She needed to fill her basket with jarred vegetables, smoked meat and dried fish. The market would be unsettling. Everyone knew her dismal fate. She decided to ignore the peculiar glances and whispering. She would have to carry on.

"Nothing has changed, nothing has changed," Taska said quietly.

She had left so early for the market that she missed the watchman's important message. She paused on the lane that passed through the woods. It seemed like a good place for contemplation. The council members would come to her cottage and she would be forced to listen to their laws and their excuses. They would bring the staff and the chains. A council of eight men decided the fate of one woman's life — forever. That made her burn inside until her cheeks flushed and her jaw hurt.

Then the council would cast him into her care. She would understand everything and accept her duty with honor. They would tell her, "This is the rite of womanhood."

Taska's heart broke beneath the cover of the forest trees.

Anger and frustration settled in like frost heaves in her bones. The cold feeling beneath her skin was covered and concealed by her dress, her cap and her shoes. Her garments would hold her together like a pillar of fragile ice, waiting to break apart into small flakes of ash and snow; to blow away on the wind in a whirlpool of redemption above the council and its laws.

Taska looked up at the sky through the tangled branches, like cracks on a mirror of blue and white.

"When will I know of the honor, the feeling that this is my duty? I feel despair. I feel as if all is lost."

Taska made it to the market and found it very busy. She waded into the crowd of villagers, minding her basket and searching for winter supplies. The villagers in the market watched her with fear, pity and selfish relief. Taska was calm. She had buried her overwhelming emotions on the wooded path. She approached the carts and looked for the choice vegetables. She heard whispers, "At least it wasn't one of us," and, "she has no life — she is suited for it." Then they would help her find some of the better beans and sprouts.

Some of the women, their names passed over in the lottery, appeared almost gracious to her for what she was doing, not for her duty or honor, but for sparing them the life sentence that seemed so incredibly cruel. Mrs. Jarod, wife of the council member, spoke to her with a frankness with which Taska was unfamiliar. And if this wasn't disturbing enough, Mrs. Jarod spoke to Taska about her missing parents.

No one spoke to Taska about her parents.

"Perhaps your life was meant to be hard, child. But there must be something more for you that just isn't clear. Your father and mother always knew in their hearts that you were

the strongest of them all. Your father once said, 'our little
girl could survive anything that we have seen in our lives —
and more.' That is saying so much."

Taska was surprised at this unfitted speech that
rekindled memories Taska had forgotten in recent days.
Mrs. Jarod didn't care about her parents or their lighthearted
manner, which made their family happy. Honor was
something that Taska learned in school. Nobility was
something she read about in books; an abstract ideal those
fat, spoiled children were born into. Nobility and honor
came from some foreign land, while love, hard work,
affection and intimacy were sacred beliefs given to her by
her mother and father.

It infuriated Taska to hear anyone speak about her
parents. She tried to calm her whirling thoughts of anger and
speak calmly.

"I will need cabbage and some of those yellow tomatoes
you often have. I need seven or eight," she said patiently.

Mrs. Jarod frowned and helped her find her vegetables.
She pitied the tragedy and the hopelessness of Taska's life.
Mrs. Jarod kept thinking how she might describe Taska to
her husband — hollow and lost in her world of loneliness
and despair. There was nothing more tragic to Mrs. Jarod
than to see Taska alone, orphaned from her family only to
have this terrible fate laid across her, like a fallen limb of
civil service. Mrs. Jarod's sympathy was mustered up to
mask the sheer relief that her daughter was spared from the
lottery.

Taska tried to pay for the vegetables. Mrs. Jarod refused
her money and said, "Just take what you need — I'll never

make you pay, dear."

"Thank you — but...."

"Please don't refuse, it is all I can do," she said.

Taska walked away swearing she would never return to her cart, or ever look in her direction again.

All the villagers would fill her day with misunderstood considerations, as they attempted to show her their grim gratitude for serving a sentence of eternity.

She looked toward the next cart with guarded optimism.

After completing her shopping, she sat by the open barn door where the blacksmith was working. She liked to listen to him whistle and clank his tools around the forge. She liked to watch him pound and shape metal into horseshoes and farm tools. They never carried on a long conversation, nor did he shoo her away. He accepted her occasional visits, sitting close to the fiery forge on cold mornings and offering her some warm coffee.

Sitting with the blacksmith, Taska looked over her full basket. She still needed more to get through the winter.

Katherine Colberton, the daughter of the murdered council member came to Taska and stood there like a frozen statue. The sun glistened in her tearful eyes.

"We buried my father this morning. While we were walking to the cemetery, someone told me that you were chosen as the staff warden for this monster. Then I realized that my name was also in that barrel, along with other women who... would have to live with that thing. My mother is so bitter. The blood... you have to understand how terrible it was, the murder... it is more than an animal, it was evil. I saw my father... and what killed him and it is

evil. But, that is not why I came to see you. I have come to
tell you how sorry... I am...."

Katherine flung herself around Taska's waist and
sobbed. The blacksmith walked around the forge and past
the two women. People from the square were staring at the
pitiful scene. The blacksmith pulled the barn door shut, like
a curtain drawn upon a stage, leaving the two women
together in their tangled miseries.

Emmit walked toward the church and looked up at the
sparkling afternoon sky. He was late for the meeting. He
wanted a confession, answers — something he could report
to the council. He rushed into the meeting hall. Langston,
Jarod, Philip, and the four other council members on the
meeting riser were waiting. He shook his head in
disappointment as he approached. Although Cain wouldn't
confess, the only known fact was Colberton's wife
witnessed the killer leaving the house when she came in.
Cain was the only person nearby; he must have been the
one. He is unknown to everyone in the village, until this
beating and subsequent capture. Where did he come from
and what more did he want?

Out of breath, Emmit stood in front of his chair.

"I've just come from questioning the killer. He has
offered nothing more. The doctor claims he has memory
loss — he cannot remember his crime — but he also can't
remember his name, his life before, his identity, how he got
here and why. This greatly complicates the situation."

Langston mumbled, "He is trying to play games."

"I believe the doctor," Jarod said, "that man has no idea of himself. You questioned him... he is empty inside."

Philip Lazarous leaned forward in his chair and spoke, "If he doesn't know what he has done, and can't remember any of his life, then send him away. His punishment will be in vain. Taska Valimar will be the ill-fated."

Jarod agreed.

"No. He cannot be allowed to walk around this town — the Colberton family will rip him apart," proclaimed Emmit. "The law in the past must be the law now. If one warden serves the staff, then we must continue. We must decide this like we have decided all previous cases, rule equally among all."

The silence was awkward and desperate.

Jarod looked around to the other council members and then down to his lap. He tried to suppose what each person was thinking. Jarod was a smart man, but he never wanted to make a decision for fear of opposition, so he followed the majority. It seemed hopeless. Philip, however, spoke up, "We need to replace James Colberton as councilor or everything we vote on will be deadlocked."

"There is no time to find someone to serve. The process of selection must be fair and well thought out. Now we must settle the terrible issue at hand with the members we have," said Emmit.

Jarod spoke up, "What about the prisoner? Can we punish a man who has all but fallen into our hands, with blood and treachery shaming everything that he touches?"

Another councilor added, "What if something happens to Taska Valimar? Sickness or death? This village will not tolerate another lottery?"

Emmit waited for everyone to finish. It drew quiet before he spoke.

"We cannot change a system that has been so successful. We cannot change what many already suffered through, and disrespect those whom died serving their term. Do you recall Slavanka Kyler, the only warden to die during her term of the staff? You must agree to continue. Somehow, late at night Amerset Loomer, her prisoner, had figured out how to break free of his chains. Gentlemen, you know the story. We must continue, we must agree to this and abide by the law!"

Emmit used this graphic horror story of the murder of his wife-to-be like the Reverend used the Bible to preach his sermon. It was his great tragedy, like the great sin in the garden of his own personal Eden. The poison was forever in his veins.

He continued his rumination, "Loomer pulled out his chains. He was free. He rose from the bed — careful not to make a sound. He walked quietly out of the room he knew so well, into the room where Slavanka slept. She was defenseless. He must have unlocked the front door, poised to leave, but freedom was not all. He stood over the sleeping woman and held the staff in his hands; the one weapon that kept him a prisoner would now free him. He pulled apart the handle of the staff and revealed the blade. It must have been a great power for him to wield the one thing that made Slavanka the keeper, and Loomer the prisoner... he slashed her to bits... my soon to be wife... everything... cut down."

Emmit choked up and then cleared his throat. Everyone

on the council had heard the story before — and witnessed Emmit's performance of tears and bitterness. Everyone waited until he was done.

Emmit's breath quivered. He composed his fury into discourse. Slavanka Kyler was his absolute and total loss in life. He returned his eyes to the tired, distant council before him, "If we change Taska Valimar's duties, what will become of Slavanka, what becomes of those memories? It is a tradition that we are here to defend and keep. We are not here to sympathize with Valimar; we are not here to pass judgment upon anyone. We are here to agree upon a course that cannot be altered. Our laws cannot be discarded. The lottery was executed. Valimar shall serve. It is her fate. If she fails, then we will have another lottery."

Jarod shook his head, "The village won't stand for it. They will turn on us, they will refuse the staff and abolish the council." He was working himself into a verbal tantrum, "Slavanka Kyler had made a petty thief into a murderer by damning that man to a daily hell, which no one could endure... we are repeating our mistakes over and over...."

"Enough!" Emmit's voice boomed like thunder through the hall. He turned sharply and plunged his fist down on to the table with a tremendous crash, "No more!"

Philip sat up at attention.

Jarod closed his eyes in frustration. It was tragedy in the past which fated tragedy now. They could all feel it. Jarod was young when Slavanka Kyler was killed. It was different to recall Emmit when he was young, in love, with his very overpowering nature of persuasion. But without Slavanka, without his youth, Emmit sustained only bitterness and abusive control. If anything could have saved Emmit from his own deviant ways, it was Slavanka. When she was killed, Emmit committed his life to gaining power, strength and fine possessions — trying to fill that empty space. Nothing else mattered.

Langston rose from his chair, "I think we should bring her the staff and begin what is inescapable."

Emmit barked out in disgust, "This meeting is adjourned!"

Taska went to the depot knowing that Sophia would be working. Sophia's father, Philip, ran the storehouse, which was the only large warehouse for storage and supplies. Being such a reliable and fair merchant for so long, granted him a seat on the council. Fishermen and people from the village brought things for trade or sold things for coins. Sophia worked as a clerk for her father, keeping inventory and filling out receipts; however, she had mastered her job so well that most of her time was spent reading or sewing.

Sophia sat working on her needlepoint, stabbing the thread through the fabric again and again. Taska came through the door. Sophia leapt up to help her with her basket of food.

They juggled the jars of jam and tomatoes and threw her cleaned goose on top of her basket.

"Taska, have you heard?"

"I have heard nothing. What is it, Sophia?" she said dimly.

Sophia followed Taska's rich black hair across her brow

to her copper forged eyes.

"No one mentioned the news?"

The assassin must be awake. He couldn't plead himself into guilt. It all remained ambiguous — like so much of her life now. Did Emmit and his cronies go to the cottage to find her gone for the day? Hillmond Wenner was choosing a staff for her, while Emmit and his followers — Jarod and Langston were waiting for her to return.

Taska brought her eyes down to her thin hands and rubbed them softly upon her black dress. The apron she was wearing was pure white, without streaks of dirt from cooking or working in the field. She didn't want to hear the words, but before she could stop Sophia, it was blurted out, "The man that killed James Colberton woke this morning."

Taska swallowed hard, trying to suppress the fear and anxiety trying to escape. She turned away to avoid Sophia's eyes. She tried to look very calm, but she couldn't hide the wretchedness as her last breath of freedom ran out of her.

Sophia was choked by her pity. Her gray piercing eyes were filled with tears.

Taska turned, "Have they been looking for me? I have been around the village all day, the council did not come to me."

Sophia nodded and thought about her walk from home to the depot, "Perhaps they are having a meeting. I saw them all by the church earlier. My father has been with James Colberton's family all day. They buried him this morning. He was a good friend to my father."

"Katherine Colberton came to me in the market. It was so dreadful, Sophia. She is a strong girl, but holds little faith in her own actions. What could the council be deciding? I am their lifelong warden," she said.

"I don't think anyone knows."

"I should go home then," Taska said.

"I can go with you."

"I must go alone Sophia, but you have always been kind to me. I find it your finest affection. You have been like a sister to me since my parents left. I still miss them... after all this time... I still miss them like the day they disappeared. I don't want you to see them administer the staff. It will make you sick, Sophia."

She rose quickly and gathered her basket and the goose. Sophia searched for something optimistic to say. But as Taska shut the door behind her, she remained silent. She wanted to chase her, tell her not to go home. She wanted to tell Taska to run away — never look back.

Emmit sat in his small house drinking warm brandy, aggravated by the meeting at the church. He was concerned about seeing Taska at her cottage at nightfall. Langston came in with a worried look on his face.

"We may have trouble."

"What do you mean?"

"I was riding down by the marsh inlet, and I could see smoke in the swamp. They are out there waiting. We must get him out of the village," Langston said.

"What if they come looking for him?"

"We still have choices to make," Langston said. "If Valimar is smart — she will do what the council cannot and cut his throat. If they come looking for him, then we can simply say he is gone. They will never find him in Valimar's cottage in the woods."

"Then we must get him out of town tonight. I am going to Taska's cottage now to have the staff administered to her. We have to get Cain out, tonight."

Langston nodded, "Tonight."

Hillmond Wenner held the staff in her hand. The wood was polished to a satin finish. The staff was an instrument of power and honor. The seam that concealed the blade was where one would place their hand on a walking stick. When pulled apart, the blade was revealed, which could pierce any man and swiftly end a man's life. She also carried the belt and chains in a burlap sack. When the village charter was created and the staff laws were placed into effect, three wooden staves were made. They were kept by the council and issued by Hillmond Wenner's mother until the duty was passed on to her daughter before she died. It was soon decided that the serving warden should be given the staff as a warrior might mount his sword and shield over his fireplace in retirement. It was a token of honor. However, it wasn't always received with such respect. Some of the carved, wooden staves were thrown into fireplaces; others buried the weapon and bid farewell to it. It was done quietly, like the dropping of a twig or misplacing a spoon. It disappeared from memory. The council of men preached honor and the staff as a trophy while the women wardens wanted nothing but to dispose of the vindictive symbol of civic bondage. Picking out the staff for Taska, Wenner noticed that the sharpest blade came from the staff that killed Slavanka years ago. She hesitated and took it anyway.

Outside of Taska's cottage the sun was beginning its westward descent behind the mountains. Emmit looked at his feet, waiting. He was lost in the thoughts of the past.

He recalled the lottery when his dear love, Slavanka, was assigned as warden to Loomer. Slavanka was Emmit's future. He recalled Slavanka's promise of their life together when her sentence was complete. Before he could plunge deeper into daydreams, Jarod broke his concentration.

"Here comes Valimar," he said turning from the cottage. Langston rose from the stoop. Taska noticed them as soon as she emerged kicking up the carpet of leaves.

She drew close and said, "A killer must be alive if you are all assembled at my door."

Langston looked stern, with eyes set back and his nose pronounced like an eagle, atop a body shaped like a withering beanpole. He seemed remorseful. Hilmmond Wenner shifted the staff in her hand.

"He is awake. We have come to bring you what you need," Emmit said as Taska walked past them and on to the stoop. The four villagers followed her in.

Taska placed her basket near the fireplace and put the goose in a wooden pail.

She peered at the staff in Hillmond's hand. Emmit held the belt and chains meant for binding the prisoner. She didn't have to recall the use of these implements.

"If this is all you have come for, then place them down in the corner and be gone. I have no time for idle talk," she said as she pointed to the corner. She waited for Emmit to place the belt down.

"There is more, Miss Valimar," he turned, the chains clanked as they fell. She fixed her eyes on Emmit's bulging neck and his crack of a mouth gaping between his jowls.

Langston looked around the room, finding comfort in anything but Taska's indifferent glare.

"He has no recollection of the past. He won't remember the murder, his life before the incident, or who put him up to this. This might unnerve you. I suppose it would unnerve anyone, but your duty has not changed. We cannot change the law, regardless of his memory loss."

"It will be an interesting marriage, with no future," Taska said.

"You know that isn't true."

"I know the truth, Hillmond. I've spoken to other wardens. I know you think I'm an outsider... a bit odd... but, you hardly understand the position I am in," Taska said sharply.

Emmit went on with his duties, "The assassin will come tomorrow. He will be cooperative, but you mustn't show him pity, his crime must be punished."

Hillmond showed her the staff in the corner. The length came just below Taska's shoulder. She offered it to Taska.

"Put it back in the corner," Taska said. Hillmond Wenner was ready to give a speech but it was deflated.

"Can you handle this weight, its size?" she asked looking for some compliance with her own tradition and position as the staff rector. Honor and courage were intertwined in every fiber of the symbolic weapon.

"Put it the corner, Hillmond. The staff is what you choose to make it. Perhaps you see it as protection, and a symbol of honor, but I see it as my last line of defense in a series failures."

Emmit appeared confused, "I hope you are prepared. We cannot wait. The townspeople cannot wait — this has been a terrible time."

"When will the post be driven?"

Langston turned, "I will bring them tonight. It will be done quickly."

She nodded.

"Then that is all," Taska said and walked to the door. She wanted them gone.

"I will come with Langston tonight and make sure you have received your final instructions. Tomorrow, in the morning, they will bring the assassin named Cain," said Emmit in a formal, calculated tone. They all walked out of her house and into the falling twilight. Hillmond Wenner stopped at the door, "I will come back to help you prepare for the prisoner. I am here to guide you through this. Do not refuse me — it would be improper. You will need someone to confide in."

Taska shut the door and realized that something was coming. It came through the woods, in the coming darkness, bringing a wicked feeling to accost her life, and ravage her delicate soul. She realized with a shudder that her last day of freedom was spent with trivial errands and busy work.

Taska prepared some leftover soup, remembering that she

needed to alter some of her dresses for the next few days.
She had to sew a pocket on the inside waist of her dresses to
wear the belt that would restrain the prisoner when they
went into the village. They were to be chained together all
the time in public. This belt was attached to a chain that
reached out to the prisoner's waist chains and locked
binders, keeping the prisoner close to her all the time.

Cain would have to be bound to her all the time when
they were in the village. Working in the field, she could
allow him to be free from the chains, but she would keep the
staff close. In the cottage, he would also be free until he
went to bed, chained to the stake next to the bed. Those who
escaped from their warden in the past had done so at night
from their bed. Taska held the keys that unlocked the
binders piled in the corner. This was another possession her
life would never be without. The ring of keys would become
a personal effect, like a small child's hair ribbon or an old
man's pipe.

She completed the sewing of two dresses when
Langston returned. He came with five men whom Taska
knew only by sight. They were village crewmen. Crewmen
were poor, dregs always looking for work — working for
food — eating to live — living to work in a vicious cycle of
survival. These men worked their bones to dust and their
muscles into knots every week for their masters, Emmit,
Langston, Jarod, and the few other men with enough to pay
them. The crewmen's wages came in the form of food or
shelter, but they were never given money to better
themselves. These men were forever bound to their masters
and bosses. This was accepted. This was the lower class.

Langston was shown the bedroom.

Taska left the room while they proceeded with their work. The crewmen pulled up a few floorboards next to the bed and brought in an eight-foot post. They drove it into the earth below the cottage floor. They drove it down three or four feet and filled in the earth, packing it tightly. They created a brace on the base of the stake that would prevent it from being pulled up through the floor. The men replaced the floorboards. Standing next to the bed was a thick post of raw wood — the binding post. Four metal rings were attached to the top to bind the bed chains. The wood and rusting metal rings looked harsh and malignant next to Taska's soft pillows and wool blankets on her bed.

When the crewmen departed after an hour of work, Taska walked into her bedroom to see what the careless men broke and what they constructed with their tools. She saw the large post erect, next to her bed. It made her stomach turn with disgust. She looked down and spoke quietly, "I can't sleep here ever again."

Taska knew Sophia had an old cot in the warehouse. She decided that she would bring the cot to the stake and move her plush mattress into the storage closet.

She walked in the damp, cool night to Sophia's cottage and found all the lights on. She dreaded the idea of speaking to the entire family. Sighing, she rapped on the door and waited.

Sophia answered the door, "Is everything all right?" Taska nodded. She ushered her into the house to Sophia's mother, sewing at the table.

"What a surprise," said the mother and began rushing around to fetch a cup of soup left from dinner.

"Drink this and warm your bones," she said and directed her to the empty chair by the fire. When Taska sat down, a black cat jumped into her lap, discovering a brief sanctuary in her presence. Taska held the soup in one hand and stroked the cat with the other. She listened to the purring of the cat without realizing that everyone was silent.

When Taska was orphaned, the villagers thought she would not survive in the cottage out in the woods alone without her parents. She refused to live in the hamlet after the villagers invited her into their families. Taska Valimar lived and thrived year after year on what she was taught by her parents. It was hard work just to survive. The only person who befriended Taska Valimar when her parents disappeared was Sophia Lazarous. Sophia and her family helped Taska in small ways when she was young. Everyone else thought she was touched and wicked for living alone with the wolves in the desolation of the woods.

"I was wondering if you still have the small bed in the depot. I would like to purchase it from you. They erected the chaining post tonight right next to my bed. I cannot sleep there tonight. And this killer won't sleep in my bed."

"Of course, but I must insist on you taking it," she said. "It is musty and falling apart."   "That bed is meant to fit in a boat," Sophia's mother added.

"It is a bed for him. He will not be sleeping in my bed," she said. Sophia nodded and said, "I will have it brought to you by morning."

"I would like it tonight. I don't know when they are bringing the prisoner. Is that possible?" she said knowing Sophia would not refuse.

Sophia's mother walked into a different room in the cottage and spoke with Philip about the bed. He came through the door to see Taska, "We will get the bed for you. They won't be moving the killer until morning."

Taska stood up, throwing the cat from her lap. The feline looked back from the floor with a slight flicker of the tail. They all marched down toward the warehouse on the water.

Sophia led the way to the pier and into the depot. The clanking and creaking of the fishing boats overpowered the sound of the lapping waves. The tide was going out to sea. No one from the village was stirring, leaving this late night errand unnoticed. Some nights, the men would drink up in the loft of the depot, play dominoes, and reminisce. Sophia opened the door to the depot and paused to listen, but everything was quiet. They walked into the back of the warehouse. It looked like the large hall attached to the church, but instead of clean, orderly benches and the council riser, it contained boxes, rope, crates and tools all arranged in an order only decipherable to Sophia and her father.

Although they brought lanterns to light the way, they still found the warehouse ominous and dreary. Sophia found the bed and the rolled up mattress. She found a small door on the side of the building and forced it open with a show of strength, startling her mother.

Philip found a crewman who offered his assistance bringing the bed out to the cottage in the woods. As the two men carried the wooden bed frame and the mattress outside, Sophia looked it over. It will be fine for the manslayer.

Philip and the crewman agreed to bring the bed to Taska's house via the country road. They didn't want to deal with any rumors or gossip concerning the bed. They headed off in that direction. Philip was somber and distant from the long wake and the funeral of James Colberton that carried on all morning.

The three women walked through town. They spoke softly in the night air, seeing their breath crystallize into vapor as they sauntered through the empty roads and alleys of the village. The leaves that rustled under their feet seemed disobedient to their intention of being solemn and quiet.

"When are they bringing him?" Sophia asked.

"Tomorrow, at daybreak I suppose," Taska replied. Her emotions were wearing thin with the exhaustion of a long day. Her freedom, like her breath in the autumn air, would evaporate at morning's first light. Yet, somehow she could endure it all.

"Don't fear him — he is nothing more than a man. I can tell you that there is nothing to dread," Sophia's mother said.

"Did they bring the staff to you?"

Taska nodded.

"They say it is an honor just to gaze at the staff, is it beautiful?" Sophia asked.

"I didn't study it. It stands wherever they left it, this afternoon."

"Is it heavy, thick...?"

"I have not touched it," Taska said. They walked along

in silence with nothing more to discuss beyond the tragic murder and the lottery. When they arrived in front of the cottage, they noticed that Philip and the crewman were not yet there with the bed. Taska led the women into the cottage.

Inside, Jarod rose quickly from the table. He had been waiting for her.

"What is the meaning of this?" Taska shouted. "Because I am to be a warden doesn't mean that my home becomes a meeting house for council members."

Her anger was drawn out by her surprise.

Jarod was unaffected by her anger.

"Miss Valimar, I must bring the prisoner tonight — as soon as possible," Jarod said. "He has been threatened. Someone sent a message to the doctor's cottage expressing a wish to kill the man named Cain."

Early in the evening, Emmit created a note and had it sent by messenger to Jarod and Langston, who were at the doctor's cottage. It read, "The assassin must not live to torment this village and continue to plague the eyes of all those who have witnessed the horror of murder. His death will be a salvation for Taska Valimar, James Colberton and the entire village." Emmit did not sign the letter.

When Langston received the note, he quickly recognized Emmit's handwriting but knew that Jarod would fall into the paranoia of an anonymous letter. So, it was agreed that Cain would be moved quickly that night. Jarod came to inform Taska on behalf of the council.

Sophia looked to Jarod and back to Taska, her face animated with anger, "My God, you are asking her to protect a killer from another act of violence!"

Sophia's mother lashed out, "Everyone knows where the assassin is going to be, and everyone was at the lottery. If she is left alone without someone to help her then she too will be prey to a killer. She can handle her prisoner but not an unimpeded madman. Isn't this getting out of hand?"

Sophia was jolted with fear when the door was tossed open and her father came in, "We are here with the bed." He waited outside.

Jarod spoke firmly, "It is the decision of the council."

Sophia turned in disgust. She shook her head. But nothing could be done.

"I shall return with Emmit, Langston and the prisoner, Cain," said Jarod as he walked out into the dark. He walked past Philip and the crewman standing with the bed.

Jarod explained the new development to Philip.

The crewman and Philip struggled with the bed frame, but said nothing to one another. Taska watched them work. She directed them to take the large bed and put it in the storage room, then put the small cot in the vacant room next to the post of solid pine. It was happening so fast. It was hopeless.

Taska went to her bedroom and looked around. She had to work quickly to take all her possessions out of her bedroom and into the root cellar. She began work, with the help of Sophia and her mother.

Sophia's mother prattled on, "This is an outrage. The council decided this and the council decided that — I don't care what traditions we are protecting. Philip never had a say in moving the prisoner, and he is on the council. This is terrible."

Sophia looked into the root cellar where the crewman reassembled the bed. It hardly fit at all. Taska had slept in that bed since the disappearance of her parents. There was barely enough room to walk around the large bed and keep her possessions safe. The high window was nailed shut. Dirt and grime coated the glass.

Sophia and her mother continued to bring things to Taska in the small room, quickly transplanting Taska's life — from humble living to meager existence.

Finally, Taska had the bedroom entirely empty of her possessions. The crewman put the cot next to the chaining post. They nailed the wooden legs to the floor and stood back to look at their work.

The room was bare. The small portraits of Taska's family and her needle point work were gone. She was glad it was gone. No trace was left of her life. The room was ready to receive the prisoner — it was ready to become his cell.

They made him stand. Although it was painful and he felt dizzy, he was standing. He looked at the men that were binding his hands in cuffs of iron, hinged at the wrist. The hinge was then attached to a belt that kept him from raising his hands upward. His shoes were old and worn; blood still stained them from the murder and his thrashing. His shirt was clean, but it was still damp from the wash.

He was shoved into the main room of the doctor's cottage and stood before Emmit, Jarod, Langston and three crewmen that were to assure that Cain would not escape during the walk. Each step he took shot pain up his leg from his left knee. He lumbered along, trying to stave off the burning soreness of his injuries.

"What is happening?" Cain asked. Emmit turned and looked to Langston. He didn't know what to say.

Jarod stepped forward, "You are being brought to your warden. You will be the ward of Taska Valimar now."

"I am to be watched over?"

Emmit approached him, "She is a woman chosen by this council."

"A woman?"

"Obey and we won't have to hurt you all over again." Emmit turned, "We must go."

They all filed out of the cottage spilling into the lane. Emmit and Jarod held lanterns, illuminating the way as the procession walked toward Taska's cottage, which would take them by the old maple trees, over the hill, past the church and through the forest. It was almost two in the morning, yet people came from their homes to see the assassin in the lane. Some of the villagers were still fully dressed in their work habits, while some came out in sleeping gowns and heavy wool blankets. Neighbors woke others along the street until most of the village was up to watch the assassin march in a macabre parade to his lifelong prison beyond the woods.

Jarod was nervous that the one who sent the threat would be out in the crowd, watching them and waiting to strike. He was surprised at Langston's calm demeanor. Emmit led the march. Jarod grew weary. Would someone attack the killer from the crowd? All the villagers were up

— it could be anyone.

"This place is not familiar to me, where are we?" Cain asked as they walked. His shackles clattered and tangled around his feet. The sound of Cain hobbling across the stone and gravel sounded out of place, as everyone else walked quietly toward the edge of the village. No one answered Cain's question.

"This crime which you say I committed, I would like to know more. If I am accused, then I would like to know what I did and the implications, whatever it might be?" Cain found his thoughts flowing clearly and without hesitation. The cool air was clearing his mind.

Before Jarod could turn and tell him to keep quiet, James Colberton's wife came rushing through the night screaming at Cain.

Jarod turned quickly — she was the one. Langston turned and stepped away from Cain. He remained standing alone when Colberton's wife clawed at him and scratched his face. Emmit, completely surprised, raced to quell the attack. Before they could get her clear of Cain, he had fallen on to the gravel and blood poured from his stitched face.

"Someone get her home!" Emmit yelled and pulled Cain to his feet. Langston pushed him on, "Let's go, walk faster."

Jarod spoke up, "She was the threat. She sent the note."

Emmit looked at him with surprised eyes, "It seems that way."

They arrived in front of Taska Valimar's house. The night had turned cold. Sophia and the crewman stood outside. Sophia's mother and father came out as soon as the party arrived.

The villagers followed, staying some distance behind. Some villagers carried lanterns or candles, with semblance to an outcast band of vagabonds looking for a campsite. Once they saw the cottage, they all crowded toward the steps and the bound assassin.

Taska Valimar came out of the cottage wearing a heavy wool cape. She bundled it tightly with her hand to keep warm. She walked down the steps to the assassin. She looked sternly into his eyes and saw nothing. This was the killer. Cain knew nothing of what he had done to this village or to her as a warden. She could see his feeble-mind through his disconcerted gaze. A trickle of blood ran down his face.

Taska looked around her. She was surprised at the crowd.

Most of the villagers had never frequented her cottage, and she felt it was wrong for them to show their dim faces now, in the lamplight of this odd procession.

Widow Colberton's attack that night was perfectly coincidental and quite helpful to Emmit's own prevarication. He was proud of his incidental success.

Jarod walked to Taska and whispered, "It was widow Colberton who sent the letter. It's safe. There is no danger."

"Why are they all here?" she asked, making her voice just audible. She looked at all the faces. What have they come to see?

"No one here wanted to be chosen at the lottery," she said. "Nobody wanted to face what I am about to face. So why are you all here? Emmit, what is this?" Taska felt like she was in a morose dream.

She approached Emmit and looked at him with a cold

stare.

"What is happening here? Am I to be a spectacle, some display for the village?" Taska said.

Jarod peered shamelessly into the lanterns of the people around him. He saw his own wife and his daughter spared in the lottery. He wept for joy that she was not chosen. Now, he felt guilty for such joy. He drew his head down as if to pray.

Emmit proclaimed, "We present this man to you in the eyes of the council, as to uphold your duties as the chosen warden."

Jarod pushed Cain forward. He stood before Taska, favoring his bad knee to ease the pain.

Taska looked beyond him. She didn't see what she expected in him. He was afraid, with no vivid compulsions for murder in his eyes.

"I have taken my duties upon the recognition that I must live by the laws of this village, but I will not share my life with the rest of the village. I will not be curried favors and I will not be considered more or less. I have taken my oath and I shall serve as God watches over me. If it was someone else, I would not stare at them in the middle of the night, but I would understand the depth of their sacrifice. You have come to watch me lose a part of my life for the sake of this man. This you shall see because the law must be executed, but I shall not move from this place until you are all gone from here. What did you expect? Did you expect me to weep — beg for mercy before the council?"

She approached Mrs. Jarod, "Did you come to watch me beat him? Did it seem as if I might wither into a heap on the ground and beg for my death at this instant? Did you?" She walked back into the center of the villagers.

"You don't know me. You never did. You should all be ashamed," said Taska.

She walked to Cain and looked at him, "We will wait until they leave — each and every one."

She spoke without feeling. She pulled her hood over her hair and looked down to her feet, waiting. Emmit studied Taska for a moment, considering what she had said. Her hands folded together under her cape. She refused to look up.

Emmit looked to Jarod and said, "Everyone, please...."

They all looked around and finally began walking back through the path to the village. Some of the villagers came to Taska, but she focused her eyes upon her shoes and waited until everyone was gone. She didn't even seek Sophia's condolence. The footsteps shuffled away like the pattering of a rain shower coming to an end.

Everyone was gone. Finally, she stood alone with Cain. She brought her head from the earth and looked into Cain's clouded eyes. She looked for his fear, but there was nothing.

There was a boy in the village that nobody spoke to because they all knew he was an imbecile. He never spoke or laughed when someone would try to amuse him. He would wander around the village and do things that seemed like that of a curious child, but he wasn't playing as the other children did. He would never go and explore the woods, or walk around the rocks and look for crabs by the ocean. The only thing he truly seemed to enjoy was jumping up and down. He jumped off things, he jumped in place, and sometimes this queer child would jump until he could barely stand.

No one knew of the child's family and it was thought that whoever bore this child would never lay claim to the daft youngster. The child survived by stealing food from the market, and sleeping in woodsheds or under porches. Sometimes when Sophia was feeling compassionate, she would let him sleep in the warehouse and feed him what was left from dinner.

On Sundays, when church was in service, it was odd to see the entire village in the church, singing their prayers and devotion up to God while this boy stood next to the posted fence jumping up and down. He would follow the crowds as they came out of the church and back into town. The jumping boy was always where the majority of the village gathered.

So he jumped.

The sun rose over the ocean and the fishermen were coming down to rig their boats for the day. Emmit walked down to the depot to find Philip. He paused for a moment to watch the fishermen preparing for the sea. The fishermen were different from the farmers and the merchants; they were filled with vigor, while acting out shrewdly to the other villagers. It seemed that taking to the ocean and leaving the village everyday had filled them with a vitality that was missed by the other villagers.

Emmit went to the depot and knocked on the door. Sophia greeted him, shielding her eyes from the sun. The warehouse was always much darker inside.

"Emmit, what is it?"

He squinted his eyes and pushed his glasses back upon his chubby, bulb-like nose. He turned his face to the sun, "I'm looking for your father. I need some things."

"Well come in then."

He stepped into the small shop that led into the warehouse. Leaving the sea soaked air, Emmit noticed the musty, rotten smell of rope, tools and other supplies that filled the depot.

Sophia went to the inventory ledger.

"He isn't here this morning. Perhaps I can find what you are looking for?" Sophia said. His request was a secret.

"When do you expect him? It is important."

"Soon, but I don't follow him about," her tone was sarcastic sensing Emmit's secrecy. She knew what was in every box, barrel and jar in the warehouse and it was an insult to exclude her from Emmit's request. His demeanor was suspicious.

"If it is so important then I shall fetch it for you."

Emmit shook his head in disgust, "I shall return."

She watched him disappear. "What an irritable man."

Her thoughts went to Taska. After the spectacle in front of her cottage, she didn't dare go to her, but she was concerned.

She couldn't help but think that Cain was causing her trouble, and that Taska was in a constant struggle with the killer.

Hillmond Wenner came in and greeted her a few moments after Emmit's theatrical departure.

"Good morning, Sophia," she said in a mournful test of Sophia's state of mind.

"What brings you to the depot, Hillmond?"

"You are close with Taska — you know her well. I wanted to ask you: has she always been so solemn?"

"Of course not. I have always known her as very kind. She was content in her seclusion."

Hillmond Wenner paced the room a few times, distress tumbling through her mind.

"Many of the villagers have come to me, worried that if Taska fails — then another lottery will draw in a councilor's daughter or some of the most respected women of this town. It is becoming a panic among everyone."

Sophia didn't care to discuss the fears of the village prima donnas when Taska was serving to keep Cain away from them all. Apparently, this wasn't enough. Hillmond Wenner was almost fifty now. She seemed wise and very commanding with the girls when she taught them the rules and laws of the staff. Her position was taken very seriously — yet she was eccentric and stubborn. Preserving the integrity of the staff and the wardens became her traditional station in life. She recalled village history by serving wardens. She learned everything from her mother — the names of all the older wardens — and spoke of them with respect and honor. If she hadn't been given the position of staff rector, Hillmond Wenner would have little purpose or direction in her life.

Sophia watched her pace, "I have heard that Taska is the

perfect match. She is alone, with no civil or social place in the village... her life has little consequence - she is the perfect warden for a lifetime prisoner."

Hillmond whispered, "Do you believe that?"

"Of course not," Sophia said. "Taska has the sense to stay out of our petty treachery. I admire her independence."

"I want to help her. I want to ease this transition, but she is so cold."

"Leave her alone" Sophia suggested. "The village has what it wants, just leave her alone."

"It is wrong," replied Hillmond. "Where is her honor, her respect? Please try to convince her that I want to help."

Hillmond Wenner left with a gesture of thanks.

Sophia agreed — everything was wrong, but it had nothing to do with Hillmond's view of honor or respect. It was wrong to steal away freedom by coupling murder and captivity to innocence and fortitude.

That same morning, Langston stood next to his large barn where he worked. Lumber and carpentry was his life; his tools hung on the clapboard wall were his trophies. He pushed over a large wooden tub filled with brown rainwater. He pulled the tub to the front of the shed. The morning air was still cool as he tried to keep working so the chill wouldn't bother his old, stiff joints and weary frame.

His gray nag stood in the shed waving its tail, a habit from the summer flies and mosquitoes. Langston took a small pail and walked away from the shed toward the well beneath a tree. The path he had worn down in the knee-high grass. He took the handle of the pump and began churning it. As the water sputtered out, the bucket filled slowly.

He had a series of chores he had to get done before going to the village that afternoon. He thought of Cain. He lifted the pail of water and began walking back to the shed. He thought about the ignorance of the assassin and Taska Valimar's furious eyes in the black of night. He suspected that Cain was a murderer and that his memory loss was a way of buying time until he could find a way to escape.

Langston had always been suspicious of people. He trusted no one. The fewer people that knew of him, the fewer people would have to suspect. He waited for people to betray him.

He reached the shed. The gray horse turned its head and tried to step around to the water. The rope attached to its harness restricted the horse's movement.

Langston threw the bucket of water into the tub and looked at the horse. He despised the nag, knowing that it was a matter of months before it would be dead. It wouldn't survive another bitter winter. He walked to the horse's harness and untied the rope. He peered into the horse's black eye and coughed hard from his throat. Not dead yet, he thought. He led the horse to the tub and tied the beast off on a fence post nearby.

Langston walked behind the shed and out into the field that had been plowed over for the winter.

The horse brought his head down to drink, but couldn't reach the water, the rope was too short. The horse jerked his head up quickly, enraged that he couldn't drink from the water bucket. The horse tried to bend down again and again with his long and muscular neck, but the rope held tight. The horse tried to nudge the tub with his nose, to draw it closer. When frustration set in, the old nag simply pawed the ground with his front hoof until it dug a crevasse into the rocky dirt. The horse finally managed to tip the tub over and watch the water run through the dirt and disappear.

Langston stood in the middle of the plowed field, looking out over the red and gold trees at the foothills of the mountains. He gazed at the peaks that cut off the village from the rest of the world. He could never make it through the mountains, and then through the vast wilderness beyond. If he wanted to run, he should've done it a long time ago. He would never make it. But he knew of the red ribbons that marked a path. He had so many chances to take to the woods, into the foothills, following the red markers left by hurried hands. It was always in his dreams. He might pick his way through the woods, looking for the next red ribbon or using the stars for guidance, living off what nature allowed. He dreamt of escape, but it was all too late. He even brought the horse as a contingency for escape, planned out years ago. His hopes were rickety and dilapidated like his old horse, his shed, and his cottage. He had wanted to leave the village when he realized that nothing he made with wood and tools would make it beyond his legacy. All the wood and timbers that he could cut and shape into something useful would fall to pieces or rot. Everything was degenerating. It was his great disillusion of the world. It fed his bitterness, his deception, and his allegiance to Emmit.

As he stood facing the great peaks, Langston felt the cold earth under his feet and the warm sun on his back.

Never had the peaks seemed so close.

Generally speaking, Philip Lazarous was a man who tried to do the right thing for people. As a businessman, he felt that being fair kept everyone happy. He also had a healthy fear of the annual tax collection. But, he didn't fear the council and what they were capable of doing. Philip tried to manage his warehouse for the benefit of the villagers, with money subsequent to the importance of trade and survival. He would always have enough money to support his family, so he was rarely bothered by financial difficulties. Now that his daughter, Sophia was old enough to help with the business, the burden of financial straits had subsided over his thirty years of running his business.

Although he wasn't as prosperous as he had imagined when he was allowed to open thirty years ago, he was content with his life. He was also forgetful of his youthful dreams of becoming a wealthy merchant.

Philip arrived at the warehouse, but noticed Sophia wasn't in the front room sewing or reading her books. He walked into the warehouse and shouted for her but he couldn't find her. He slowly walked to a crate and put his arm over a wooden hold to rest for a moment. Where had she gone? Perhaps she went to see Taska, he thought. He was wary of Sophia's involvement.

He heard the shop door open and then slam shut.

He could tell that it was Sophia by her footsteps. He knew her gait on the wooden floorboards, and the way she moved swiftly from place to place with her firm young legs and her furious tempo.

"Sophia, is that you?"

She walked to the door, "Yes, I went to check on Taska. I was worried."

Sophia pushed her hands into the smock over her dress. She spoke with a calm, matter-of-fact manner, "Emmit came looking for you. He wanted to speak with you of something important, but he didn't say what it concerned."

He nodded, "I shall see him later today."

Philip's mind searched for a reason that would bring Emmit around. He dismissed the thought. He sauntered to Sophia, "How is she?"

"She is different now that she is captive... with the prisoner."

Before he sat down to his ledger and ink, he turned to his daughter to ask her another question about Emmit's visit, but paused. He didn't want to seem anxious. She picked up her sewing and began working the needle. Having Emmit so eager to speak with Philip made him cautious.

He didn't want to wait. Outside the warehouse, the carts were assembling for market and the commotion increased as the sun rose over the square. The clop of horses on the cobblestones seemed to announce the coming of the daylong market. It was very busy by mid-morning. The children too young for school at the church ran between the carts and around the legs of their mothers. The sound of seagulls called out over the village, echoing from the buildings and sheds that butted one to the other to make the square, sheltered from the cold north wind. The only thing visible from the center of the village was the fishing fleet and the ocean beyond. Most of the fishing boats were out working their nets.

Other than the market, villagers went to the few established businesses that were not wheeled in by cart and horse: the blacksmith, the depot and the cobbler.

The blacksmith was very diligent, with his forge raging from four in the morning until dusk. The blacksmith had come to believe that shoeing horses was the most lucrative business, but the fisherman kept him busy everyday with their worn and broken tackle from their boats. He would reshape and mold what was broken on the waves of the sea, and accepted fish as payment. He didn't mind being paid in food — it was a living. The cobbler fixed old shoes and leather harnesses, which was his most common work. The carpenter, although he preferred to help build barns, make furniture or mend a fallen roof, would always profit the most from the coffins he made. Some of the proud villagers would make their own casket for their dying relation, but most, who were too busy farming or fishing, would have the carpenter make a respectable box.

Mrs. Jarod always came early and set up in the same location in the village square. But she often wandered about, gossiping to her friends, leaving her cart unattended. She knew when she returned nothing would be missing. She couldn't imagine who would be silly enough to steal from a councilor's wife.

Philip came out from the warehouse looking for Emmit. He noticed that Mrs. Jarod was speaking to some of the other women. Taska and the late night vigil at her cottage was the morning gossip. He felt misanthropic about seeing the same faces that appeared in front of the Valimar cottage in the woods. He wanted to betray them. Perhaps it was his agitation with Emmit that boiled over into bitterness.

He walked slowly across the cobblestones, hoping that no one would approach him, and that he could make it to Dr. Keller's cottage up the road. He didn't want to find Emmit; he just wanted to know what he was looking for. He worried over Emmit's deceptive mind. His unpredictable rages at the council meetings were odd. He was more calculating than that. Something was overshadowing his rage — something was happening beyond the scope of the staff and the killer.

Taska put Cain to work. She wanted to test his loyalty, his disposition and his strength. Taska directed him while tending to her late-coming squash.

Cain picked up a bale of hay and brought it back to the edge of the vegetable garden. She kept the patch of fertile land and its modest harvest since her mother and father disappeared. It was her mother that started the garden, teaching Taska the importance of growing what one needs to be self-sufficient. It was important not to depend on other people, and Taska's mother structured their lives to work alone, set into motion forever like the spinning wheel, perpetually turning through time. But, it wasn't that simple when Taska was little. Once the Valimar family began a life of self-sufficiency, they would have to fend off anyone who tried to stop the spinning wheel of their secluded life.

Taska with her hair tied back under a white bonnet, used

a spade to pull and turn the soil over. The harvest was gone — reduced to stalks and dried leaves. She raked the dead vegetation into the soft earth. Cain said nothing to her.

She found his obedience a comfort, but she watched him carefully. She wanted to predict what he might do before he did it. She wanted to know him well enough to predict his thoughts before he considered them.

Taska dropped the spade to the ground. She had turned over the entire garden. Cain was spreading hay over the freshly turned soil. She looked at his face, at his curious eyes.

"Are you planting hay?" Cain said.

She shook her head, "No, it keeps the soil from washing away during the rain over the winter, and it protects the seeds underneath." When she spoke to him she held a tone of authority.

"It is not a waste of hay?" he said. Taska bent down and pulled apart a raked clump, "Hay is something I can waste. I have no animals to feed. The soil, which becomes our food, is what I must protect."

She turned away from Cain, listening for his movements, listening for his words. She heard nothing. He could walk up behind her, or catch her off guard. She didn't want to appear wary or frightened by him, but when her back was turned — she was aware of him.

She glanced over her shoulder and noticed how he stood over the bundle of hay, like a scarecrow drenched with rain, slipping from his makeshift crucifix. His injuries were painful, so she made his chores and work simple and easy.

Cain spread the hay. The sun was warm. Taska felt the

heat through her blouse. She liked the feeling of the sun's warmth upon her face and shoulders, and tried to absorb as much as she could. The raw winter months would wear her down. Winter always tested her forbearance.

Everything had now changed. Taska realized the winter would be difficult with Cain. Anger erupted in her like a crackling tumble of thunder. It was painful to change her life after living alone for so long. Her anger came from the throwing away of freedom and self-sufficiency, like a stone tossed into an incoming wave of civil obedience. The council had enveloped her entire life with one cresting motion, halting the wheel of her perpetual life, set into motion by the only images that she could find comforting — her parents.

Winter would seem like years, in the company of a stranger. What would she say to him? She was always content with her books, her own writing and the sewing. His constant presence would violate her solitude, making the long dark nights uneasy and harsh on her nerves. He was appalling. She was desperate to be alone.

His heavy breathing would obscure the crackle of the wood in the hearth, his movements would distract her thoughts. Taska clenched her teeth, flexing the muscles along her jaw at the thought of this misery. She glanced at his face and thought of something to say, something to humiliate him — deceive him. She could kill him and no one would know. That sounded so remote.

She felt lost.

All she could manage in her deepening anger and distrust was, "We must finish by dark. Move along, move along."

She walked to the side of the garden in the knee-high
grass that was still green and lush. She watched Cain do
what she had done for so many years, alone. His hands
spread the hay, covering more and more of the garden until
the rich, soft brown earth was smothered in a dim yellow
blanket.

She wanted to undo all his work in the garden, then do it
again. That patch of earth was her well-tended legacy. Her
work was more than a series of chores; she was performing
the rites and prayers that blessed her life, befitting the hopes
of her parents and desire of God.

Emmit looked out at the road from his office window then
back to his desk. He decided he would go and look for
Philip again. As he glanced over his desk, he saw the
proclamation that Taska Valimar penned to uphold for a
lifetime. The yellow parchment was ripped in one corner,
but the ink was fresh. The red seal of the village council was
stained into the paper, revealing the head of a lion and a
peacock. It was odd, but nobody knew what this stamp
meant or where it came from, yet it was the only seal to be
found in the village. It was an old relic of a life passed into
the wrenching hands of history. Someone must have carried
the stamp during the original journey to the village.

Emmit studied Taska Valimar's signature on the
parchment and tried to imagine signing a life away for the
sake of a half-breed killer. He whispered, "What a pity."

The door opened and Langston stomped into the office

and took off his hat, "I saw the warden and her prisoner out in the field today."

Emmit smiled, nodding his baldhead, "Is he a problem?"

Langston turned his head to the floor, "I saw nothing."

Emmit laughed ironically.

"What is so funny?"

"Cain is a problem. There is more to this than you might think."

Langston looked at the windowsill and then around at the books and the rolled up scrolls and proclamations. He didn't know what Emmit was trying to say — so he waited.

"Langston, your complete confidence in the staff and lottery is foolish. And did she have the staff when they were working in the field?"

"I don't think Valimar will hesitate to cut his throat should he get unruly," Langston said with a tone of annoyance, "You should allow the girl to do the keeping. Give her some consideration."

"Do you think this whole affair should be a consideration? Do you think it should be easy for a man to come and slaughter someone? Should it be easy for him to break free and come after us — to hunt us down?"

Langston turned his head, "He doesn't know his crime. He is an imbecile."

Emmit snarled, "Suppose he is not and he is playing a clever game. I spoke to Dr. Keller. He thought it was very doubtful that this outsider would remember anything, he showed me a book with a medical case in it. A man was hit in a fistfight over a woman, and lost his memory. This poor fellow couldn't remember a shred of his life. A year later, he was clocked in the head with a lifting boom and his head was split open. He survived the injury and regained all his lost memory. A person's memory is a tricky affair."

Langston shook his head doubtfully, "There is no hanging him now."

He wasn't sure what point Emmit was coming to, but it made him nervous. Emmit appeared to have complete composure, but something was burning furiously in his eyes. He came around the desk and took his hat from a hook on the wall.

"I have something I want you to take care of for me — discreetly."

Langston turned and walked to the door. He was bothered that Emmit would suggest killing or attacking Cain. He knew this is what he was planning. He wished that the villagers just killed Cain and then it would be over.

This realization made Langston furious, "I will not go after Cain."

Emmit turned with his voice already raised, "Do not be a fool, Langston. There is a time and a place for everything. Your accusations are rude."

By the hook where Emmit hung his coat was a sack on the floor. He picked it up, with a shifting clatter inside.

"Take this sack and destroy it. Leave it tied, do not open it. Burn it."

Langston took the sack and sighed with relief, "That is all?"

Emmit laughed, "I just need you to burn some old receipts that are now obsolete. I tied them well so nothing would fall out. I know you are often... uncomfortable with my methods, my tax collection, our meetings out in the woods, but we all must survive somehow."

Holding the sack, Langston nodded, "This killer is a difficult thing. We all need to go about our business."

"We have, Langston."

The church bell tolled four in the afternoon as Philip walked toward the church. The open land that stretched beyond the church shimmered in the autumn light as the sun was slowly descending. The edges of the meadow were still lush with grass and a few wild flowers that were now decaying in the cold, frosty mornings. The wind rustled through the grass carrying off little seeds to the north.

Philip reached the door to the church when a voice boomed from behind him. He had found Emmit.

"Philip, over here!"

Through the damp grass, Philip walked to where Emmit stood, concealed in the shadows of twilight. His eyes were red and dry, and his face was a gray pallor.

Philip looked around to be sure they were alone. Emmit coughed hard and spat on the ground. The stone and the dirt seemed to crunch under their shoes as they approached one another.

"This is very furtive. Are you all right?"

"I am fine. I haven't been sleeping well."

Philip looked at his own trembling hands. He didn't like to meet Emmit alone — in such a remote place. He folded his arms across his chest to stop the trembling.

"I will be curt," Emmit said, "A few years ago — I

brought you a box. I need that box, I need it soon. I realize what being in possession of that box means, I know it is illegal, but I feel that I need protection."

Emmit averted his eyes.

"Protection from what?"

Emmit did not answer. A long silence made Philip weary. He changed his tone to a more businesslike manner.

"I am not sure I can locate that box, it has been a long time. I doubt they even work," Philip said trying to talk him out of it. Philip knew exactly where the box was, inside two other boxes on a shelf behind some stacked crates.

"You must find them. I need them. Soon. In a few days."

Philip nodded his head. He couldn't deny him what he wanted; after all, the box belonged to Emmit and he had a receipt for it. Philip had volunteered to keep the box in his warehouse for Emmit, and conceal it from the men of the Annual Visit. If Philip refused to give Emmit his box, he would quietly and very astutely punish Philip for his disobedience, through blackmail, legal tactics or physical threats.

"What is this about... what has brought this on? If they come for the Annual Visit and find you in possession of those pistols — there is no telling what they will do."

His fears spun around in his mind, kneading and churning in him, but he knew not to speak of his fear and treachery. Yet, somehow fear had spoken to Emmit every night, and he had to find a measure of security. He never used weakness unless it was a tool for gain.

"I suppose it is a matter of salvation," Emmit said.

This made little sense. Emmit's words were hollow and

desperate.

"I will do my best to find them. But mind you, the consequences are yours once you take them back..."

Emmit gruffed hard, "I don't need your morality, Philip. I know what means to bear these arms."

Philip remained calm, "At least wait for the Annual Visit to come. They will come before the New Year. Then I will pass them on to you."

Emmit looked at him with determination, "My concern is not with the Annual Visit. Only people who have something to fear, or something to hide, fear the Annual Visit. I must arm myself against the killer."

Philip turned and walked away, disgusted. Emmit walked up behind him and put his hand upon his shoulder firmly, "Do not dismiss this. I don't need your reverence, and I'm not asking for it. You should be pleased to get rid of that box."

Philip tore away from Emmit's grasp, "You'll get your precious weapons."

His mind raced with rage as he walked away from the church, then he turned, "You think that you are above all of us, above God." He pointed to the church. "Somehow you think you're above everything, Emmit. But you aren't above them, when they come, and don't ever believe you will be. Your power over the village is a threadbare cloak you cast off when they arrive."

Philip's trembling hand pointed to the ocean — to the harbor.

They parted. Philip walked down the road back into the village. Hearing a noise, Emmit turned to the church. He paused for a moment and let his anger simmer. When he looked around the corner. The jumping boy jumped down the steps of the church and then back up each step.

He watched the child throwing himself into the next jump. The child, known as the town mute, jumped and spun in the air. He studied the jumping boy silhouetted upon the steps of the church in the autumn twilight; once the box was in his possession, he would have something to hide when they came for the Annual Visit. He would also have a set of pistols to manage his foreseeable offensive against Cain or anyone else that might test his benevolence.

He turned to the road and began walking slowly, with the words of Philip Lazarous buzzing and swirling about in his thick head. There was no other way.

He left the jumping boy jumping.

Taska wrote in a journal. It wasn't a binded journal, but rather, sheets of parchment that she kept in a pile on a wooden shelf in the corner of her cottage. She sat at the table in the center of the room writing. The fire blazed brilliantly, splaying light across the walls and ceiling. Cain sat on the floor, in the corner, staring into the fire. He preferred the floor where he was able to stretch his legs out before curling them up upon the tiny fisherman's cot in the other room to sleep. He sat staring into the fire with a daydream look on his face, trying to locate a point of reference in his empty mind.

Taska was reading over her writing. The ink well was often dry, and her writing was hard to read on the blotted and bleeding parchment that Sophia gave her from the warehouse. This was her record. Through her words, she took careful account of her actions day to day. Being alone, she opened a dialogue between her mind and soul. She feared that her life might be forgotten — without anyone knowing that she lived a significant, however simple life. She had no family to pass on her feelings, her life, or her possessions when she was gone. The parchments were her entire legacy now that he parents were gone.

Taska often looked back through the pages, searching for new perceptions of her past. Having a record of her own state of mind as she made decisions, along with a report of its outcome, was critical for Taska to live a life of singularity. She was able to read her words from ten years ago, when she was young and missing her parents so much. She encased her feelings within words and let them weep out upon the parchments. She allowed anger and loneliness to twist and turn with pain from her mortal heart into immortal dialogue, perpetually echoing her life back to her as she read. Upon the pages, she continued to look for the signs and premonitions from her past that would sanctify an order of living that she could endure; she was searching for a rhythm or pattern that created a divinity of hope.

Cain coughed. She turned her head slightly to listen for more motion, or his disruptive voice. But nothing more came from the corner. He sat staring at the flames. She didn't want to attract his attention. It was like having a ghost in the corner — occupying space and time in her mind.

The purpose of her journal had changed now with Cain's arrival. Taska knew the pages of her past could sustain a life that was peaceful and affable, but now the pages would document a future of uncertainty. The flickering firelight seemed to brighten as the wood crackled and popped.

When Cain spoke from the corner, his voice was weary from plowing up and down the field rows for the past week. She looked at the flickering light upon his brow. He darted his eyes to her face to notice her combed hair and the lace cap she always wore.

"The wind, it is blowing hard — you can hear it rattling the door."

Taska nodded, "The mountains offer a harsh taste of early winter. Those mountains make the fisherman angry. In a few days we will shutter the windows."

He focused on Taska's nose and her round, smooth chin. He turned his eyes away. Cain tried to focus on his own feelings and memories. He had been wary that his gaze would intimidate or anger Taska, yet her face was familiar to his clouded memory. Her brown eyes seemed to inspire Cain while bringing about a dim sorrow that could cast a cold, lasting shadow over any ignited happiness. His mixed emotions didn't come from Taska but from the dim corners and crevasses of his conscience. Taska's face reflected a feminine tenderness that sparked his absent mind. His head was filled with scattered images and emotions, but he felt removed and detached from it all. It lacked a cohesive timeline of cause and effect. It was terribly frustrating and depressing.

Cain laid the palm of his hand on the cool floorboards.

He looked at his hand on the dusty floor. It was very difficult for him to understand the assimilation between the fishermen and the cold mountains. His mind searched for connections and meaning between words and ideas.

While Taska wrote on her parchments, Cain rubbed his hand slowly on the grit of sand and dirt. He grated his hand over the wooden boards, allowing splinters and sand to lodge and dig into his palm. It was his only immediate connection to his feelings and sensations — everything else felt numb.

He could feel life returning to his body day by day, slowly. He could see clearly what was around him. The autumn air, the fields, rejuvenated his physical body, but nothing could spark his memory. He felt emotions that he could not name. He saw images he could not approximate or even comprehend as they erupted from his waking subconscious. He sighed often as he tried to connect ideas together.

Taska flipped through pages of her journal and found phrases that she was searching for. She wrote some ideas down, and pondered their significance. She sought out her freedom that was now broken and discarded. Her words, her own intimate depiction of life would somehow illuminate her current misgivings. All she had to do was keep writing.

Her past, written on the brittle page would become a refuge for her broken spirit mended when she woke each morning, but ripped and tattered into shreds by nightfall. She often began each entry addressed to her mother or father. Most of her writing was long letters to them explaining her life, her decisions, her setbacks, and her love for them. They would be able to read her words as they looked down from heaven to her, and she often thought while working in the fields, that their spirits were inside the cottage reading about her life, consuming her anguish and her small victories.

But when she rushed in, believing in her vision of blessedness, the cottage would be empty and the parchments undisturbed. This was part of living outside the village.

The villagers had a different perception of Taska Valimar and when rumors came about that she was touched, after her father and mother were gone, no one came to the cottage. Taska encouraged them to stay away, so that she could live in peace.

The next morning, it was dreary. The overcast morning reminded Taska of the misery of winter. The shorter days and cold mornings made her worry. She wasn't ready for six months of solitude. It was common for a blizzard to come in the beginning of April, mocking the villagers one more time before warmer weather would arrive. Winter seemed to perpetuate late into the spring, while summer quickly faded early in the fall. The villagers, however, continued with their lives regardless of the weather.

From her window, she looked out to the plowed field and the turned over garden. It was coming quickly. She had to cover the wood, and get to the market to increase her stock of food. If a snowstorm came, the cottage would remain her entire world for days, maybe weeks. With Cain, it would be difficult. She would have to carefully ration out her food supply.

Taska walked out of her cottage and around the house.

Cain was gathering firewood into a pile. She wondered if Cain, with his strength and his diligent work could make a wood shelter to keep the wood dry during the winter.

The soft, wet ground reminded Taska of how bad the weather was last winter. She used all her firewood by February. Then, she had to burn the woodshed to make it through the cold. She had to survive and sacrifice was part of survival. That was when she was alone. Now that she had the help of another person, she could gather more wood, make a woodshed, and make it through.

Cain could have a value after all. She found this amusing; Cain was a valuable tool for the betterment of her own life. Although she would find ways in which Cain would make her life easier, it would never replace her happiness.

Taska's gray outline approached out of the fine mist. He wondered if something was wrong. He feared Taska's anger, although she never allowed him to see her furious. This anxiety that overcame him stemmed from the attack by the villagers, the council and Emmit's constant verbal assaults.

Cain bent over and picked up a few logs and threw them onto the growing pile. She knew where to find lumber to make a woodshed; it could be taken from the old abandoned cottage down the lane.

The wood would be poor and rotten, but she might find enough to make a shelter that would keep the wood dry. It was odd that when a cottage was abandoned for years all that can be salvaged is enough to make a small shed. What pieces of life remained inside, left to the will of nature for so long? She felt good about her venture, aflame with curiosity.

She went inside the cottage. She put her hand upon the staff and paused. The law stated: the warden must restrain the prisoner when not within the bounds of the warden's property, but Taska thought that the manacles were unnecessary. They wouldn't see anyone on their walk down the country lane. Would carrying the staff and the lumber back be too cumbersome?

The staff felt light as she took it from the corner. She could wield the weapon with the motions memorized from her teachings, like steps to archaic folk dancing. She imagined herself, many years ago, in the springtime, laughing and making fun of a duty that she would not likely face. Those who learned how to use the staff with Hillmond Wenner never thought that they would be chosen as a warden. It became fun to learn, as one learns to weave or thatch. She realized how naive it all seemed as she clutched the weapon.

She held the top portion of the staff, twisting it quickly, revealing the long knife concealed in the handle. The metal blade glimmered with polished perfection. Did Cain understand what the staff was for, and what it was meant for? She decided not to tell him that it was more than her walking stick, leaving her safety and protection a secret.

She slipped the knife back into the handle. She wanted to be off before the drizzle and rain set in.

They began down the road — sauntering along. Cain walked in front of her.

"Are we going to the village?"

"We need lumber to build a shed for the fire wood," she said. "The firewood can't be wet or it will not burn well. Or we could store it in your bed." Taska smiled at her quip, but Cain didn't understand.

Down the lane, Taska and Cain turned off into the woods and down the slope. Hidden in the woods was a gray, dilapidated structure, overgrown and falling apart. Nature had invaded the empty spaces that once held its inhabitants. The leaves in the autumn canopy above were colored in yellow, orange and fire red, while the leaves under their feet made up a carpet of brown rot. The dark eves of the cottage had been obscured by nesting birds in its hollows. Time had stopped, leaving the forest to have its way with this vigilant structure. The forest, the mountains and the sea always encroached on the villagers.

It was fitting that the old wood was being consumed, back into the overgrowth and the forest. The beams of the roof belonged to the birds while the floorboards became homes for field mice and garter snakes searching out slumbering dens for the oncoming winter.

Cain walked through the leaves toward the cottage door. The interior of the cottage was dark. The door was not hinged, but lay flat on the floor inside. He saw nothing distinguishable inside the cottage. Toward the back of the cottage some of the roof had collapsed. There was certainly enough lumber, but could they carry it all back. Cain disappeared into the darkness of the cottage. Fear sparked in her; without him in sight, he might flee.

She panicked.

She brought the staff up and shouted, "No! Wait!"

He didn't reappear. She marched through the leaves with her hands firm upon the staff.

When she reached the porch, his figure emerged from the darkness. His arms filled with a bundle of wood. He said, "There is plenty of wood in here for a shed. Most not too badly weathered."

Taska's eyes burned with the fire of her anger, the staff was across her chest, and her knuckles were tight across the bones in her hands. She was prepared to strike.

She lowered the staff and walked over to Cain to study his eyes. Although she believed Cain truly knew nothing of his past, she was suspicious of his mind — suspicious that he may ultimately deceive her.

Taska was standing at the door. It was dim inside the cottage. Cain walked down the front steps of the cottage and threw the wood down in a clank and fumble of lumber and earth.

She stepped inside. In the rafters, forest doves had made a nest. The walls were broken and fallen. There were stains on the standing wall, which at first inspection, she didn't understand. Finally, she realized that pictures had stained the wall where they had once hung. The sun, over time, came through the windows and faded the wood around the picture, leaving distinctive marks on the wall — oval, rectangle and square. It confirmed life there.

Taska shifted the staff to her other hand and scuffed her shoe upon the floor. She pondered over the ant-eaten floorboards that appeared unreliably weak, yet after all these years they held their strength.

Taska walked back out to check on Cain. He looked at her oddly, "Did you know who lived here?"

"I did not know of the people who lived here. I suppose

it was a family."

Cain was struggling with the concept of getting the wood back as he looked to the path that led to the road, "I do not think it will be hard to get this wood back. Maybe two or three trips."

Taska was troubled by his phrase, although it sounded innocent enough. Cain was 'thinking.'

Now that the cottage was explored, all that remained was the chore of building the wood shed. Taska turned back to the door of the cottage and peered at the dark shadows inside. She wondered if her cottage looked that dark inside. She had glimpsed into the human heart, dark and foreboding.

Cain posed a curious question, "What if the people who live here come back?"

Taska examined the falling roof line atop the house, "What do you mean? There is nothing here."

Cain agreed, "That is all people have sometimes."

Taska looked into his eyes. She turned away quickly so Cain wouldn't see her surprise. He was more than a shell, lost in the blood and swell of his thrashing. His perceptions enlightened Taska's tangible portrait of the human heart, empty, rotten and fallen into ruin. He was "thinking." His mind was filling with ideas and concepts — for him better, and for her — worse.

The point of the staff was sitting in the leaves. Cain was not stupid, just incomplete. She pitied the fact that his mind created the sardonic sense of his own capture and applied it to something remote like the abandoned cabin, but not himself. His mind was capable of treachery and a rational awareness of his life. She had to remember that. She turned her eyes from the staff to Cain's pondering face.

"Carry all you can. We will come back for more," she said. He gathered up the wood in his arms while Taska took a few pieces, carrying the staff in her other. It was cumbersome.

They returned back to Taska's cottage. As they piled wood, Langston approached on his gray horse trotting along the edge of the woods. She threw down the lumber and held the staff firmly. He was spying on her. Her anger simmered. Would they always check on her — watching the prisoner? Cain dropped a pile of wood in the grass.

Cain saw the gray horse, and turned to see her reaction. He felt frightened, but Taska's calm was conspicuous. The horse and rider approached through the heavy mist, crossing the muddy field. Cain went to Taska's side. He stood a few paces behind her, fearing the coming conflict.

Langston approached by the vegetable garden. The horse was fighting, twisting its neck as it fought at the bit under Langston's hard hand. He barked as the horse spun in a circle. Langston had to turn his head to look at Taska as the horse turned round and round.

"Your prisoner is spooking the animal," he said bitterly.

"What is it you want, Langston?" Taska shouted over the blowing horse, now prancing in circles. He looked at Cain and turned his heavy eyes to her.

"I am going to the village. I wanted to check on him," he shouted. He was eyeing Cain.

"The council should not waste their time worrying about him," she rebuked. "He is obedient. Don't come here again unless you are ready to take him with you."

Langston shook his head at her scornful voice. The horse spun around in a tumult of gray fur, leather and human flesh.

"I saw you walking on the road without him chained. You were breaking the law. I see no chains now."

Taska was stern, her voice commanding, "He is not off the property, he need not be chained on the property. I know the law, and I am aware of the charter, although you and your council may not think so."

Langston, now out of breath from fighting with his gray nag of a horse pulled up the beast with a violent jerk and said, "I don't want to see him without chains again. What I saw earlier will be our little secret. We are watching you. I know what you are doing."

He rode across the small field to the road. He would soon be reporting to Emmit and the rest of the council. Taska saw Cain's fear.

"Am I to be chained?" he asked. Taska dropped the staff and began gathering up the wood.

Cain looked back at the woodpile, avoiding Taska's eyes. She didn't answer immediately. The staff was lying in the grass among the other scrapes of wood. It was all falling apart, like the old cottage in the woods.

"I am afraid when we go into the village, you must be chained," she replied. "It is not safe for you, but it is the law. It is public humility. It is part of your sentence."

Cain squatted down to the lumber to find the best pieces to build with, "Is it safe?"

Taska looked at the horse off in the distance as it

disappeared into the woods, "You have been attacked twice. Everyone knows the crime you have committed. You will be defenseless in chains."

"You must get supplies. And they want to see me," he said. "I am not afraid."

"We will go in time. Let us deal with our shed today, and the village later."

They began building the woodshed. They both proved quite capable of building the shed. After finding some rusted nails and a hammer, they began building the wooden shed. She did not allow Cain to use the hand saw, but allowed him to pound nails. By dusk, under the overcast sky, they completed a rather large wood shed. She would have plenty of firewood and plenty of time to gather more before the first snow fall.

In the village, Langston rode in on his horse and climbed off before they hit the cobblestone road. He knew the horse would spook when his wide hooves began to clatter and clack on the cobblestones. He tied the beast to the tree and walked down the road.

He headed down to the doctor's cottage. Reverend Conrad and his swarm of children from the school were coming down the hill. Langston didn't like the tumult of children yelling and running around through the afternoon solace. The children were running around the big trees lining the road, singing and calling out names. The Reverend always took pride in his students. He was stern and often harsh with the children, but he was devoted to them. The Reverend caught up to Langston before he could hurry off.

"Langston, I hope all is well with the council now."

"Yes, things are fine."

The school children ran down the hill, passing the two men.

"School is out for the day so soon?"

"You can't keep them like animals. They need to run wild before it gets too cold."

"I suppose."

The Reverend cocked his head, "Is something wrong?"

"Children make me uneasy," Langston said.

"You don't look well. If you need to talk, I am always...."

"I hate the little runts... it is nothing more," he stammered.

"Fine. Well good day to you then," the Reverend said.

Langston marched off down the lane, cursing and swearing under his breath. Reverend Conrad looked out to the sea. It was a wide bank of heavy fog pulling into the village, like a smoldering fire spreading all around them.

Sophia stopped to speak with the Reverend for a moment. Seeing her white cheeks and her copper hair, he was reminded of her as student. He felt like he could at least tame some of his children and make them into good villagers. Sophia was one of his few good-natured students.

"It was a lasting sermon you gave last Sunday. Your best yet," she said. The Reverend found inspiration in her youth, while she found inspiration in the Reverend's holy bond.

"You are kind to say that. But, it was like any other sermon," he said gently.

"It was very moving."

"I must say I am surprised that you haven't settled down and started a family. I am sure your father would like nothing more."

Sophia blushed and then laughed, "I am not sure if I am ready to settle down, although Claas, the fishing captain has spoken to me on occasion. I think most of the men in the village are wary of my father's position on the council. It has been difficult to think about anything since the Colberton murder and Taska's service."

He perked up with curiosity. "How is she? I have been saying prayers for the girl."

"It has been oppressive, but she is putting him to work."

"Do you think she will return to church?"

"There is no way to tell. I will tell her you were asking about her return to Sunday services. She will be touched by your concern," Sophia said. "I must be off, sir. My father gets anxious when I am late."

He stopped her with a hand on her shoulder, "Taska is pure. Apparently, she has never connected our history to her family, her remote home and her desperately hard life. People believe that she is blind — or the one fortunate soul left in the village. She never attended classes at the church. Her parents taught her to read and write before they disappeared. Rumors suggested that she is wicked, but she is quite the opposite. Forgive me for keeping you, but you should see Taska Valimar as I see her. God bless, child."

Sophia hurried down to the warehouse. She didn't understand what the Reverend was saying. She saw Taska as self-reliant. Taska spoke her mind and cared for the

people that cared for her. Why did he call her the one
fortunate soul left in the village?

> *Dear Mother & Father,*
> *I have missed you of late, because of the*
> *prisoner I have been forced to acquire. It has*
> *been difficult to move from living alone to*
> *living with a lifelong servant. The staff and*
> *Hillmond Wenner's gibberish of honor and*
> *service never meant anything in the past —*
> *now it all just seems absurd.*
>
>   *I have been susceptible to hardship*
> *since your departure. I have never once*
> *questioned these difficulties. However, this*
> *selection as a warden for this hollow, non-*
> *feeling killer seems to be the cruelest.*
>
>   *I have been thinking about our*
> *conversations, before you left. You spoke of*
> *salvation — away from the church — a city*
> *where the streets are silver and gold and the*
> *water sparkles like gems floating across the*
> *sea. You spoke of the gardens and the music.*
> *You said it was filled with art and theatre,*
> *brimming with culture. I have been thinking*
> *of a golden world in my mind. I have been*
> *catching moments in time, believing the*
> *images in my mind like those of holy visions*
> *— and I now believe the golden city is my*
> *future. Escape from sorrow and injustice is*
> *not idle amusement — but my only hope. I*

have come to believe... that if I realize and
see this golden world in great detail, perhaps
it will pull me closer, draw me away from
misery. I wonder if I might find you among
the streets, among the people and beyond.

    I suppose this is all sacrilegious to
the church, but I have found little shelter
under the wing of religion. These thoughts
are pure. They allow me to be hopeful. If the
villagers read my thoughts and devotions of
the golden world, they will cast me as a
heretic. I find it difficult to believe that they
could cast me in a fate worse than my
present state.

    The prisoner remains obedient.

    Taska stopped writing and put her pen down. The door opened. It was Sophia. She let herself in. Her cheeks were flushed from the cold September night. The brass tip of the pen, still shining with wet ink stood suspended over the parchment, poised to strike. She placed the pen on an old piece of material that she used to clean the pen tip. The ink bled into the fabric.

    "I hope I'm not disturbing you."

    Taska shook her head, "Of course not. Come in."

    Taska took Sophia's cape and hung it on a hook near the fireplace. Cain sat with his back against the wall and his eyes peering up at her.

    "Is he being punished?" she asked. Sophia noticed his scars were fading and his hair seemed longer.

"No, he sits on the floor," Taska said.

She sat across from Taska. The parchments were sprawled out on the table. She looked at them. The tips of Taska's fingers were dotted with black ink. Sophia knew about the parchments, but never asked what was on them or why she was writing. She didn't want to appear too curious, or overbearing. She was thoughtful and considerate in obtaining anything that Taska might need from the village, yet she was still part of the interwoven social strands which created the village web and its mediocrity.

"He seems very pensive tonight," Sophia said looking at Cain.

"Yes, I have been working him. I managed to finish a wood shed a few days ago. It was something I needed for the winter. He is gifted with tools. Must be something of his past. He is good with his hands."

It was difficult to continue long conversations with Sophia. Taska's mind was clouded by her thoughts inked in marks on the page.

"I hope the market is still gathering in the village?" Taska asked, renewing the conversation. "I must get to the market before the first of October, winter is coming quickly."

"Oh yes, it will gather for another two weeks. They discontinue with the grounding of the fishing fleet. They will ground the fleet in the third week of October. You have time. When they ground the boats for the winter, no one has room to set up the market."

Taska nodded and recalled the boats in their cradles of wood, covered in brown canvass and burlap, nestled all about the waterfront for the winter. Most of the boats were stored behind the warehouse and the cobbler's shop.

Her memories of the winter always seemed gray and dark like the season itself. She knew she would have to get to the market to stock up for the winter with things that she did not yet have in storage: canned tomatoes, canned fruit and some alcohol.

"But the blacksmith won't close," Taska said with sentimental knowing. She used to walk to the blacksmith's shop at dusk last winter and speak with him. She would stand near the coals of red fire flickering in the blacksmith's forge. She would keep warm while the blacksmith repaired tools or boat-tackle. The red, soft glow that came off the burning forge fell across the new, soft snow at dusk, serving as a vivid memory of winter. The cobblestones faded quickly into the even blanket of white. Black slate and wooden roofs became white and clean like soaked muslin still wet from the wash tub.

"I think everyone in the village is wondering about him. They haven't seen you in a few weeks now," Sophia said, pulling Taska from her recollection.

Taska shook her head in disgust, "I thought they would be happy to forget him out here."

"They fear what they don't know. If they don't see him every day, then they think he is behind every tree, in every window, waiting. He is the village spook."

"That would explain why they keep coming out here — Langston, Jarod, and Hillmond Wenner."

Cain looked at the flames and mused over the terror. His eyes turned to Taska. He could not comprehend the fear he instilled in the village. The one thing Cain feared was making Taska's life worse than it had been. She was all he knew. Taska looked quickly at Cain without feeling, without worry. It brought him dim consolation.

"I'm glad you are getting along out here. I worry."

Strands of her rich, black hair obscured Taska's cheek and her small ear lobe. Cain had tried to please her with complete obedience and respect. Although Cain didn't know what to call his emotions and his desires, he was faithful to Taska, like a child to a mother. He admired her. He noticed the strands of hair that escaped Taska's cap and shimmered over the fair skin down her cheek. He admired her tolerance and compassion for him, although he didn't understand precisely what to call it.

He continued to rub the palm of his hand on the floor. He imagined the murder over and over in his mind, not of which he knew by memory, but a story made up in his shadowy mind by the badgering questions and innuendoes of the council as they shaped him into a monster.

Sophia gazed to the pressed red rose in the frame on the wall, "I suppose I should tell them that they need not bother you."

"They know where their assassin resides. Langston and Emmit have been poking around here. They want to be sure their marriage of innocence and guilt has not been troubled," Taska said. "But, if they fear him, as you say, they will continue to come back. Some will bring gifts that I won't use, while others will come, less the hypocrite and just ask me where he is and what he is doing. One by one the entire village will come to me out of curiosity"

Taska's fury was slowly building with discipline and direction. Cain was not the evil monster that Emmit and the council professed. The village always bent and twisted reality.

"They want to see the evil. They want to see what you do to protect the village," Sophia said. She was shameful for saying that as she rubbed her thin hands together with discomfort.

"The night they brought him, they came with no feeling of guilt or condemnation; they came to see a deplorable act in a tragic performance of life that they were so happy to be spared from. I could see it in their eyes. They were waiting to see how fortunate they were, measured against my misfortune," Taska said.

Her voice was hollow as she stared off to the staff leaning in the corner by the cupboard. "They will continue to come."

The crackle of the fire covered the silence, keeping time in the cottage. The smell of burning wood and must hung in the air.

"Don't think I am angry with you, Sophia. I've become very good at being angry and shooing people away. I often forget how to speak among friends."

"They come to see what they fear. They want to keep him in front of them, their eyes always upon him, so they don't have to look over their shoulders. But they have no regard for your peace."

"But why don't they trust the honor and the privilege that comes with the staff? They don't even trust their own laws, I don't understand that. I want to know why I can't be trusted," Taska pleaded.

Sophia looked to the pages spread out on the table. That was where Taska sought out her answers. She peered at the black ink on the tip of the pen. The ink held all the answers — all the nobility, all the freedom — all the contentment that was stripped away during the lottery. Sophia wondered how long she had been searching, and how long she would continue.

Late that night, Sophia walked home in the cold night air. A half-moon shined dimly, giving her guidance in the woods. But she never worried about walking at night. It was sometimes a comfort to walk in the darkness where no one could see her.

She admired Taska's seclusion from the village. She saw Taska as a saint in her detachment, living away from the rest of the village, unspoiled by the village drudgery. Sophia often wished that she too was away, and that a few days could lapse without seeing anyone.

However, the women in the village assumed Taska lived alone because of her unsettled mind. It was just recently that Mrs. Jarod called Taska a half-breed. She said, "No woman can live like an animal. She is hardly a woman at all — she is deranged." The village created and spun out their own stories when Taska refused to supply them.

Sophia could never explain to her what was said about her in the village. Taska lived her life unaware. She didn't understand the intricate web of deceit that spread about the village. Taska should have immunity from their social treachery.

Sophia had a strange way of recalling people. She

remembered faces without faults, unmindful of their flaws; but upon seeing them she was reminded of their blemishes, a scar, or a broken tooth. Yet, when Sophia saw Taska in the cottage, she seemed radiant. Taska was beautiful and she found comfort in knowing Taska was pure, just as she appeared in Sophia's mind. Taska was a true vision, without fears, without cracks in her porcelain skin.

It was Taska's beauty that made Sophia adore her. It was her freedom that beckoned Sophia's never ending devotion.

She came out of the woods to the opened field. The steeple rising above the hill was silhouetted against the stars. The church was some distance away but the tip of the steeple could be seen. As she came down the hill, her eyes gazed at the light in the church where the Reverend retired for the night. She felt uneasy with his unyielding conviction of the pure evil within Cain.

Sophia walked past the great maples that lined the top of the road leading down into the village. She could see the lights in the cottage windows and even on the fishing boats. Each light illuminated a different face in Sophia's mind. She passed familiar trees and the cottages that she saw every day. An unsettled feeling came over her. She wanted the vibrant feeling of the woods instilled in her bones. She longed for the smell of must and mold. She wanted to gaze upon Taska's brow and caress her flawless cheek. Sophia imagined the touch of Taska's cheek upon the back of her hand. The touch was so lucid and real in her mind. Allowing her vivid dream to resonate for a moment, she paused as it began to slip away like a match, brightest at first strike until it vanishes by the slightest breath, into a stream of pale, dissipating smoke. The back of Sophia's hand tingled with desire.

The town was taking over again. She felt herself becoming immersed back into the murky waters of the village that always left a film of nervous agitation and hypocrisy upon her pale skin.

Sophia was happy to get home. The night air chilled her. She wanted to get close to the fire and talk to her mother about Taska and her quiet life on the edge of the world.

Sophia turned the corner of the family cottage and found someone standing there waiting by the rain barrel. It was Claas the fishing captain.

"I've come to see you. Come to talk. Have you been with Taska?"

"I have."

He didn't reply to her answer. Claas had a broad chest, thick arms and coil rope legs that seemed to flex with a rolling sea. His face was deeply rutted with the sun and the wind wearing his features into relief. He squinted even in the dark — a force of habit from the open sea. Sophia was the antithesis of this fishing master. She was thin; her skin pale, like powder and her mind was refined. Claas admired her fragility and her beauty, but often feared her educated mind and political father. He never knocked on the door, or asked for Sophia; he waited outside until she came out, or she passed by to go in. Sometimes, he would spend hours waiting, only to find that she had gone to bed. Philip, coming back from a meeting in the church would see him leaning against the corner of the cottage. "She is taking inventory at the warehouse," or, "she is gone to bed — not feeling well."

Philip sympathized with Claas. Sophia never pushed him away. It was a tenuous relationship. Although Sophia never sought out his intimate love or companionship, she was satisfied with his devotion to her and his silent, perceptive manner.

"I am sorry for your friend," Claas said. "I will not stay, I just wanted to see you and let you know I have not been lost to the sea."

Sophia nodded. He turned and sauntered back down to the water. Something about that fisherman stung her heart. It would be safe to say that if any fisherman were lost at sea, the whole town would know and attend the funeral. Claas was like that. He spoke in vague, riddle like statements. She felt her stomach tighten as affection sometimes can do, pausing to watch him walk down the lane.

"Sophia, is your father home?" said Old Kavner hobbling from the other direction.

"I suppose, I have yet to go inside," she said.

They went inside. Philip and his wife were sitting at the table. Philip was looking over some papers and his wife was sewing. Old Kavner stepped right in, "I am sorry — to barge in, but I need you to see this Philip. I found something you might want to see."

Philip nodded, "All right. Let me get my cloak and we will go."

"Anything serious, Kavner?" said Mrs. Lazarous.

"I am not sure. Your husband will confirm it for me."

Philip nodded, "I will be back soon."

Sophia chimed in, "May I go along?"

"Wait here. It is getting cold out. You have been out all night as it is."

Mrs. Lazarous asked, "Who were you talking to out there?"

Sophia sat down where her father was reading, "Claas came again."

"He is a nice man."

"Yes, he is."

Philip took a lantern with him.

They left the cottage and walked up the lane. Old Kavner took him to a place beyond the church and out into the tracts of the open fields. They came to a small pavilion between two open fields. The farmers and the croppers used this pavilion for gathering, meeting or just to rest during the harvest time. Old Kavner was out of breath as they walked down the path to the small, opened shelter.

They shined the lantern under the pavilion. They looked around at the benches and tables. To the left was a small open fire pit where men could cook food, heat their brandy or just warm their hands. Old Kavner brought him to this pit. Philip shined the light into the ashes and the grate. Old Kavner lifted the grate out and tossed it aside.

"What is it? What am I looking for?" Philip said getting tired of being led all the way out to a farm field.

"Here — look at these."

Philip looked closer. He saw an old burlap sack that was burned and charred. Most of it was ash. In the corner of the pit, scattered about, where small wooden tiles. He picked one up and realized what it was.

"These are the tiles from the lottery barrel. They have the names of the eligible wardens on them," Philip explained. "This one is Taska Valimars."

Old Kavner pointed down into the pit.

Philip reached in and grabbed a handful of tiles. He pulled them up and looked at them, "This one, too. And this one. They all say Taska Valimar."

Philip threw them down, "Mother of God, they fixed the lottery."

Philip and Old Kavner collected the tiles and wrapped them in Philip's cloak.

"Kavner — not a word to anyone. Not yet. You are one of the oldest men in this village. You have seen treachery and tragedy. This must be kept secret — until we know who was behind this."

"I will do anything for you, Philip."

Philip nodded and patted his friend on the back.

Taska stared out the little window encrusted with dirt and cobwebs, waking to the dim light of the rising sun. She wondered why she didn't hear the church bells. The tones always woke her no matter how deep her sleep. She thought that perhaps she was so tired that she didn't hear them.

Taska's mind wandered away from the church bells. He would soon wake up. She would have to prepare Cain for the day ahead. The market would assemble in the cobblestone square. Her stomach turned, "I must go today."

The charter spelled out that Cain must be chained. Once

she affixed Cain to her side with chains and shackles, her freedom would be destroyed. The leather belt was new and stiff, while the chain seemed like part of an old boat mooring, rusty and tired. The two belts and the chain remained in the corner where Langston put them when they came weeks ago. Taska saw the increasing color of dawn brighten the root cellar that was now her bedroom. Three weeks, she thought as she raised herself up out of bed.

She sat up in bed and looked at her dress slung over the hook on the back of the door. She mused at the dress, remembering the first few nights with Cain, when she wore her dress to bed. She was so worried that she would have to get up in the middle of the night and tend to him, or catch him as he tried to escape. But slowly, she realized he would never escape his chains. She began to trust them.

Taska took her dress from the hook. She had spent the previous night stitching together a dress with a rip in the shoulder that tore while walking through the dense brush by the abandoned cottage a few days ago. The sparrows and their endless squawk didn't allow Taska to slip away into her dreams of the old abandoned cottage.

As she tied the back ties of her dress, she glanced down at her shoes, worn and splitting at the soles. She laced them tight and thought - my shoes can wait, but I must buy my winter supplies.

Taska walked out into the common room and fetched her dirt and soot stained apron that she wore every day. She looked to the dark corner where the two belts tangled in metal links and a rusted lock.

Cain moved about in his bed. She could hear his bed

chains clattering. It was time to unlock his restraints. The staff stood next to the cupboard, her parchments stacked on top. Everything that Taska could call a possession could fit in that cupboard. On the wall near the cupboard, she had a small pressed rose in a clean, polished frame. The brown flattened rose, which appeared like a blot of spilled crimson ink, was given to her mother by her father when they were married. That is what they told her. But when a very young Taska would ask her mother to see her wedding dress, her mother would say, "I used it up." Taska assumed that meant it was used for fabric in a tablecloth or a common dress. Taska, as a child, wondered where it went, a table cloth, a gown for someone else. Even now, she wondered how much of her parents life was still here, still cut and reused around her. It felt like most of it was gone now.

Taska continued to look for that dress, always dropping subtle hints, "What color was your wedding dress?" But Taska's mother never answered.

Taska took the staff from the corner next to the cupboard, deciding it was time to unlock Cain. The council would be upset if they knew that she didn't sleep with the staff next to her bed, but she couldn't bear to see it when she first opened her eyes. She didn't want to make her stomach feel worse than it already had been when she woke every morning, another day with him.

Beyond the door of the bedroom his empty eyes waited for her.

She appeared at the door as Cain's eyes turned to her and changed. She stood with the staff in her hand and her keys in the other. His odd look continued as if he knew something she did not.

"Your bindings, give them to me," she said. Taska then feared he might be free.

She let the staff fall away, slamming to the floor. She brought his wrists up quickly. She heard the chains. He was still bound in the iron cuffs. Her fear was becoming obvious as she stood back.

"Your white cap. You aren't wearing your cap,"

Taska waited until she understood his words. She realized she had not put on her cap. The strings that always brushed her cheeks - were absent.

"Give me your bindings. I will free you," she commanded. She was frustrated. She was angry that she forgot to put on her bonnet, getting caught up in her hazy dreams, oblivious of every detail.

"Are you angry that I have seen you this way?" he said as he rose from the bed and buttoned his shirt together. Taska ignored him as the pain in her stomach twisted hard with sharp cramping pain.

"I do not care," Taska feigned indifference.

"But you have never shown me your hair before. Not without your bonnet."

"My hair is not something that I hide from you, or anyone. We must tend to the fire wood."

Cain heard her command, and he would not disobey her, but he wanted to say something more. Not because he wanted to defy, but he wanted to reach out to her without a physical touch.

"Don't be angry. Suppose I did not see your hair," Cain's voice dimmed in his attempt to appease her. They walked into the common room and to the door. Taska opened the door to see the sun illuminating the trees of the nearby forest, brilliant with gold and red. The crisp morning air was invigorating. They walked out by the garden. The frost dampened Taska's hem, although she held it up with one hand.

The sun was just cresting over the trees. The mountain faces glistened white and gray, and the snow was blowing off the highest peak.

Cain returned from the woodpile with a few logs for the fire. He noticed Taska's engrossing gaze over the mountains. He looked to the high precipices.

"What do you see? It is as if you have never seen the trees and the mountains. Have you forgotten about them?"

Taska turned her head down. She thought — *he will take everything.* But she tried to calm her panic, "If you look, and carefully observe, you will see that it is different every day. The season is changing."

"What is different? Out here? The mountains are different?" Cain said in disbelief. His voice came to life.

Taska brought her hand to her waist and slowly rubbed her aching stomach. The twisting would not stop.

"I don't understand," Cain said glancing quickly over the woods and the field before him, but he didn't see any change in the mountains. The tree looked the same to him. He couldn't discern the subtle difference that a new day would bring. He could see change, like her hair without the bonnet, yet he couldn't understand its complete meaning.

"Today we are going to the market."

"I will be chained."

"It is the law."

He put the four logs he was carrying down on the ground. He felt nervous and irritated.

"Will you go with your bonnet on?" he asked. Would the villagers follow him and create a spectacle? All he knew of the village was assault and bitterness.

"I will wear my cap."

"Will they kill me?"

Taska slid her hand down the smooth handle of the staff. She knew that some would fear him. His scarred brow would make him seem like a monster. Taska took a deep breath and rubbed her stomach.

"They will look at you," she said calmly, "but they won't fear you, they won't attack you."

Cain nodded and gathered up the wood again. Taska stood peering out to the mountains. Perhaps her parents where there beyond the great range of snow and ice.

"Will they fear you?" said Cain.

Compassion came from his lips, which was a newfound feeling he couldn't describe or control. Cain was bound to what Taska showed him. And what was worse, she was bound to how he felt.

Taska turned her head quickly with revelation and stabbed the staff hard into the soft grass, entangled with leaves and sticks, "The chores will not wait."

Cain walked back to the cottage with the wood. Taska walked behind him. Her stomach loosened up, but each day it was getting worse.

Sophia had to begin the dreadful task of inventory at the warehouse. It was a chore she had to perform every year. Her father always wanted it done and documented in the ledger before the Annual Visit, which was never announced but happened in late fall or early winter. By law, the warehouse had to have a complete listing of its total contents. This was a difficult feat because the contents ebbed and flowed constantly. Sophia had to count every nail, every coil of rope, and every crate. It would take at least ten days. What made it worse were the people who would come and purchase things that she had already documented, which made amending her inventory difficult. She would have to change the list again and again.

Sophia could hear the jumping boy outside the door on the wooden steps. The repetitive sound was reassuring, although she couldn't understand why. She listened to his rhythmic jumps, three jumps, and then a pause. As he began the cycle again, she wondered if anyone ever listened to the boy and his jumping.

She rose from the table and put on her smock. She thought of where she might start her inventory. It was such a monumental chore, that she often compared it to counting grains of sand on a beach. She looked at the first item on the list: the old sea cot. She had given that to Taska. She scratched it off the list.

Philip came from the back of the warehouse, exhausted.

"Father, what have you been doing?" she said.

"I am looking for a box — with two old pistols in it. They belong to Emmit. I want to find them before he comes again for them," he said short of breath and covered in dust.

Sophia nodded, "A brown, wooden box with a rusty lock on it?"

"Yes, you have seen it — recently?"

"Emmit came early this morning — claimed it was important. It took some time, but I found them."

Philip stomped his foot down hard, "Ugh!"

"What is the matter?"

"I wanted to destroy the box."

"He doesn't have a key for it," she said. "He will have to break it open."

Philip calmed himself, "What is done is done."

"What does he want with two old pistols?"

"God only knows," Philip said and went out the front door of the store.

"They are illegal. He can be hung by the Annual Visit if he is caught," she said. Her words followed her father down the stairs. Sophia went back to the warehouse to begin inventory.

Philip came back in, "Sophia, you might come out. Taska is coming."

She threw down the inventory list, "Are they at the market?"

"They are coming."

"Are they bound together?"

"Yes," he said stepping back outside.

"Oh, good God."

Sophia turned her head down. The women of the village would harass her. Say things and offer her nothing but stares and sidelong looks. Sophia looked for her cloak. She wanted to greet Taska before she waded into the busy market with

Cain.

She wondered, Mrs. Colberton — where was she this morning?

Sophia tossed her cape over her shoulders. Coming out of the shop, she almost toppled over the jumping boy. Sophia sighed in frustration, forgetting her visceral thoughts earlier about the curious child. She searched around the busy market. When she arrived at the warehouse every morning, the market was not yet assembled for the day. But when she came out — it was as if a caravan of gypsies had come and set up camp while she was working.

She walked down the steps and passed Mrs. Jarod. She smiled to her, "Good morning, Sophia. The market will stop gathering in a few weeks. I dread the winter solitude."

Sophia smiled and glanced up the hill towards the tall maples. She could not see them coming. Maybe her father was mistaken.

"I look forward to the winter," Sophia said as she looked over the cart of blankets that Mrs. Jarod was peddling. Also on her cart were glass canisters filled with tomatoes, fruit and cucumbers, the brass lids shimmered in the mid-morning sun.

"Your mother hasn't come for her tomatoes yet. I hope she hasn't forgotten," said Mrs. Jarod.

Sophia smiled, "No, I'm sure she won't forget. I will remind her."

The doctor came out of his cottage and looked up the lane. He had gotten word that Taska was coming. Sophia moved up toward his office. This was the first time Taska had come into the village since Cain was delivered to her forest cottage.

She turned and walked across the market, her shoes clacking on the cobblestone. She wondered again, where is Alice Colberton? She scanned the crowd of villagers. She didn't seem to be in the market. She would throw herself into fits if she saw Cain in the village.

Dr. Keller walked slowly down the steps and across the lane to Emmit's office and stood by the door. Emmit came out and spoke with him. Sophia walked casually up toward Emmit and the doctor. She wanted to turn Taska away. She thought about what she would say — don't come — they will tear you apart — just let me bring you the things you need. But she just waited, watching.

Dr. Keller turned to Sophia, "Good morning." But, Emmit said nothing, training his eyes on the two approaching figures.

"He is chained," said Emmit.

If she stood with Dr. Keller and Emmit, it might imply coercion. Turn back, please turn back, Sophia whispered.

Sophia moved away from Emmit and the doctor and approached Taska and Cain. She heard Emmit ask the doctor, "Where the devil is Alice? I hope she stayed home today."

She looked down at her feet, trying to extinguish her regretful apprehension before she greeted Taska. Nothing will happen — nothing will go wrong — she thought, concentrating on the rocks and the pebbles in the road. All of a sudden, fear came across her chest and up to her cheeks like a sheet of rain. She felt the blood rush through her complexion. She clenched her hands tight to hide their nervous shake. She thought not of the villagers and their perceptions, but the fragility of Taska's nature.

Taska was carrying a large basket in one hand and the staff in the other. Cain pulled a small wooden rickety wagon, rattling along the road.

"Good morning," Sophia said with a pensiveness that flushed her cheeks.

"Sophia, good morning, we've come for the winter stock pile."

Taska's voice was clear and crisp, strengthened by the morning walk through the woods. Nothing from the village had touched her yet. Sophia tried to say something simple, something that would seem ordinary.

"They are all down there," she said. Her voice fluttered somewhat as she looked back over her shoulder to Emmit and Dr. Keller. They were walking down the lane to take up a better position in the market and deliver the news — the assassin and the warden were coming.

Sophia slowly walked with them while the sound of the cart crackled and scratched across the dirt track. Taska was bound to Cain as the law deemed essential, but Sophia never thought that physical binding would be so vile. It was the law, but to see the chain, strung between them like an umbilical cord from mother to son, brought a deep feeling of grief. A waistband was wrapped around Cain. The chain disappeared into her dress just below the small of her back. They could only pull away a few feet from one another before the chain tightened.

Cain's hands were not bound at the wrists. For some wardens it was a precaution. Most criminals that were bound at the wrist were being punished with wrist shackles for crimes like stealing or indecent fondling.

Taska held the staff like a walking stick. Sophia found a hint of Taska's conformity in the way she carried the weapon, with refined dignity. Now, Taska had to walk into a sea of bitter approval and cruelty. It was difficult to be part of this act. They reached the cobblestones of the village center. Cain looked around with apprehension. He was looking for Emmit, Jarod and Langston — his accusers.

"Are you working today?" Taska asked in an amiable way.

"Yes, I am taking inventory. My father wants it done before the grounding of the fishing fleet," said Sophia.

Taska swung the basket in her hand slightly, "I am sure it is not easy in such a large warehouse."

The Reverend was approaching. Sophia thought of intercepting him. Her mind ran wild with fear knowing the Reverend's quick tongue and malevolent feelings aimed at Taska's bond to Cain.

The Reverend marched his frail bones to Taska. He had a purpose. Sophia's eyes were so wide that she seemed to have a continuous gasp captured within her expression.

He noted that Cain was chained, "So he has come back to town, he has come with his guardian."

Cain's heart raced and his cheeks flushed. The old man's profile was one of the first impressions etched into Cain's blank white memory, with his wrinkled forehead and white hair.

"Reverend, this morning, I didn't hear the bells ring out," Taska said clearly. She turned slightly, then focused upon his white collar that gave him his distinction above the other villagers.

"I hope the bells in the church are not in disrepair," Taska queried.

The Reverend turned up his head. His eyes squinted in the shadow of the morning sun. He chose his words precisely. He wanted to provoke a rage in Taska that would humiliate her martyrdom.

"It was decided... the bells need not ring... only on Sunday. The council decided that no one could hear them so far from the village, so why bother with the burden," the Reverend said.

Taska brought her chin up and twisted her brow, "I am able to hear them clearly from my cottage."

Sophia looked at Taska and then to Cain who kept his face turned to the ground.

Taska continued, "I suppose, if you believe that, then we should only have faith in Our Father on Sunday, while the other days we can believe in anything that we wish. I thought that those bells were a gift brought a long time ago by the people who founded this village. Every time those bells toll, they bring out a small accolade to their kindness. That is what you have preached to us, it is not for us to listen to the bells, it is a voice of our past being sent to God. It is selfish to think that because you are deaf to the bells, so is our Holy Father."

The Reverend pulled back his hasty words. He knew that Taska, while walking with evil in the guise of an absent-minded assassin, also lived her odd life not knowing anything about the history — the ancestry — the Annual

Visit. The Reverend pitied Taska's ignorance.

"It wasn't my decision to make. It was decided by the council, and it was written." His words were clean and to the point. He turned to Sophia and nodded, "I must return to my work. No time to prattle on here."

He meandered away in a hobble that seemed like that of a three-legged dog, lacking a sense of fluidity in his step.

"Let's get what we need Cain, before it gets too late."

Taska appeared unaffected by her meeting with the Reverend.

The market was crowded with people from the village, stocking up with food and supplies to get them through the winter. Taska looked at all the villagers that she knew trying to place names to faces. Being away from the village had made her forgetful of all the people. She looked at Cain and his cart to make sure he wasn't struggling.

Taska walked to the edge of the crowd. Some people looked at her with blank indifference. Some didn't notice her at all. Cain walked directly behind Taska concealing the chains that joined them together. Sophia walked behind them both, mindful of the cart Cain towed behind.

Taska had to find wicks for her oil lamps. Mrs. Jarod would have them. But, Taska couldn't bear to speak with her after she had made such a spectacle the last time she visited her stall. Sophia could purchase them for her. Taska continued over to Mrs. Myler's cart. She was a frail old woman who had once been a warden when she was fifty-two years old. She was also Claas Myler's mother, the fishing captain vying for Sophia's affections. Her sentence was four months. At least she had served. Taska went to her cart and looked over the dried herbs that she had hanging all over her cart. The scent of herbs and smoked fish hit Taska's nose with severity. She looked at the scallions and thyme.

Mrs. Myler watched her look over the cart, picking over her herbs.

"If there is something you can't find, I might have it back at the house, dear," said Mrs. Myler.

Taska found some herbs, "This bunch will be fine. I cannot go without seasoning. Your garden seems to produce the greatest of taste. You must work magic over the seeds." Her voice was mundane but touchingly jestful. Miss Myler broke into a dispirited smile, "The boys bring seaweed, from the outer sand bar. It is the fertilizer."

"I knew it was magic," Taska said gazing at her leathery face.

She paid Mrs. Myler and looked back to Cain. She went to the next cart knowing that Mrs. Loupon would have the jarred vegetables and fruit she needed.

Emmit stormed through the crowd. His belly seemed to push and move people around him in a way that he was quite use to. Emmit faced Taska and Cain, while disregarding Sophia entirely. Taska continued to look at the hundreds of glass jars filled with fruit, vegetables and meats.

Cain brought his eyes to Emmit. He couldn't take his eyes away from the jowls, and the folding chin of Emmit's rotund face. Cain brought his fist tightly together and waited. Sophia, waiting for someone to speak, watched Cain and Emmit locked in a long stare. The scent of fear hung heavy.

"Emmit," Sophia said quickly, "my father is looking for

you. I thought he would have found you by now."

Emmit's eyes were fixed on Cain.

"I spoke with your father," Emmit said.

Taska turned when she heard his voice, low and imposing.

She could see Cain and Emmit locked in a terrible stare. Taska stood between them, as Emmit brought his head up to Taska, inches higher than his own.

"Do you want him back?" she said quietly. Her eyes were wide and pensive. She was impressed by his intimidation, staged for the other villagers. Taska brought the staff up close to Emmit's body, leaning it to him like an offering. Emmit took a step back.

She glanced at Cain while she pointed to the jars, "Pick out the tomatoes."

"It was proper to chain him here. I understand you have been letting him run free in the forest. Don't be foolish with him. If he turns on you he will kill as many as he can," said Emmit. "He will kill us all."

Taska ignored him and spoke quickly on another topic, "I must say I am sorry I missed the vote concerning the church bells. Perhaps the bells could continue ringing if the Reverend could find someone with enough strength to do his job."

"What is the point in having the poor Reverend work so hard to benefit so little?" Emmit said. He knew she could hear them from her cottage.

He turned and meandered through the crowd. Sophia looked at Taska and watched her white bonnet strings flutter in the light breeze. Taska's pale thin hand was wrapped tight around the staff. Her grip funneled her tension, like lightening through a rod.

Taska turned to Cain, watching him load jars of canned tomatoes into the cart. She squatted next to him, "Look, not this one, it has bad tomatoes in it. Look at each one."

Her voice was gentle.

Cain took the jar from Taska and placed it back on the wooden shelf. He began looking at each one. Taska moved down to the bin of onions. The skins peeled away and blew under the cart, but the onions inside were firm and tight.

She took eight onions and placed them in her basket.

Cain rose from the tomato jars and awaited further instructions.

"The cucumbers are there. Look for the smaller ones. Take four jars," Taska said pointing. Her voice was not hindered by her tiff with Emmit.

Sophia placed her hand upon the ties on the back of her dress. She looked closely at Taska's eyes, close enough to see the black pupils among the pools of rich, dark brown, "Come to see me before you leave."

Sophia's whisper hit Taska's cheek.

"Of course."

Sophia walked through the crowd and back to the warehouse. There was nothing more that she could do.

The market was somewhat overcrowded with crates of food and canned goods. This was the last great sale before the winter. The noise from the blacksmith clanked out across the great courtyard. The seagulls, usually perched on the boats and the pier, were waiting for a spare crumb or morsel to find its way into the open. The chickens and the goats were corralled or penned up in a ruckus of whines and clucks. Upon layers of sound, smell and color came the voices of everyone who needed to buy, sell, or survive.

Taska realized things had changed since she had been gone, but she couldn't decide if things had physically changed or her perceptions had changed.

Alice Colberton came up to Mrs. Loupon who owned the cart. She spoke loudly without consideration for Taska, "She shouldn't bring him here."

Alice Colberton noticed Cain who was busy picking out jars. Taska concentrated on her basket. She did not want to have a shouting match with Alice Colberton. Taska accepted her unabated slander without dispute, knowing she suffered the loss of her husband. This was a grim fact that still remained, regardless of what she thought of Cain or his ambiguous guilt.

Mrs. Loupon was obviously embarrassed, but she couldn't appear disobedient to Alice Colberton.

Alice lashed out, "You should not be allowed here!"

Taska turned her shoulder to Alice Colberton and brought the staff up to her breast, "We will be gone soon enough, I hope you would extend us a similar courtesy."

Alice Colberton flared with the fury of Taska's engagement.

"You flaunt this beast like he is your prize, while I suffer without a husband and a father for my children."

Her tongue eagerly awaited Taska to strike out again.

"Your husband's death was unfortunate and I am sorry, but I cannot be responsible for what has happened. I must be responsible for what is yet to happen. We must not forget who is guilty and who is performing a service to the council," said Taska. "With your husband's long service to the council, you should realize this civil union...."

Alice Colberton snipped, "You think what you're doing is honor? You call living like a hermit out in the woods — letting him walk around, free to kill, you call that honor? He should be strung up. How dare you mention my husband in our time of mourning?"

She spit to emphasize her disgust.

The pop came quickly and the glass tinkled across the cobblestones. Taska looked down and saw a broken jar with only the lid intact. The marinated peppers, red and green stained the cobblestones. Cain was already on the ground, picking up what he had dropped.

Alice Colberton laughed, "He is a wretch." She stormed away.

A crowd soon gathered and the villagers all stared at Taska and Cain. Cain tried with intensity to make the accident disappear, working as quickly as he could, only to smear and spread the mess.

Mrs. Loupon, the cart owner, came to them, shaking her head in disgust. Cain continued to gather up the broken glass. Taska found her purse, pulling out a coin that would buy four jars and paid the woman.

Taska looked down at Cain.

"Leave it, and get eight of the squash there," she said pointing to the jars of squash.

Cain released the spilled peppers and the broken glass. As he rose, he wrapped his hand around a piece of glass that fit in the center of his palm. He concealed the bit of glass that was shaped like an odd triangle. He wrapped it tightly within his palm. His mind churned with nervous agitation. He knew that she would be so angry. He obeyed but clenched his fist tight. His palm stung as the sharp edges of the glass tore into his hand.

Taska ended up buying thirty-four jars of vegetables and fruit from Mrs. Loupon, making her forget the vinegar mess in front of her cart. Cain pulled the cart along the cobblestones, stopping at the wooden steps of the warehouse. He had never been to the warehouse.

Cain was wary of Taska's unseen temper.

"Leave the wagon there. It will be fine," said Taska.

Cain let the rope go and walked behind Taska up the steps. The chain that connecting them was long enough to let them walk comfortably, but with little distance between their strides.

They went into the warehouse and greeted Sophia. She was waiting for them. Cain was often anxious around Sophia. Her perceptions seemed spiteful. He knew that Taska would tell her about the broken jar and her complete embarrassment with him. He was desperate to prove his obedience.

Sophia smiled, "Sit down, I will make some caraway-seed tea."

Taska placed her basket upon the floor, with the staff placed over the basket.

"I hope we are not a bother. Your father may become angry with us for disrupting your work."

Sophia shook her head and disagreed. She brought three cups to the table with saucers. "He won't mind. He will be happy to see you," said Sophia.

Taska looked at her spoon and the cloth napkins that Sophia placed next to each cup. Her mind raced with the images and conversations of the people she saw in the market. She didn't expect their ferocity.

"I think I have been away from the village too long," said Taska dimly.

Cain looked at Sophia who stood behind the chair, waiting for the water to come to a boil.

"I don't think you should come at all. You have proven to them that he is well kept, but don't let them say those things to you."

"I cannot stay away. I must come to the market, the cobbler. It is impossible to live without the village," said Taska.

Cain tightened his fist and let the glass tear slowly across his palm. His fear and his anger smoldered slowly in his chest. His own disgrace was complex and hard to control.

"I am grateful for having you as a friend," Taska said graciously.

Cain turned his face down. Taska could see his shame. She felt pity for him. She wanted Cain to see her face filled with contentment; without animosity.

"It was not your fault — they had to say something."

Cain brought his glance to her eyes, but he couldn't forgive himself. His clumsy hands and Emmit's intimidations had rattled his nerves. His disapproving eyes fell to the chain around his waist.

Sophia came to the table with the kettle and filled the

three cups. She set it on a pad of fabric, used as a potholder. She joined them at the table.

"Soon, the grounding of the fleet and it will be over. It was a quick summer. Then everyone will be getting ready for the winter festival," Sophia said over her steaming cup tea. She noticed Cain's somber face and his sour mood.

"I suppose I won't be here for the grounding of the fleet," said Taska. "Perhaps I will come in after to see the cobbler and visit you on occasion."

"I hope you come often. You are always welcome."

"Then again, maybe I can stir up the villagers by coming to the grounding of the fleet. Perhaps the more they see me, the more they will come to accept their own sentence," Taska said.

"They are trying very hard to dismiss it. The fact that he comes and goes like a bothersome specter is frustrating them. They don't find justice in their own system, not until it suits their desires," said Sophia — frustrated.

Taska realized that asking the entire village to forget would mean that she would have to disappear forever. Slowly, something greater was being asked of Taska and her service: dispose of the alleged killer or make it all go away. It did not matter what happened to her.

"They want to forget his treachery, Taska."

"They will never forget, not until we are both gone." Her eyes wandered over to Cain. She could never kill him, although that is what the council had suggested to her. Nor, would she alienate her life from all the others. It was the village laws that shaped the dissension and the shame of their civil failures. Some saw the failures and knew that nothing could be done to change them. Others used the shortcomings of the system to manipulate and control the rest.

Taska gazed upon Sophia's delicately sculpted neck and her glimmering strands of hair that hung down like auburn silk.

Outside the warehouse, carpenters, laborers and volunteers were building the stage and the podium for the ceremonious Grounding of the Fleet. Similar to the christening of a ship, the ceremony involved praise and prayers for vessels and crew of the fishing fleet. Almost forty, twenty-foot dory fishing boats made up the fleet of rugged and hard-worn men who pulled their catch in with pulleys and back breaking work. They put off the weather and the elements to harvest the waters around the village. The farmers had never been able to supply enough food for the village because of the rocky fields. Their harvest of wheat, corn and barley were meager compared to the buckets and buckets of fish that came from the sea. The only harvest that the farmers could really profit from was the fall apple and gourd season.

The fishermen and the crews that went out to sea knew their position of importance in the village and took pride in supplying it with fish for a year. Smoked, dried, poached, steamed, fried and baked — cooking fish was so common that most of the hearths and pantries in the village reeked of it. In the lanes where the houses were close together, the smell of cooking seemed almost intolerable.

The proud fishermen, who slaved over the nets and the

cold water of the sea, would take the time at the Grounding of the Fleet and seek the reverence for their hard work. Of course, Reverend Conrad would bless the entire fleet and the crews.

Philip helped prepare the stage, donating hammers and nails, canvas and rope. He spent the day busy with the construction and the festival preparations. Now, as the evening twilight came, he grew tired and weary. He was preparing to leave for the night.

Sophia had gone home early. Beyond the stage, the fishermen were building cradles and stilts to keep their deep-keeled boats safely grounded for the winter. They sewed canvas together and made tarps that covered the decks and the rigging of these sailing catch boats.

It was forbidden by law to leave the village, so building a ship fitted for any extended journey was illegal at best. This meant that most of the boats were small, one deck fishing boats, durable in the rough surf and bad weather, but within the limits of the law. All boats were inspected by the voted harbormaster. For the eighth consecutive year, the position of harbormaster remained vacant while Emmit made the vessel inspections as a proxy. He charged a fee for the boat inspection, which he put in his pocket. This was another medal on his coat of arms and his armor of respect and power.

Philip looked out the small glass-paned window, down to the cobblestone square in front of the warehouse. The market was sparse and ill-attended now that the cold weather was becoming unbearable for some of the older villagers. Soon, Emmit would be upon the wooden podium, in front of the first fishing boat to be pulled out of the water. As leader of the council, he would be master of ceremonies. The stage was complete — with exception of the blue bunting and the corn stalk decorations in the front. In front of the village, the voice of the council leader, the harbor master, the property master, the trade minister, the cemetery warden and the probate judge — all one odious man.

It should be mentioned that most of these positions were vacant and Emmit slipped into them to collect money or to control his friends and fellow villagers. A few positions like the cemetery warden and the trade minister for example, were his own inventions. Every dead body needed a death certificate and a digging fee, which was split between Emmit and Reverend Conrad. He profited from the living and the dead alike. He found no shame in it. Yet, why would someone want to collect so much wealth when the town was so simple and sparse? Money could control his influence along with his ranks and titles. He was considered by most to be the Governor of the village, although no such position had yet to be invented.

The only genuine portion of the Grounding of the Fleet was that of Old Kavner's ruminating speech. He was the oldest fisherman in the village and certainly the most outspoken. Philip and James Colberton had helped Old Kavner with his speech from year to year. He was articulate and very poignant when he spoke about time and the changes in the village. It was sincere. He had come close to death four times while fishing and lived to tell the harrowing stories.

His boat was always chosen to be the honorary boat,

grounded with the pomp and circumstance marking the end of a successful fishing season. After the celebration, all the boats were pulled out of the chilly ocean, cradled on stilts and then covered for winter. When the last boat was stored away safely on dry land, the Reverend would bless the fleet in a somber and exclusive ceremony for the fishermen alone. The springtime blessing of the fleet was a great celebration of the spring, filled with color and music, compared only to the winter festival in its size and grandeur. This is how the village celebrated life, with festivities of change. They cherished days of celebration, breaking the routine of manual labor, the harsh elements and wretched living.

It was a time for children to throw down their brooms and shovels, forget their studies, leave the fields and their crops, and gambol and frolic with other children. The older villagers laughed, danced, and spoke of the great times at bygone celebrations. Everyone ate until they were full and drank until they were silly. But every single villager knew that this was a time, if not to celebrate, then to live that day with purpose and hope.

Long shadows of late afternoon splintered through the windows and the breaks in the walls of the warehouse. It was getting late. Philip had to stop to visit Old Lady Gertrude on the way home. The days were getting short and the nights were bitter cold.

Philip went to the back room of the warehouse and fetched a few things for the old woman. It was getting dark in the warehouse, so Philip lit a lantern and carried it with him. He found a bottle of liniment and a jug of linseed oil.

He quickly looked for a gift he could bring. Philip always offered her a gift because she was so poor in her old age. After she paid her taxes — she had little money for comforts. He found an oil painting of a ship. On the frame was a small brass plaque that read — *Lucifer's Wing Under Full Sail.* The ominous ship was plowing through heavy seas under heavy storm clouds, the devil himself carved out of the bowsprit. The colors of the oil painting still seemed clear and vivid. He took it without any further consideration.

Philip arrived at Old Lady Gertrude's door carrying the two bottles of linseed oil and liniment in a sack, the painting in the other hand. He went right in, for the door was never locked. It was warm with the glow of the brilliant fireplace. Old Lady Gertrude sat in her chair with blankets wrapped around her from her neck down to her feet. Her watery eyes and her shaky smile noticed Philip. Her cheeks were hollow and her frail frame was that of a twig. Her face was bony and somewhat emaciated, showing the true dimensions of her skull beneath, an outline of a fading life. Hillmond Wenner sat at the table. They were keeping each other company. The cottage was a simple square with a wall that hid the old woman's bed. Now, she spent most of her days sleeping in her chair, rocking herself to sleep. She would cook stew or something soft to eat. Every few days she would venture out in the fair weather and shuffle down to the market or walk up the hill to see the church in the distance.

A calico cat sat up from under the old woman's chair, startled by the draft. It began licking its coat. Philip shut the wooden door and put down the things he brought with him.

Gertrude smiled a toothless smile. She brought up her thin hand from the blankets that twisted and turned around her figure, making her true body indefinable. She was slightly deaf and could hardly walk, but her mind flourished without detriment.

Philip raised his voice slightly, "I have come with your liniment and your linseed oil." He pulled the bottles out of the sack and placed them on the table across from Hillmond. She motioned for him to come closer. Philip looked down at the picture and brought it with him across the room. Gertrude motioned for him to sit on the bench. Philip sat down. He watched her grinning face, wrinkled with time, each year bringing on a new mark and a new pain.

"You must take some money. It is there in the canister upon the mantle," Gertrude said.

He wouldn't receive her money. Philip lifted the painting, "I brought you this as a gift. It is a painting of a ship named *Lucifer's Wing*."

She turned her eyes to the painting. "It is a great vessel, a beautiful painting. But I cannot afford to pay you for this," said Gertrude — always blunt, which made her seem harsh sometimes. She was simple and without regard to the sensitivity of others.

"It is a gift," he said and got up from the bench. Philip looked around the room for a place to hang the picture.

"You know, they came to collect my tax money a few days ago — always more to pay each year," she said.

Hillmond Wenner spoke up, "I was explaining all the recent happenings to her - with the killer and the warden."

Philip nodded, "Tragic acts often haunt this town."

The old woman raised her voice, "How can she serve a life-term? How can someone live forever bound?"

Philip found a place for the painting by the window, "It is the law. The laws deter people in the village from committing a crime — because we all know the punishment. This outsider had no idea what his punishment would be. He never planned to be captured. Our laws do not afford such a situation, and therefore we must abide by the rules already established. We never thought we would see an outsider, never mind have one murder someone."

Gertrude looked over to the dark corner in the back of the room. Standing in the corner was her old staff, like an uninvited ghost. She had served for six-years when she was younger.

"I remember my time, Hillmond. Your mother assigned him to me after the lottery. I was ward to a thief. Time has stretched across my long life. It all seems like a long dream — passing quickly. But, like a pit in time, I remember those six years vividly. Time stood still and belabored my life. It was a great burden. Taska won't survive."

"You have witnessed terrible things," Hillmond said. "You were part of the original bloodshed and treachery. Surely your duty to the staff was simple compared to your trip to this village — the complete loss of your life, the destruction…"

Philip hung the painting on a rusty nail and leveled the frame the best he could. He stepped back and checked its position.

"Sophia Lazarous, your daughter, knows the Valimar child?" the old woman said.

"Yes, Sophia is the only one Taska speaks with in confidence in these trying days," he said. Hillmond shot Philip a bitter glance. She had tried to visit Taska and gain her confidence. For all her attempts to reach out to her, she was thwarted by Taska's disdain. She had all but given up.

Philip was frustrated that no one checked on the old woman from time to time. Hillmond came once a week, otherwise he might see her meandering about the market or sweeping off her stoop. It haunted him to see her deprecated life in the village. Her seclusion and neglect would someday be his future as a feeble old man.

"I would like to speak with Sophia. Have her come and see me, Philip," Gertrude said.

"I will tell Sophia," Philip replied. "Taska is reluctant to come to the village. She will not come to you. And now, I must be off."

"Take your money and don't refuse," Gertrude said firmly.

"Fine, I will take your money," Philip said. He went to her tin box on the mantle and opened it. It was empty. He looked to Hillmond and showed her the empty tin. The old woman had her eyes turned down. They took all her money when they collected the taxes. Emmit and Langston had pilfered money from an old woman. He burned with a simmering rage. He pulled a pocketful of coins out and put them in the tin. It was his earnings for the day, but he owed it to her. He felt like he was paying into his future fate where all good deeds are returned and all bad acts are washed clean.

"Sophia will come! Tomorrow!" he said replacing the

tin to the mantle.

Old Lady Gertrude smiled with Philip between her new painting and the window, "I never noticed that painting before. I must be going daft or something." Her smile widened at her own jest. Philip laughed out right and shook his head, "I am afraid you are still sharper than an ax."

Hillmond glanced at him with embarrassed gratitude. She admired him.

Philip disappeared out into the roadway. Gertrude shouted, "Thank you for the gift..."

Knowing that he couldn't hear her anymore she spoke quietly, "...it is beautiful."

She brought her eyes down to her lap.

"Taska Valimar is pure," said the old woman. "She knows nothing of the village legacy. She believes that we still possess free will. She knows nothing of our captivity."

Hillmond didn't reply.

Philip's eyes concentrated on his steps that would take him home, but his mind began refining his anger down to a very intricate design of deceit. He would have to wait until time blended together to create a fate that would end his own anger and abolish Emmit's reign of treachery. This was the first time Philip ever lived so filled with horrific intentions and unpure thoughts. It was the first time Philip felt like he was doing exactly what he was chosen to do in his life. The evidence was building from journal entries, empty money tins and lottery ballots. He had to forge his frustration into something new — something determined — something like revenge.

He wondered what time it was, he knew that it was

about seven o'clock, but without the church bells, no one knew the time for sure.

Philip walked through the door of his house and found six women hemming dresses and garments for the upcoming celebration. Philip looked at all the faces and noticed Mrs. Jarod, Miss Myler, and Sophia all sewing diligently. Philip placed his hand on his wife's shoulder and walked to Sophia, who was tucked into a corner. He tried to hide his face from the other women so they would not suspect his burning rage.

Sophia looked up to her father and waited. But he took her hand and brought her outside, shutting the door.

Sophia became anxious of her father's secretive manner, "What is it, Father? Is something wrong?"

"No, I just didn't want them to hear us," Philip said, "I spoke with Old Lady Gertrude, tonight. She seemed adamant about seeing you. I believe she wants to speak with you about Taska Valimar. I don't know if you have time tomorrow, but I think you should go to her. She is very thoughtful. You should go if only to humor her."

Philip retreated into the cottage.

Her eyes tried to define the old maples that marked the top of the hill. Why would Old Lady Gertude want to see me? Claas was coming down the hill. He approached and stood next to her like a statue. The leaves rustling by in the lane gave off a musty scent. Sophia looked up at the stars and the smeared clouds that blocked out portions of the celestial map above the old maples.

Sophia stole a glance at Claas looking at the stars. "Claas?"

"Yes?"

"If ships navigate by the stars, how do they find their way when the storm clouds obscure the sky?"

He turned down his star-speckled eyes, "No one has ever asked me a question like that."

Sophia put her hand on his arm. "I rarely say things like that. I suppose standing out here every night has its rewards," she said quietly.

"Good night, Sophia," he said and walked down the lane, whistling a popular dance tune. Sophia had never heard him whistle before.

When the cottage door opened, it startled Sophia, but she quickly regained her composure as she glanced at her mother, "Come in dear, before you catch something wicked. It's too cold out to be dressed like that."

She looked down to Claas walking down to the water and then back up to the celestial map of fate — blotched out here and there by wispy clouds.

"I'm coming."

Taska heard Cain shouting to her from outside while she was tying bundles of herbs to the nails that she had pounded into the wall. The arid heat from the fireplace would dry them quickly for seasoning.

Taska turned from the herbs on the wall and looked out the door. When she didn't hear Cain call a second time, she wondered what he was up to. She went to the door and saw Cain by the road that led to the village.

"What is it?"

She sheltered her brow with her hand. The sun blinded her.

"It is a child. He is jumping," Cain said. Taska looked around to see what Cain was going on about. She went out to the road with Cain and saw the jumping boy. They watched, like they were watching a curious possum or a squirrel.

The boy's head was bald. The stubble of his hair outlined his tan face. The villagers gave him frequent haircuts to avoid infestation. Now that the first frost had come, the boy was allowed to let his hair grow for the winter to keep him warm.

"Why is he doing that? Why is he jumping?"

Taska watched and tried to understand the child's madness.

The boy would make a jump and check the spot from which he took off. He would turn his body at the waist and look at the spot where he had taken off. Then he would look ahead and make another leap.

"Perhaps he is measuring each leap," Taska said.

Cain turned to the woodshed, "I will go back to work."

Taska continued to watch the little boy who was partially obscured by the tall weeds that lined the road. She took a few steps, "Boy!"

The child stopped. His face was blank; his motion still. He had been spooked, like an animal. He didn't expect villagers out that far in the woods.

Taska yelled again. Her voice was clear and crisp this time, "Boy, come here." She waved her arm letting her sleeves fall back to her elbow. What could be said to such a dumb child?

The boy smiled a playful grin and shook his head. Taska waved again. She posed as if she would go to him if the boy refused.

Finally, the jumping boy came through the weeds and leapt towards them. He would run a few steps, stop, and leap and then run a few steps. Taska turned from the approaching child and walked back to the steps of the cottage. She went to the water barrel and filled a tin cup, then turned back. Cain watched the boy carefully. The child appeared brave like a wolf coming from the woods on the scent of food. He stopped his approach at the edge of Taska's immediate yard where flattened weeds marked their daily routines and habits. Taska brought the dripping cup to the tall weeds. She stood holding it out to the boy, poised on the edge of the meadow.

"Come here, I have something for you," Taska said.

Although the boy might have been dull-witted, he survived at least five years on animal instincts. He knew some things were dangerous, and others acceptable. He smiled dimly and took one leap from the tall weeds to the dirt, gravel and grass. He paused, waiting to see if Taska was teasing him, but she held the cup steady. There was no reason to distrust her.

Cain waited. "Why doesn't he just come to you?" he said.

"He doesn't know us. He is cautious, as well he should be in the village," she said.

Taska didn't move her outstretched arm. The tin cup dripped with water. She cocked her head and nodded, which brought the boy a few steps closer. Cain looked at the water, "Maybe he will take it."

Understanding and trust joined in a mysterious trance between the wild boy and a woman resolved to help a fellow survivor. She calmly brought the cup down and walked it over to the boy. The boy took it and drank without fear or uncertainty. His fear evaporated in her gaze as if a primitive message was sent to the boy.

"Of course he will," she said as she brought herself to her knees next to the boy. She studied his dirty face and his shaved head. Cain stood like a statue. A language was spoken in verse which came from simple animalism; eye contact, posture and movement which read like poetic conversation, filled long verses of understanding that a woman and a child could speak to one another regardless of birthright and bloodline. The boy was mysterious. He knew a secret dialect of action and reaction.

The boy wiped his mouth with his sleeve and looked at Cain with a sinister smile. The boy pointed to Cain and nodded, bringing his mute insight to Taska's attention.

"What does he want?" Cain said uncomfortable around the boy.

"He wants you to jump."

Cain turned his head down in embarrassment.

"Jump? You want him to jump?" she said as a primal interpreter.

The boy laughed. His small lips turned into a tooth yellow smile.

Taska smiled. It was the first time she had ever really smiled. Cain studied her expression, and her cheeks now pulled up tight into a laugh. The stunning beauty of her face was like the golden glitter of the sun on the ocean. He felt his stomach tremble as a rush came over him.

"Jump?"

Taska laughed outright, "Yes, jump!"

Like jumping into an ice-cold lake, Cain came alive with the vigor of Taska's laugh. It was lyrical. Cain bent his knees and leapt from the ground with a great burst. The boy laughed hysterically, with squeaks and chirps. Cain jumped over and over again. He did not smile or even grin with the excitement of his feat. He was focused on his movement and the agreeable feeling it brought.

The jumping boy laughed and began jumping along with him. He was so happy to be leaping about that he released the cup, letting it flounder on the ground. Jumping was a contagious, spontaneous act. Cain didn't know if he should stop, but the immense feelings continued, keeping him bouncing off the ground. Each time he left the ground, he tried to savor the feeling of being free of the earth. He occasionally shut his eyes to feel the motion without the distraction of sight. It made him dizzy and disorientated.

Taska took a few steps back and watched Cain and the boy jumping together. She began clapping to the jumps and leaps until they were jumping together. The boy was laughing hysterically and could hardly continue. Finally, Taska began jumping and clapping, her hair tossed about her shoulders. She was caught in a rapture of happiness. She hadn't felt this light and easy for years and years. So many difficult and tragic events had belabored her sense of happiness. It had been so long.

The boy, used to jumping for hours, continued to keep Taska and Cain laughing with his silly sounds and apparent ecstasy. She took the boy's hand and quickly took Cain's large paw. She told Cain to take the boy's other hand. They formed a circle, as they faced each other, jumping to the left, then to the right. They jumped and danced until Taska fell to the ground laughing between gasps of exhaustion. The boy fell to the ground, mocking Taska, laughing and making his own sounds.

Cain, on one knee smiled, "I am exhausted."

She watched the boy spin around in the grass then bring his body up, only to tumble back, head over heels. Taska laughed with the boy, although she could no longer frolic as he did.

Taska's eyes were bright as she laughed and played with the child. The light in her eyes showed her intensity, which did not depend upon happiness or rage. It was a look of great strength and venerated power. Cain looked away from Taska's gaze when she met his eyes.

"Never have I laughed like that," he said like he had confessed a sin.

"No, not that you remember," she said softly. Taska watched the boy, his body tumbling and swirling like leaves spinning in the wind, twisting and turning.

She laughed and enjoyed the child's abundant youth. Although the boy never spoke a word to them, he made them happy. He even smelled like earth and leaves.

Taska gave the boy more water and heated up some soup, which he accepted. Cain looked into his soup, indulging in the happiness that permeated his heart. The same soup that he consumed day after day seemed so tasty that night. When the boy was finished standing in his chair and licking his soup bowl clean, he jumped down to the floor and went to the door that Taska left open for him. She didn't want to spook him if he had never been confined.

He stood in the doorway for a moment, turning back only to wave his tangled hands over his head in a farewell gesture. The jumping boy was gone.

Taska let out one final laugh as he disappeared into the falling twilight.

For a long time they sat in silence. Words would have only interrupted and trampled the ardent happiness that the heart held captive for the rest of night.

Taska stood in front of the fireplace stirring seasoning into a stew. Cain sat in a chair at the table. It had been a long day in the field, but the last field was finally tilled to Taska's satisfaction. Now they could let winter bewitch their lives. Taska took two large bowls from the cupboard and put them on the table. She also found spoons. She retrieved a large loaf of bread from the shelf behind Cain. His appetite was growing vicious as he waited for Taska to pour out a bowl of stew.

She placed the loaf on the table. Little spots of mold slowly began covering the brittle crust. The black and green spots were speckled upon the crust in a random pattern. Most of the bread was uninfected, but where it was infected, it ate away the crust in a vile deterioration, like disease.

Taska returned with two bowls of soup. She placed

Cain's bowl in front of him and sat down. She studied the soup. The scent and the steam of the stew drifted to her nose. Her stomach ached all the time, not allowing her to consume the thick stew of tomatoes, mushrooms and cucumbers. It was a stew that her mother favored when Taska was little. Alone in bed, Taska had nothing but memories of her family — old recipes and her written words to keep her company. It was little consolation. Now, with the twisting in her stomach and the sharp pains, even the stew of motherly comfort was unbearable to consume. She felt a slow physical decline.

She remembered the jumping boy and his raggedy grimace. Everyday her vivid perceptions of the boy would fade little by little. She would wake early in the morning, still lying in bed thinking about where the boy might live, and what he might be doing that morning. She worried about him when the autumn rain would pour down in torrents. She hoped he was in someone's house, or tucked in a woodshed somewhere. Colored in a different hue and transfixed into her heart by her imagination, the boy was her own; while the real memories of the boy were fading. Every detail of the child had become smooth and dull like a stone washed by the sea over thousands of years. Eventually, the boy and her happiness would become featureless, until it was forgotten among her other dreams. It was how time shaped memories.

Sitting at the table over her stew, she wondered if Cain was living in the same shapeless haze.

"Cain, do you recall any of your life. Has anything come back to you... memories?"

She wasn't accusing him, but asking him how he remembered the past and the health of his mind.

"I recall it all."

Taska looked up with suspicion, but Cain was still tired and sullen.

"What do you mean?"

"I never forgot my life before I came here — but I lost the context of time and space. I have these images of people and places that are so vivid and real that you can almost touch them. I can even relive memories in my mind — but nothing connects one memory to another. No one has a proper name that I can remember. The little moments in time are so clear, so important, if I could just relate them to time and this hollow body."

Taska felt sorry for him. She wasn't afraid at all.

Her obsession with the boy brought on a realization that happiness crumbles away. She thought back to the day when they jumped and danced with the mute child. The moments of happiness, which seemed spontaneous to her at the time, now seemed contrived. She compared her moments of happiness with the moment of standing before the entire village, after her name was drawn from the lottery barrel. Although her fear of the lottery and her happiness with the jumping boy where opposite emotions, they both sent a vivid shudder through her soul. Those two moments created a lasting impression on her desperate heart. Those two moments, although experienced differently, were still worn away with time. Those two moments reminded her that she was different from everyone else. Happiness could feel like complete abandonment, making every emotion a reminder that she was bending her conscious into something remote and radical to the expectations of the villagers and the council.

Every time she thought of happiness, it became a pinnacle from which she would look down upon her wretched life, driving the pain closer to her heart. Taska could stretch her soul between absolute happiness and complete self-worthlessness in one moment of being. This contortion of her soul would pull her further and further apart until she disconnected from her life.

Her eyes trained on the specks of mold on the bottom of the bread.

Cain was down to the bottom of his bowl. His stomach was full and his bones warmed. He hadn't noticed her lack of appetite.

He walked over to the tub of water, washed his bowl and his spoon then wiped them out with a rag. He didn't want to speak. Taska's stare forewarned him that she would begin writing on her parchments.

Cain sat upon the floor. His back rested against the wallboards while he watched the flames of the fire dance across his muddled conscious. This was his place in the cottage. He placed the little piece of glass, shaped like a triangle, in a crack between two floorboards. He would twist and turn the glass over and over with his fingers, while rubbing his other hand on the floor, like someone swiping gently at a cat. He would fall into a contemplative state — struggling to connect one memory to another.

He also thought of the little boy. Cain had forgotten happiness. It was beaten from him. And now, he wanted to bring laughter to life again, but he knew nothing of what caused it, or how to ask for it. It was peculiar that so many people from the village came to see Taska, but only that little boy brought her real happiness.

Cain recalled the motion of his feet to the dance; the little boy with tears rolling down his face from his laughter; Taska's dress swirling and moving in a jubilant frolic; all connected in Cain's mind by clasped hands.

He looked at his hand, flat on the floor and he studied the veins, the scratches and his clear fingernails. He imagined Taska's hand in his fingers gently holding on to her soft palm. He could feel her compassion and her happiness emulate through this touch. He could recall her warm fingers entangled within his, the pulling and the jumping. She possessed something that could change him. He knew that now.

He touched Taska in a time of happiness, and he too was touched with a passion that he could not understand or conceive within his newborn mind.

Cain continued to rub his thumb over the glass that was shaped like a bent and crooked jewel. He didn't look at the glass for fear that if someone saw him with this token it might be taken away. It was his possession. It was the one thing that he could touch, the one thing that fate had made his own. Now, he wanted to reconnect memories again. Visions intertwined like fingers laced with another hand.

In the cottage, Taska and Cain fumbled with dark notions in their minds. Cain was searching for his disconnected past, while Taska scribed out her future salvation.

Cain spoke quietly, "That child, the jumping child, he reminds me of something. Of something missing. Something sad."

Taska paused, "Like a memory?"

"Like a sad memory."

Although she should have been alarmed by his emerging memories, she just felt his loss.

Along the lane where the cottages were close together, Emmit and Langston walked together with a lantern. They were collecting taxes. That night, they were paying a visit to the horse trader, Karl Hallaphan. He was a small man, but still healthy and spry. He wrangled and tamed horses for riding. All the horses in the village came from the quiet equine trader.

His wife, cooking on an old cast iron stove was a rotund woman who laughed when she was nervous.

Emmit stepped into the cottage. He was carrying a lamp, the tax ledger and a bottle of ink. The straight pen was inside the ledger.

"We are here to evaluate your taxes."

Langston came in behind him. He was carrying a thick stick of wood. It was a suggestion of intimidation, although he swore he never used it.

Emmit went to their table and sat down. He spread out the ledger and opened the inkwell. He looked over the long column of numbers and names. The tax collection was another ill-fated civic responsibility that Emmit enjoyed.

"Answer me truthfully: how many people are in your

family?" he said.

"It is just me and my wife."

"No children or extended family?" he said.

"Of course not, you know us," said Karl Hallaphan.

Emmit dipped his pen in the ink well and made a mark in his ledger. "How much money, property or merchandise did you profit from since my last tax collection?"

Karl Hallaphan looked to his wife. She fetched a book and brought to Emmit. He opened the pages and looked at the ledger. Emmit shook his head and chuckled a little. He turned the pages, searching for more numbers and transactions. He shut the ledger and handed it back to the horse trader's wife. She grinned and held back a giggle.

Emmit looked around the room at the blankets, the books, the glassware and the large duck roasting in the hearth.

"I guess horses are a poor man's business. I noticed you only sold eight horses in a year," Emmit said.

Langston leaned against the doorway.

"It has been a hard year for us. The livestock business is not very lucrative," said Hallaphan. It was not quite the truth. Emmit knew who bought horses and it seemed that more than thirty horses had been sold from Hallaphan's barn and field. He shook his head and wrote some figures on a sheet of paper. His writing was quick and nervous. The others watched on. Karl Hallaphan paid eight gold coins last year for his taxes," now he waited while Emmit tallied his bill for this year.

He finished the receipt and stamped it with a read mark of the council. He handed it to Hallaphan and looked down to the ledger. He checked to see if the ink was dry. Gently, Emmit closed it over.

Karl Hallaphan looked up from the receipt, "Does it say I owe twenty-seven gold coins for the purpose of the taxes? I paid out eight last year."

Emmit nodded, "And you sold only a few horses last year. You did not have three boys living in your barn."

"This is an outrage."

"We cannot pay it — we will not pay it!" said his wife.

"Those boys mind the stable for me — feed and clean the stalls. They are not my family — just hired help," Hallaphan said. "I will not pay for this pillage. I simply do not have the money."

Emmit nodded. His hands were steady. Langston shifted his weight and held the stick up higher.

"I know you have friends on the council. Jarod speaks highly of you, and Philip Lazarous says you are a fair horse trader. You were a pallbearer at James Colberton's funeral — were you not?"

Hallaphan nodded and his wife turned away to sob.

Emmit continued, "By law, I must have enough gold to match the number of people in this village. When the Annual Visit comes, they will pour over this ledger — they will check and see you have two adults and three children. If you do not match the money to the names — then they will come directly to you. In the past, the soldiers have been lenient, but if they suspect that the money and the bodies of the family are disproportionate, they have the right to take things away. If I have to place you on the list — they will come to you. Will they take your wife? I do not know. Will they burn your barn? I do not know. However, it is simple to resolve your greed and pay the money — but that is your choice."

"I refuse," Hallaphan said.

"I will add your name to the list."

Langston shook his head. He moved out to the street. Emmit collected his lamp and his book. He looked at the mortified horse trader and his wife, "It is a shame that you will be the first on the list — they always go to the first one on the list. But your morals and your integrity seem more important."

Emmit laughed and shook his head. "We are all that is left of our bygone country, our religion and our faith. We are the prosecuted and the criminals. This is our village, but by their rules and by their laws and by their faith — this is their prison and we are the ghosts from a world gone by," said Emmit. "Odd that you hold your principles of fair and proper above all else. Beyond the council and this village — there is nothing. Your appeal to a higher order is a delusion, not to mention a waste of time. I am the highest order. So, have some respect for yourself and save what little you have before they come and collect the taxes. We are kept by the mountains and the sea — and we have no liberty or expectation of justice in the eyes of the soldiers and the tax collectors. They see us as animals. And right now, you are the first sheep to the slaughter. "

Emmit walked out to Langston and shook his head. Mrs. Hallaphan continued sobbing inside. They walked up the lane together and whispered, "I think we frightened him. If he does not pay after the Grounding of the Fleet, we will burn his stable down."

Langston nodded, "His payment will be prompt after he loses his horses."

"I have a crewman that might be useful — I have sent him on a few errands before. They will set the fire — if it comes to that."

"Perhaps he will pay in a few days," Langston said without concern.

Emmit and Langston approached the office and spoke about other taxes they had to collect in the coming days. Langston was carrying a small sack of collected coins on his belt.

Langston saw a small sack in front of the office door. "What is that?"

"Maybe Hallaphan had a change of heart and paid his taxes," said Emmit with a laugh.

Langston put down his intimidation stick and picked up the sack. It didn't feel like coins.

"What is it, Langston?"

He opened the burlap sack and looked through it. He pulled his hand out and saw the dark soot on his fingers. He reached in again and pulled out the tiles, "It looks like burned paper or wood."

Emmit took the tiles from Langston. He knew what they were. He sighed hard, "Lottery tiles... Taska Valimar's lottery."

Langston stood up, "I burned these tiles."

"You were not very thorough. There is a note attached to the sack," he said. He pulled the paper off the sack. He read it aloud, "Lottery for one — not a lottery for all. That it sedition — now we are watching you."

Langston gruffed, "Who signed it?"

"There is no signature. Perhaps we can figure out who wrote this message by comparing signatures on some of the documents from the tax register. Now finish burning these -— and be sure that nothing is left. I am disappointed in all this," Emmit said. They parted in silence. Emmit went into his office and sat down at his desk. He opened the tax register and began comparing the hand writing to the signatures in the ledger. Would the villager sign with his real mark? Would it be that simple? He began searching the tax register, but nothing seemed conclusive. He began looking through land leases, deeds, receipts, and funeral certificates. He stayed up all night searching for the one villager that now knows the truth about the lottery. Emmit knew that Taska Valimar was the only woman who lived a life worthless enough and simple enough to live with a lifetime slave. He needed Cain out of the village in case the others came looking for him. He needed to be secured, far from the village. It was deplorable and depraved, but it was his plot all along and he had to see it through to the end. If he couldn't convince the villager who discovered the lottery tiles that he did what was best for the village — he could always do away with the situation.

The Grounding of the Fleet would begin around midday. The steady, soaking rain had subsided to a light mist and a heavy fog out on the water. The smell of low tide hung in the air, suspended in the shrouding fog. The masts of the fishing boats slowly disappeared in the rolling fog. A bitter chill cut to the bone.

The entire village slowly accumulated in the town square, facing the newly constructed stage. The council filed in and took their honorary seats on the bench on stage. They sat looking out into the crowd. The overcast was dim and dreary. Philip rubbed his raw hands together. The last time the entire village gathered was during the ill-fated lottery for Taska Valimar's life. Emmit stood next to Langston at the other end of the stage. This panoramic view of the village filled Emmit with delight. He felt like he was the epicenter of the village — the focused control of state and civil propriety.

The cobblestone square was filled with faces familiar and vague, gathering in their Sunday best for the ceremony. Some of the women wore bonnets, others wore their best caps. Little girls wore bows in their hair, minding their mothers not to run around in their best shoes. The fishermen, a sordid bunch of ruffians and hard working men, gathered in a group by the front of the stage. This ceremony was for them. Although everyone came to the celebration, only the fisherman knew the honor and the courage that comes from working on the sea. The fishermen went out, regardless of the weather and came back with adventure and tragedy upon their breath. The calm days when the water was flat and the sun was mild made everyone forget the strength of the sea and the great cresting waves that rose and fell in a vicious, unforgiving thrash. Philip noticed Claas standing with his comrades, mingling with the captains, the net handlers, and the crewmen who hauled and gutted the catch. He was well-dressed in his suit and tie.

Reverend Conrad mounted the slippery steps and reached the top of the podium. He looked out to the villagers and back to the council. He was carrying his book of prayers with a marker of green ribbon fluttering in the breeze, like a child's hair ribbon.

Emmit moved forward, "Ladies and gentlemen. We gather for the Grounding of the Fleet, an occasion that marks the new and the old and brings generations together for reflection and praise of the brave men that went to the sea, and brought back plenty for all."

Behind the podium was Old Kavner's fishing boat that would be the ceremonious first pull. The other fishing boats were behind it. The clanking of the halyards rang out like the muted church bells. The ocean stretched out behind the boats in the fog. The gray water heaved and churned.

The village had become quiet. Emmit began his speech. Philip Lazarous stood next to Jarod with his hands behind his back. Philip found it difficult to listen to Emmit's stoic speech. His oration was not trusting or fluid, but that of a spoiled child always getting his way. Emmit's large hands flailed to his over-acted ego. But the villagers accepted this, and drew pleasure from the pantomime of public speaking that was second nature to him. There was no question of his brilliant performance in front of everyone in the village.

"...The vocation that these men choose," Emmit said looking down to the men in front of the podium, "is a vocation of great courage and honor, and great responsibility. With this work comes the fear and the reality of death. The Reverend will say a prayer for those men that did not come back to the village this year. The sea would be their life, and too, the sea would be their death. We honor Quinn and his son Vessler for their bravery on the sea and in the face of death, so brave."

"Reverend."

The Reverend opened his book of prayers and began reading. Emmit took a few steps back. The Reverend's voice was not as hard and dramatic, but rooted in the formality of a psalm. Without the hollows of the church to echo and reverberate his voice, the Reverend's blood of Christ seemed misplaced upon the podium, away from the stained glass illumination of his blessings. He stood on Emmit's platform of power, ego, and greed that made his heavenly altar of souls and holy spirits seem insignificant and inferior.

"Oh God, who didst bring our fathers through the Red Sea, and bear them through the great waters singing praises unto Thy name: we humbly beseech Thee to vouchsafe to turn away all adversities from Thy servants at the sea, and to bring them with a calm voyage unto the heaven where they would be, with you, O Father. Amen."

The entire village whispered, "Amen."

An altar boy stood in front of the steps and rang a handbell twelve times. The twelve bells tolled every morning when the fishing boats left the harbor. In the evening, the twelve bells rang out again, announcing the safe return of all the boats into port. When the wives of the fishermen heard the bells, they knew that their husbands and sons were safe. If someone perished in the sea, no bell would sound until they were put to rest.

After sounding the bell, the altar boy moved aside. The Reverend moved to the edge of the podium. He made the sign of the cross in front of the fishermen, with a sad pall of reverence.

Emmit stepped forward again, "Thank you, Reverend. I have a proclamation from the council, deeming this day, November third, the day the fleet is officially grounded."

Philip picked his wife out of the crowd standing with Sophia. He looked for others he might notice. Karl Hallaphan was standing near the front with his eyes averted down. Old Lady Gertrude was propped up by her cane as she stood with Hillmond Wenner. Taska Valimar and Cain stood in the back of the crowd, detached from the tight knit community — but present. Cain appeared slightly cockeyed in the shoulders. Philip's attention returned to Old Kavner as he walked across the podium, careful not to slip on the slick stage. His back was bent over and legs bowed awkwardly. He was wearing an old hat that was grand and elegant, however ragged and stained.

Old Kavner's voice trembled as he settled into his key speaking position.

"Today we ground the fleet. I have lived to see many years of fishing come to a conclusion like this day. We thank our Lord and praise him for his gracious power to protect those who we have lost, and guide those who continue to take to the sea. The men that I have taken out into the ocean, have seen the eyes of God. These men work like horses in harsh and violent seas without complaint. With the ocean comes a freedom, given and permitted by the village and the council. This is a gift that every man cherishes, and protects because his life is nothing but the sea," said Old Kavner.

The village applauded and even cheered for the old man. Some of the children, restlessly standing in the crowd, dreamt about the ocean and its never ending freedom.

Taska stood with her back stiff. When the speaking was over and the ceremonial ship pulled from the water, everyone would turn to leave, seeing her there. She was content with standing in the back of the crowd. Taska could participate and control her immersion into the village hierarchy. When everyone would depart and go to the church for the festivities, Taska would take Cain back to the cottage for dinner.

Taska kept the staff in her right hand and held Cain's chain in her left. Cain listened to the praise showered upon the fishermen. The voices were hardly audible from the back of the square. The Reverend and Old Kavner shook hands with the entire council, then walked down the podium steps to the hull of the fishing boat. The bow of the ship was held in place with ropes and pulleys.

Cain noticed the little jumping boy. He was trying to gain Taska's attention. He smiled at her with a grimy smile. The jumping boy remembered her. The boy awed over the chain that connected warden to prisoner, but he didn't touch it. He continued to look up at her face, unable to spark her attention. Finally the boy walked to her side and took hold of the edge of her apron hem. She glanced down. He was lost in a forest of human confusion. He was a simple boy.

On the podium, Emmit shouted, "As we prepare to pull

this boat from the water — I say to everyone of the village, let happiness burn into our hearts while the bitter winds chill our bones. Let the snow be light and the ice thin for this winter. Let our vast supplies of food serve as our gifts and our glory under the watchful eye of our Lord. Amen!"

Emmit turned to the ship behind him and waved his plump arm. The drum began to roll and the pipers began their ritual tune. Everyone began cheering as the boat came out of the water, slowly sliding over large timbers. Twenty crewmen pulled and turned the ropes through the giant winch. The seaweed and the barnacles on the bottom of the vessel gushed out from under the boat. Philip leaned over the podium to watch the ship shift and grind, along the timbers. It was odd to see the boat list and grind along. It was meant to glide through the water, not scrape its spine across the rocky shore. The boat churned up mud and sand. Philip saw something entangled in the green and brown weeds and the mud. The pungent odor was that of fermentation and waste. A mass of gray eels, writhing and digging into the putrid mud, caught his attention. Philip was disgusted by this carnal mass of twisting flesh and mud, but he could not turn away. He was a witness to dark earthly pleasures. Watching the twisting mass, he knew that he was capable of discerning the worst of all things in the world, from the darkest sins of man, to the work of the devil himself, who tainted this ceremony with the scales and blood of a tangled mass of evil.

The low thumping of the drums kept time for the heaving ship — while the shrill notes of the bagpipers wove a melodious tune. A sea shanty sung out among the villagers and the fishermen near the podium raised their caps on to sticks and waved them for the village to see their salute.

The boat came slowly, creaking and scraping against the wood timbers beneath. Old Kavner stood by, with his feet in the seaweed and water. He nailed the blessed pendant to the side of the boat.

"Under the eyes of God, I bless this ship, grounded!" Kavner proclaimed. Around his feet, Philip noticed the tangled mass of slithering life, thrashing and hiding just under the surface.

The village let out a cheer and the drummers picked up a marching beat.

The entire village applauded wildly as Old Kavner nailed the pendant to the hull. All the fishermen made their way to the pendant. A prayer and the sign of the cross were the usual blessings.

The council filed out of the square behind the pipers. The rest of the village fell in behind them. They marched through the village, past the old maples and to the church where the celebration would go on all day and well into the misty night.

Taska stood aside and watched the pipers march out. She then looked down to the little hand clinging to her apron. It broke her to let go. It wrenched her stomach, her heart, her soul, but she pulled her apron away from the boy, and turned from him.

The boy bent his brow hard, glaring up at Taska with a look of betrayal.

No one noticed the daft boy. No one noticed the daft boy did not jump when he held the warden's hand. He was calm;

he was just a boy.

Cain, however, looked at the child's face as Taska turned away. He saw the boy's reaction. Watching the child's face wounded Cain greatly with a pain that he felt through his chest and down into his legs. Not like the pain of the glass triangle, piercing into his hand, but that of something incomprehensible. It was a deeper pain that emerged from the pit of his chest and spread all over his body, dissipating into numbness at his fingertips. The concussion of his feelings broke him.

It was cold.

So, the celebration began at the church. The fog and mist had turned into a steady rain. Inside, the music reeled, the food was spread out and the wine began to pour. The fishermen drank their stout and cheered on the dancers. Violas, a flute and two bassoons now replaced the pipers and the drummers of the marching group. Although the instruments were old and dilapidated, the music was rich and the tones were pure. The players made music above the flat sounds and broken instruments. It was sweet and refreshing. Without a single gong from the church bells recently, music was a welcome treat.

The council sat in the pews of the balcony, with their grins smiling down upon everyone. They spent a few hours looking down on the village, so people might come to them and ask for their guidance or council. They were left alone while the rest of the village danced and walked around to meet friends and neighbors. Sophia sat next to her mother, below the eyes of the council near the dancing couples. Her cheeks were flushed from spirted dancing. In her hand she held an apple that she began to devour. Mrs. Myler approached Sophia and said, "I knew that she would come. Did you speak with her?"

Sophia rose quickly and caught the eye of her father in the upper pews that looked over the festivities, "If you mean Taska and Cain — no, I did not have the opportunity to speak to them."

Putting the apple to her mouth and piercing the skin, she walked away toward the steps to the balcony.

Sophia reached the top of the steps and looked down upon the crowd and the dancers. It looked different from above. She walked behind the chairs, all lined upon the railing, filled with the odd shapes and sizes of council members.

Philip saw his daughter in her gray dress and black hair ribbons. He greeted her with a smile. Langston turned, seeing him go to his daughter. Philip and Sophia retreated to a dark corner of the balcony to speak away from the other members.

Emmit turned to Langston, "They speak of Valimar. She was there."

He kneaded his hands together and gazed over the festivities below. The noise from the dancing and the music below muted out their words. Emmit brought his mouth to Langston's ear and gave him specific instruction.

"We have made it clear that Taska Valimar can kill Cain without an ounce of suspicions. Is that correct? Yet, she refuses to end her sentence for her own soul and the good of this village. Now, we must seek out another solution. We have to…."

Before they finished whispering — someone tapped Emmit on the shoulder. It was Karl Hallaphan. Emmit shook his hand and offered him a chair, but the horse trader refused. He pulled a small sack from his belt. Emmit took the sack and opened it immediately.

"It's all there, Emmit."

"You are wise to remove your name from the list — the Annual Visit will be quite satisfied with your prompt payment," he said holding the horse trader's fortune in his hand. Karl Hallaphan was disgusted.

"My wife has been bed-ridden with worry — I hope you are satisfied."

"I saw your wife at the ceremony — she must be feeling better now," Emmit said.

"The taxes are inappropriate — quite a leap from last year," said Hallaphan. "Perhaps a different tax collector should be appointed for next year."

"Take it up with the collectors when they arrive — perhaps they will be sympathetic, or they will take you with them for being a hindrance."

Langston smiled and looked away.

"Rumors are circulating that you and the Reverend are sharing profits above the money deposited for the taxes," said Hallaphan

Emmit smiled, "I hardly live in luxury — careful of whom you accuse — you might offend the good Reverend or God himself — what's worse you might offend me."

Langston chimed in, "Let it go Karl — it is only money

— which you owe."

"Thieves to the end."

Emmit stood up seriously, "You are trying my good spirits."

Langston put a hand on Emmit's shoulder to draw his short temper back.

The horse trader stormed off. Sophia and her father watched the transaction, but couldn't hear the spoken accusations. Langston leaned over to Emmit when he sat down, "Shall we burn his barn anyway?"

Emmit shook his head, "Of course not — I am a man of my word... just poison the feed. And we will leave his name on the list for the Annual Visit."

Langston leaned back in his chair, satisfied. His eyes focused upon the people below. Poisoning horses would be simple — but solving the warden problem complicated and difficult.

Philip Lazarous sat back down after dismissing his daughter. Sophia walked back down the steps and into the crowd. The children ran all about the hall, playing and feasting on the sweets. Usually, the children spilled out into the grass to play and run around the church grounds and cemetery, but the rain kept them indoors. Jarod leaned over to Philip.

"How is Taska Valimar?" he asked.

"Everything is fine — they were at the ceremony," he said.

"'Tis a shame," he mumbled.

Philip looked down at his wife, who was speaking with her closest friend, Venny. They stood on the edge of the dancing. Watching his family from a distance brought out a thrill in him. The festivals always made him content with his life, bringing fourth an upwelling of love for them. It was a love that sat idle for too long, erupting in his chest like a storm of emotions. His emotions brought to mind moments in time that linked his family together — tragic and happy alike. He never lingered on the years that rushed by him, but the moments that were so vivid and real to him. Years were abstract and undefined.

Philip avoided the council and their sidelong looks. He wanted to be among the people, dancing, laughing and drinking. He went down the stairs, under the council's scrutiny. He greeted a few people and made his way through the crowd. He stopped at the gentlemen who played the music upon the council riser, "Would you be so kind as to play your most animated polka?"

The player with the viola smiled, "Yes sir."

Philip thanked him and quickly found Sophia.

He approached her with a broad smile. Sophia was surprised. Philip opened his arms, "Will you have the honor of dancing with your old papa?"

His manner was silly.

His wife laughed and some of the villagers applauded. The violas began, and the other instruments fell into rhythm as they began dancing. Sophia was dressed in a gray full-length dress that flowed and billowed with her dance steps. The bodice of her gown was velvet black brocade that accented her slender waist and her modest bosom. It was a fine gown — glimmering with costume jewelry and bleached periwinkles in her hair. He studied her pure skin

— free of wrinkles and creases. Her eyes were still youthful and brilliant. She was untouched by the inner darkness that Philip had recently acquired. She was wearing a shimmering pendant attached to a thin gold chain around her bare neck. The entire council gave her the necklace as a gift when she was baptized at three months old. It was her dearest possession. It matched her tin broach that was pinned to her dress in the shape of a flower, painted gold.

Philip danced along with contentment. Emmit and Langston where watching with envy. Philip often flaunted his strong family bond and his beautiful daughter. It was all he really had. As Philip and Sophia moved about the dance floor to the sound of the music, he felt a great inner power ignite in his chest. This feeling of trust quelled Philip's burning anger to strike out at Emmit and his treacherous ways. Philip's power came from love, compassion, and never betraying the trust of his wife and daughter.

Emmit had trampled and defiled love when he buried his wife to be, twisting compassion into a tool of deceit. His one lust was for power and money. In Emmit's mind these bonds of simple humanity where unsavory ideals for misled minds constantly dwelling in idyllic fantasy. Emmit watched Philip and Sophia with bitterness and envy.

"Father, you dance as well as you did when I was little," Sophia said.

He nodded, "I have to dance while I am still on my feet, before these bones become all too brittle."

"Your bones will dance forever," Sophia sang out to him. "Isn't that an old folk song?"

Philip laughed with her and continued their dance.

The polka came to an end. Everyone stopped and applauded the musicians. Emmit stood and waved down to Philip, complimenting his fine dancing.

Philip ignored his gesture. Philip and Jarod were the only two members of council that were agile and bold enough to dance. Jarod danced with no one but his wife.

When the music began again, Philip resumed dancing with his daughter. The slow waltz allowed them to rest and speak as they spiraled round and round.

"You seem so brilliant tonight," Philip said.

"You seem so outspoken. What is it that makes you this way?" she asked. Before he could blush, he looked down to his feet — serious and quiet.

"I am worried about the council," Philip said. "I fear an abuse of power — unfair tax collection and worse. With Cain away from the village, they fear they cannot watch him. And the Annual Visit."

Sophia laughed, "Please father, you always become so morbid before the Annual Visit. But when they are gone, nothing has really changed and then you unwind."

She smiled. She wanted him to be happy again.

"It will be over soon enough. Hopefully before the winter festival," Sophia said.

Philip agreed with his daughter, if only to appease her. Yet, he knew that the village would change, it was inevitable. The death of James Colberton started the maelstrom of trouble.

Philip saw a prophetic vision of change. It was catastrophic. While dancing with his daughter, he realized with perfect clarity that fate would soon provide opportunity to strike at the root of his ultimate evil.

A warm smile came to Philip's face. Emmit had never suspected Philip of coercion. His plot against Emmit would be a precise and pure action, like leaving the anonymous note with the charred ballots on Emmit's doorstep. It was simple and effective.

"Like times when you were up to my knee," said Philip. "You could still out dance your old papa. Where is your suitor, Claas — it is about time to dance with him."

"I will dance with him — but my dear father comes first," she said teasing him.

"You need to think of marriage and the future. But, if you could stay young forever...."

Sophia laughed with embarrassment. She fell into step with the intoxicating music.

A few days after the Grounding of the Fleet, word began to spread that a tragedy was unfolding on the Hallaphan farm. Eight of his horses had come down with crippling illness. He turned all fourteen horses out to the large pasture and waited to see if they would shake the illness. Karl Hallaphan thought it might be rotten grain that made them sick. By giving them plenty of water, he hoped that the illness could be purged. Soon, the first horse fell in the field and by dawn the next day, most of his horses were laid to waste. Those that clung to life, writhing in agony, were eventually put down. Rumor was spreading that a plague had arrived that would kill everyone in the village. The doctor tried to quell everyone's panic.

In a madness that no one really understood, Karl Hallaphan built a funeral pyre — gruesomely hacked his animals into pieces and burned them all. His hands were stained in blood for weeks. An entrepreneur would have skinned the animals, cropped the hair and cut away the hooves to sell for profit. But, the horse trader and his wife were ruined, and the madness was all that remained of their business.

Sophia and her mother had walked out to the farm to bring Mrs. Hallaphan a basket of food and a small sack of money collected from the neighbors the night before. The crystal blue sky was marred with the black, thick smoke of the burning equine corpses. They shared their condolences and left without a long stay. Karl Hallaphan was standing by the pyre throwing more fuel to his wasted livelihood. Sickened from the smoke and saddened by the sobbing horse traders wife, Sophia and her mother retreated to the church.

They walked through the doors of the church mournful and tired.

"It has happened before. Horses have sickness like we do. It is a decree of God. It is a test for us all," said Mrs. Lazarous.

They walked into the cavernous church. It was empty. They thought they would find Philip there. He was visiting Reverend Conrad about the loss at the Hallaphan farm.

They walked down the center isle of the wooden pews. Sophia gazed upon the altar and the stained glass that stood above. The shapes and fragments of color made the glass seem to glow with pulsating color to the muted landscape that was falling to the stern grip of winter outside.

It was quiet in the church. The sound of her mother's dress swished with the clattering of their shoes upon the marble floor. This was not only the foundation of the church, but as the Reverend so often said, "the foundation of the village." The great marble slabs were gifts from a Bishop in another country at the time when the church was being built. The marble was smuggled across the border and brought to the Reverend at a substantial price. The village was small and church foundation took four years to lay into place.

Now, the marble was worn smooth and polished by all the treading parishioners. The cracks and veins in the floor were like an archaic map, sealed in time as it was imprinted by nature. The villagers often sat in the same place at church year after year. Sophia always sat on the end of the isle so that she could inspect the marble veins and colors that allowed her imagination to seep into the crystalline textures. She sat in the eleventh pew on the right. This was her vantage to all the other villagers, where she developed her opinion, her fondness and her dislikes.

The two women reached the altar in front of the church where Sophia's mother made the sign of the cross. Sophia followed.

She turned to look at the back of the church where the balcony and the door to Reverend Conrad's quarters rose above the church common. Great columns held up the ceiling, decorated with etched leaves and turning cornices atop each column. Between the great columns, the organ pipes cut in long metal shafts to the ceiling in staggered cuts. The sun was brilliant through the side windows, splaying light in defined shafts across the pews.

The door upstairs opened and Philip came out. He walked down the steps and greeted his family. His face was long and morose. He sat in the front pew and leaned back.

"Did the Reverend offer some alms for the horse trader?" Sophia said.

"He gave me a few coins to pass on to the family," he said. "I will take it to his wife tonight."

Philip sat looking off into the colors of the stained glass in front of him, "He certainly lives among many comforts."

"What did you say, Philip?" said his wife.

"Reverend Conrad has quite a study. I wonder where he has accumulated all those books and furnishings."

Sophia put her hand on her father's arm, "I always thought that they were gifts."

"From who?" he said.

"We shouldn't speak of dishonesty here in the church," said his wife.

They began walking down the aisle when Philip mentioned, "Do not forget Old Lady Gertrude."

Sophia nodded, "Yes, I will go there tonight."

"What do you have to see her for?" her mother asked.

"I have to drop off some supplies that she needs. Linseed oil and some other things. She asked me for them on the way to the warehouse a few days ago, and I have been forgetful," said Sophia. She didn't really know what Old Lady Gertrude wanted, but she didn't want her mother to be suspicious or she would force herself to come along.

"Philip, you should let Sophia rest a little," she said with concern.

"Oh, mother. I cannot sit idle for long. I have the dark days of winter to do that."

They walked out to the front of the church and down the steps. Philip left them to go back toward the black smoke and the empty barn.

In the clearing near the church, among the grass and the short weeds, Hillmond Wenner was with a class of six girls — administering the methods and the rules of the staff. They all stood in a circle, each with their own staff. Sophia looked down to the steps and carefully watched her mother climb down. Sophia held her mother's arm so that she wouldn't fall.

At the bottom of the steps, Sophia paused to watch. They were learning the ways of the staff — protection - defense - pride - honor and courage. Sophia thought of Taska holding the staff at the ceremony and the chains that tied them together. She could hear the girls laughing, holding the staff like a toy. The chirping laughs filled the meadow. Hillmond Wenner had a way of handling the girls - — making the history of the weapon exciting and amusing. It was now marred by the murder of James Colberton and the subsequent imprisonment of an innocent woman for the sins of a stranger.

Sophia and her mother quietly sauntered down the gravel road.

"More girls for the lottery. It seems like this village has a knack for giving birth to more and more girls. We always have a few more naive girls to take up the staff," said Sophia's mother. Her sardonic tone matched Sophia's sadness.

"Perhaps a generation will come — devoid of women — no one to take the staff and no one to participate. Then they will forget this tragic test."

Sophia decided that abstinence would be the only way to abolish the annual study of the staff. What a whimsical idea - — a village without women, girls, ladies, or lasses. Life would be extinguished, year by year, man by man until the whole village vanished. Then it would be over. Sophia looked to the small rocks and stones in the lane, confident that another daughter would be born to someone. Life always thrives.

"I will see Old Lady Gertrude tonight. Perhaps I will see Taska tomorrow," said Sophia. She wanted to see her, but wished she noticed her at the Grounding of the Fleet and spent some time with her.

Sophia's mother added, "It would be a fine day if it wasn't for that putrid black smoke."

Old Lady Gertrude lived near the top of the lane, by the old maples. She was neighbor to Emmit up the hill and Old Kavner just next door. Sophia was slightly blinded by the sun setting in between the trunks of the old maples. The leaves had completely covered the road in a colored carpet. The setting sun was golden as it drew up long, autumn shadows. Twilight was quick to that of the long summer evenings. The sun was still warm until it finally tucked itself behind the mountains, then the air turned cold.

Sophia lifted her skirt and stepped over the threshold of

the door to Old Lady Gertrude's cottage. She paused and knocked. A voice spoke out but she couldn't make out her shaky words. Sophia stepped inside. She looked into the dark room, now illuminated partly by the reflecting sun upon the door.

Old Lady Gertrude smiled, "Sophia, I am glad you have come."

She turned to close the door. "No, please, leave it opened for a while," said the old woman. Sophia left the door wide open. The sun poured in.

The interior of the cottage was warm. The leaves from the road spun around her door stoop in a rustle that spooked her cat. Along the floor, a cool draft invaded the cottage.

Sophia took off her shawl and folded it neatly, as a matter of habit. Old Lady Gertrude rose slowly using her wooden cane. She erected her body and balanced, wavering slightly. She was hunched over as she walked to the bench near the table. It was painful for Sophia to watch the old woman move about the cottage.

"Come and sit down. You must be tired from working all day, come and sit," she said.

Sophia watched the frail woman make her way to the table. Sophia put down her shawl and took a seat. The old woman brought some bread and used a knife to cut the heel off for Sophia. She placed it on a plate and poured a saucer of oil for dipping. She shuffled over to the corner, and returned with a jug of spirit. Old Lady Gertrude poured some into a glass and set it down for Sophia to quench her salty, dry mouth.

Old Lady Gertrude sat down on the bench next to her.

She sighed with the release of her muscles. "Oh, it is a hard thing to live to an old age. I'm glad you came, Sophia. When your father told me that Taska Valimar was now a warden, I feared for her, and I worried about you, too."

Sophia pressed her lips together.

"The situation seems to be quelled. Taska is heavy handed with Cain," she said.

Gertrude didn't argue. She had so much time and history to draw from within her mind. "Tell me about her prisoner."

Sophia rubbed her cold hands together and thought for a moment, "Cain is harmless. He has no recollection of his crime. He was beaten senselessly when he was captured. He is frightened most of the time."

"Do you think he understands what he has done? Do you see him as a trickster?"

"No — he only knows of his crime from Emmit and the council. They have asked him about the crime. They tried to get him to confess," said Sophia.

A calico cat leapt up to the table. But instead of bothering with the food, the cat sat down and swished its tail. Sophia broke off a piece of bread and put it to her mouth watching the cat licking its silky coat.

"But the assassin had no answers," Gertrude said softly. Her reflections were distant. Her eyes had watched generation upon generation move her station in life up the ladder until she sat atop, waiting for her final leap into heaven.

"Are you saying that without the council's interference, the criminal wouldn't have realized his heinous crime? Yet, now he lives every day, slowly becoming what the council has created. Oh, it is true that he probably is a criminal. He is most likely a monster. He will fill the shoes that fate has laid before him," Gertrude said. "The actor must play out his part."

Sophia interjected, "Cain is no more than a shadow of the council's misdeeds — he is forged by Taska. She does more than keep him away from the village — she lets him thrive — unhindered by terror."

The cat blinked. Everything in the cottage seemed slow, tired and fragile. Yet, there was a comfort among the simple life of this old woman.

Gertrude continued, "Suppose no council gave him the details. What if he became a villager, unaware of his unlawful ways?"

"Perhaps he would think himself to be innocent," Sophia said, wiping the crumbs from her mouth.

Gertrude was trying to get to a point. She was steering Sophia through the maze of passing generations, of actions over time and consequence that brought them to this day. The old woman continued, "Cain would be innocent, while a councilor is murdered. Beyond the surviving family, Cain might live his entire life working hard on his farm, or maybe taking to the sea and bringing the catches in every night. He would go to church, join the festivities — and live a happy life — she might be happy."

"Did you say she... I don't understand," Sophia said.

"Yes, Taska — I am talking about the Valimar girl."

Sophia broke into an odd look, "What do you mean?"

"Her parents never told Taska that we are all prisoners — that we are all outcasts. They kept it from her. Taska

Valimar never went to the church for school — her mother taught her to read and write at home. They never explained to her that we were persecuted and moved like slaves in blood soaked ships, and the screaming... such terrible times. We have always remembered the past; a bad legacy is passed on like the bloodline of a tyrant. Taska knows nothing of how we came to be here or the bloody revolution. All she knows of history is her parents. They chose to wipe away the bloody history. And then they disappeared."

Sophia looked down to the bread and the yellow oil that stained the hard crust, slowly absorbing into the tender, soft inside of the flaky bread. She pondered, "How can I have been so blind. What does this life mean if you do not have a picture of history — the legacy of this village — this prison? She has so much innocence."

Gertrude nodded, "Like the assassin?"

"No, he was told by the council. He was told outright, when he woke from his thrashing," Sophia said. "They forced his guilt upon him like food thrust down his throat."

Gertrude continued, "The council told him. Before the interrogation, however, he was free of guilt. He was free from everything. When the council painted his criminal acts over and over in his mind, they made him into a killer. How did he react when they told him he had killed?"

"He was desperate. He was confused. He did not know of James Colberton. It was incomprehensible to him," Sophia said.

Gertrude looked down at her knotted and crippled hands. "Your father has told me that you are close to Taska Valimar. She lives with the staff as her way of life, yet she lives in the woods, alone. Her parents didn't want to tell her because they were ashamed of being outcasts. They didn't want to live with the brandished mark upon their lives. Taska was innocent to our misery and our treacherous past. So Taska has lived like the assassin, unknowing of the past. She has lived her entire life, working hard on her farm. She prays in the church, she sees the rest of the village, and she comes to the celebrations. She lives a happy life. If you tell her that she is a prisoner — that she can never leave this village — she too will realize that everyday has been shrouded in a veil of lies."

Sophia's gray eyes dimmed into tiny pools of light. Her spine, her limbs, and her fingers lost their feeling. She clenched her hands tightly. Old Lady Gertrude looked away. Tears fell from Sophia's cheeks — dizzy with pure emotion spilling over in a confused cascade.

"I thought I knew her so well. I am a fool."

In the darkness of the cottage, Sophia couldn't sleep. She was searching through her memories with Taska — not recalling one instance where Taska questioned life in the village. Even as childhood friends, Taska seemed unaffected by the past. When her parents disappeared no one wanted to mention any memories for fear of upsetting the isolated child. Sophia was devoted to Taska and her free will, but freedom came from ignorance.

Sophia couldn't sleep knowing that by morning, Old Lady Gertrude would conspire against Taska and send her a note. With curiosity, Taska would respond by going to see her. She will be told of the death and the persecution of an entire generation. Taska, sensitive to the past, will suffer terribly.

Sophia turned on her side and brought her quilt up close to her cheek to ward off the chill. She had found a calm, even nature to show to her mother and father after visiting the old woman. Her eyes, although red and bloodshot from crying, were convincing. She spoke clearly and answered their questions. She tried to eat, but it didn't feel right. Finally, she spoke of going for a walk. But when Sophia got outside, she didn't feel like going anywhere. Her legs seemed tired and weak. She sat upon an overturned bucket, down by the blacksmith's barn.

Claas found her and spoke for an hour about the distress of Karl Hallaphan and his equine massacre. Yet, even his deep voice and concern for the Hallaphan family, didn't break her feverish worry. She loved Taska and couldn't begin to fathom the Hallaphan disaster.

While Claas continued, Sophia let her mind wander. She conjured horrific visions of the future. The flames of hell would lash up and scorch her small feet. She had led Taska through a perpetual falsification of life. She recalled her studies in the Bible. She recalled the nine ways of being accessory to another's sin: By counsel - by command - by consent - by provocation - by praise of flattery - by concealment - by partaking - by defense of the ill done... by silence. Sophia's guilt was in her silence. But who created the sin which made Sophia an accessory? Her mind searched until she realized that it was not just one face, or one person's wrong doing, but all the names and all the faces in the village. The village legacy was locked within them tight. It would never seep out. No one could possibly know they were a village of exiles. More so to that of an outsider. Only the revolutionaries on their Annual Visit could validate the past. All the misery and blood shed was passed on like multiplication factors and spelling lists taught in the church classrooms.

Sophia left Claas to the remainder of the night and climbed into her bed for a solitude. She was trying to devise a way to amend her sins. No matter what was to be done — Taska's life would change and all that Sophia loved in Taska would be gone.

Her eyes grew heavy and she finally fell asleep. An immense feeling of space unfolded in front of her until she was suspended in the middle of the open sky — nothing attached to her. Below — she could see no earth or firm ground. All around here were clouds and the sun. Suddenly, like the moment between the flash of lighting and the roar of a thunderclap, she realized that she was falling. But without an end, or a bottom, or fear; she was not afraid. Sophia didn't know where she jumped from or where she was falling. Without a crime to remember, Cain would not be guilty. Without knowing the village was a troupe of exiles, Taska would remain free from their persecution. The rushing air blew back her hair and penetrated her skin — she was still falling down through emptiness.

Sophia was jolted awake. She had chores to do and the warehouse. She felt the affliction that she left the night

before, pour over her and darken her mood. Sophia felt tired
and weary.

Her tired body walked to the fireplace. She was alone in
the cottage. She took some hot water from the kettle and
made tea from mint spears. She sat and drank it slowly
thinking of the cold air that had crept in overnight. Sophia's
emotions had become an untamed beast last night. Like a
drunkard ashamed of a binge, she couldn't find the same
meaning that moved her and upset her the night before.

Weariness had not forgotten what had happened, but had
left her feeling numb and indifferent to what she knew. The
morning felt static and trifling. Sophia could bear any
hardship in the morning with a cruel indifference.

She dressed, finished her tea and gathered her cape. She
threw it over her shoulders and began her walk to the
warehouse. Her mother and father were already there. When
she reached the cobblestone square, she noticed the last of
the fishing boats were being pulled from the water. The
masts of all the ships were gone, the sound of the halyards
clanking in the night breeze were mute. She found comfort
in the bellows and hollers of the fishermen, working on the
boats in the morning. She might even see Claas hard at
work. Now, only the wind would moan through the bare
trees, like the whispers of a thousand voices.

She arrived at the warehouse. Her father was going over
the large inventory books, being careful everything was
accounted for and written in the ledger. He was a thorough
man.

Sophia took off her cape and looked at the books
quickly. Her father didn't speak.

A fisherman came in asking for thirty yards of canvas. When she turned to her father, he attended to the fisherman.

"It is probably all we will have until the Annual Visit. You have used it all up. I don't think I have much left," Philip said.

The stubby fisherman smiled, "Whatever you have I will take. Soon, we will all just have to barter with one another."

Sophia walked into the warehouse to fetch the canvas. Philip followed to help with the cumbersome roll. She pulled the large roll down and let it fall on to the floor.

"Just give him the rest," said Philip as they carried the roll to the fisherman. "This is all we have." The fisherman paid with two bills and left the warehouse, dragging the roll behind him.

Sophia sat down at the table, watching her father stuff away the bills in his pocket.

"Is the inventory book in order?" she said looking at the old bindings that created years and years of stock, sales and trade.

"Of course. You take great care of the inventory books, my dear," Philip said.

Like Sophia, Philip didn't speak much in the morning. It was a good time to work, with clear thoughts and precise judgment.

"Old Lady Gertrude, did she need anything when you saw her yesterday?"

"She was fine. Father," Sophia said diverting her eyes to the ledger. "Why do you think they have yet to come for the Annual Visit?"

"I don't know, but sometimes they are late. They won't

tell us when they are coming. They seem to enjoy the element of surprise. I dread it more and more each year."

Sophia added, "They come so late at night, frighten the villagers and send the town into panic. They are terrible."

"And, they are not soldiers anymore. When I was young, every man that came, dressed in full uniform, they marched in lines, with fifty men. It was like a drill. It was almost like a ceremony," Philip said. "The revolution was blood fresh upon their lips, but now they come with eight soldiers and thirty scavengers from the lowest of cesspools, mercenaries and thieves."

Philip let his mind wander. Sophia stared at the books. On the page she noticed the old cot she had given to Taska just after the lottery.

"Sophia — is something wrong?"

"No, perhaps I will go to see Taska this afternoon. I would like to see her as often as I can before the heavy snow," her voice seemed to flow out smoothly like it came from the wooden reed of a fine musical instrument. She thought about what she might say to her. Gertrude's words haunted her, "Someone should tell her. She must not find out from a stranger... but from someone she can trust."

Sophia wanted to be the one to tell her that her life had been a farce. She needed to tell Taska the truth, before Old Lady Gertrude summoned her. Sophia wanted to tell her without anger, without regret, without fear. But, she would have to see Taska's reaction and her plummet from an innocent precipice into the calamity of deceit. It had been looming over her since she was born. This was the only way Sophia saw redemption from her sin.

By the time Sophia convinced her father that everything was in order for the day, it was already late afternoon. She hurried up the lane, passing the old maples. She noticed the jumping boy standing in front of Old Lady Gertrude's house, just below her window. He jumped up and down under the window, trying to see in. She considered shooing him away, but she was in a hurry. The boy was daft and bound to live that way forever. There was not much sense in bothering the child.

Sophia walked up past the church. Some workmen were finishing their work for the day — putting a fresh coat of paint on the clapboard façade. Now that the fishing fleet was grounded, the fishing crews could paint and do other chores around the hamlet. They stood around the front door of the church talking and laughing now that their work was done for the day. They watched Sophia hurry by, giving her a friendly greeting. The cross upon the tall church spire made her feel driven to go to Taska and release her soul form the treachery of her unknowing sins.

She hurried through the woods, piecing together something to say that would explain the village and their eternal imprisonment. Her whole life was about to shift, shocking her entire collage of memories and contemplations. She may even deny anything that Sophia explained to her — leaving her distrustful and angry.

She could feel her limbs become numb and her teeth grinding hard together. She came out of the woods. Taska's cottage was in the distance.

Sophia trotted through the plowed field, drawing close to the cottage. She felt the moment rushing to her like a distant fate was waiting inside. She looked around the fields and the yard for Taska, hoping they were collecting and chopping wood or spreading hay over the turned fields. No one was outside.

She approached the door, took a deep breath and walked up the stoop. She took her thin, pale hand and knocked loudly. She waited and listened for someone to come to the door, but there was nothing. She lifted the latch and stepped in.

"Taska?"

She peered into the dark cottage. She stepped in and shut the door behind them. She called out again. She looked over to the fireplace and saw only the red coals left from the morning fire. She looked in the corner, near the cupboard — the staff was gone. She checked the room where Cain was kept. They were gone. When she came back out to the table, she noticed the red rose pressed in glass on the wall. She walked closer to examine the wrinkles and the shape of the flower, mummified for Taska's family inheritance.

She found a note on the table. She walked over and began reading it: "Dearest Taska, I did greatly hope that you would come to me today, for I wish to speak with you concerning matters of the past. Your fate as warden has made your life difficult — so I will understand if you cannot come to me. Respectfully, Gertrude."

Sophia let her eyes rest on the word "respectfully" wondering if this note was a trick, created by her own fear, and her devout love for Taska, releasing her from having to explain to Taska what she could hardly stand to say out loud. She was in Gertrude's cottage when she hurried by.

She turned quickly and rushed out of the cottage, leaving the door opened. She held the hem of her skirt up as she ran to keep from falling. She wanted to rush to Taska and protect her from all the treachery the village could muster. She wanted to press her between a piece of glass, like the rose on the wall, saving the delicate folds and delicate veins of Taska's innocence. She was still pure. If she ran through the thickest of woods and down to the shore, then followed the shore to the village, it would be quicker than going past the church and down through the village.

She knew how much she was about to lose. She picked her way quickly through brush and fallen trees. Her feet pranced through the fallen leaves like a deer gliding through the woods.

At the shore, she found children playing on a giant piece of driftwood that had been part of the shallow stone shore since she was little. They watched her rush down the beach — panting. She picked up her run, knowing the obstacles of the forest were now behind her.

Night was close, but the sky was still a dim red and yellow. Sophia ran through the field behind the blacksmith's shop and finally to the cobblestone square. There, Langston and Jarod sat with the blacksmith. She hurried through the square, clattering shoes across the cobblestones. She looked up the lane, but the cottage was still around the bend.

Sophia drew up when she saw the jumping boy, spinning and laughing in the lane like a mad child possessed by animal instincts. Old Lady Gertrude came out on her stoop, looking up the lane. Sophia was too late. Her chest heaved and her legs trembled beneath her. Hillmond Wenner was trying to have them come back, but they were too far off.

Sophia ran to the scene, up the bending lane. Taska pulled Cain behind her as she stormed up the lane, the staff carried brazenly in her other hand ready to fend off another assault of her memories and her convictions.

Sophia took a few steps, "Taska! Wait!" Her voice echoed off the structures and the cottages in the village. She turned quickly, "Did you tell her everything?"

Gertrude said nothing. Hillmond Wenner came back down the road. Other villagers had come from their suppers and stoves to witness the disruption.

The jumping boy was laughing and spinning out of control. He was drunk with the frenzy and the emotion of Taska's disenchantment. The shouts and denials that poured from their lips in a bitter exchange had elated the daft boy.

Even from a distance, Taska's eyes were empty, her black hair in disarray in the midst of her furious retreat.

The monster and its keeper retreated. Sophia was afraid, but her fear erupted from what she had failed to say and do.

Sophia watched Taska flee. She had been witness to the murder of Taska's innocence. She would become the warden to Taska's soul — not by lottery, but by faith.

Sophia stood in the middle of the lane and wept into her hands.

The jumping boy ran after Taska and Cain, laughing and spinning in a surreal dance, mocking the severity of the wounded souls.

Philip had been reading through James Colberton's official papers. The pile of crumbled papers and stiff parchments concerned his affairs of village law, land rights and inheritance claims. In the past he was a shrewd legal councilor, but lacked an official court in the remote village. He was the last of the legal men, bringing civility and judicial decisions to matters such as land use and property lines. He relied on good record keeping, using hand-drawn land maps and previous records to prove where property began and where it ended. He executed wills and testaments to the villagers, making sure that all the property, money and titles where transferred properly, and given to the correct survivors. Most of the transactions that went through James Colberton's office were merely matters of writs and notices. Very few disagreements and disputes went to the council to be weighed and voted. The council was the last resort to any decision. If someone refused to move off someone else's property, for example, Langston, Jarod, Philip and James Colberton would make the law clear and then force the decision upon the family. If they refused, they were summoned to the council meeting and reprimanded. Sometimes, they were physically evicted, or burned out of their house. If someone had to be imprisoned, a sentence was given and a warden selected — they would serve the term away from their families and their land. When the condemned returned to their house (if anything was left), the boundaries of their property had changed and a fine had been levied. That was how the system worked — civil until it was brutal.

It rarely came to enforcement. Furthermore, now that James Colberton was dead, no one followed up on the disputes. Someone would have to set up the office and take up the role of James Colberton's council. All that remained were piles of his legal documents, notes, books, and dusty ledgers.

Philip rubbed his eyes and peered across the piles of paper. He had found a diary that was bound in leather. It was the one thing that Philip kept separate from the other papers — it was kept at the bottom of a locked drawer. It documented Emmit's deeds and misdeed in the council. Philip didn't realize that James was keeping documentation on this adversary. Creating a history of deceit was all he could do.

The journal documented things Philip never considered. It shed light on how Emmit collected tax money and extorted a bit more for his own pocket. Philip had heard the complaints from Karl Hallaphan that Old Lady Gertrude had been picked clean when Emmit and Langston came for the tax collection. He had illegal weapons, and fixed a landmark lottery in the village. He was corrupt. Yet, you would stop him?

James Colberton, before Cain killed him, had been following Emmit around. This is what he found. Late at night, Emmit and Langston would load up the gray nag that Langston kept in his yard. Filled with money and trade goods, they would go into the foothills of the mountains, and meet with rogue groups. According to James

Colberton's accounts, they would buy books, gunpowder, weapons, jewelry and maps from these traveling men.

Taking their newly purchased loot and stockpiling it in the Reverend's office and living quarters, they managed to keep a small fortune in precious gems and rare manuscripts. It was the Reverend who wanted the scripture and the books. Emmit and Langston kept the weapons and money. They even acquired maps that would lead them out of the wilderness that imprisoned them.

Philip read with shock that every six weeks, they would arrange to meet a small band of mercenaries and trappers. If Emmit and Langston had made outside contact, which was illegal, why didn't they leave?

Philip shut the leather bound journal and leaned back in his chair. His eyes were burning. There was more to this. The meetings, the rigged lottery. Something was happening. The flame of the candle sitting on the table in front of him wavered in the drafty room. Like a poison, coursing through his veins, Philip attached his verdict to his suspicions — to counteract the venom of deceit. Cain had come from the trappers and the mercenaries. Emmit and Langston paid him. James Colberton was a threat, because he knew the law and could root out Emmit's corruption. He had been clashing with Emmit and Langston for years about land and the rights of the villagers. He had fought them on the taxes — and argued to reduce the tax payment for the poor and raise it for the well to do. James Colberton had been suspicious of Emmit's underhanded dealings. When he drew close to the proof, he was murdered. It was a theory. But something didn't sit right with it. He was missing something.

Page after page of writing described James, quietly stalking through the woods in pursuit of the secret affairs of the Emmit and Langston. He followed them out into the foothills, stayed hidden in thicket and trudged through streams to catch a glimpse of their misdeeds. He had to fight off a wolf, and stayed out in the woods for days on end tracking and hiding.

An example of the passages appeared as follows:

"After waiting in the clearing for some time, men arrived and met Emmit and Langston. Rugged men who trap and kill were greeted with handshakes and obvious tidings of affection. They laughed and traded goods. I saw weapons, rifles and long knives draped over the trappers and mercenaries. They made a fire and spent a few hours, laughing and trading books, jewelry and rolled up maps. These men dressed in fur and leather knapsacks. Langston bought three knives and a long blade that night. Emmit loaded the horse with books for the Reverend. I have always wondered why Emmit was so deceitful and hungry for power. I never understood why he pillaged our own village, and had no place to spend it. Why accumulate power and wealth if it can't be spent? He has a great plot. Does he send messages to the outside world? Could he send word to the world that we are forever captive? If the trappers could make it to us – then we, too, might find our way out. If a large group left it would be terrible. The soldiers of the Annual Visit would massacre anyone left behind. They would know of our sedition. They would burn down the village and begin a search for us. They would wipe us out. I must reel back my spinning head. Emmit sees me as a threat. He fears that I will dethrone him from his high and mighty position. If I bring the charge and hold the evidence – I can turn him over to the Annual Visit. Then he will be taken away. I must find more evidence. There is another full moon coming. They will meet again. I must continue to document his deceit. I might need help, an extra pair of eyes, someone I trust and someone who knows the woods."

Philip thought for a moment. He counted the weeks. He mulled it over. This next meeting was around the time when Cain came to the village. What happened? Did James find someone to go with him? Was there someone else who knows?

This was the last entry in his leather bound journal.

Emmit sat at the table in his cottage, with a large, round candle in the center. It was close to midnight. He looked over the large ledger that contained all the minutes of the council meetings over the last few months. He reviewed passages, looking for faults or flaws in the judgments made by the council. Although he could never publicly change the outcome of a vote or decision once it was voted upon, Emmit could bend and change the way people thought and the way they reacted. If he didn't like the outcome of a vote, he would change the outcome of what was being voted upon by his influence alone. The village was his to rule. Looking over the minutes of the meetings and the verdicts was to leisurely judge and rule over all the villagers.

When the Blutchard family wanted to build a barn, it

came to a vote. Emmit voted against it because they didn't have sufficient cause to build a barn. They had no animals or large crops stores. But the rest of the council thought it was harmless. When the barn was in the middle of construction, it burned down. Without enough money to build another barn, the scorched earth remained dead. The source of the fire was never known. The spot remained black and dark, nothing grew in its place.

That was how things happened. Emmit used phrases like, "accidents happen," and "careless people need to take heed." No one asked why, they just accepted the fate they were given.

Yet, as his eyes scanned over the name Cain, his mind became turbulent. This issue was unfinished. He looked at the council notes and the outcome of the vote. The name Taska Valimar was on the next line of the yellow parchment. It haunted him.

When Cain was handed over to the arbiter, Emmit was wary. He failed at killing him when he was captured. Emmit looked over to the wooden box on the chair. He clung to those pistols. Cain was among the villagers. The assassin was clearly mocking him each day he lived with his amnesia act. The pistols loaded and placed near his bed allowed him to sleep. Emmit knew that he could point the long barrels at his greatest fear, away from his own insanity, and outward to anything that obstructed his way. The trappers and the mercenaries could also come to the village, searching for Cain, demanding answers from Emmit and Langston. But, the outsiders believed that the village was full of malaria, typhus and other maladies, so they stayed away.

He looked back down at the book. The candle flickered. He turned and looked to the door. Langston stepped in from the pitch-black night and took off his hat.

"I thought you should know, Valimar is in town — she is speaking with Old Gertrude. I do not know why she is here at this time of night," said Langston as he lumbered to the table.

"Cain is with her?"

"Of course."

Emmit folded his hands upon the table, "What do you think this is all about?"

"Perhaps she knows about the crewman that I hired."

Emmit shook his head, "No, that is your business. No one knows of that."

"Perhaps the crewman told the old woman," Langston said.

Emmit sighed deeply, "No, not at all. Just pay the old woman a visit tomorrow and ask her. She is harmless and constantly trying to keep out of harm's way. Hillmond Wenner would tell me if the old crone was suspicious."

Langston wouldn't fail in his plot.

"Most of the village has a great respect for that old hag," said Langston.

"She is the last one. She is the last remaining person, give or take a few of those old sea leeches. She is the last to come on the boats. Everyone else lives in the shadow of the second generation. Our parents explained and pleaded with us about how difficult it was and how many perished. I tried to encompass their fear, their anger, but I just do not feel so affected. They tried to preserve too much of the Old World."

Langston seemed to agree, "Our families left us nothing. They passed on tales of wealth and happiness, without the inheritance. All we have, we must earn with twice the labor and half the profit."

Langston put his hat on and opened the door, "I will speak to the old woman."

Emmit leaned back in his chair, "And let me know when they leave tonight." Langston latched the door as he left.

Emmit looked at the box where the pistols were kept. It was irksome to know the assassin was close by. Finishing the business of Cain once and for all would return authority and rule into Emmit's grasp. He let his mind wander to the Annual Visit. Like everyone in the village, he wondered why they hadn't arrived. He would have to hide the weapons well when they arrive — randomly checking houses for contraband. Emmit rubbed his eyes after removing his eyeglasses and whispered, "We must obey."

Gertrude woke from her half-sleep. She tried to get up when Taska returned late at night.

"Please don't get up. I had to speak with you again. I won't sleep until I know more," Taska said placing her hand on her shoulder. She was calm and solemn, but something was simmering hot beneath her skin.

The old woman felt weariness sink into her heart.

"When you left, Taska, I came in and I grieved for the sadness that I afforded you. But, you must know about your past. You must know what everyone has accepted," she said recalling how desperate everything was that afternoon.

Taska turned and told Cain to sit upon the bench near her. She knelt in front of the old woman. The chain draped over to Cain. Taska had lost her rage and replaced it with a craving for the truth.

"Tell me again...."

Gertrude looked into Taska's eyes. The truth had to come from the beginning. She no longer had to shield Taska from the tragic past. But Gertrude couldn't remember exactly when it began. The white haze of the old woman's history clouded her mosaic past. She began quietly.

"It was when I was young. I knew nothing of this village. The only people who thrived here where criminals, banished here as a punishment. The old men that where here when we first came told of crimes and treachery that they had committed. Some died. Some we had to kill. This village was a kind of penal colony. Some called it a work camp, but that wasn't why we were sent here. They didn't want us to work; they didn't care what we did when we got here. If we stood in the village square and died in our tracks that would have suited them fine. It didn't matter. But we survived. Among the wilderness and the killers, rapists, thieves and degenerates, we began our lives again."

Taska composed her mind. She wept in her cottage. That was done now. She couldn't sleep and her wretched stomach wouldn't tolerate food. So she came to listen.

She never considered her past important beyond her parents because they were all she knew. Now, she conceived a greater tragedy, which defined the evil and the viciousness that permeated the village.

Gertrude continued, "Your parents were kind people. I

knew them when they were young. They had a great deal of pride and loved you very much. They knew that the past had little to do with your future. But, when they were children, they saw their parents murdered and the world thrown into chaos. Let me start in the beginning."

"It was a political coup. It began with a series of assassinations in the streets of the capital. The religious and pious statesmen where slain or taken away. It had all failed. The government superseded all divinity and religion in the country. Churches were burned and any faith was abolished as a criminal act. The churches and mosque were plundered for their gold and treasures. A few cathedrals remained and a call went out. If you could not turn from your faith and believe in the dictator and his henchmen — then go to your faith and embrace it. You will not be harmed. And we were not arrested for lining up and entering the church, but once inside — they marked who we were and wrote our names down. Four thousand people were recognized by the state. Other religions and faiths suffered similar fates. One by one like trees for the lumber mill, we were fallen and taken to holding pens by the wharf. We lived in squalor and terrible condition. It was wintertime. They could not move us on the ships until the ice in the harbor broke up. I was young so I slept for a few hours and then went to the fires and warmed up. Some of the older people froze to death, stuck to the ground like stones in the mud. Some say they just gave up. Taking away the dead was hindered by the fact that they were frozen to the bone."

So we prayed. What else could we do? Our own judges, magistrates and civic leaders damned us. All those men of

political and social prominence turned from their faith and
gave a blood oath to dictators and tyrants. Your parents
were children, hardly knowing of the hardships and killing.
Langston was a young man. I was just becoming a woman.
We lived in the bitter cold camps for three months dying of
hunger and exposure. Some of the new citizens, who
renounced their faith and lived for the will and want of
autonomous dictatorship, came and spit at us through the
fence — screaming political slogans. We prayed and waited
for death."

Your mother's family was aristocratic, so your
grandmother was hoping to be pulled from the camp by her
family. Your mother was a child and stayed closed to her
mother. Your father was an orphan who wandered about the
camp looking for food and trying to stay warm. Your,
grandmother kept Viviana, close to her. She was a little girl.
Your grandmother was visited often by her upper class
family and they told her to forget her husband — a flour
mill operator who was down on his luck. She refused to
leave him alone in the camps. Your grandparents and your
mother stayed together and prayed for the killing to end and
the spring to come. Before it got too warm — the ships
arrived in the icy harbor."

At night, they would take fifty or sixty people away. We
never saw a ship leave. We never knew what happened to
the people taken away — but we assumed they were
murdered. Men came into the camps to ask us to convert
and believe in the new regime. No one really turned to
freedom. Finally, our night came and we were marched
down the pier. I knew for sure we were to die. We watched

a line of prisoners face archers. The muskets were too loud
— so they shot them with arrows, and they pushed them
over the side into the harbor. We knew that our fate would
be similar. We would end our lives on the killing wharf. We
tried to stay together — your grandparents and your mother
stayed close. Letzen, the orphan somehow attached himself
to our group — playing with Viviana and staying close to
our constant fire. We began a march to the executioner's
ship. They loaded us onto three ships. We were on the last
boat. Screaming and waiting for death, we thought for sure
that we would be killed and tossed over the side. People of
the new state were screaming out terrible things at us from
above. They were so glad to see us die. Some waved the
new flag and called us traitors and heretics. Some of the
people in line were attacked and beaten — then thrown to
the crowds. They were torn apart. But it got worse. At the
end of the long wharf there was a litter of dead bodies, by
the hundreds, piled by the red stained wall. They refused to
acknowledge the new system — and refused to get on the
ship. Soldiers with swords, knives and muskets lined the
pier — keeping us in order.

"Four men appeared on a high podium — they were our
judges. They were adorned with jewels and fine robes —
pillaged from the religious artifacts that remained. They
asked us to embrace the new system and never again put
faith in God and spirit. Those who could turn from God —
stepped out of line and were walked back down the dark
wharf."

"But we all stayed together. Our families were gone.
There was nothing to go back to."

"The judges condemned us as enemies of the new system and told us to board the ships. Some knew they would die, so they dropped to their knees to pray. This was the wrong thing to do. Soldiers beat them, dragged them to the wall and massacred them with swords and clubs."

"Three ships were loaded. They all left just before daybreak. We were on the last ship. The first ship to leave went out into the harbor. There — they killed everyone on the ship and tossed them over the side into the freezing water. Bodies by the hundreds were floating in the harbor. The second boat left the pier and moved out into the harbor. A few smaller boats moved in and removed the captain. They proceeded to burn the entire boat into a furious fireball of burning wood and flesh. Bodies flew from the ship and the masts crashed down wickedly. They poured oil over the swimming victims and lit them ablaze. No one survived from that ship.

"We prepared for death as well. Our boat was allowed to leave. When we reached the outside of the harbor, we realized that they were taking us away. We pushed through the floating dead and watched the fires burning in the harbor. It was a sea of blood. Finally, after two weeks, we arrived here. My family and my legacy are piles of bones at the bottom of the harbor near the capital. Those who were on that one ship arrived here."

"What of Emmit? Did his family come on the ship?"

"When we arrived, criminals and other tawdry types had lived here. I am not sure if anyone knows Emmit's parentage. He probably doesn't know himself. Likely, he was a bastard to a criminal."

Taska was numb. She could hardly speak, "This village is not what it seems."

"Your parents remember the fire and the death and they never wanted you to live with such terror. That is why they never told you. Your parents, Viviana and Letzen, grew up together in this village. They were destined to be together. They loved you so much. Most of the children were too young. If they were lucky — they were born here in the beginning when the village was just a few houses and a church. We have tried to preserve something of what the church once was. We are privileged. Reverend Conrad is blessed to be alive."

"I live in a world of outcasts and criminals," Taska said. "Now, I will spend the rest of my life protecting all of the villagers from one of their own."

Gertrude cupped her cold hands under Taska's chin, "Do not lose faith in God. This is all that we have to remember the past. It almost disappeared. We are free to believe in the church. Is that not a powerful act?"

Taska rose from the table, "We are not free."

Cain and Taska prepared to leave, "I will come again with more questions. I will come late at night — when the village is quiet."

Gertrude nodded, "You are welcome here anytime."

Taska hurried Cain out into the street. She was filled with frustration.

Cain was in bed staring up at dark shadows scattered over the ceiling. He was tired from listening to the old woman

and her tales of murder and persecution. Taska was crying
in her room for a while but now her sobs had subsided. Cain
tried to sleep, but like Taska, his past was obscured and
uncertain. His memories were a hodgepodge of images and
emotions that lacked any time or reason. His tried to
recognize faces and places in his dreams. He often dreamt of
riding a horse in the snow, through sheer mountain passes.
He dreamt of swimming in beautiful lakes of crystal blue
water and seeing an entire city across the rippling waves.

Each time he heard Taska moving about, he became
aware of the cottage, and Taska's sadness. The betrayal of
the past had permeated like smoke settling into cloth. Cain
didn't know how to reassure Taska or settle her frayed
nerves. Somehow, like a puppet — manipulated by its
strings, Cain wanted words of comfort to come through to
him. But this was all a dream, like the odd visions that could
only be his past.

Cain's bed was against the wall. The boards that made
up the wall stood loose next to one another, which afforded
Cain slivers of light from the fireplace. Sitting up, he could
press his face to the wall and see the main salon of the
cottage. Cain heard Taska's door open. He looked through
the cracks. He listened to her shoes tap across the floor.
Taska threw more wood on the fire.

He couldn't see much of the room through his little crack
in the wall, but he knew what she was doing by the sounds.
She went to the cupboard and took her parchments to the
table. Cain could only see her back when she sat at the table.

The logs began to burn and brighten the room. Taska's
hair draped down to the ties on the back of her dress. He

noticed how the firelight illuminated her black silk-shiny hair. He could hear the parchments being turned over and shuffled. He found comfort in watching her.

He watched her until he fell asleep. He didn't realize that sleep had overcome him until he woke and Taska was no longer there at the table. The fire burned dim and now he could hear a whisper. For a moment he thought he was dreaming. His dreams were a collage of voices and faces disconnected from his life. He knew he was awake, he knew Taska's voice even as a whisper. But was someone else in the cottage or was she praying?

Taska was reading from the parchments, "I am a shadow, a person brought from the darkness by the illumination of truth. But I don't feel that the truth has enlightened, but rather imprisoned my soul with more chains and more locks. I have no desire to live with my uncovered history. There is no freedom when your life is predetermined by the actions of the past. Mother and Father gave me freedom, knowing that they had lost so much already. I forgive them for withholding the truth, wherever they may be. This cottage is the same; the village is the same, nothing has changed, only my perceptions — nothing more. That is what gives me comfort. But someday my perceptions will change and so will this life."

Her voice was slow and her words clear. She sat back down and crossed out something on the paper. She inked something else. Taska was composed; her tears distant, her passion for her pen afforded empathy.

Cain wasn't an intellect, but he had a few questions that puzzled him as he tried to rationalize Taska's anger and her sorrow. Why didn't the Reverend speak to her if he knew that she was unaware? Why did her only friend betray her?

Cain couldn't understand why everyone remained silent in the shadow of such oppression. Pain without suffering and weeping without tears made no sense. But, it explained why Taska was unaffected and different from the villagers.

Cain looked through the seams of the wood and saw Taska musing over the parchments near the hearth. He felt his body release his nervous tension, knowing she was calm. He fell asleep and slept through the night.

The next morning, Langston knocked on Old Lady Gertrude's door. He knew she wouldn't come to the door, but he didn't want to intrude. He waited for her voice to invite him in. When the door did open, Langston looked at Old Kavner with surprise.

He turned to the old woman, "It is Langston. I will leave you. Thank you for speaking with me — I will check on you soon."

Langston grinned, "Do not leave on my account, old man."

Of course Langston was only ten years younger and well into his twilight years, but he knew Kavner hated to be called "old man."

Old Kavner threw out his hand and gave a disgusted "ack" as he walked out into the lane.

Langston walked over to the bench and sat down as Gertrude smiled, "Langston. What do I owe the honor?"

"I noticed that Taska Valimar came late last night. I

wanted to make sure everything was peaceful. She isn't causing you any trouble I hope?"

"She is not any trouble. She is very earnest in her views and her ways," said Gertrude.

Langston looked away from the woman tapping his shoe on the wooden floor, "She seems that way, but I often wonder. She is often disobedient to our wishes as a warden."

The old woman laughed and turned her eyes back to Langston who seemed so young to her, although he was well into his sixties.

"Of course, but you cannot take her entire life. She fights for this life; she fights for something individual and unique to her own. Let her scratch and claw, after all, it's all you've allowed her to do."

Langston rose from the bench, "I suppose you see what you want to see."

Gertrude looked up quickly with a stern face, her anger was quickly revealed, "I see what she allows me to see, which is not to save much grace for you and the council. Some of the villagers are so angry for coming to this village. Perhaps some people wished they had remained in the city of blood. They are so bitter that this is all they have. I would rather live with faith and poverty than despotism and riches."

He shook his head and walked to the door, "Everyone was wary of the lottery. Now it is resolved. Fate picked her. We cannot allow her to deviate from the law."

The old woman shook her head, "Fate is nothing more than rhetoric for the council. You all hide behind fate, and lawful votes, but when your masks fall from your faces you will be proven guilty in God's court and council."

Langston left the old woman, haunted and spiteful. Something was being planned. Something happened that he had missed. He could see the footprints and the broken branches from the ruckus, but he couldn't see what happened. Trickery and deceit seemed to be dancing around him. He looked down the lane and saw Sophia speaking with the blacksmith. Sophia noticed him but quickly looked back to the blacksmith's forge. He knew the only way to break the vengeful spirit that seemed to spill out from Sophia, Gertrude, and Taska was to do away with the source of evil.

Emmit's plan suddenly went from a chore to a joyful act, bringing about a feeling of excitement and dim happiness. He seemed to froth with excitement at the thought of killing Cain.

Old Kavner hurried to the warehouse to speak with Philip. He had gleaned a few minutes with Gertrude, before Langston interrupted him.

Kavner came in and saw Sophia leafing through the ledger. She was double checking her own handwriting and making sure everything was accounted for. The ledger and its completeness was a festering concern until the Annual Visit was concluded.

"Sophia, where is your father?" he said.

"He is behind the warehouse, patching the stone wall," she said. "Is something wrong? You look harried."

"No, nothing serious. Just wanted to ask him his advice

on a matter. Since James Colberton's death — I have no one to speak to about my taxes."

Sophia nodded, but still remained suspicious.

Kavner walked around the warehouse. The sun was held in a web of wispy, white clouds. Philip was mending a small stone wall that had fallen when a tree came down last winter. He had pulled the tree away from the wall. Stone by stone he was rebuilding the collapsed portion.

"Philip, I spoke to Gertrude this morning."

Philip turned from the wall and slapped the dirt off his hands, "She was all right?"

"She is a resilient old woman."

"What did she say about Emmit?"

"I told her what we suspected, a fixed lottery and the stealing of money above the tax collection. I even suggested foul play in Hallaphan's barn disaster. I told her we had no real evidence. I told her that it was all a secret. So, she told me about Emmit.

"She began back before we all came here. Emmit was sixteen. His family had been killed. He began to grow fanatical about leaving the church and joining the new regime. They allowed him out of the camps — after he promised to renounce God and work for the cabinet of the state as a page. He vowed his allegiance to the leaders. This is where it gets interesting. He worked with a group of young men — ransacking rural churches and pilgrimage sites. His band of boys burned churches, killed priests and... raped the women of the church. It was a test of his allegiance."

Philip gasped and then shook his head, "He was a

despot?"

"His band of boys — armed with torches, knives and
horses, marched through the countryside — traveling from
one holy site to another. There must have been forty to fifty
men in the pack of killers and pillagers. They were a terrible
band of death and destruction. On his eighteenth birthday —
Emmit and his band received word that they were to be
honored at the capital for their work in wiping clean all
religion in the rural countryside. When they arrived in the
capital — they were given a great feast. When they were
done eating — they were all taken away to prison. Most of
the men fought and died in the palace courtyard. No one
wanted to go back to the camps, but their plunder and
murder were getting out of hand. They were becoming a
vicious force. Although they were merely forty or so men,
their reputation was getting dangerous. The government
feared that they would create a militia and start to rebel
against the ruling army. Emmit was sent back to the camps
until he was sent to the village."

"So much blood on his hands," said Philip.

"We are among the tyrants. And it would explain why
he has been out in the forest meeting with trappers,
destitutes and traders. He may even know them from his
youth. Yet, something still puzzles me — if he knows that
there is a way out of this wilderness — why does he stay?"

Philip was quiet.

"I do not know," but it seems clear that Cain came from
these people. Although he may not remember — he ran
among these traders, thieves and cutthroat bandits. We have
never met an outsider wandering around. We live in a

remote location. The only way someone like Cain could find a small village in the vast wilderness was if he was directed here."

Kavner agreed. Then he paused, "As long as Cain lives — he could still accuse Emmit of hiring him to kill James Colberton. Why has Emmit allowed the assassin to live this long?"

"He must be convinced that Cain cannot remember," Philip said.

"What do you think?"

"Cain has no memory... but it might prove lucrative just the same. But, something is keeping Emmit here. What is greater than money or power?"

Old Kavner was stumped, "That is all he thrives on."

"But, beyond that — what would keep him here?" He paused, "A woman."

"Who?"

"I am not sure just yet. Emmit's life was almost perfect in the village until his wife-to-be was killed serving the staff. It is the one part of his life he cannot obtain with power or money — love has alluded him."

Kavner and Philip worked on the wall together, whispering and plotting. They were diligent in the fall morning sun.

The Bible lay opened upon the table. Cain was learning how to read now that his chores had diminished and the weather turned cold. Taska sat across from him as he read passages out loud, but it was slow and laborious. Taska, who knew most of the Bible, listened and corrected his mistakes. She would speak quietly, correcting a word or assisting him in finishing a phrase. She had grown tired of reading to him, followed by his question.

He was reading from the book of John when a faint knock came to the door. Taska dropped her sewing down to her lap. She looked at the door and shook her head. Cain stopped his slow reading, expecting Taska to answer the door.

She watched the wooden door and waited. Cain looked oddly to her. She shook her head again, and looked back down at her sewing. The rapping on the door came louder. The latch of the door was lifted, but Taska had propped up a log to keep it shut. Now, no one could come in without an invitation.

A thud came to the door as the visitor tried to force the door open.

The door didn't give at all. Then a voice came, "Taska! Are you in there?"

Taska looked back to her sewing and continued her stitches.

"It's Sophia."

"Continue reading," said Taska. She listened to Cain while Sophia called out a few more times.

Finally, it was quiet. Cain continued his reading. Taska didn't want unnecessary contact with the village. It was deceitful. They would only bring her more misery. Sophia would worry about her, but she would also go back into town and tell Philip, who would eventually tell the other council members to stay away.

Cain stopped reading, "Is Sophia an enemy?"

Taska felt a heaviness fall upon her breast.

"Don't say that, Cain. We should be left alone. It is not Sophia I hate. She has been kind to me, but if she comes all the time so will the rest of the village," said Taska.

Cain leaned back in the chair, unsettled, "But she will go back and tell the village that there is trouble and they will come anyway. Not Sophia but Emmit, the council."

She seemed to agree, "They will come one way or another. We are not breaking the law, so they will have to come and stand outside."

"Their curiosity will break the door down. The more they don't see you, the more they fear me," Cain said.

"This bothers you, so it seems?"

He thought for a moment and shook his head, "I don't know. But it makes you angry." Taska found his words childish. She had witnessed his hollow body grow into an image that was resoundingly familiar, but to what or to whom, she couldn't identify. She spoke low, "Why don't you read a little more."

Later that night, Cain laid in his bed listening to the wood crackle and burn in the fireplace. He listened to Taska as she sat writing, but he heard something unfamiliar which broke him from his conscious wrestling. He sat up and looked through the cracks between the spaces in the boards, trying to keep his chains quiet. He watched Taska looking at the stack of parchments, and then she took another and crumbled it into a little ball. She turned and threw it into the fire. The fire plumed in a glare of yellow and red.

Taska read another sheet; a sheet from her past. She was

rewriting it on a separate parchment, editing and changing her own history to fit into her new perspective. The pages of her past became useless and outdated. She was trading one sheet for another, shifting her perspective from diffused to clear — from innocence to experience.

Cain wondered if his eyes deceived him. He couldn't comprehend why she would foster so much sentimentally, and keep her life so fully recorded, only to disregard it now.

He couldn't feel what Taska felt, and he couldn't understand what her fear had now become. It frightened him.

Taska had lived according to village life. Her life was suited for the little piece of land she tilled, and the common laws that she tried to up hold. She did these things to please her mother and father, and God. But her parents and her friends had deceived her. Her life was not predestined or chosen. It was a catalyst for the council, the village, and the church to use as a weapon of self-destruction.

The council constructed the laws she followed of an outcast band of leaders, puppeteered by the Reverend and the Doctor, who controlled a village branded as heretics and non-conformists. Taska was never marked as an outcast, nor was she accepted as a villager. She had failed in her hollow, useless station. The parchments, her declaration to God and her parents had betrayed her. She was clutching a simple, monastic existence with the delusion that it was the proper way to live. Upon the pages, Taska was creating a new religion, based on her own voice, her own laws and her own vindication that her life now demanded. Conformity and civility were all paper-thin masks that were now torn away.

Now, it was up to her to define peace, happiness and a civil order.

When she slept, she had visions, like that of a saint. They were foretelling her of her new life. She saw unrecognizable faces, a world that was alive with feelings and ideas, new to her. Like Cain, dreaming of a disconnected past locked into his subconscious, Taska was having visions of a future disconnected from her life now. She would wake with tears of happiness in her eyes, after dreaming of a life that was safe and blessed. She often called her visions of this new life the golden world. Her parchments were the only way to get to the golden world. She knew she would get to this ethereal place if she believed the words she put down on the parchments.

Everything else was a lie.

A few days later, Sophia stopped into the cobbler's shop. She was overwhelmed by the smell of glue and the smell of fresh hides the cobbler stored in his shop. The old cobbler looked up, his glasses hanging low on his nose.

"Sophia, what do you have for me today?"

"I brought my boots from last winter. They have worn through on the sole."

The cobbler was a quiet man, and he kept to himself and his business. Although he was asked to join the council, he kindly declined saying that his shop was all he could keep up with at his age. The council wanted him to fill Colberton's place — but he knew of too much deceit in the council. He was never married and lived in a room behind the shop.

He looked the boots over. He noticed the hole and the scuffed leather. The heel was pulling off the left foot. Shoes and boots wore out quickly in the village. Hard work and constant wear destroyed footwear and crippled feet.

"These boots are of a soldier. They have lasted very well."

"I have had them for some time," said Sophia.

"Leave them and I will get to them as soon as I can. I hope you have some other shoes to wear?" the cobbler said. He looked down to what she was wearing.

She smiled, "Of course."

Sophia noticed the pile of shoes he had to fix, stacked in pairs next to the bench where he worked. It would be some time before she saw her boots again.

"I will come in a few weeks, perhaps they will be done," she turned to leave.

"No, no, come tomorrow and they will be done. You will need them when the bad weather comes. I am always quick to repair the shoes people need, while other shoes can wait until time permits. It is a matter of necessity. I was just telling Taska Valimar the same thing when she brought her shoes in. They will be done."

Sophia nodded, "She was here? When?"

He thought for a moment, "Let me see, I suppose... early yesterday morning. Yes, that is it."

Sophia looked around at the workbench, filled with tools, odd shapes of leather and fabric.

"I went to her cottage a few days ago and she didn't answer, I thought she might be sick," Sophia said.

"She appeared well and spirited when she came in. Well, as much spirit as one can muster up with a killer attached to her," said the shoemaker.

"I will stop to see you late tomorrow, on the way home from the warehouse. And when you see Taska, ask her to come to the warehouse to see me."

Sophia stepped out into the lane. She was met by Jarod and a fisherman. She had to walk around the two men as they blocked the doorway. She didn't care to speak with Jarod, so she darted around them. But Jarod spoke up.

"Sophia, I want to ask you about Taska Valimar," he said as he dismissed the fisherman to follow her. She stopped, almost standing in the center of the cobblestone square. Frustration broke across her face.

He approached her and lowered his voice, "I spoke with your father this morning and he mentioned you were concerned about Valimar. How long has it been since your last visit?"

Sophia was annoyed by Jarod's mettling ways.

"I went to see her a few days ago, but she wasn't there. Nothing to worry over."

Jarod knew she was concealing her true thoughts.

"Well, if you think nothing is wrong, then I won't worry over it."

"You shouldn't," Sophia's tone was aggressive.

Jarod tipped his hat to her and walked back toward the fisherman by the door of the cobbler's shop.

Sophia walked away furious. She desperately wanted to see Taska in person to apologize to her, but Sophia knew she would be denied. Someone might go out to the cottage and check on her.

She went into the office of the warehouse. Philip was sitting at the table with the ledger. Sophia was angry with him for telling the council about her personal visits to see Taska, and how she worried. She would have to leave him out of all that she said and did concerning Taska. Yet, she had no idea that Philip was unraveling the wrath of Emmit's deceit.

Snow was falling lightly, floating by the little windows of Taska's cottage. She knew that it was late. She could hear Cain's heavy breathing as he slept. The fire was now dying down. Her contemplative words on the page created sufficient comfort for her ravaged soul. Every new word, every new revelation that she scratched into the parchments drew her closer to the golden world of her dreams. She believed her dreams as epiphanies of the future. She knew her destiny had changed; no longer could she live a befitting life before the eyes of God and her parents, but for something more prolific. She could not dismiss God completely. It was impossible after her lifelong service. The scriptures, the ceremony and the devotion were part of her life. But, she turned from Him, as everyone had turned from Taska. Her discovery would bring to life a vision that constructed a realm of comfort and happiness in her mind, while skirting the gates of heaven. She had to write out and explain every detail.

That night she scribed: I have deferred my deliverance to the gates of Heaven. I have deferred my faith in our

Father, for that of something smaller — more tangible and real. Perhaps I am not ready to accept the invitation to Heaven; perhaps I will forever stand at the entrance of God's domain, but never be allowed in. There is a place where I've been — common to that of Heaven, but so complex and filled with human emotion. It is a city — intricate and filled with enlightened people. In this Golden World, I have visited with a companion — a friend. She has offered me a new life in her house near the river. She loves me without conditions, like Sophia and my mother have tried. She has offered a salary and quarters there — she has promised to show me society — something I have only read about in old books. Forgive me, God for deferring my fate to the hands of my sponsor — with respect and duty. Some of the villagers will read my admonition and call me a heretic — someone who had the devil in her soul and wickedness in her heart. Yet, on these parchments — I can speak to anyone — my parents, my creator and my own emotions. I can speak to freedom and hope — I can speak to a feminine salvation beyond the wrath of my illicit and wanton sins.

Taska saw evolution in every word she put down, defining parameters, laws and values. She was puzzled at times, asking herself, "Is this all just the devil's trick? Am I defiling God?"

She would clarify more boundaries, viewing her creation vividly, longing to live among the people she adored. Her writing brought about great comfort, an even temperament, and a desire to leave for this newly created life, whether it was a sin or a gift from God.

Taska stood up and stretched her back. She always left

her parchments sitting on the table overnight so the ink would dry evenly. It was important not to distort what was written. It was as if she could create gospel and psalms for her life beyond the wooden walls and natural boundaries. Stretching her physical body felt good. She was sore from mapping out her words and thoughts. Thoughts of her bed and sleep were overcoming her with great comfort.

Taska walked by the front door and into her room, forgetting the log that she jammed under the door latch to lock them in. She forgot Cain went out earlier in the evening to bring Taska a few faggots and three logs for the fire that evening.

She went into the room where her bed was made. She unknotted the back ties of her dress and slipped it off. She left her petticoat on and wrapped a flannel blanket around her. She took off her cap by removing her hairpins and hooking it on the brass armlet where she hung her dress. She pulled back the wool blankets and climbed into bed. She extinguished the small oil lamp she carried with her. She always left her door closed. But the light of the fire still seeped in beneath the door and through the cracks and spaces of the plank wall.

As her hair spread across her pillow and her eyes finally closed, her ears listened to Cain's breathing and the pop and crackle of the fire. It took but a few moments for her mind to begin to drift off.

Something was bothering her, something she might have overlooked, "Does Cain have enough blankets? Is he warm enough?" The sound of the snow brushing lightly against the window reminded her.

She thought of getting up, but her tired body remained motionless. As she dozed off with concern for Cain, a noise erupted.

Thinking perhaps that it was a dream, she woke herself completely. Her eyes were wide as she turned her head up to the ceiling. She thought it might be Cain, restless for another quilt. But she didn't hear his chain's rattling about in the room. It came from the front door. Perhaps a frozen mouse was searching for warmth.

She propped herself up on one arm. She peered at the fire through the slats in the boards, loosely butted to one another. Perhaps it was the wind? Then she noticed some white flakes of snow blowing under the door of her room. The swirl of white upon the floor didn't make sense. When Taska looked back to the broken image of the fire, she saw a shadow pass by. Someone was in the cottage. The door was open.

Taska got out of bed without hesitation and flung open the door to her room. She saw the front door of the cottage wide open. Maybe the wind? She could hear Cain's door open. She looked to the white footprints on the floor. Before she could do anything, she had to fetch the staff in the corner. She dashed across the room. Cain's bed-chains were clanking and clattering frantically.

Taska pulled the staff out from the corner. She turned and saw a shadowy figure in Cain's bedroom. She pulled the dagger out of the staff and held the stick firm in her left hand. She rushed into Cain's room and threw herself upon the figure. The two images merged into one mass on the floor. Cain was crouched in his bed, trying to fend off his attacker.

A thunderous bang ripped through the noise of the struggle and the flash from the pistol charged the room. Cain gasped hard. He tried to pull himself from the post. He wanted to help or get away but his chains would not give.

Taska was able to get to her knees to wield the staff around, trying to flog the intruder into submission. The shadow pushed her away, against the wall. She feared his strength. Taska watched the figure get to his feet and start toward the door. She could let him go, but with the dagger of the staff still in her hand, something possessed her to lunge at him. The stranger fell. She brought the dagger of glistening sliver up and pierced it into the back of his knee, pulling it down through the muscle in his calf, down to this ankle.

The stranger shrieked and staggered out toward the fire. Taska rose up with fury in her eyes. She left Cain and chased out after the stranger who was stumbling in pain, knocking over the table, and a chair. Taska saw her parchments fall to the floor.

She pulled the stick portion of the staff around to her chest to break it over his head.

Taska hesitated and the stranger darted out the door, slipping and stumbling on the snowy stoop. Taska's swooping staff hit the door and bounced down to the floor. She rushed to the door to follow after the intruder, but the falling snow would quickly obscure his tracks, and freeze her bare feet. She left a substantial wound on the stranger, making him quite easy to identify. His blood was stained and smattered on the floor in a trail from Cain's room out into the soft snow.

She slammed the door and looked back at the toppled table. Then, she looked to Cain's room. She rushed in and saw Cain trembling on the bed. His eyes were wide with fear. Gunpowder filled the air.

"Did he hurt you? Are you wounded?"

He shook his head and tried to cover his fearful eyes with his hands. Taska retrieved the keys from her room and unlocked his chains. She told him to sit by the fire and calm down. Cain did as he was told and didn't move from the warm hearthstones.

Taska looked around the room with a lamp and found the discharged pistol that had been fired. She carried the weapon out and put it on the floor. She up-righted the table and the chairs, and collected the scattered parchments. She laid them back on the table so they could continue to dry. She took the pistol and put it on the chair. She wiped the blood from the blade of the dagger and put the staff back together. Taska stood the staff in the corner.

"What is that?"

"It is a pistol. They are illegal in this village. Illegal because we are outcasts. We are not permitted to have weapons."

Taska pulled a chair close to Cain and sat down. She looked closely at his face, "Are you sure you're not hurt?"

"I am not hurt, I just don't know what happened. Was this because you didn't let Sophia come in the other day?"

Taska shook her head, "Oh no, not Sophia. This reeks of something hateful. It was someone who could get a hold of that weapon. Someone who could afford a weapon."

"Someone you know?"

"I do not know."

She put her hand on his cheek, allowing her fingertips to run through his hair. She closed her eyes slowly, then looked upon his brow again, "As unfortunate as we both are to live as condemned and keeper, you are not responsible for what just happened. I've watched you become angry when I am mistreated. I know you try very earnestly to appease me."

His dim scars were healed over and his hair was getting long. For the first time since she had been with Cain, she found comfort in his being there.

"Why don't you try to sleep? I won't chain you. Just go and lie down."

She brought her hand down to her lap and nodded for him to go. With his mind still fluttering with excitement and his body still rattled, Cain stood and held out his hand, trembling next to Taska. She took it lightly and looked up to him, "Try to sleep. I will be here."

Cain remembered Taska, laughing and dancing with the jumping boy. It was too far gone.

"I am not afraid with you here," said Cain.

Taska released his hand and stood up. She walked him to his room. She watched him get into the little cot. She pulled his blankets up to his chin, "Call if you need me."

She walked out to the table and examined the pistol. Before her anger could build again, she realized Cain was no longer an empty shell, but like a boy, still afraid of the dark — and rightly so.

It was still snowing in the morning when Taska bundled her cape tight around her neck. She made sure Cain was well protected from the biting cold they would encounter. She made sure his chains where loose and comfortable. Taska took the staff and the burlap sack and they began their trek to the village.

The snow was about eight inches deep. It had continued lightly all night. The sky continued to spew more, dusting their shoulders and frosting their hair. The new fallen blanket muffled the world. The wind was light, but bitter. Cain huddled with his face down in the scarf wrapped around his neck and face. They didn't speak as they marched through the virgin snow toward the village.

The snow covered the rooftops and cobblestones leading into the village center. It was beautiful to see the town brightened by a coat of fresh snow. Fall was so stark and brittle, while winter snow so clean and pure. Taska and Cain walked down to the village square and noticed the blacksmith at work. She gave him a friendly wave. She walked over and stood in front of his shop near the flames of the forge.

He was busy making tools, so Taska didn't stay very long. They stood in front of the forge until they could feel their fingertips again. As they turned to leave, he smiled, "Come anytime and warm up."

Looking out over the piers, now empty of the fishing fleet, the water was a frigid gray. The big rolling waves dominated the sea as they moved across the horizon in large swells.

She stopped at the warehouse, hoping Sophia still made it to work through the snow. Tracks in the snow gave proof that someone had come to the warehouse. She climbed the steps and opened the unlocked door.

Sophia rose quickly from a chair by the fire, "Taska, I didn't expect you here with weather like this."

Cain walked in behind Taska and shut the door. The room was dim, but the little windows allowed enough gray light to see Sophia's startled face. She was like a pale apparition in a dark, heavy cloak.

"You must have been to the cobbler,"

"No, I haven't, is there something wrong with the cobbler?"

"No, it is just that I asked about you.... It doesn't matter. Would you like some tea, or rum?" Sophia said, "Let me take your wet things."

Taska didn't care for hospitality or courtesy. Her face was tight from the cold. Her seething anger from the incident the night before made her appear despondent. Her eyes were empty.

"I do not mean to bother you. I need to speak with your father. It is very important," she said and raised the sack in her hand.

Sophia placed her hands upon the back of a chair to brace herself. Sophia could see that something had happened — something was wrong.

"He is at home. I can take you to him."

She turned to fetch her shawl and her gloves. Taska had changed — it was obvious that Sophia's lies and deceit had taken its toll. All she could do now was comply with Taska's wishes.

They walked up the hill, trudging in a wake of snow. The snow was becoming heavy. It was blinding. By the time they came to Sophia's door, they all were trembling from the cold — fingers numb and cheeks stinging. She opened the door and Taska and Cain filed in.

Philip was sitting at the table with a bowl of soup in his hand. His wife stood up from the rocker in the corner, throwing her sewing down in a basket.

"Father, Taska needs to speak with you," she said.

He turned and acknowledged Taska with Cain. He picked himself up from the table and moved out of the way, "Come here, closer to the fire."

They drew close to the heat. Cain peered into the flames. He stood behind Taska, always feeling safe tucked behind her, out of direct sight.

"Sir, I need to meet with the council,"

He nodded, "What is this about?"

"Respectfully, sir, I would prefer to wait until the entire council convened. It is very important. There was an incident last night at our cottage."

"With him? What did he do?" Philip exclaimed.

"No. Please sir, gather the council," Taska pleaded.

"I will have them together in the church in one hour. Stay here until then," Philip said.

He took his coat and left to gather the other council members. Sophia turned to Taska, "Are you all right?"

Sophia's mother sat them down while she put on some hot water.

Taska didn't wait for the entire hour to pass. She

finished her tea and thanked Mrs. Lazarous. She thanked
Sophia for beckoning her father.

"May I take you to the church?"

"Of course, anyone can come," Taska said with an odd
softness. Mrs. Lazarous asked, "Should we collect the
neighbors?"

"No, don't trouble them. The weather is miserable."

They departed for the church in the snow, which
continued its relentless accumulation. At the meeting hall,
the Reverend and the doctor were sitting in the front bench.
The council was stirring about, but when they saw Taska
and Cain enter, they took their seats. This had been the first
time Taska had returned to the church since she was chosen
as a warden during the lottery. Philip looked on nervously.
Taska took off her cape.

Emmit stood up and pounded the meeting hammer down
twice. He was annoyed at being rousted out of his warm lair
for an impromptu meeting. Sophia and her mother sat next
to the doctor. He leaned over to Sophia and asked, "What is
this about?"

She shrugged her shoulders, "I know nothing."

Taska and Cain stood before the riser and the table.
They looked up and waited for Emmit to speak. Cain
glanced around, still afraid of their power and their
conviction. Langston was irritable and leery. Jarod
whispered with the other members about the snow and the
treacherous act of getting to the meeting hall.

"This meeting is called by Miss Taska Valimar. It is
consider a priority meeting hailed into assembly by Philip
Lazarous. Now Miss Valimar, I hope this is something of

217

importance. We have risked life and limb to gather here. Now, what is your great proclamation?"

Emmit continued to stand. Langston leaned back in his chair and rubbed his hands together as if he were washing them under an invisible water spicket.

Taska began, "Last night a stranger came to the cottage while we were sleeping. He came in and tried to murder Cain."

The council gasped and commotion stirred in each face. A murmur began among the council.

"When the intruder entered, I tried to stop him with the staff. He escaped, only after I cut his leg, very badly," she said.

She turned to the doctor and Sophia to take in their reaction. She continued, "There is a killer in this village, and he is easy to find. But that is not all."

She laid the staff down and lifted the sack with two hands. She pulled out the pistol, "He tried to kill Cain with this pistol, an illegal weapon."

Philip peered at the pistol and allowed his mouth to drop open. His rage turned into fear; a terror that turned his limbs numb. He tried to contain his emotions, and appear calm. Emmit nodded in mock disbelief. He was sure to notice Philip's reaction.

Sophia was weeping silently, with tears staining her chilly, white cheeks. It broke him to see his daughter suffer — to see Taska holding the pistol. Philip realized his guilt in giving those weapons to Emmit and he accepted his responsibility.

Emmit turned on one foot, "Doctor Keller, has anyone

reported a wound like Miss Valimar has described?"

The doctor shook his head. Then he thought for a moment, "But, if it is as bad as she has mentioned — then he needs immediate help."

Emmit nodded, "So, we should be looking for someone who came to the village, an outsider perhaps, a rogue thief with a bad leg wound."

Then Jarod spoke up, "An outsider wouldn't know where Valimar lives. It was someone who lives here. Perhaps this attacker also murdered James Colberton."

"We have caught Colberton's killer. He sits right there. But where would someone get a weapon like that?" Emmit said. He knew to be very careful. Philip realized his problem was a growing vine, tightening around his neck, constricting tighter and tighter.

Emmit turned, "We will find this person. I can assure you that this crime will not go unpunished. If he is still breathing, he will be condemned."

Taska looked to Jarod, "What will the punishment be?"

Jarod spoke out, "He didn't kill but he tried, so he would get at least ten years with a warden."

Taska nodded, "Another lottery — and so it goes."

"Yes, another lottery," Jarod repeated. Then Emmit pounced, "Do you want another lottery, Miss Valimar? Suppose you are still a suspect. Perhaps this was your weapon and now your acts are forcing another lottery — you sound spiteful and angry. Perhaps you want to see others suffer as you do?"

"We were attacked while we were sleeping!" Taska said slamming the staff down like a gavel.

"How can she be guilty?" proclaimed Sophia. "There is evidence; the assassin is in this village. Why would she want someone else to suffer as she does... the pistols, father. Please...."

Emmit laughed out of spite, "Is this all a plot from the warden or from a real assassin? It all seems ridiculous."

Sophia stomped her foot, "What happened to honor Emmit? The staff is about honor — and now you admit that Taska now suffers bitterly and seeks revenge? What happened to serving her sentence with honor? Where did the pistol come from, Emmit?"

The council mumbled and spoke in whispers.

Philip rose and turned to Emmit, "No! This will not continue — we cannot turn on her, not like this."

Emmit brought his hands up, "Please, everyone calm down. We are not here to accuse anyone. I apologize for my outburst, but we must consider all aspects of the case. James Colberton always said just that to the charges of a criminal matter. We will look for the wounded man and when he is found it will be resolved."

"I will help you search," Taska said as she looked to the other council members. Emmit chuckled, "No, that won't be necessary. I'm sure his wounds are bad enough to find him without much of a search."

Philip shouted, "No, that is a good idea. We should all look around and search — we may find more evidence."

Langston finally rose, "I think Miss Valimar has been through enough. You and Cain should retire for the day to your cottage and we will come and tell you what we find. This weather is too oppressive for searching. We will look when the weather breaks."

Philip shook his head and sat down. He began thinking out the plot — knowing where the pistol came from — that Emmit has constant contact with the band of trappers and thieves. This was clearly his plot — according to Colberton's diary and the guns from the warehouse. Sophia all but said so. He knew that the injured man wasn't a villager. He was an outsider. Philip looked down to Cain, sitting behind Taska as she stood before the council. He came from the woods too. He covered his face with his hands.

"Reverend," Emmit said. "Say a prayer for peace and calm."

A brief prayer was said and Emmit adjourned the meeting. Taska didn't bother saying "amen."

Most of the council members assured Taska that everything would be resolved. The last person Taska spoke to was Philip. He leaned close to her and whispered, "I have my suspect in mind. We will find him." Taska took Philip by the hand, "Thank you Mr. Lazarous."

Philip left the meeting hall. Mrs. Lazarous took Taska's hand and asked if she needed anything. But Sophia could not hold back her emotions and began to cry. Taska took her shoulders and pulled Sophia close to her breast. They wept for a while — until the frustration and anger subsided.

Langston and Emmit went back to Emmit's office. Hillmond Wenner sat waiting for them. She wanted to know what had happened with the warden and Cain. When they got into the

office, Emmit took off his coat and sat down at his desk.
Langston left his coat on and stood before him.

"What happened?"

"The killer was attacked. The pistol was left behind.
Philip knows I had possession of this weapon."

"What are we going to do?" said Langston.

"Where is he? Is he alive?"

Langston looked over scrolls, rolled and tied in a heap.
"I haven't seen him. I thought he was planning to wait and
kill Cain after the Annual Visit."

Emmit rose, letting his belly stick out over his desk,
"Where is the pistol?"

"Jarod took it from Valimar. I suppose he will burn it."

"Clearly, it was stolen from your office, you can not be
accountable for a thief and perhaps a murderer," Hillmond
said easily weaving a lie.

Philip Lazarous walked in without knocking. He stood
with his hair wet with snow and his eyes aglow with anger,
"Langston. Hillmond. I would like to speak with Emmit
alone."

He nodded, "If I find him I will let you know." Hillmond
followed him out of the office.

Emmit and Philip were alone, "So, you jump to
suspicions. You assume that because I was the last to have
those weapons that this was my plot, this was my
treachery."

"Of course. If you didn't plan this yourself then you
allowed Langston or Jarod to work out the details. I am not
a fool," Philip said bitterly. "Your deceit runs through and
through."

Emmit knew he would have to appease Philip. This was difficult. He had to cede to Philip for the moment.

"Well, it seems that someone stole a pistol from the cabinet. How a thief uses my weapon is beyond my control. But this is not the time to yell and scream in the streets. This is a time for simple actions," Emmit said. "The other pistol is back at my home."

Philip asked, "Why? Why is it so important to kill Cain?"

"If he becomes free, if he ever breaks free of Valimar, he will come after all of us. Valimar is so lax with him that it would not be difficult for him to escape. The council will perish. He will try to kill us all," Emmit said. "Don't you fear for your life when you look up to the ceiling from your bed, wondering if tonight is the night that he is going to come... don't you fear him?" He sounded truly worried, truly afraid.

Philip turned and looked to the window. He didn't trust Emmit, and this was just another manipulation.

"If anything happens to Cain, then I will see to it that you pay the same price. You find that killer, and bring him before the council. Then the lottery. Make it happen, and if he is dead, then cut someone's leg up and have the lottery anyway. This is not a matter of council protocol, this is my protocol. If these events don't occur and nothing is done, then I will reveal all I know — regardless of what crime I may have committed. Taska Valimar is not going to be disregarded and tortured as you would like her to be," Philip said with fists clenched. "We will have a lottery."

Emmit became angry, "I gave her chances. She was too

damn proud, mistaking honor for simple release from her terms as warden. We made it clear that if Cain had an accident, then she would not be held in contempt, and that no questions would come about. But she told Jarod that she was above the law, above killing even for her own freedom."

"She knew that you would trick her. She knew that murder is murder and you would hang her for it. She is not as dumb as you might think," Philip said as he turned and walked to the door, "So many people in this village want to believe that Taska is insane, but she knows. And if the attacker isn't found, then I will tell her all I know. She will know you have the matching pistol. You will be under my scrutiny — and I am prepared to see this through. I just hope it is all figured out by the time the Annual Visit comes, Emmit. I will not lie to them. I will tell the Lieutenant and his men what I know of the illegal weapons. I will tell them everything."

Emmit laughed, "Your coercion and your threats almost sound convincing. I will find the man responsible for what Valimar surely deserves, and then it will be resolved."

Philip stood outside of the door, "With a lottery, Emmit — a fair lottery this time."

The door shut. Emmit said quietly, "What did he say?"

Taska and Cain were asked back to the Lazarous cottage. Sophia, still distressed, made her way silently from the church, through the snow back to the cottage with the others. Cain followed the bottom hem of Taska's skirt through the accumulating white powder.

Back in the cottage, Sophia sat down and covered her face with her hands. Cain stood behind Taska near the fireplace. Mrs. Lazarous quickly put out a wedge of cheese and some bread.

"Let me take your wet capes," she said as she rushed around the cottage in a fury of domestic comfort. Taska put her hand upon Sophia's shoulder, "We are fine, and they will find who did this."

Sophia took her hands away from her face in a blank stare. Taska told Cain to sit down. She sat next to him. Mrs. Lazarous brought cups to the table and went back to the fireplace to check the kettle.

She turned to Taska, "Eat something, it will make you feel better."

"I am afraid I don't feel well to eat, but thank you."

Taska looked thin and pale but Sophia attributed her ill look to the attack and the trek into town in the snowstorm.

Taska pushed the cheese in front of Cain and cut a piece for him. She then broke off a piece of bread and put it in front of him. She looked at him, "Eat a little, it will be fine."

Mrs. Lazarous turned, "I cannot believe that they accused you of staging this. It disgusts me to think that one cannot seek justice without being accused in this village."

Cain took a few bites from the flaky bread.

"It doesn't surprise me at all. The council hides their own guilt, and their devious ways behind accusing eyes and outrage. They try to shout and make noise to divert attention from their silent deceit," Taska said.

Cain didn't look up from the cheese and bread but said,

"They didn't seem to care until you showed them the pistol. They weren't going to believe you, until you showed them proof of the crime. Then they started getting nervous."

The door flung open and Philip spilled into the cottage. He brushed off the snow from his shoulders like pesky insects. He spoke with a loud tone to his voice as if he had been shouting for some time, "Don't worry, we will find this person that attacked you. He is here, somewhere."

Mrs. Lazarous helped with his coat.

"No, I am going back out, to the doctor's cottage. I want to begin a search party and start looking."

"You're not the one who should be looking, let the younger men go and find him. You don't need to go tromping about in this bad weather," his wife said.

He shook his head, "I am going back out, if I don't go, nothing will be done and after a few days, they will say they couldn't find him. They never asked Taska for a description, they never asked her what he said. Nothing. Emmit and Langston have no plans to help."

Sophia spoke softly, "If they know where he is, why would the council try to hide him? Just bring him for sentencing after he is well, like they did with Cain."

"Do they know where he is?"

"Someone does," Philip said.

"If they know — why would the council try to hide him?"

Taska answered quickly, "Perhaps it was their plot."

"Perhaps the council is afraid of what he might say when he is caught. I must go. I will report back from time to time," Philip said. "Are you going to stay here for the day?"

Taska rose, "No, we are going back to the cottage soon."

"I will send someone with word of what is happening," he walked out into the snow-covered lane. Taska spoke up, "Mr. Lazarous, thank you."

He pretended not to hear her as he shut the door, but Taska's cause was not the only reason for his diligent work. He began walking to the doctor's cottage. If the council was harboring this wounded man, and his leg was cut badly the doctor would be seeing to him.

He noticed Emmit standing in the doorway. Philip knew, something was happening. The water was flowing rapidly under the smooth and unmoving ice.

Down behind the blacksmith's shop, where all discarded lumber and wood was stacked, stood a small shed where some of the fishermen stored nets, and tackle from their boats. The shed was set back among the wood scraps and overgrown weeds, which poked through the carpet of snow.

Langston had been careful in coming to the shed, being sure no one observed him coming or going. As he stood by the door, about to let himself in, he noticed the white smoke that escaped from the back of the shed. This made him furious.

He threw his shoulder into the stubborn door and it flew open. Inside, he saw his hired assassin and his grim state.

"I told you no fires, someone will see the smoke," he said as he stomped on the small fire of twigs and leaves smoldering on the dirt floor. The injured man lay upon the fishing nets, motionless. Langston looked at the mangled leg. He saw the blood was dark red; it flowed easily from his mangled leg. Langston turned back to the door to be sure no one saw him come in. The blood had soaked through the netting and pooled in the dirt on the floor.

"It is time to change your bandages, wake up...."

Langston turned the man over. He was dead. The fire must have been a last attempt to save his own life from the freezing cold and the unstoppable flow of blood. The bandage did little to help. Langston was satisfied he was dead, knowing that now he wouldn't have to kill him by his own hand. He looked around the shed. Langston was looking for anything that he might have left behind which could accuse him of being part of the crime.

Langston picked up the frozen body and dragged it out of the shed.

Philip entered the cottage of Dr. Keller and looked around. The doctor rose from his desk, "What is it, Philip? Is something wrong?"

Emmit didn't speak, he just walked out of the cottage. Philip was suspicious. This is what he expected. Philip was predictable. If Emmit was standing around the doctor's cottage — something must be happening there. It was Emmit's diversion, while Langston was out at the woodshed.

Philip opened the door to the back room and looked inside. The bed was empty. He turned from the door and faced the doctor, "I suppose I cannot be accused of not looking in the obvious places."

Dr. Keller smiled dimly at him, "If he is mortally wounded, as Valimar has described, he may be dead by now. If this man has failed at his duty, knowing he is now marked as a killer, then he would not allow anyone to find him."

Philip turned to the door, "Where is Langston?"

"I don't know, I saw him walking toward the church a little while ago," said Dr. Keller.

Philip nodded, "I'm sorry about the intrusion." He walked out on to the slippery steps where he met Jarod. He stopped and looked up at Philip, with his hand over his brow to keep the flying snow out of his eyes.

"I've come to help you look for the assassin. Emmit told me you might be looking for him, I want to resolve this now. I don't think that Valimar needs another assassin to worry over," Jarod said.

Philip agreed, "Let's check the boats around the warehouse. Now that they are up on land — a boat might be a good place to hide."

Claas met them down the lane. He had heard the news from Sophia when he went to see her. He joined the two councilmen as they headed to the waterfront. The snow was light and kicked up easily under their feet. When they got to the side of the warehouse, near the icy seaside, they inspected the wooden ships cradled and covered with canopies. The wind was whipping hard from the water.

"It would be easier if we had a ladder," Jarod said as he walked down the small embankment near the rocky shore.

"There is one at the warehouse we can use," Philip said. He turned back to his warehouse. The men marched back up the embankment.

Langston walked into Emmit's office and took off his hat.
He sat down near the door in an old wooden chair. Emmit
sat at his desk, reclining back in his chair, with his black
boots up on the corner of his desk. Hillmond Wenner stood
by the window.

Emmit cocked his head, "Tell me something
encouraging."

Langston grinned slightly, "When I got to the shed, he
was frozen dead, but still bleeding. He wasn't breathing so I
knew he was gone. His arms were frozen to his body. I
brought him down to the beach and threw him into the
outgoing tide. Last time I saw him he was drifting out to
sea."

Emmit nodded, "Good, the damn fool deserved worse,
but at least he is gone."

"What about Philip and Jarod, are they still looking?"

"Let them look for a while, they will get tired and go
home," said Emmit. "But we have another problem. The
man was a crewman. A local. But, Cain's brother and
friends have been sited at the marsh. They set up camp. If he
comes looking for his brother, he might explain the whole
plot to one of the villagers. Everyone will realize that we
have been using outsiders to kill and supply the village. By
law — we could be hanged."

"What do you suppose we do, Emmit?" Hillmond said.

"We have to stop trading and meeting the caravans in
the woods. We have to go to the mercenary down by the

marsh. We have to explain the accident."

Hillmond, who was standing near the window, noticed something.

"What is it?" Emmit said.

"Valimar and Cain. She must be going back to her cottage."

Emmit rose and went to the window. He felt a fear well up inside. Emmit knew that nothing could rattle his well-established life, yet Cain was volatile. He watched them walk up the lane where the old maples were covered with snow.

Hillmond spoke quietly, "She has a strong will. She knows what happened; she saw how upset the meeting became. She was watching, trying to see who looked suspicious, and who looked surprised."

Emmit felt nothing more than hate in his chest as he began breathing harder, "Taska has the youthful mind of her parents. But she won't run like her mother and father. She won't run blindly into the wilderness, running to a ghostly city over the mountains. She is now tied to this village forever. At least she is not as foolish as her parents, perishing in the mountains."

Langston nodded, "Probably didn't make it that far. The wolves got to them before they reached the foothills."

"I am not concerned with her. Philip is the person to watch. He knows the pistols are mine. He knows. We must be careful. Philip is becoming dangerous, like James Colberton was," Emmit said. He turned from the window. He no longer had full control of the council. The council was splintering and changing. He tried to think very clearly for a way to regain complete control over Philip and somehow gain the confidence of Valimar. This was the only way he could continue his rule, and do as he wished for the remainder of his life. But fear had driven Emmit to make a mistake, giving Philip permission to govern Emmit's actions by fetching the pistols. It was a desperate move that left him vulnerable. He still had one pistol left.

He thought of the disappearance of Taska's parents. He knew that they had no chance of making it through the mountains. But they left a marked trail, with red ribbon. Those ribbons still remain. Langston never told anyone about the ribbons and the marked trail for fear that Emmit would find out about them.

For Langston, knowing that perhaps an escape was possible from the village, made him content with life, knowing if he had to run, there was a direction to pursue.

"There is a simple solution," Emmit said. "One more meeting in the marsh."

Claas and Jarod pulled the ladder out of the warehouse as the snow blew in the wind. They both took one end of the ladder, with Philip leading the way. They walked down the slippery slope leading down to the fishing boats. They came to the first boat and stood up the ladder. Claas scurried up the side. Jarod and Philip followed. As they climbed over the gunwale of the boat, Philip looked around, pulling back some of the canopy.

Jarod looked around, "I will climb under on all fours and take a look."

Claas was already beneath the canopy — searching in the fishhold. He disappeared. Philip could watch his progress by the lump in the canvas, moving slowly across the snow covered fishing boat. Philip looked back to the center of town, toward the blacksmith in his shop. Then, he focused on his own warehouse. He put his hands to his waist. Everything seemed futile. Whatever Emmit and Langston did to obscure the botched attack and hide the attacker — it was done.

When Jarod came out from under the canvas, he shook his head, "Not under there."

"Perhaps it was too hard for him to climb into a boat with a bad leg. I don't think it was possible," Philip said.

Claas appeared from the fishhold, "Nothing."

Jarod agreed and gazed out at the ocean. Philip fixed his eyes on something, "Look. There."

He scurried over the side of the boat and down the ladder. Jarod looked out to the ocean, at a mark on the water, bobbing up and down. There it was, just around the last pile at the end of the piers. With no boats in the water, it was easy to see. There was something large floating in the water.

They clamored down the ladder and tried to catch up with Philip. His heart raced and he thought, "Could he still be alive?" While Philip ran down the snow-covered pier, Jarod ran to the side of his warehouse and found two long poles.

He walked down to the pier with Claas. He handed a pole to Philip and looked to the dark mound in the water.

As they pulled the black mound closer to the pier, they

could make out a hand. Using the wooden poles, they pulled it close enough to lie down on the pier and pull the body up. As Jarod lay across the snow-covered boards, he tried to reach out, "I think we can get him." Claas got down, assisting them.

Philip also lay on the pier. At the same time, the three men plunged their gloved hands into the icy ocean and pulled with all their might. The waterlogged heap of clothes and flesh weighed more than they expected. They lifted him high up, but Jarod lost his grip. Philip let the body splash back into the water. The cold drops pricked Philip's cheek.

Claas swore under his breath.

"Try again, Jarod. We have to have proof."

They pulled again, and got him up to the pier.

Philip wasn't so quick to rest. He turned the unknown man over and looked at his face. His eyes were staring out into eternity. His skin was pale white with blue under his eyes, "He hasn't been in the water that long." Claas appeared disgusted.

Philip straightened out his legs, taking the twist and turns out of them in a matter of fact manner. He could see the rip in his pants and underneath was the wound, deep and gushing with muscle and bone, just as Taska had testified.

Philip spoke quickly, "Go get the doctor and maybe a few men to carry him back. We have something to show Emmit."

Jarod rose and shook his head, "Why would he try to swim?"

"Go, get them now," he said to Jarod. "He did not swim — he was tossed in."

Philip rose from where the body lay and looked out to the water. His hands were numb and purple. He pulled off his wet gloves and threw them down to his feet. Claas was shivering. He looked down at the body and tried to identify his face. He looked like a crewman he knew, but he couldn't be sure. He knew the doctor could identify him.

Quietly Philip mumbled, "Emmit, you were so close to letting this one go out to sea."

Mrs. Jarod held a very serious position in the village every year, although her endeavor was not of a serious nature. She was the winter festival vanguard, and she made sure the entire festival came to be perfect, without missing a detail.

The winter festival was always held in the center of the village. Never a year went by when snow wasn't upon the ground, and a giant pyre was made to light off at the beginning of the festival. This great fire shed a glorious light upon the entire party, and gave warmth to those who did not dance.

This festival started at nightfall and ended when the last person found their way home. It was said that some festivals, years ago, lasted almost three days. While no one believed this story, it was also meant as a challenge. Some would say, "Let's make this one last three days." But after a few dances and some wine, the one who was so enthusiastic would be the first to stumble home. The winter festival set everyone into action by way of cooking, sewing, and rehearsals for the musicians. The village square was cleaned and prepared. The children ran to and fro gathering wood for the great fire. They considered this their sole purpose until the festival came. The children had sled races and skated by the church pond. Having this festival outside in the middle of the village was symbolic for casting off the cold weather and celebrating life under the stars.

It was still another three weeks away, but Mrs. Jarod decided it was time to start the wheels into motion. Now that the afternoon brightened and the snow had subsided, she decided to check with the Reverend about the music. He had all the sheet music for the holiday songs and dances. Although he did not approve of the songs, calling them tempting, he allowed them to be played at the festival for the merriment of all.

Mrs. Jarod was surprised to see the oil lamps lit upon the council riser as she walked into the large meeting hall. She walked up to the balcony, toward the Reverend's quarters and knocked hard on the door.

The Reverend came to the door. His eyes were tired as he pushed his eyeglasses to the bridge of his nose.

"Good afternoon, Reverend. I wanted to ask you about the music for the winter festival. I know you are kind enough to keep it for us, so I wanted to know if I could take the sheet music back for the musicians to practice in the next few weeks," said Mrs. Jarod.

The Reverend's wrinkled face cracked into a smile, "Is it that time already? Let me see if I can find them. I am sure all this snow spurred you on to begin preparing. This is our first big snow."

He allowed her to come in to his office. It was very formal and foreign to Mrs. Jarod. It was where he would read, study and receive anyone who wanted to see him. This room was perhaps the most lavish in the entire village. It even seemed greater than the church itself. He was permitted these extravagance because of his position within the church. Beyond his privileges, the Reverend knew that the Annual Visit never went to the church. It was not worth pillaging when villagers, councilmen and prisoners were better victims.

The floor was covered with a fine rug, which hid the warped and darkly stained boards beneath. The rug was bordered in red and green colors, the center depicting a scene of a knight in saddle among people gathered around him. Some of the people were holding up gifts of praises, others holding up small children. The scene sprawled itself out under a great old willow tree that disappeared under the Reverend's desk.

The Reverend looked through some books and papers on a shelf in the corner, pulling out books of hymns and songs.

Mrs. Jarod noticed the thousands of books stacked on the shelves that seem to make up an entire wall. Mrs. Jarod knew how to read, yet couldn't make out too many of the titles. She noticed the small table next to a chair in the corner where a small tray of coins were displayed. All the metal discs where different, some large, some small. Mrs. Jarod tried not to stare at one thing for too long. When she looked at the small fireplace, and the cross, which magically seemed to hang upon the brick and mortar, she seemed to gasp at its beauty of gold.

Where did this all come from? She wondered if this was what he brought with him when he came here?

He turned with a stack of paper and books, "This should be all of it. I hope you might also consider a few traditional hymns. I believe I have them here."

He handed her another stack of books that almost matched the size of the festival music. He knew she wouldn't use the hymn music, but perhaps she would incorporate a few into the dances and jigs, waltzes and ballads to be sure everyone was entertained by the music.

Holding the stack of books and loose music, she turned as if she forgot, "Don't forget about the oil lamps downstairs. They are still lit."

He nodded, "Thank you, I don't know if the council will be back today or not."

"What was the meeting about this morning? I have yet to see my husband," Mrs. Jarod asked.

He looked at her and walked her to the door, "I believe something happened with the assassin Cain, and the warden."

She looked down at the books and said quietly, "With all due respect, Reverend, I knew that she would make a problem out of all this."

"Someone came into the cottage and tried to kill Cain. Valimar chased him away," he said.

"Have they found the person who is responsible?" she said in a voice of outrage.

"I don't know. If they have, God help the poor wretch," the Reverend said. He smiled slightly, "Good day Mrs. Jarod."

"Good day, Reverend."

When she walked out into the church hall, she looked

down to the council riser and then whispered, "Not another lottery...."

Taska and Cain returned to the cottage. After Taska freed him from the chains, he went outside to gather three or four logs from the woodshed. He also brought some smaller scraps to rekindle the flames.

Taska sat down and felt the tremendous pain in her stomach swelling and receding like sheets of summer rain. She tried not to clench her stomach or give Cain the impression that anything was wrong. When he came in the door, she sat quietly while he worked at the hearth, rekindling the fire.

"What do you think will happen? Will they find the man?" Cain said.

"I don't know. Sophia's father is not someone who can be dismissed lightly. I don't know what they will find."

Cain watched as the fire danced and leapt beneath the new fuel, "At least it has stopped snowing."

This brought a glint of hope to Taska's eyes as she felt her stomach turn and twist. Eating something would make it worse. The thought of food made her tired, but she had to make something for Cain.

She turned to him, "You mustn't be hungry yet. I will roast some potatoes later for you."

"I shall read to myself at the table," he said and walked into his room to retrieve a Bible. He returned and opened the book to a marked page.

After a few minutes passed, a pounding came to the

door. Taska opened the door to Sophia, her father, Claas and Jarod standing at the stoop.

"Come in. Did you find the man with the cut leg?" Taska said.

As everyone came in, Cain shut his book and stood.

Jarod nodded, "We found him floating in the ocean by the docks. We checked his leg, it was cut as you said it would be."

Philip then conjectured, "Someone must have thrown him in. I would assume that he died and when someone went looking for him, they found him dead from his wound. They threw his body in the ocean."

Sophia looked to her father, "Emmit won't accuse Taska of murder will he?"

"No. I wouldn't worry over that, Taska. You clearly acted in defense of Cain and your own life. But now that he is dead, we cannot convict the attacker. It will have to end with an unmarked grave," Philip explained.

Sophia spoke up quickly, "Who is to say that whoever is responsible for this plot won't do this again. Perhaps it is Mrs. Colberton who has been plotting to kill Cain?"

"No, I have seen Mrs. Colberton — she is in deep mourning and lacks the conviction for revenge. It is clear that Emmit was connected to this terrible event. That pistol that was left behind was one that he owned. He wanted them for his own defense — but now it is the weapon in the hand of a killer. Emmit can't afford to lose another pistol," Philip said and went to the door. Jarod looked at him oddly. He didn't know Philip was accusing Emmit of these acts.

Claas shook his head, "The attacker isn't a crewman. I

know the fishermen — this was a stranger."

"Lock your door from now on, and I will try to find more traces of who also had a hand in this attack. I cannot have you living in fear. You have done this village a great service by being warden," said Philip. "Emmit will claim he did not know the attacker and that the pistol was stolen from him. He will explain everything away."

"Please let me know what you find," Taska said.

She shook his hand.

Sophia spoke softly, "Come to the village if the weather permits."

The four figures walked out into the muted white color of the snowy afternoon.

That night, as Taska sat at the table, the warm fire to her back, she felt worse than she had during the day. She tried to concentrate on the parchments. When her mind couldn't focus and make sense of her thoughts of the future, she asked Cain to read out loud to her. This kept her mind somewhat preoccupied with correcting his words and helping him with biblical pronunciation.

Later, she put Cain to bed, and tried to comfort him. She decided not to chain him because of the incident the night before. He agreed.

Taska returned to the table. She read some of what she scribed. Her knotted stomach and her aching back made her somewhat troubled by what she was creating.

She defined the parameters and scope of the golden world. She divided up laws and charters, and she knew every last detail of her new world. This was an all-consuming job that took her mind from the simplest emotions to complex moral questions of faith and truth. If the parchments were read by anyone from the village, she would be judged by the church and given a prison sentence. Her words defied the church, but didn't condemn the villagers or the Reverend.

Maybe that is what was troubling her? Perhaps allowing the Reverend to question every motive, every sinful word, would test her new faith. But how could she trust (even the Reverend) in completely condemning her vision — trusting him to give her a sacred evolution to the golden world. She did not want to become a martyr in the eyes of the church; she wanted to be free.

She shook her head. It wasn't her lack of devotion that troubled her; it was a question of how she was going to move on to the golden world. If she could find the answer then, like a butterfly breaking from its cocoon, it would reveal its beauty.

She pondered her dilemma. But her stomach wrenched hard, and without warning Taska spewed vomit upon the floor next to her.

Half sick and half disgusted with the mess she made, she walked quickly to the door, kicked out the axe handle she used to lock the door, and vomited once again out on the stoop.

Cain woke when he felt the cold air streaming from the opened door. He had been asleep for only an hour or so. He walked out and watched her by the door. She knew he was there when she came back in.

"Is the pain bad?"

She nodded, "I just need to catch my breath." She walked back to the chair and sat down. She was pale with pain. Cain walked to the barrel in the corner and pulled the lid off. He took a large cup of water to Taska.

She slurped it up, dissolving the burning and the bitter taste in her mouth. He watched her drink and then fetched the bucket next to the hearth. He filled the pail with water and returned to the table. He got down to his knees and began cleaning the patch near the chair. Taska watched him and put her hand upon his back, "No, don't bother. I will tend to that in a few minutes."

Cain looked up to her, "Why don't you sleep, you can't continue like this. You haven't eaten in a few days. You need rest."

She waited until Cain had finished cleaning the stains from the floor. She threw the filthy water out the front door. She made sure he got into bed and then she went into her room. She shut her door just as Cain put his head to his pillow. He had never seen Taska sick. He reached between his mattress and the bedsprings, pulling out his triangular glass shard and began rubbing and fumbling. This was always a comfort for Cain, like an old woman in a rocking chair. He was afraid for Taska now that she was really sick. He wanted to tell her to stay in bed all day, but he couldn't muster the words, and the command. It was hard for him to speak out of turn to Taska, even if it was for her own good.

Taska would never sleep unless he was in bed. Taska could never completely trust him. He was the condemned and she was the warden — she would maintain those boundaries — even if it killed her.

Old Kavner was sitting with Old Lady Gertrude and Hillmond Wenner at the old woman's cottage a few days after they pulled the attacker from the water. He was talking about old times, but the warmth from the fire and the wine they drank, made them all very sleepy. Old Lady Gertrude always slept in her chair now, so she was comfortable. Hillmond Wenner and Kavner spoke for a while, until he checked his timepiece.

He should be going home. He said good night to Hillmond Wenner and stepped out into the lane. The frigid air woke him up. It was late and the village seemed completely abandoned. Up the lane — he heard hooves moving on dirt. He could see a few shapes moving and then the horses moved off. He stopped and listened. The horses were moving out through the woods. Curious, Old Kavner closed up his cloak and walked up the lane. By the time he got to the tracks in the snow, the horses and riders were gone. Reverend Conrad was heading back up toward the church. He followed the tracks.

He went through the woods, listening as he traced the prints in the snow. The tracks were running north toward the stream and the creek that led out to the ocean. The partial moon and the still air made it easy to follow the fresh tracks. He could hear the horses picking their way through the woods. Even for an old man, he knew the way through the woods to the creek. He just followed the tracks and paced himself. Although he was cold, he was curious to see what was happening. Philip had warned him that Emmit and Langston were dangerous. They rigged the lottery. He even suggested that they tried to kill Cain. Old Kavner didn't know what to believe.

Along the creek, the ground leveled out and the open fields were easier to walk. The tracks moved toward the edge of the field. There, Old Kavner could see the flickering of fire on the trees.

He moved closer. He was careful to approach quietly. As he arrived close to the fire, he saw Emmit dismounted from a horse. He approached a stranger and greeted him with a solemn handshake.

Langston remained on his old gray nag. The old man was too far away to hear what was being said. He moved up closer. He wanted to hear the discussion. Emmit pulled a sack of coins from his pouch and proffered it to the man at the fire. He had a cart and a single horse with him. Pots and pans were simmering near the fire. Emmit held out the money. Yet, the odd man didn't accept it. He flew into a rage and yelled and screamed about his only brother — his only family. His voice was hysterical.

Emmit dropped the sack of money and pulled out a small dagger. He ran toward the distraught vagabond and tried to attack him. A struggle began, wrapped up in cloaks and limbs, punching and hitting. Snow clouded up around them. Emmit was thrown back. It spooked Langston off his horse and he fell to the ground.

Langston stood up slowly and reached into his coat. He pulled out a pistol and limped his way toward the vagabond. He fired the pistol — hitting the stranger in the chest. The

boom of the blast made everything quiet as it echoed out.
They took the dead body and threw it on the fire. Emmit had
sustained some blows to his face from the fight. They let the
horse go and they took some things from the cart. Anything
that they couldn't bring back went in the fire. Before The
fire was burning like an inferno and the flames and the
smoke shot high into the sky, like a portal of hell had been
opened from the dark underworld. Old Kavner made it back
to the village before sunrise. He went to the shore and
walked back along the beach — so that Emmit and
Langston riding back from their night of murder and pillage
wouldn't spot him. Old Kavner began to realize that the
village wasn't so isolated. Stories of people disappearing
might have been true.

But were they killed? Or did they arrange to escape with
outsiders who led them over the mountains? The Valimars.

The day the attacker was buried in an unmarked grave,
Philip said little to his daughter at the warehouse. He was so
angry and frustrated thinking of Emmit's plot and Taska
alone in the cottage. His misery came from disappointing
Sophia and Taska in bringing the attacker to justice, and
exposing Emmit for orchestrating the entire scheme. He
knew there was little he could do or say to Emmit now that
the attacker was dead. He knew, however, he would
somehow have his moment.

Philip sat at the table in the cottage looking over his
ledger. He knew everything had to be just right for the
Annual Visit. Some thought perhaps the Annual Visit would

not come this year at all, but Philip knew that tax money was never forgotten, even if the money came from outcasts and killers.

Philip's wife sat near the fire knitting a blanket, and trying to stay warm. She always had poor circulation in her feet and found it almost impossible to warm them once they became cold.

Philip tallied all the things that were stored in his warehouse, making sure it was all in order. The tax collectors always stayed for a few days going through everything. They only spent a few hours in the warehouse. Philip's job was to greet the Lieutenant and his band of men. The Lieutenant picked him because it was the first place they checked when they landed at the wharf. So, Philip Lazarous was the intermediary, showing the Lieutenant and his men the entire village. This was a privilege and an advantage for Philip. If this were an elected position, the council would have voted him out and replaced him with someone sympathetic to Emmit and his deceit. But Philip, by making peace with the Lieutenant and his men, created a position that no one in the village could change or alter, even Emmit in his high and mighty court.

When the pounding on the door started, Philip raised his head with a snap, unaware that he had fallen asleep.

Philip opened the door and saw Langston standing before him with a bottle in his hand. He was drunk.

"Langston, come in before you freeze," Philip said.

He came in and put the bottle on the table. Mrs. Lazarous smiled but didn't speak. Philip walked to the table and looked at the bottle, "What is the meaning of this?"

Langston sighed, as his weary frame collapsed onto the bench. His eyes looked distant and thoughtless. He had a bruise on his brow. He looked beat up and tired.

"I came to have a drink with you Philip. I thought I would just come and sit. Is it all right?" Langston said looking over to Mrs. Lazarous. She nodded, "Of course." But she knew he was Emmit's proxy and that he had a hand in what had happened with Cain's attack. But, she also trusted her husband. Philip wouldn't tell Langston anything that Emmit didn't know already, over a few drinks.

It didn't seem like Langston had been drinking. He didn't smell of liquor and he was steady on his feet.

Philip closed the ledger book from the warehouse and placed it at the end of the table, away from Langston. He fetched two cups and returned to the table.

He gave one to Langston and waited for him to uncork the bottle.

"Are we celebrating?" Philip said.

"No, we will get our fill of that in a few weeks. The winter festival is coming."

Langston's voice woke Sophia, sleeping in the next room. She lay in bed listening to the two men talk about the trivial things that had been going on in the village. Langston was very careful not to mention the attacker. Taska's name had yet to come up.

Sophia lay in her bed staring at the ceiling, listening, waiting to hear what might be said about her.

After a few drinks, Langston spoke about Emmit. This was where Philip had to use caution.

"Emmit is a good man. He is good at leading us on a

steady course. He is our navigator," Langston said. "Just a bit anxious sometimes."

Philip nodded and looked down at his empty cup, "I like to look to God for that kind of direction. The council cannot define the course of a man's life, or a village. Let God tell us where to go, and let Emmit be up on the bow with his finger pointing the way."

Langston laughed, "Yes, I agree... I do agree."

"What happened to your head? You have a good welt there."

Langston touched the lump gingerly, "That old gray nag threw me again."

Philip poured another cup of wine and topped off Langston's cup as well.

"Do you remember Slavanka Kyler? She was a whimsical woman. She and I used to sit in the summertime down by the blacksmith's shop and prattle on like we are now, for hours we would talk about any old thing, waiting for Emmit to come and join us. But, that was when we were young, and work didn't take such a toll on us. Those days went by so fast. What happens to friends?"

Slavanka's death might have been Emmit's great loss, but everyone missed her when she was killed. She was a dear woman with many friends. Philip felt sorry for him.

Langston continued, "How about Stoddard the fisherman. He was always yelling and singing on his boat; he was a silly man. He used to take fish from his catch, the ones too small to eat and he would put them into the pockets of the children that were being mischievous. After a while, all the children in the village had a smock or a coat that

smelled like tinker mackerel. It was a silly practical joke,"
Langston's laugh was deep.

Philip also laughed and then nodded. He remembered
Stoddard and his antics.

"That is the uncle of Claas the fisherman. He has been
seeing Sophia from time to time."

"Strong family. Yes, I recall Sophia dancing with the
fellow at the Grounding of the Fleet," Langston said. "And
the Valimars, they were such nice people. Do you remember
when they would come to the festivals and dance — it was
always marvelous to see them dancing, perfectly in step —
seemed like the only thing that was out of place was the
fellows playing their music on those old instruments."

Sophia remembered Taska's mother and father. They
were shadowy images, never real, never alive, just images in
motion when she was little.

"Yes, I remember the Valimars, Langston. They were
kind people. But they wanted something more than the rest
of us," Philip said with a distant tone in his voice.

"Oh, they wanted something else. They wanted it so
completely that they ran after it. It is funny Philip, but no
one knows. We never worried about Amerset Loomer when
he killed Slavanka and escaped. A few weeks later, we
found him in the hills, nothing more than clothes and bones.
Looked like every animal out in those hills found him."

Philip looked curiously, "Does Emmit know that you
found him dead, did you tell him?"

"No, I was with two other men and we thought if we
told Emmit or anyone that we were out in the foothills then
we might get punished. We never said anything. But when

the Valimars left there was something more...."

Sophia brought herself up from the bed. She listened carefully, letting the blankets fall from her arms. Her eyes widened.

Philip shook his head, "No, they faced the same fate as Loomer. It is wilderness out there. They never could have made it. Viviana Valimar was too fragile to make it through the wilderness."

Langston nodded, "Maybe your right. But it was a long time ago. When you look at Taska, you can see her mother's grace and her refinement. She came from an upper class family. It still bothers me now. So many times I have thought of going, but never the strength to go. The Valimars were strong — defiant."

Philip nodded, "So many times you thought of going where?"

"I suppose I can tell you; it is so far forgotten now. The day they were to leave, someone spoke of the Valimars running away. It was gossip. Someone knew, or someone was told. Whoever they trusted to tell they were leaving, they must have spoken to others. Well, Emmit and I were up by the old maples and we saw Taska running around and around with the other children. She was a child. She did not go to the church school, but she played with some of the other children. Emmit was jealous of Letzen — he was in love with Viviana. But, she thought him ugly, mean spirited. He was a killer. So, when Taska was in the village — Emmit acted out.

"When we asked her what she was doing, she said she was playing. Emmit knew of the rumors that the Valimars

were leaving which would have been a criminal act. But
Emmit only half-believed the gossip. He told Taska to go
eat dinner with Jarod and his family. When she went with
them into town, Emmit told me to go out and check on
Letzen and Viviana Valimar. Viviana would never leave
without her daughter — or so he thought.

"I went out with the doctor to their cottage. We knocked
on the door and finally, just went in. We found the cottage
empty, but nothing was taken. They packed nothing. I
thought that perhaps they were looking for Taska in the
village. But upon the table, there was a note."

Langston finished the half a cup of wine and poured the
last bit out of the tall glass bottle. He nodded, "It said 'Your
father and I have gone. We know that you will follow when
you return and find this message. In the woods, where we
always walk, you will find a red ribbon in the mulberry
bush. These will be your markers. Follow the red ribbon as
your guide through the woods and you will find us. We will
be waiting in the clearing, just before the stream. Waiting
with love, mother and father.' That was all the note said."

Langston continued with his stone face, but his voice
was flawed, "The doctor took the note and threw it into the
fireplace and burned it. We spoke about it and left. On the
walk back to the village the doctor and I swore that we saw
nothing and we saw no one. We have always kept that oath.
But it was difficult to watch little Taska, unaware, never
knowing — all by herself. Jealousy and his unfulfilled love
made Emmit a bitter spiteful man."

Philip's eyes were wide, "They were waiting?"

"Since then, I have found that path. I suppose it leads to

a spot somewhere in the woods where two piles of bones sit together. But I found the path. Many days, so many, I have thought of getting a few things together and following the ribbons. Even if the markers take me to some desolate place in the wilderness, it seems so beautiful to go where Viviana and Letzen have gone. It is like a dream. It is an end to our madness."

Philip was awestruck with Langston's empathy and his illusion.

Sophia quietly wept, covering her mouth with her quilt. Everything that Sophia had been told was filled with half-truth and deception. Her past, which she thought was filled with truth, honor and faith, had so much despair, blood, fear and deceit. Sophia could no longer find comfort in anything that was around her or anyone she saw. She thought of Taska and wept. She promised herself she would never tell Taska of her parents, although she was committing a sin. She couldn't make her suffer anymore. She would rather perish in hell.

Philip looked at his wife who wiped her tears away from her eyes. She looked down at her sewing, pretending ignorance. But, Langston's words had changed them all, placing the burden of truth upon their shoulders.

Langston was leaving when he said, "I feel better that I could speak to you, Philip. You are a true friend."

Philip shut the door and listened to Langston's footsteps in the snow, crunching into the distance. He turned and looked to his wife with a helpless look on his face.

"Philip, was Langston drunk? Did he mean what he said?"

"Yes, he was drunk — and I believe every word."

The cottage was warm. That was odd. She got up and
slipped into her dress. She reached around to tie the back of
her dress and felt her head spin while her vision grew dim.
She stopped for a moment and put her hand upon the foot of
the bed. The sensation overcame her entire body, then
slowly faded. She finished dressing with caution. A sickness
was upon her. The aches and pains erupted all along her
back, legs and neck. She knew that illness was coming.

She put her cap on and held it in place with a hairpin
given to her by her mother. She walked out to the table and
stopped, surprised to see Cain sitting at the table reading his
Bible. She recalled the previous night and her decision not
to chain him. Cain must have rekindled the fire when he
woke. He heard the door open, "Are you still sick?"

Taska rubbed the back of her neck with her cold hand, "I
am fine."

She filled the kettle from the barrel in the corner and
hung it on the hanger in the fireplace. She sat down to watch
Cain. His eyes continued to make pass after pass over the
lines in the Bible. Cain was becoming a personality, and
every day he lived with Taska, she could see him change
from hollow and dumb to thoughtful. Each word he came to
understand from the Bible brought him closer to being like
everyone else in the village. Every word that Taska wrote
upon the parchments took her further and further away from
being like anyone in the village. Devotion and faith could
conform or transform. This was the vital difference between

the warden and the prisoner. They were both devoted to two very different ideologies.

She was responsible for Cain's life and what he thought. Every day she lived with him, he would think new thoughts and new reasoning related to the stories and the plots in the Bible. This enlightened her, but often compromised her control over him. He was intrigued by the Bible and its teaching, but something more was emerging from Cain. He mimicked Taska's walk, he watched her pose herself, and speak with others. Cain was becoming a mirrored apparition of her own physical being. When he first came to Taska, she knew that Cain would take everything from her. He would live her life as she did, moment by moment, with the exception of her own thoughts and dreams. He was already impressed with the Bible. And she had her devotion to the Golden World.

Yet, as she watched Cain struggle through a passage in the Bible, she was surprised at what she saw in him. She had inadvertently defied the punishment of the law by making Cain a defiant entity of self, with no feelings of remorse or guilt for his crime. He never took freedom away from her, but rather, Taska had fostered a sense of being in him that resonated in her strong will and passion. Watching Cain in the most trivial jobs, she could see bits and pieces of her life woven into his clumsy, forgetful shadow. Her physical actions weren't fluent or unique until she saw them placed on a clumsy, thoughtless shadow. Cain had become an extension of Taska's freedom and solitude.

She would have to find a place for Cain before she left for the Golden World. She held a responsibility to him, sitting at the fire reading his Bible.

This brought her back to her main concern, "How will I know when it is time to go to the Golden World, and which way shall I go to get there?" It would come to her. Somehow she would find the answers, and her future would become self-evident.

"Soon, I will get some different books for you to read," Taska said.

"I don't mind reading this one. It allows me to think. I sometimes think of what it might be like in heaven," Cain said.

Taska was surprised, "Is Heaven a good place... when you think of it?"

He looked down to the book, for an answer.

"No, I mean what is your perception? Do you like to think of heaven?" Taska said.

"Sometimes. But, I don't like to think about how I might get there; it troubles me," he replied.

Cain knew what she was thinking. His ideas of getting to heaven and Taska's escape to the golden world were so similar, that she thought Cain had read her parchments, stacked on the cupboard.

He noticed her face and looked back at the page, disregarding her glare. But after a few moments he spoke softly, "What is it?"

"What do you know about that. What did you read... where did you read that?"

Cain turned from her, "You have to die to go to heaven, like the man with the cut leg. You can't go to heaven alive, can you?"

Taska turned her nose down, "No, but you shouldn't worry over it. You will get there. You will not find me, but you will find your happiness there." She realized that his misguided eyes did not understand or even comprehend the parchments.

Cain brought his elbows up to the table and folded his hands together, "Of course you will be there. They will make you an angel. How can I be without you to help me? You have not sinned."

A welt of sorrow for Cain's misguided tone grew in her. She thought of the Golden World, which was a vision greater than any heaven she might imagine. She looked to Cain's folded fingers intertwining one across another, "Some people do not want to go to heaven, but somewhere peaceful."

"You must go to heaven," Cain said as he looked at her with abandonment.

"No, heaven is too far for me. I'm going to a place that is simple. I have walked the roads where I am going, over and over, and each time I meet another new face, another new idea. I have looked into the eyes of people who I can trust. Anna, and the others are there."

Cain bent his brow, "Anna? I don't understand."

"She is a woman Cain, like me. She is different than anyone you have seen. She wears her hair in braids that are long and they flow down her back. When she walks, she walks as if she is carried through the air by glass birds, very difficult to explain. She once gave me a glass crystal that she told me to keep. She told me when I come to stay forever, I will be able to smash it open and inside is a gift."

Cain was puzzled. Where were these images coming from and how did she meet these people? Taska was living beyond his comprehension. But where did it come from?

Taska continued, "I felt a gloved hand in my palm and it took me up these great stone stairs, thousands of steps, and when we reached the top, Anna brought me to the edge and....and she points to the sky where the sun is setting. I can see the world turning from yellow to a golden color as the sun pauses in time. It feels like... we are given permission to stand on the edge of the world. When I look to Anna, her eyes shine and glimmer, and she smells of all those flowers and trees of the forest below, reading and writing letters, and she smiles lightly and says, "it's beautiful."

Cain looked at Taska's distant gaze, "It is like you are there already. How do you know of this place? How do you know it isn't heaven? You see it so clearly. My dreams are distant. When I dream I see a face, but all that remains are feelings, like a reaction. I know that I should love the faces in my dreams, I should act differently, I should be something different among the faces in my dreams, but all I can do is look at them oddly, and just feel the emotions that they make inside me. Faces have no names; they have no relation to anything I can recall. They are just emotions masked with faces of familiarity. They tell me things that I don't know, and they weep because I cannot react to what they are saying to me. But you see a world that is defined by who and what you are. I remain in the shadows."

Cain was motionless, waiting for Taska to see him, waiting for her to return from within. Cain had envisioned his past over and over again, night after night. Perhaps a wife, perhaps children called for him to recite their own existence from within his hollow mind. The memories of his past were clear. Cain's comprehension of those images became the barrier he could never cross over. He truly lost his memory of the past.

With a somber look in her eyes, Taska thought, "What have I done to him?"

Sophia and her mother were pulling out all the dresses for the winter festival. Some were kept in large trunks and cases. Others needed mending or alterations. They had picked out a dress to bring to Taska. They knew she wouldn't come unless she had a dress and perhaps having a nice dress would nudge her along to come to the winter festival, even if she had to bring Cain with her.

"We should find some clothes for Cain," said Mrs. Lazarous. She thought for a moment. "I think I have his coat. It wasn't stained all that much. I washed it but never returned it to Taska."

She went to the cupboard and opened it. She rummaged about and looked through clothes. She drew out an old, heavy coat. She held it up and looked it over. "It should go back to him." She brought it back to the table and laid it out. She opened the coat and let it fall open. She looked around the stitching, looking for stains or rips. In the lining there was a small tear.

"We can sew that rip." She ran her hand over the lining. She paused and felt something inside. She moved her hands over the lining. Sophia watched her, "What's wrong?"

"Feels like there is something in there." She moved her fingers around the edges. She felt around the edges. Sophia put her hand on it.

"What is that?" Mrs. Lazarous took the shears and cut the lining. She slipped her hand in and pulled out a thick letter with a seal on it.

They stood astonished by the name on it:

Taska Valimar

"What is this?" Sophia said. They flipped it over and looked the entire envelope over.

"I think you should go fetch your father. He should see this," she said. Sophia nodded. She grabbed her cloak and headed to the door. "Sophia! No one knows about this."

"Yes, mother."

Sophia left the cottage. Mrs. Lazarous went to the door and locked it. She went back over and sat down near the hearth. She broke the seal and pulled out the document. It read:

Taska,
I know it will seem almost impossible to believe, but we have sent this man to fetch you. We are alive and living in a small town near the capital. We have tried to send people to bring you to us, but they have met with grave endings. This

man will take you back to us. Trust him. He is a friend and
someone who can bring you to safety. He is a good man
with a family, a son — they call him The Wolf. If you are
reading this letter, you have met this man. We trust him, and
we know he will bring you back to us. Take the few things
you need and go with him. Tell no one that you are leaving.
Just leave. And come home to us. We have missed you and
we have longed for this day. Come now, so we can put this
dark time behind us. Come home.

With Love - Viviana Valimar

Mrs. Lazarous drew in a breath and let it go. She wept, letting a tear fall on the paper. She tried to compose herself when she heard the knocking on the door. She wiped her face and went to the door. She opened it and saw her husband's face.

"What is it?"

Sophia and Philip came in. They locked the door. Philip took up the letter and read it to Sophia. They all sat in amazement. Sophia consoled her mother.

"What do we do, Father?" Sophia said. "They are waiting for her."

Philip considered the elegant script. What could be done? It all felt hopeless and somehow possible.

"I'm afraid we have broken the key inside the rusted lock," Philip said.

"What do you mean?" Sophia said.

"Cain doesn't know the way back. He doesn't remember why he is here. He doesn't know them anymore. He doesn't know the way back. He doesn't know his own family."

Sophia shook her head, "There must be a way to get him to remember, get him to know. Can't you speak to him? Explain that he is here to take her away. Tell him. Perhaps he will remember if you just tell him."

Philip looked to his wife, doubtful. "I can ask him. But if he doesn't remember, why would he believe us. It wouldn't make sense to him."

"Then show Taska the letter."

"And tell her to wander into the wilderness with Cain?"

"This is terrible. He was sent to take her home."

They sat looking at the parchment, thinking. Finally, he took the parchment and threw it in the fire. Sophia gasped. "What are you doing?"

She tried to pull it out, but it was too late. "Why destroy the letter? That belongs to Taska. That is her family."

Philip took her hands, "It is a shadow. I will speak to Cain, see if he remembers. But Taska can never know. It is a darkness that will consume her. They will send someone else. They will."

Mrs. Lazarous looked at Sophia, "You can never tell her. It is cruel. It will break her. Promise me, you will never tell her."

Sophia wiped a tear from her face, "I will tell her nothing. But promise me you will try, Father. Perhaps Cain will remember. And then they can go."

Philip nodded, "I will give my word to speak to him."
They sat quietly around the table. The Valimers had made it
out somehow.

At the church hall, Sophia and her mother came late to a
meeting of the winter festival. Mrs. Jarod was quick-
tempered by then and told them to take a seat quickly so
they could begin. The meeting assembled to discuss the
festivities. So many things had to be done, so many people
had to come together to make this festival exciting.

Sophia pushed her lower back hard into the stiff bench.
Listening to the preparations and organization of the festival
became frustrating with the chatter about food, costumes
and the music.

Disgusted by everyone's inane bickering, Sophia shook
her head and got up, "I don't feel well."

Sophia couldn't stand to listen to others prattle on. She
could hardly stand the sound of her own thoughts. She
thought about the letter, the man that came to save Taska,
and the shadow now shackled in the cottage.

She walked through the wooden door, into the church.
She looked up to the high ceiling, untouchable and
cavernous. The stained glass was now just a muted array of
colors blackened by the darkness outside.

She walked to the front pew and sat down. A few
candles were burning softy upon the altar. The golden
crucifix was sparkling in the candlelight. This changeable
symbol never failed her. She wore a small silver cross
around her neck all the time. So many men, so many people

had sinned, and then asked for forgiveness. How many were truly forgiven? She studied the veins in the marble floor. She followed a vein that twisted and turned, mocking destiny, passing from one point to another, never ending, regardless of confession or forgiveness.

The stained glass colors were hardly distinguishable. She noticed a red spot low in the window of stained glass, reflecting off of the candles on the altar. Her mind thought of the red markers that Langston mentioned. She could see them so clearly in her mind, hanging upon a branch, wrapped around a tree, frayed and weathered from the years of posting the trail.

That was all that remained of Taska's legacy, color without substance. The pressed rose in the frame that hung in Taska's cottage and the red rags hanging upon the trees, a forgotten moment of great intensity, and hope, crumbled and thrown into a fire by Langston's deceitful hand. Sophia turned her head from the stained glass and looked into the light of the flame upon the altar. She thought of ash and the smoke. To know they were waiting for their daughter, was tragic. It brought her to tears thinking about it.

Sophia didn't know where forgiveness and humanity dawdled, or when her heart would crave those things. But it made her bitter to listen to Langston's voice, over and over in her head, explaining the note that he discovered so long ago, and that he might take to that path one day, to Viviana and Letzen Valimar. He thought nothing of forever fracturing a family that needed only a few moments to escape this life.

Sophia could no longer trust her past; it was warped and

altered by constant lies. She knew that the faith that was instilled in her life, from this house of holy worship was nothing more than a guise for hungry, sour men. Sophia was allowing her trust in God to fall away, like the final leaf falling to the ground from a great tree of humanity that Sophia had tended her whole life. It now stood rotten and cold, awaiting a strong stormy gust to topple it over.

A few days passed and Philip hadn't seen Old Kavner for some time. He went to cottage one morning and found him sick with the shakes. The doctor told him it was nerves and gave him some chalky pills to take with water.

"How do you feel today?" Philip said.

"I feel very sick. I went out to the creek."

"The creek? Why?" said Philip.

"I followed Emmit and Langston to the creek. They met a man out there — an outsider. They traded with him… "

Philip looked at him with amazement, "They are waiting."

"They fought with this man, something about his family… Emmit fought with him and Langston shot the man. It was terrible. They burned him and destroyed the camp. I was afraid they would find me and kill me too. I hid in the icy swamp for almost two hours before I found my way back. If they know about me… if they know what I saw — they will come for me. They will kill me."

Philip patted Old Kavner on the shoulder, "Come now, if they thought you were there, they would have come here looking for you by now. I am sure you were undetected."

Old Kavner then mentioned, "Who are these men? I keep asking myself — why doesn't Emmit leave with these outsiders? Why must he continue to torment our lives and destroy the council?"

Philip nodded, "I have been wondering about that too. I was wondering what is keeping him here. I think it is Hillmond Wenner."

"No, she is not like him. She has no inclination to the man. I have spoken to her on many occasions at Old Lady Gertrude's cottage. She is not affiliated with his deceit."

"On the contrary, my old friend — she is always with Old Lady Gertrude and she lives next door to Emmit's cottage. She stays late with the old woman and then steals away to Emmit's cottage. She has been seen close to him during these days of uncertainty. She defends him. I am sure she had a hand in fixing the lottery. She has had a hand in all his deceit. He will never leave her."

Old Kavner pushed his head back into his pillow and moaned, "So much treachery. Nothing is what it seems any more. Who can we trust, Philip? It is all so uncertain."

"Trust me as I trust you. Everything else is uncertain."

Old Kavner agreed and shook Philip's hand. He would be in bed for weeks with his shaking nerves.

When it rained, and the snow was still on the ground, a mist would creep down through the village from the woods. The rain was lifting, but the mists continued to stream through the trees and haunt the village.

Old Lady Gertrude had just opened her door to let her

cat out when Dr. Keller came out to sit on the stoop of his cottage. He watched the old woman shuffle out a few feet and look up toward the old maple trees in the lane. Dr. Keller waved to her. She went back into her cottage. The unusually warm night was refreshing after the recent snow. The frail doctor was tired.

He had been to three homes with fever-sick children. He would be called a few more times before he retired for the night. When illness broke out in the village, it never took a single patient, but rather three, or four at a time. He stretched out and threw his hands over his bent knees.

He yawned, letting the musty air settle deep within his lungs. Then he stood up. That is when he heard someone running down the road. It was Hillmond Wenner. She met him in the middle of the road.

"What is the matter?"

She was out of breath and still looking back to the top of the lane, said, "I... I was coming from the church after saying my prayers and speaking to the Reverend. While I was walking back, I heard someone coming through the woods. I couldn't see where the sound was coming from. Then I saw the assassin. He came out of the darkness and attacked me. I broke free and ran away. Emmit. Call Emmit. He must have killed Valimar. The assassin is free!"

Dr. Keller spoke calmly, not believing her hysteria, "Are you sure it wasn't someone else?"

"No, I saw him clearly."

Dr. Keller looked down to the warehouse and saw Claas and two crewmen sitting on barrels, talking to one another and whittling. He hurried down to solicit their help.

Dr. Keller looked up the lane for something to emerge, a figure, a voice. He walked to Emmit's cottage across the lane.

Emmit opened the door and looked at Dr. Keller with tired eyes. The doctor, still looking up the lane, turned and spoke with a skeptical tone, "I don't know if this is true, but rumor has it that the assassin was seen, alone, coming this way."

Hillmond forced her way into Emmit's arms crying and holding him.

Emmit stepped out of his cottage, "Where is he?"

"She mentioned something about the church. If it is true, we should find out where he is and what has happened to Taska Valimar...."

"I will be out in a moment. Find Jarod, and Langston... and someone should get out to Valimar's cottage. She is probably dead," Emmit said. "I knew this was coming."

Emmit brought Hillmond into his cottage and shut the door.

His hand's trembled and his brow began to perspire. He walked quickly into his bedroom and began loading the pistol. Hillmond was sobbing, "He came after me."

Outside, the doctor, the cobbler and Claas came up the lane and met in a circle. Two crewmen joined them.

"Is it true what is happening, Doctor?" Claas asked. The doctor who was listening for a voice or footsteps, took a step back to listen carefully. They all could hear him coming, but the mist still concealed his location. The crewmen spread out a little and listened.

As the footsteps came closer and closer, the cobbler

became agitated and nervous. One crewman went next to the doctor's cottage and found a stick that he might use to subdue the assassin. When a figure came out of the fog. Dr. Keller peered at him with squinted eyes, "That is him!"

Claas advanced with the other crewmen, "Let's get him."

Cain saw the group as he began stumbling forward. He was soaking wet and his hair was plastered to his face from the rain. His voice was crazed from running.

Before the first crewman got to him, Cain shouted in a hoarse, broken voice, "Dr. Keller, come quickly...."

He was hit in the head twice, which brought him down to the muddy cobblestones. Cain tried to protect his face and head when he fell. Claas got in a few good blows.

Emmit came from his cottage wearing a long cloak, his hands tucked under the long garment. Hillmond Wenner stood behind him, fearful but curious.

Dr. Keller stepped away from the crewmen who fought with Cain in a pile on the shimmering cobblestones. People emerged from their houses, hearing the screaming and scuffling.

When Emmit walked past Dr. Keller, carefully watching the three men wrestling and punching one another, he had a blank look to his face. He stood before the pile of men and shouted, "Enough, move out of the way!"

The three crewmen looked over to Emmit and then scrambled out of the way, leaving Cain on the ground, balled up in pain and confusion.

Emmit's arm came out from under the cloak holding the pistol, like a long, dark extension of his hand. He watched Cain wincing in pain, blood running out of his mouth.

Emmit felt a swell of power pouring out to his limbs, an intoxication similar to ecstasy. His anger was uncontrollable as he peered at the entity that had caused him so much fear, so much pain. It wasn't Cain that brought out this rage. It was the council — it was Amerset Loomer running around the countryside — it was the gypsy trader he had murdered at the creek.

He lifted the pistol with his hand steady, not allowing his anger to shake his aim. He looked down over his outstretched arm, over the barrel and glared for a moment.

"To end all murders!" Philip Lazarous said as he ran by Emmit and threw himself over Cain. He turned back to Emmit and waited. The pistol was still poised upon them. Emmit smiled slightly as he mused over killing Philip Lazarous.

Dr. Keller finally broke the silence, "It's over, Emmit...."

Emmit brought the pistol down and concealed it within his cloak. Philip looked at Cain's blood-smeared face. His dark eyes seemed to have lost their sense.

"Cain, where is Taska, why did you come alone?"

When Cain heard a voice speaking to him, his eyes met Philip's. He began to recognize him. Philip waited and looked back to Emmit who still stood over them.

"She is dying. She has been sick. Now, she is getting worse."

Philip called the doctor over and looked back to Cain, "He said that Valimar is sick." He spoke loudly to Cain, "How is she sick?"

"She vomited a lot today, and when she sleeps, she speaks out loud. Finally tonight, she woke and told me to get the doctor. Her vomit was red with blood. I ran to the church. I asked Hillmond Wenner for help, but she screamed and ran off."

The doctor, now soaked by the drizzling rain shook his head in disbelief, leaving the two men.

Jarod soon showed up as a crowd of villagers emerged. Philip helped Cain get to his feet. Philip faced Emmit with bitterness. "Did you think he was coming for you? Did he call out for vengeance when he came, or did you beat him before he could say why he was here?"

Jarod advised Emmit, "Not in front of everyone."

Cain shook his head, hoping that he would stop yelling at Emmit. But Philip continued, "If I hadn't rescued him, Cain would have been floating under the piers, with no notice of the missing bullet in your case, or the hole in his head. Where is the other pistol, Emmit? What happened to it?"

Jarod shouted, "Enough! Take him into the doctor's cottage."

Emmit sneered, "It should be over ...."

Philip turned and saw Dr. Keller waiting. By then, Sophia and her mother followed the commotion to see what was happening. Sophia saw Cain being led by her father into Dr. Keller's cottage.

She stopped the cobbler, "What happened?"

"The assassin was running loose, Claas and the others beat him, and...."

She ran to her father's side, "Father, what is happening? Where is Taska?"

After the doctor took Cain by the arm and sat him down

just inside the cottage, Philip consoled her, "She is sick. Cain came to fetch the doctor. He was attacked by some of the crewmen."

"Claas?"

"Yes, I saw him on top of Cain, thrashing him."

Sophia looked up the steps, "Doctor, you must see Taska... I will go..."

"Let me fix up Cain and then we will get out to the cottage. Find someone with a horse. If we have to bring Taska back, then we will use the wagon."

Philip looked over to Langston and Emmit as they disappeared into the cottage. Hillmond Wenner was back inside. The pistol would soon disappear. Old lady Gertrude stood at her door. Sophia quickly walked around asking people for a wagon that they might use. Mrs. Lazarous explained the commotion to Old Lady Gertrude.

Philip went to Cain and spoke with the doctor, tending to him, "Is he all right, Doctor?"

"He will be all right. Just beaten a little."

"Don't worry anymore. No one will hurt you," he said as he spoke with disgrace in his voice. "We will go to Taska very soon. Don't worry, you are safe."

The doctor rubbed some ointment around his eye, which was now beginning to swell. His mouth still spewed blood. Claas approached Sophia and tried to speak with her, but she pushed him away.

"How could you beat him like an animal?"

"He came running at us, like a deranged killer — it happened so quickly."

"Your hands have his blood on them," she said. "Get

away — leave me alone."

A wagon was wheeled in front of the doctor's cottage. More curious villagers came from their houses to see what was happening. Everyone listened to others repeat the story.

Philip stood by the wagon, waiting for Cain to come out of the cottage so they could leave immediately. Sophia stood near her father, insistent on going to see Taska with him.

Jarod told everyone to go home, but as soon as word spread about Taska's illness, everyone started talking about another lottery. Without a warden, Cain would need another keeper.

Jarod continued to yell, "Nothing will be decided until morning... everyone just go home!" But no one left.

Cain walked down the steps and was helped into the shabby wagon. Dr. Keller came out with his bag of medical instruments and supplies. The farmer, who brought the wagon, helped Sophia get onto the back. She sat in back with her feet hanging over. She tended to Cain as best she could in the dark, holding a stained handkerchief to his bloody mouth.

Langston emerged from Emmit's cottage with irons to bind him. He stepped to the back of the wagon and took Cain's wrists.

"No, let him rest. He is my responsibility," Philip said putting his hand upon Langston's shoulder. With a sharp turn of his head and rage in his eyes, Philip said, "Don't get in our way, we are performing the law... something you disregard so quickly."

Langston gave the binders to Philip, hitting him in the

chest. The chain fell to the ground. If Langston's anger was burning, then Emmit's was raging. Philip whispered to Jarod, "Just throw the chains in the back, we will be out of town in a few moments."

Emmit stood in the doorway of his cottage, the light from the fire inside illuminating his silhouette, while Langston stood nearby, watching the group prepare to embark. Philip looked at his round face, knowing they would continue to clash over and over until only one remained. Philip wasn't frightened by this notion, but rather obsessed with it. He wanted to finish it, once and for all. Langston would never turn away from a lifelong friendship with Emmit. Langston was two-faced, trying to win Philip into his favors by sharing a bottle of wine and his misery. Philip shook his head and turned his glare from the two figures in the doorway. It had been going on for so many years.

The rain was still drizzling down. Philip, Jarod and Dr. Keller walked behind the cart as the procession began up the hill toward the big maple trees.

The fog was thick in the woods, making the trip surreal. Trees and branches appeared like distorted human shapes frozen in poses of great distress and pain. The cart rolled to the front of Taska's cottage where the fog was thick and the white streaks of snow and ice appeared like petrified clouds hanging in a brown and black sky.

Sophia and Dr. Keller went right into the cottage, Cain following behind. His face was broken and swollen. Philip, still bitter from his clash with Emmit, stood by the cart for a few moments. He opened his coat to allow the damp, cold air to wake him up. Jarod was afraid to speak.

Philip walked into the cottage, looking into the room where Taska laid in bed. Her face was white like the fog outside. Her face was damp with the fever burning in her cheeks. He turned from the door and walked by the fire to warm himself. Sophia worked with the doctor, while she tried to speak to Taska, but she was despondent.

Jarod walked to the table and sat down, "We must find another warden until she is well."

"A lottery? Did you hear the villagers tonight? It will be a riot."

Jarod looked to Cain who stood by the door to Taska's bedroom. Then Jarod turned back to Philip, "We must follow the law. She cannot care for him; she can't even speak. We must use our judgment, not our sympathies in this matter."

Philip laughed, "If we are following the law, then perhaps we should have a meeting to decided how to punish Emmit for having unlawful weapons. Perhaps that is the first order of business."

Jarod rose from his chair and stoked the fire with a poker, "You often think that you are untouchable, but when you need the council, when you fall into trouble, you won't have their support. You are making too many enemies," Jarod said.

"The council is not what it seems. Abuse after abuse has been recorded since the death of James Colberton. It will soon come apart at the seams, for no power, prestige or intimidation can stop this infernal destruction."

"Philip, you are losing your mind. You are part of that same deceitful council. You are the two-faced ass, and you will be exposed when you bring your unlawful weapons to the attention of the council. I have heard that they came from your warehouse."

Philip laughed and clenched his fist, "They were always his... I was the only one who could hide them for him, so the Annual Visit would not find them."

Jarod walked closer to Philip and spoke softly, "Don't start a fight with him. Emmit will always shout louder, stoop lower and then, if you are still standing, he will knock your teeth out. Everyone sees him as a supreme ruler of this village."

Philip shook his head and walked out on to the stoop of the cottage.

Sophia watched Dr. Keller as he made a small incision on Taska's arm, allowing the blood to flow into a bowl. He listened to her breathing with his stethoscope. He walked out into the large room, and sat down in a chair. Sophia came after him.

"What is going to happen, Dr. Keller?" she asked as she turned to tend to Cain. His lip was swollen and his eye was black and blue.

"You will have to stay with her, Sophia. She must take this medicine every half of an hour for at least a day. She is very sick," the doctor said.

Sophia's hands continued to tremble, "Will she make it?"

"I think she will, but I have seen this fever kill, so you will have to be here all the time."

Cain nodded, "And I will be here... to help Sophia...."

Jarod who was still by the door, turned and laughed, "No, you must come back with us."

Sophia turned back to Dr. Keller and spoke lightly, "He cannot go. He is better off here. I have spent time with Taska, here from time to time, I know what I must do to chain him at night. I am eligible for the staff."

The doctor spoke with a grim voice, "I will not be the one to make political decisions. The council must decide. Hillmond Wenner must approve of your responsibility to the staff."

"And the council has made its decision. She is not succeeding Valimar; it is not the law. It comes to lottery," Jarod said.

Philip came in having heard the conversation and looked to Cain, "No, he stays here. He will face more trouble in the village. It is apparent that Emmit's intentions are to see him dead."

Jarod burst out, "You are putting your own daughter at risk. This is just what he wants. Maybe he will tear her apart like he did to James Colberton or Slavanka Kyler, maybe worse!"

"He has had every opportunity to kill Taska and flee, but he has not. You don't understand that this man came into town tonight to save Taska's life. He will stay," Philip proclaimed.

"You seems so righteous, always changing the law for the rights of humanity. What the hell is wrong with you?" Jarod snapped.

"I have seen enough. I have heard enough from the

council, and from you. They don't trust you. Don't think that you are an outstanding member of this village. You are just like everyone else, ruthless, selfish and untrustable."

Jarod walked by Philip without saying a word. He knew that it was a worthless fight.

Dr. Keller walked back into the bedroom and Sophia followed. When Cain and Philip were the only two left in the room, Philip said, "You're not going anywhere. Not to worry."

Cain sat down at the table. He was noticeably shaken by the bickering. His face still hurt from the fight earlier. Philip sat down across from him and listened to them in the other room, moving around, speaking quietly to each other.

"You were brave to come to the village."

"I knew they would think I had escaped."

"But you came anyway. You are a brave man to help Taska and risk being hurt yourself. You seem like a man who would do what is right, you seem like a wolf. Fierce, strong. Family man. Anyone every call you that?"

The sounds of the fire crackled a bit and then settled.

Cain looked at him oddly, "What do you mean?"

"Strong and fierce like a wolf."

"I am not sure what that means?"

Philip looked down to his hands. "It is just a thing people say when they are brave. You were brave coming to seek help. You were fierce like a wolf."

Philip sighed. The key truly was broken off, the lock rusted into place forever.

Sophia had been sitting in the bedroom watching Taska. She seemed to sleep well now. It would be a long night of sitting up, being sure she was given the syrup the doctor had prescribed, every half-hour. It would be another fifteen minutes before she would have to wake Taska for another dose of thick medicine.

She walked out to the other room where Cain sat at the table. Although the Bible was opened on the table, Cain wasn't reading from it. Sophia sat down next to him. She wanted to comfort Cain, but she wasn't sure what effect this would have on him. She didn't know how he felt. His eye was swollen.

"You can read? That is good," Sophia said.

"She taught me, but it took some time. She went over almost every word in this book with me, but she taught me well. She showed me my name and what it means to be a manslayer. She isn't going to die?"

Sophia looked to her hands, "She won't die."

"If she dies, life will get worse. I dare not think of what will happen to me," he said.

"She isn't going to die, and if she did you would see her in heaven," Sophia said.

Cain shook his head, "She is not going to heaven...."

"Don't say that, you haven't the right to say that. You don't know what you are saying."

Cain didn't want to debate with Sophia, although he was reciting Taska's opinion. She had spoken of visions, ideals, and described intimate details that created a place different than heaven, a place where only she could be happy. Taska had allowed Cain to glimpse her visceral paradise, and although he feared the images she described and the people she seemed to know, he knew that it was her vision. "It is hard for me to explain."

She nodded. "Do you have memories before you came here?"

"I do not."

"You must remember something?" she said pushing him.

"Like broken fragments of glass. They never fit back together. Just shadows."

"Why did you come here?" He peered at her with a sad tired look on his face. She watched his eyes search the empty space between them. And for a moment, thought he would just blurt it out in a ramble. She watched for a few beats. Then she looked away. He was falling apart in front of her. "Where do you sleep?"

He looked to the door of the bedroom, "There, with the chaining post."

Sophia changed her tone, "I suppose I will have to chain you tonight. Is this what Taska has been doing?"

Cain nodded and closed his Bible. He stretched his arms, yawning for a moment. He had not been chained since the attacker came into the cottage. He had been allowed to sleep without the chains, and then Taska grew sick. Then he tended to her day and night, and spent little time in his bed.

Cain stood up and looked to his dark chamber, "I will be waiting...."

He walked into the darkness and laid out on the bed. Sophia was bothered by his tone and began to think about the staff and the murder that Cain was accused of committing. She turned to the cupboard and saw the staff leaning in the corner.

Sophia walked to the cupboard and took the ring of keys, then glanced over at the staff. She knew that the long pole would be useless if something did happen, for it had been so long since she learned the motions and the ways of the staff. She left the staff in the corner and walked to the door.

She listened for Cain, but she heard nothing. As she opened the door, her eyes widened as she searched for Cain in the room. She found his contour on the bed.

His voice was kind and soft, "Please lock the front door with the axe handle before you sleep. I am worried about who might come in."

Sophia felt uneasy. Then she looked at him, "Has she been chaining you?"

"I have been staying up to watch her since she has been sick," he said looking down at the quilt, which he huddled close to him. She looked back out the door, "I won't chain you. Just stay in bed. I will lock the front door now."

Cain slipped down into his bed and laid his head upon the pillow, "Thank you Miss Lazarous."

Sophia was taken by his politeness. She shut the door, feeling like she just put a child to bed. She went to the front door and put the axe handle under the door latch with firm kick. If Jarod or Langston came out early in the morning, they would not be allowed in to see Cain unchained. Fear crept over her. She felt alone. It was the first time that she realized how isolated and vulnerable she had become.

Sophia looked into Taska's room where the oil lamp cast

a hazy light about the room. Taska was sitting up in her bed. Her black hair had fallen around her face, and her eyes were clouded by her sickness. Sophia walked to her and sat upon the bed.

Taska's voice was broken, "What is it Sophia... why are you here?"

Sophia pushed her shoulder back down, "You are sick. Cain was watching you. When you became really sick, he came to the village to get the doctor."

Taska rubbed her eyes and looked to the little window, "How many days? I can't remember."

"I came a few hours ago, perhaps two days you have been sick," said Sophia.

With her eyes closed, Taska shook her head with surprise that she couldn't recall anything, "I have been sick for a long time. Did he have trouble? Is he hurt?"

Sophia, embarrassed about the incident in the village, said, "He is here and he is not hurt too badly."

Taska sat up again, "Tell him to come in here."

"He just went to sleep. Let him sleep."

"Did you chain him?"

"No, I did not. I locked the front door," Sophia said.

She opened her eyes wide, "Call him for me, please."

When she retrieved Cain, he had heard most of what was said, but he walked in as if he heard nothing. Cain looked down upon her. Taska took his hand and noticed his swollen eye, "They beat you — what a shame."

He didn't speak, his tears, and his nervousness broke his voice. She could see his face was trembling. She smiled lightly, "Don't get upset. Go in and sleep, Sophia will check on you from time to time. If your eye gets too swollen, you should fetch some ice from the water pails outside and put it over your eye."

He nodded, but didn't speak. He wanted to ask her so many questions. But she answered them with a few simple phrases, "Cain, go lie down, I will see you in the morning, don't worry, just go to sleep, we will be here."

When Cain left, Sophia turned to her quickly wiping away a tear. Taska put her head back down to the pillow, "Come now, sit with me. You must have had a terrible night."

She had the syrup and the spoon. "I am to give you this every half of an hour," she said holding up the bottle to show it to her.

"It was proper of you not to chain him. He is nervous after the attack."

Sophia sat down and looked at Taska's pale brow. She looked to her eyes that now closed in an innocuous comfort. Her black hair spilled out across the pillow. She studied each fine strand as it intermingled from one to another. Sophia saw her world so clearly, with vividness that created a complete understanding of time.

"I never knew that it would be like this," she said.

Taska, starting to doze off into light slumber, said, "Like what?"

"I never imagined it was this peaceful here. I often tried to imagine... the silence and the immunity that enshrouds you."

Sophia paused for a moment and looked to her own hand upon the quilts on the bed. She rubbed the soft quilting between her fingers.

"I never knew you like this...." Taska said. She turned on to her side and gazed at Sophia. She looked at her distance gaze, filled with mixed emotions.

"When you fled from the old woman's cottage... I knew that you hated me, I knew that..."

"Nonsense, it was distressful, but I never hated you, I had to find the truth. Once I found that I live among outcasts, I had to live my life all over again, in a different passage. All my memories changed, altered and were cut into pieces," said Taska.

"It is useless to scorn your memories," Sophia said. "Your life will deteriorate until even you cannot remember the real past from the imaginings of your altered perceptions. This is living with lies...."

"...which has been my entire life, there is no difference," Taska let her eyes close.

"I never imagined that it was so peaceful here. I watch Cain and he is obedient. He fears the men that speak to him as if he is half-witted, but he is heedful."

Taska took a deep breath, "Every time he sees those men, the council, he is either thrashed, taunted or condemned. He has every right to fear them, but he cannot fear everyone, or everything. I will not allow him that life. He must be the son of someone. Everyone must have repose, somehow."

Taska changed her voice, "What will happen with your father? He has taken many risks for me. I hope he is not in the council's disfavor."

"He will continue to defend your actions, and that of

Cain and what he did for you tonight. It turned wretched.
But let it wait for another time. Let it all just be forgotten for
a few minutes. My father seems to know his coming fate.
Uncertainty is everywhere."

Sophia pulled the quilt up to Taska's neck and patted it
down. She took Taska's hand and intertwined her fingers
within her own, "So peaceful...."

Just before dawn, Taska got sick, waking Sophia from a
light slumber. Sophia, who didn't realize she had fallen
asleep, rushed quickly out to retrieve a pail, but by then it
was too late.

Sophia left the pail next to the bed and began cleaning
up the floor nearby. She brought a wide, porcelain bowl
filled with water and an old rag to scrub the stain.

Taska held her stomach and watched Sophia. She
wanted the pain to go away. She knew the pain would ease,
but never completely disappear.

As Sophia took the soiled water out, Taska spoke
quietly, "I want to get better. I don't want this to go on."

Sophia turned by the door and said with kindness, "Give
it some time. Your fever has broken already. It just takes a
few days." She had to put the bowl down on the table in the
other room to unlock the front door. She kicked out the axe
handle, then went to fetch the bowl.

When she stepped outside she closed the door so the
draft wouldn't bother Taska. The morning air felt cold and
invigorating on her face and arms. She shivered. The moon
was settling into the trees, leaving the clouds and the rain to

her memory of a night she would never forget. She rinsed out the bowl in the rainwater barrel which had a chunk of ice over it. It reminded her of Cain's eye. She wondered if he was all right.

Sophia went back to Taska's room and put the bowl on the table.

"Are you all right?"

"I think so...."

She took the oil lamp and walked to Cain's door. She opened it slowly and let the light of the lamp fall upon his face gently, so she wouldn't wake him. But, Sophia could see his eyes were studying her. She seemed intimidated by his gaze, "Are you alright? Your eye is not swollen, is it?"

She stepped into his room and sat on the edge of the bed. She turned his head lightly with her hand and looked at his blackened eye.

"It has lost its swelling but it is still bruised badly. Can you see out of it?"

He nodded. Sophia clenched her teeth and took a deep breath.

"Try to rest; it is still early. If you need me just call," said Sophia.

He said nothing, but he tried to obey by lying back down and shutting his sore eyes. Sophia rose from the bed and walked out to the table. She put the bowl by the fire to let the glowing embers dry it slowly. She warmed her cold hands by the red coals.

When she returned to Taska's bed, she was sitting up.

"Were you sick again?" Sophia asked and sat down on the bed. She looked into the bucket and saw nothing.

"No, I just want to be sure it doesn't come again."

Taska wiped her mouth with the sleeve of her sleeping gown, and shut her eyes lightly. "I will get you some water," said Sophia.

She returned with a cup of water, and Taska drank most of it. She wiped her mouth again with her sleeve. She gave the cup to Sophia with a weak and shaking hand.

Sophia took the cup and placed it on the floor, "Climb back under the blankets so you don't catch a chill, I had the door opened. I will rekindle the fire in a little while so it won't be so cold in here."

Taska climbed down under the quilts, "Sophia, if anything might happen, today, next month or ever... take care of Cain, see that he isn't mistreated."

Sophia laughed quickly, "Don't be silly, I will make no such promise because you will be fine. Don't fret over such silly thoughts."

Taska pulled up her blankets with a look of concern. Sophia didn't know what to say. Taska whispered, "I want to get better... I want to be better off... I really want to be well...."

Sophia leaned back on the bed and said, "You are getting better, you just have to believe that you can get better. If you believe it completely, with complete truth, it will happen. You will make your health return because you believe nothing else."

Taska thought about that notion for a moment, peering up to the ceiling and the cobwebs in the corner, "I wish your words were true."

Sophia continued, "Of course my words are true. Look

at Cain. If you had believed he was treacherous, then you would have treated him like a criminal. If you treated him like a criminal, he would have slowly become exactly that — a criminal. But Cain is gentle and useful because you knew he was able to be what you thought he should be. This is not magic or trickery. It is the fate of your kindness and believing what you thought to be truth. It doesn't matter what you believe, or how much different it is to what others think, but if you believe it true — then it is true, the only one you must convince is yourself."

Taska knew that what she had created was real. The Golden World was spelled out on the pages, like the Book of Job and the story of Moses. She now realized, with the clarity of a holy vision, how she would reach the Golden World. It was all that mattered to Taska, and she knew it was the purest form of truth.

She rose from her pillow and wrapped her arms around Sophia. She shut her eyes and held onto her as she felt her warmth and considered her brilliant words. She knew that she was now free, and she could fly away, leaving the tattered cocoon of confusion and doubt sitting on the rotting branch.

In the village, around midnight, nothing was stirring. The snow-covered rooftops glowed dimly in the light of the moon. The ocean lapped at the pier footings and the rocks along the shore. The only sound was the splash of oars rowing a small boat toward the dock. The three men on board didn't speak. They were huddled in their coats and capes. When they reached the pier, the oars were pulled into the boat and the tallest of the men climbed up onto the dock.

Lieutenant Thadium stood looking over the village while he unbuttoned his long wool coat. The brass buttons were the only thing that glistened in the moonlight. The two other men followed the Lieutenant as he began walking down the ice-covered dock. The two men with him were not dressed in uniforms like the Lieutenant, but rather, dressed in rags. Lieutenant Thadium stopped for a moment to strike a match. He lit the end of an old rolled up cigar. Once the smoke permeated the air around him and the red glow blazed brighter than the moon, he continued with the men.

They reached the cobblestones and glanced around the center of the village. The only thing that seemed unusual was the immense pile of wood stacked in the middle of the cobblestone square. They looked for a cottage that might have a light on, but no one was stirring.

"What is the name, Lieutenant?"

Lieutenant Thadium had a way of speaking clearly while his tobacco hung in the corner of his mouth. His habit never prohibited him from commanding his men, "We are looking for Philip Lazarous."

A noise came from the blacksmith's shed, which was closed up for the night. A small figure appeared, slightly dazed, and walking awkwardly. It was the jumping boy. On cold nights he would sleep near the blacksmith's forge to stay warm. He would put down straw mats and blankets around the base of the forge. This would keep him warm all night, for the forge never cooled down. But soot and the dirt clung to him, leaving the jumping boy's appearance nothing less than filthy.

One of the deck hands approached the boy. He looked him over and turned back to the Lieutenant, "Should I ask this one?"

"Does he speak?" said the other deck hand. When the Lieutenant approached the boy he could hardly make out the difference between the boy's filth and his tattered clothing.

"Tell me boy, where can I find Philip Lazarous?" said Lieutenant Thadium.

The jumping boy examined the brass buttons on his coat and looked to his polished boots. Then quickly, he took the Lieutenant's hand. He walked quickly, pulling the Lieutenant along with him. They walked up the lane.

The jumping boy stopped in front of a door. The Lieutenant pounded hard.

Sophia opened the door and looked at the dim figures. She squinted her eyes and then rubbed them. The blanket she was wrapped in fell off her shoulder, revealing her bare skin. She realized who the men were.

"Philip Lazarous, where is he?"

Philip came up behind his half-dressed daughter. "What is the matter, Sophia?"

Sophia let the door open entirely, "They are here for you."

"I am Lieutenant Thadium. We are here for collection. Are you Philip Lazarous?"

He stepped forward feeling the bitter air streaming in over him. He nodded. Lieutenant Thadium looked back to the two men that stood behind him, "You can come with us and report to the Captain, then we will bring you back."

Philip's voice cracked when he spoke up, "Let me dress. Come in."

Philip quickly went back to his wife in bed and told her he had to leave. She began getting up, but he told her to stay in bed. Philip finished dressing. He went out to the hearth and saw the three men warming their hands. He put on his wool cloak and pulled his boots up. As he sat down to tuck his breeches into his boots, the Lieutenant queried, "What is the meaning of that great pyre of wood in the center of the village?"

For a moment, Philip couldn't understand what the officer was talking about, then he recalled the winter festival and the great bonfire. "It is part of our winter festival. We light it and celebrate until it dies out. It lasts all night," he said.

Lieutenant Thadium looked at him curiously, "What do you celebrate?"

"The season. It serves as an excuse for everyone in the village to gather together. No religious ceremonies are undertaken at this festival," Philip said.

Lieutenant Thadium nodded and spoke to his deckhands, "Get the boat ready. We will be there soon."

The two men left in silence. Philip stood up and pulled his gloves over his hands. He looked to the ledger from the warehouse on the table and he thought one last time, "Is everything in order?"

Then just before they were about to leave, Philip realized that this was the time to follow his course, which was fueled for months by anger, deception and murder.

Philip followed the Lieutenant out the door and down to

the docks with a slight spring to his step. He knew that with protocol, tax collection, the winter festival and the simple movements of his own plot — undoing Emmit would simply be a matter of execution.

The small boat carrying Philip, the Lieutenant and his men arrived alongside the great war vessel out in the harbor. Philip noticed faces looking down upon them. No one spoke. The only thing that could be heard was the lapping of the wind swept ocean on the hull and the creaking ropes and the rigging. He noticed the lettering near the bow figure. Before he could fathom the meaning of the name, Lieutenant Thadium held the rope ladder that was hanging over the side of the ship and said, "Welcome aboard the *Lucifer's Wing.*"

The climb up the damp and frozen ladder seemed like a never-ending struggle to the top of the massive ship. When he was pulled over the side and onto the deck of the *Lucifer's Wing,* Philip looked around at the shadowy faces and great masts that stood on deck like giant tree trunks reaching up to heaven. He looked to the dark corners where piles of rope were intertwined with buckets and tackle blocks.

Lieutenant Thadium reached the deck and prompted a shadowy figure, "Where's the first mate? He should be here waiting."

The deckhand disappeared toward the cabin door in the rear of the ship. An old man with a face full of whiskers and a bent nose brought the Lieutenant a lantern and passed it to the tidy and proper officer.

Lieutenant Thadium walked with Philip to the rear of the ship to a cabin doorway that led down into the ship's innards. Philip followed the Lieutenant and the light he carried. He didn't want to stray too far behind because he was unsure of what lingered in the shadows and the spaces he could not see.

Philip saw a face that made the Lieutenant stop, "Babble, you weren't there to greet us. What is happening?"

The sickly man stuttered as he thought of an excuse, "We had outbreaks of fighting all night sir; they are restless. Every time we come into port, sir."

Lieutenant Thadium shook his head, "Anyone caught fighting will be chained with the barrels for three days. I will not tolerate it."

"Sir, that is too harsh... they are restless... Just need get on shore... I will tell them...."

"You will tell them my orders and nothing more. I will not let this ship fall into chaos because men are restless and brawling. Although we are not flying battle flags, indolence and insubordination will be punished with severity."

The first mate nodded and gave out a quick and meaningless salute, "Yes sir, I will curtail any unlawful behavior." Philip watched the first mate fall away into the darkness. While the Lieutenant unbuttoned his coat, Philip listened to men whispering all around him — on the upper decks and lower bilge. He couldn't be sure where he was on the ship. He began to feel ill as the awful smells of cooked fish and oil permeated everything. Everything swayed slowly back and forth.

Philip followed the Lieutenant through a series of small stairwells and ladders, turns and hallways, changing their direction with every step. Some hallways were crowded with people, others were vacant and dark. Then it occurred to Philip that some of the hallways were quarters for the men. Ghostlike images huddled around barrels, dimly harboring life in the frigid cold. The images made Philip realize the magnitude of this warship and the immense world from which this ship had come. It made him fearful of the power which was concealed within the timbers and rigging, hidden within the ghostly men: a power that could take away everything.

When they reached a doorway, it looked different than those they had passed through. It had a glass pane in its center about the size of a man's hand. The glass was cut with many angles, like a crystal that had been pressed out flat. Lieutenant Thadium turned to Philip, "Don't speak directly to the Captain. Speak to me. Don't stare at the Captain. He won't speak directly to you. Don't speak unless I speak to you. Do you understand?"

Philip didn't understand why, but he understood his orders — don't speak. He agreed.

Lieutenant Thadium knocked on the door and waited for a powerful voice ordering them to enter.

The Captain's cabin was immense. The room spilled out like an entire deck of the ship. In the center stood a great oak table, which was heaped with papers, books, and rolled up scrolls. The Captain was standing near this great table holding a pen in his hand. Lanterns hung from the low rafters. A tea set and wineglasses cluttered a table behind the Captain in a series of indulgent drinks and tea services of bone china, silver spoons and gold tumblers. The fine tableware was bruised with tea stains and syrupy brandy. A small vault on the floor was covered in maps and documents. On the right, a partition closed off his bed, revealing the broad foot of his sleeping chamber and his dressing trunks.

The Captain put the pen down and turned toward the windows that faced the stern of the ship. Each little window was the size of a sheet of parchment, but because there were so many, it appeared to be one huge window. Beyond the windows stood the pitch-black night. Yet, the room was filled with lamplight that fended off the rats, the scourge, and the inclination to kill.

Captain Urvon was in his uniform, his coat slung over a chair decorated with gold braid and metals. His black hair was gray at the roots and his face was smooth and unhindered by the harsh weather or the bitter life at sea. He was a pampered and self-righteous officer. Although he appeared muscular and powerful, the gold and adornments of the things around him seemed to suggest he did nothing but count money along with the days it would take him to return to his lavish home and his stately dinner affairs.

"Captain Urvon, this is the emissary from the village, Philip Lazarous."

He turned from the windows and looked Philip over with a look of contempt. He then spoke to the Lieutenant.

"Is the anchor secure?"

"Yes, sir. We have secured the anchor and I will keep a watch on it until the wind dies down. No reports of ice in the area now for days."

The Captain pondered over Philip for a moment, "Lieutenant, are the taxes collected from everyone in the village?"

Lieutenant Thadium looked at Philip and waited. Philip was careful to speak to the proper officer, "Yes, the taxes are collected and the register is complete. It is ready for collection."

The Captain looked at one of the many books left open on the table. He pulled a leather-bound volume from the bottom of the stack and flipped through some of the pages. He turned his head, "How many are in the village now?"

"About five hundred and sixty," Philip said but looked to the Lieutenant Thadium, as if Philip's words came from his officer's mouth.

"So, Lieutenant, this means the amount of taxes will have increased. We have a growth in population," said the Captain and laughed under his breath. He looked over another page of the book and then closed it.

"Lieutenant, explain to our good friend about our new rule. I do not believe he knows about these changes," said the Captain.

"Sir, I am not sure what you mean?"

"No? Perhaps I can help you. When the tax collection this year is greater than last year — it is obvious that the village has more occupants and has ignored all our warnings to decrease their population. The new law: if the village is growing more than two percent — then we must take some of them away — part of our relocation laws."

The Lieutenant nodded and looked to Philip's shocked

face. He glared at Lieutenant Thadium and then averted his eyes to the floor, "I would think that more profit from a village is better, regardless of the number of people in the village."

In a moment, the Lieutenant seemed disgusted with Philip and spoke sharply to him, "We are not trying to generate revenue. This is a liquidation process. When it continues to grow, then it seems that you care to disobey us, so we must assist your council in keeping the population in order."

The Captain chimed in, "In order, we mean steady decline."

Philip could feel his heart beating quickly. He had never heard anything of this law. He found it difficult to compose himself. They were all doomed.

"I understand. I'm sure that you will find everything to your satisfaction. These actions you speak of will not be necessary," said Philip.

The Captain spoke directly to the Lieutenant, "They have increased their numbers by at least twelve if our good friend is correct with his figure of five hundred and sixty. They are very close to exceeding the population allowance."

Lieutenant Thadium spoke optimistically, "We will know when we check the register."

The Captain looked at Philip and then down at his table filled with papers and books, "Yes... I want that register. Now that our friend knows the current situation, he is likely to alter the register, keeping the count low so we won't have to take people away. So, until you get the register on this ship, Lieutenant, we shall hang on to this one for a while," the Captain pronounced.

Philip, now afraid of the situation blurted out, "I will go with you to get the register. I will bring it to the ship. We can go back right now."

The Captain laughed, "I believe our friend doesn't wish to stay with us." The Lieutenant laughed at the Captain's trifling joke.

"I will go to fetch it now, sir," Thadium said as he composed himself, but he didn't get away.

The Captain said, "No. Wait until daybreak. Then take Babble with you and bring the register and the tax money. And tell our little friend here, that if we have more taxes than names, or more names than taxes, we will account for everyone in that village. If we count too many I will sign a reduction order. And I will line up every man, woman, and child and take every third putrid wretch until we have the correct number."

"Yes sir," Lieutenant Thadium saluted and walked out with Philip.

As Philip walked into the dark corridor he realized that his forehead was damp with perspiration and his knees were trembling.

Sophia woke to the sound of crying. She wrapped herself up in a wool blanket and walked to the sound in the next room. She saw her mother with her hands over her face, sobbing.

"Mother, what is it?"

She was embarrassed by her weeping, but she couldn't break the emotions that had taken hold of her. In between whimpers she said, "Your father went with those men, and he hasn't returned. They took him to the ship...."

"He will be fine. He has been the emissary for years now. He knows what to do." Sophia said rubbing her mother's shoulder, "He hasn't been gone long."

"It has been four hours. It's too long," she cried out. Sophia decided to try and find out what was happening. She dressed and took an oil lamp.

"I will walk down to the warehouse and see if they are there."

"They won't be there," said her grieving mother.

"Then I will go to Emmit's cottage and see if they are there."

She didn't wait for her mother to argue. Sophia got out into the lane. It was bitter cold. She slowly walked down toward the warehouse and peered at the pyre of wood that would be ablaze the next evening for the winter festival. When she reached the warehouse she saw that it was dark inside.

She walked over to the blacksmith's shop. She couldn't find anyone. She thought it was odd that no one was around even though the Annual Visit had come. She noticed her breath turn to steam, spiraling into strands and wisps from her lips up into the bitter air. That is when she noticed the giant ship that appeared as pitch-black upon the water.

The giant vessel was a shadow standing unmovable in the ocean. A few lights glimmered from the ship, like dim stars.

A little hand that pulled on her sleeve frightened Sophia, as she pulled away and yelped all at once. She regained her breath and looked down to see the jumping boy. The little boy, with a grimy brow, looked at her and pointed at the ship, but Sophia didn't understand. He pointed again, she just looked at him with a puzzled look. Finally he began jumping up and down and pointing, grunting to her.

"It is a ship," she said as she tried to dismiss the child, but he continued. He jumped and pointed, trying to tell her. Finally, Sophia realized, "Did they go there... did you see them go to the ship or are they here in the village?"

The boy pointed, this time without the grunts and the jumping. Sophia looked up at the shadow of the boat. Why would he bother to go out to the ship? Something was wrong. No one had ever gone out to the ship. She tried to resist the idea that something terrible had happened. She kept thinking, "He is fine. He is in no danger. They won't kill him — they need him."

Sophia looked at the boy and put her hand out. At first he was apprehensive and shy. Sophia stomped her foot once. It was as if he could hear her speak. When he placed his grubby little hand into Sophia's palm, it was ice cold. She slowly walked with him to the warehouse. She would walk one step for his two so Sophia had to saunter along.

She didn't speak to the boy; he wouldn't understand.

She found a match and lit the lantern she had been carrying. She walked with the boy into the warehouse. She stopped at a pile of wool blankets. She handed one down to him and continued on. She turned back to the boy, who was lagging behind, to see him with the blanket draped over his head. She couldn't help but smile at him. As she pulled the blanket off his brow, she noticed how dirty he was from sleeping around the forge.

Sophia walked him back to the warehouse and fired up the coals in the stove. The dry wood started quickly. She put a large pot of water on the stove. She found a cloth to wipe his face.

Once the water came to a boil, she poured some of it into a porcelain bowl. She poured some cold water into the mix. She tested the water with her fingers and dipped the washcloth into the water. She gently started wiping away the soot and dirt from his face, staining the cloth. She wouldn't be able to get him completely clean without a bath, but she would at least restore his dignity.

The little boy didn't mind his scrubbing because the water was warm and the cloth was soft. When she finished cleaning his face and hands, she dried him. She made a little bed for him next to the stove and made sure he was content. She even found half of a teacake from her afternoon tea to give him.

Sophia cleaned up the pots and threw out the rag that she used to scrub him. She watched him as she was leaving, his eyes shut and his little hands clutched around the teacake. He would be safe for the night.

Sophia walked back out to the cobblestone square. She paused in the bitter cold and looked at the tall masts that looked like black church spires in the sky. She looked at the wide hull and the anchor chain that disappeared into the rippling waves. She had forgotten how big the ships were that came every year. It frightened her to see them by day, yet by night they just cut a hole in the sea and stars.

She thought of what she might say to her mother. She

tried to practice her words so they would provide comfort…
but it was easier to stand out in the cold.

Philip couldn't sleep where the Lieutenant told him to after
receiving a flea-ridden blanket. His hole was just outside of
Lieutenant Thadium's cabin. In the middle of a small room
that seemed more like a corridor, there was nothing but a
wood burning, cast iron stove, with a pipe that climbed
through the decking above and disappeared.

Every few minutes, a deckhand would pass by, stopping
to warm his hands by the stove. Philip stayed in a dark
corner, out of sight and with his eyes half-opened. He didn't
want to fall asleep for fear that something might bite him
while he slept. He had a continuing fear the ship would
leave, making him a permanent crewmember.

He considered what Captain Urvon said. He knew that if
he explained the situation to the council, it would bring
about panic. He began to think of his own family being
taken away on the ship for relocation. It was terrifying.

He waited for the sun to turn the sky into a gray slate
color. Although he couldn't find an ounce of light coming
down from the ship decks, he knew in a few hours the sun
had to come up. Then he would try to persuade the
lieutenant to return to the village. He knew Sophia and his
wife would be worried sick.

Suddenly, a voice called out to him from by the stove.
He sat up from his slouched bed and tried to focus his eyes.

"Who is there?" he said as he pulled the blanket down
from his shoulders. The figure drew closer to him and

scrutinized Philip for a moment.

"When you came on board, I was there. You are the emissary from the village."

Philip placed his hands on the cold deck boards, "Who are you?"

"Babble, first mate," he said in a whisper. Then he squatted down, bringing his ugly face closer to Philip. He looked around and said, "You shouldn't sleep with your back to the wall — outside is the frigid water... you will catch your death, friend. I am hiding."

"From what?"

"Sometimes, a man knows what he knows on a ship like this. But I don't care either way. So I don't want to be there when something happens. I won't be caught, I won't be blamed, I won't be anything."

Philip looked down at his cold hands and back to Babble's ugly face in front of him, ready to pounce on an unsuspecting passerby like a troll.

"Is it safe?" Philip asked, wondering what this gruesome man might be suggesting. First Mate Babble had a nose that must have been broken twenty times, if at all. His gray and black eyebrows stretched over his eyes, broken many times by scars and wounds. His left cheek was caved in and heavily scarred. He tried to hide it with his whiskers, but it was so evident that Philip could not keep his eyes on his dim portrait for more than a few moments.

Babble whispered, "Might you know someone who would want to murder you?"

Philip shook his head and looked down quickly, not allowing himself to believe what Babble was saying. He tried to strengthen his will and his fears so he spoke quietly, "Why do they call you Babble?"

"I know everything that happens on this ship. I know who is here, who is there I even know the strangers. Sometimes, I know too much. The men think I tell the Lieutenant everything, so they call me Babble, because I spew out everything."

"Did you talk about this murder?"

He laughed a little, "I pretended I didn't know about it. Now, I am hiding."

When the Lieutenant's cabin door opened, he looked over to Philip and then, seeing Babble nodded, "Be prepared to go ashore in one hour. I want to take two of my soldiers and pick out two men from the crew. When first light comes, we will drop the away lines."

First Mate Babble stood up quickly and mimicked a salute, "Yes sir."

As the Lieutenant turned to retire, Philip quickly rose and said, "Will I be returning with you? When you return to the boat ... must I come back, sir?"

Lieutenant Thadium pondered for a moment, "No, you can stay in the village. I don't want you speaking of the population tax which we discussed. If panic begins in the village while we are here, I will assume it originated from you. Have your little festival and keep everyone in order. When we come, I will speak only with you. Be there to meet us when we come."

"Yes sir," Philip said watching the Lieutenant disappear back into his cabin.

First mate Babble smiled, "A few too many in the

village... naughty, naughty."

Philip walked over to the warm, black steel stove and warmed his hands. He thought for a moment, then spoke to the deformed sailor, "I've never heard of this law before. I can't stop people from having families, trying to survive."

Babble walked closer and lowered his voice, "And what is worse, they won't take the young people, the new people. They take people like you; they take older people. But they won't take the young people; they fight too much." Babble had an odd way of thrusting his face close to Philip as he spoke, making Philip look at his deformed face and smell his putrid breath. It was intimidating.

Philip shook his head and rubbed his hands together. He wondered what would happen, who they would take and where they would bring them.

Babble smiled, showing his three or four rotten teeth, "Don't worry friend, they won't take you, they already like you."

He turned sharply, "Why does everyone call me friend... I don't know any of you?"

"We are all friends, up on deck, in the village, down below, all friends."

"What about the poor bastard that will be murdered tonight?" Philip asked.

"He has friends. He is a close friend, because he will be dead."

First Mate Babble and Philip were waiting on the deck looking towards shore when first light broke behind them. A few dim lights appeared from people who were up early to tend to a fire or their livestock. A few men were preparing the rowboats on ropes and davits. Philip asked Babble, "Why soldiers?"

He was blunt as he supervised what went on around him, "We are a warship, and we have captains and lieutenants that are targets of attack if someone were to start a war. We also transport prisoners."

"Prisoners?"

"Call them what you like. I call them outcasts. Of course, it is a matter of opinion," Babble said.

Philip watched the Lieutenant come out of the hatchway and down the deck. Four soldiers fell into a line and saluted Lieutenant Thadium.

"Did you get a few men?"

"Yes sir, they are here."

"Forgive me for saying so — but I don't think that we need that many people," Philip said dimly.

The lieutenant was amused, "Well my good friend, you don't go to your church in your work clothes, do you? It is a matter of respect. It is a show of power and possession for all of us. Don't think we are worried about our safety, but rather our image in the eyes of your people."

Lieutenant Thadium ordered the soldiers into the boat. Philip watched the top of the muskets pointed up to the sky. The bayonet tips were sharpened to a razor fine point. Babble and his men climbed in. Philip followed without being commanded. The Lieutenant climbed in and gave the order to lower the wooden boat down into the water. As they slowly slipped down to the water line, the sway of the boat hanging from the ropes made Philip sick.

The ropes were released. Some of Babble's crew pulled out the long oars and began rowing. As they moved away from the *Lucifer's Wing*, Philip could look over the vast hull and study the letters on the side of the ship. The ship's figurehead, carved and painted, wasn't in the shape of a half-naked woman like on other ships, but rather Lucifer himself. His horns were raised up to the bowsprit, his mouth frozen open in a perpetual shriek, and one arm reaching out ahead of the entire ship. It was a terrifying image. Because of the bitter cold, the figure of Satan was tarnished with blotches of ice. A long icicle hung from the elbow of the carved dark prince.

They reached the dock and pulled in the oars. One of the deckhands scrambled out of the boat and tied off the ropes.

Philip was the first to get off the boat. He looked around the quiet village and the center of town. The first light of morning was illuminating the eastern sky. He looked at the front of his warehouse, wondering if anyone was about. The Lieutenant ordered the four soldiers to stand by the boat until they returned. First Mate Babble also instructed his men to stay by the boat. Philip noticed how the village seemed small and simple after going out to the warship.

Babble and Philip walked through the cobblestone square, followed by the Lieutenant, "Now, where is the register?"

Philip looked up the lane, "Emmit's cottage. He is the head council member."

Lieutenant Thadium looked around the village in the clear light. Then he turned back to Philip, "The taxes are there?"

"Yes."

"Lead the way," said Thadium.

They proceeded up the lane. Philip walked by his own cottage, noticing the smoke from the chimney. His mind raced with panic about the tax register and what the numbers were like. If he only knew what was coming, he could have manipulated the numbers, or had someone else do it — it would have been easy.

They reached the front of Emmit's cottage. The bitter wind whistled in the trees around the lane. Philip pounded hard on the door. It seemed to rattle the picture on the wall inside. When the door whipped open, Emmit was angry, "What in God's name is this about!"

He peered at the Lieutenant's dark coat and the brass buttons. His eyes wandered over to Babble and his gruesome gaze. Philip greeted him with a dumb look.

"We are here for the register and the taxes," Philip said after an awkward pause.

He looked back into his cottage, then realized what was happening, "Uh... my office. Everything is there."

He came out with his coat and shut the door to his cottage. He pointed and began walking, "It's just up here." He fumbled with keys in his fat hand.

They reached the next door and filed into the office. Lieutenant Thadium followed him, but Philip waited on the stoop with Babble.

Sophia hurried up the lane. Philip walked down a few paces to meet her, "Sophia, what is the matter?" Philip said.

"Mother wanted to be sure you were — here," she said.

"Yes, I will be home soon. If you come across Mrs. Jarod this morning, explain to her that the winter festival will begin at five, just as she planned. The Lieutenant may bring some of his men," Philip said in a tone of authority.

Sophia's eyes widened as she feared his words. Having those dregs from the ship at the festival would be deplorable. Sophia glanced at Babble and turned away quickly. She trotted back down the lane.

"Your wife, friend?" Babble said. He laughed with a hiccup. Philip ignored his comments. He focused on the door that was opened to Emmit's office. The dawn sky wasn't bright enough to see inside, so Philip listened and waited.

Lieutenant Thadium called Babble into the office. He came out with four sacks of tax coins. He walked past Philip and down the lane, back to the boat.

"I will take this back to the ship; you may get it back," Thadium said as he came out the door. He was carrying the register and a few other scrolls under his arm. He walked down the steps and waited for Philip. Then he turned back to Emmit, standing in the doorway, "Any criminal activity?"

He stepped down the first step and paused, "There was a murder."

"Was it a villager that was killed?"

"Yes."

"Was he killed by another villager?"

Emmit paused and looked to Philip, not knowing what to say or what to keep secret. Philip turned and faced the Lieutenant, "He was one of us."

"Very good. You can kill one another all you like. Was

the criminal punished?"

Philip continued, "He was imprisoned for life."

Thadium nodded, "Where's the prison?"

"We have a warden system," he said.

The Lieutenant laughed out loud and looked down at the register he was carrying, "You people are fools. You should have strung him up by his neck."

Philip looked down the stony lane, "It was complicated."

He didn't care, "Hell is hell no matter what you call it. Let us go."

As Philip and the Lieutenant walked toward the waterfront, Babble ran up the lane, "Sir! They are ringing the warning bell, something is wrong on the ship!"

The Lieutenant sneered and followed Babble down the lane in a slow run. He turned back once and said, "Be here when we return!"

Philip stood in the lane noticing the ball of red that was coming up over the horizon, near the ship. The figures scurried back to the rowboat, climbed in and were quickly away. Philip took a deep breath of cold air. Babble's murder had occurred, a murder that had set Philip free from his dangerous position as emissary for a while. He felt tired, hungry, cold and angry all at once. These were feelings that fear had suppressed while he was on the ship.

Philip now had to consider his other plans. Emmit was terrified. It was now just a matter of interlacing the fingers of fate with those of the Lieutenant and his firstmate — demons to the end.

It had been an hour since Philip had returned to his cottage. He spent some time comforting his wife, who feared that he would never return. Sophia wanted to bring an old dress to Taska. She had convinced Taska that she would enjoy attending the winter festival, but Taska didn't want to face the entire village. She was angered by the way they treated Cain when he came into the village for help. She was tired of the innuendoes and the intimidation.

Sophia gathered up the dress that she had altered, with the hope that it would fit Taska. She gathered up a sewing basket and some fabric that her mother had set aside in the event that she had to make quick alterations. The sun was now shining through the windows, and the village was coming to life.

Finally, Sophia took a pair of old, mended trousers and a shirt from her father's chest of old clothes. If Cain didn't look presentable, Taska might refuse to go to the festival. He would feel better in different clothes, rather than the work pants he wore day in and day out.

Philip and his wife were at the table eating breakfast when Sophia announced she was off. When she walked out into the lane, most of the villagers were walking down toward the center of the village to look at the great ship that was floating in the inlet. It was a spectacle.

Sophia walked up the hill out of the village. She turned around to look at the ship, moored in the harbor. It was like a giant serpent surging from the sea. Sophia walked past Old Lady Gertrude standing at her door looking down at the ship in the harbor. As Sophia passed, she asked, "Is that the visit?"

"Yes, they came last night."

She shook her quivering head, "Your poor father...."

Further up the lane she saw Emmit and Langston coming down the way from the church. She kept her eyes trained to her feet and quickened her steps. But they still questioned her, "Sophia, is your father back at the cottage?"

"Yes, he is having breakfast."

"What time did they come last night?" Langston said as Sophia tried to walk away without further interrogation.

"I don't know... he was up very early, he should rest for a while."

Regardless of what excuse she made, they would go and question him. She walked up by the great maples and out through the woods, beyond the church.

Coming around the bend, Sophia saw Cain gathering wood outside the cottage. The sun was glimmering off the slate roof, sparkling with melting snow and ice. The trickle of melting snow pattered on the ground like rain. The sun was warm. She spoke from a distance, "I have something for you."

Cain turned with an armful of wood, "Books?"

"No, some clothes, for the festival tonight," she said.

Cain tried to hide his disappointment.

Sophia opened the door for Cain and walked in behind him. Taska was sitting at the table with her parchments spread out in front of her.

"Sophia, how are you?"

Sophia put down her things and unlatched her cape. She hung it on the back of the door. She took a deep breath, "It has been a long night. They have come for the Annual

Visit."

Taska, who now stood before Sophia, frowned, "That must be the end of the winter festival."

"No, they want us to have it anyway," she said pessimistically.

"Well, that is thoughtful."

"No, they want us to invite the dregs of the ship to the celebration."

"That is nonsense," Taska said.

Cain stood from stacking the wood and brushed off his shirt from the dust and the cobwebs. He quietly filled the kettle and put it over the flames. Sophia and Taska sat down at the table. She gazed quickly over the parchments and looked at Taska, "How do you feel? Have you been sick?"

She shook her head and placed her hands into her lap, "No, I haven't felt ill in three or four days."

Sophia admired Taska's face, her smooth cheeks and her clear brown eyes, "You look stronger. You look healthy."

Taska couldn't help but smile and said, "I feel much better. But I don't look different. Nothing has changed, merely my perceptions, nothing more."

"You were sick for two weeks. That is a long time to feel bad. It must feel wonderful to be well."

Cain sat down at the table. He had not seen Sophia in a few days and hearing a different voice was very entertaining to him. She had become friendly with Cain while Taska was ill. They worked together and nursed her back to health. Never once did Cain make Sophia nervous or concerned for her safety. He was helpful and often pitifully honest with Sophia.

She continued about the Annual Visit, "The men from the boat came to retrieve my father late last night. He didn't speak that much about it, but they brought him to the ship and he had to stay there overnight?"

"Why? Didn't they take the taxes?" said Taska.

"This is the first time he had to go on the ship. He didn't explain it, but I think he saw some terrible things on that ship. He didn't want to speak about it."

Taska looked down to the parchments, rubbing her fingers over the paper as she spoke, "I wish someday you could read these pages."

Sophia was taken aback, "Do you think I will understand them?"

Taska laughed as flattery flushed across her cheeks, "It is not hard to understand. But it is important." She paused with a distant stare, "To me — they are important."

Sophia watched Cain tend to the kettle of water, "I will read them if it pleases you. If they are important, I will certainly read them."

Taska smiled lightly, "I am glad. That makes me very happy. They are for you."

Sophia heard her speak but no longer knew what to say. Taska's face was animated with a smile, as if she had been released from some ethereal obligation. Finally, Sophia smiled lightly and placed her hand over Taska's thin fingers. Their touch met across the black ink, the words, and the conviction of emancipation. It flushed Sophia's heart in waves of love.

Cain brought cups to the table and poured the water for tea. Sophia stood and fetched her canvas bag. She pulled the azure colored, full-length gown from the bag and unfolded it. Sophia let it hang in front of her. With her eyes wide, Taska rose and felt the fabric of the dress.

"It is beautiful."

Sophia pulled out the crinoline petticoat that would give the dress a full and grand look. Taska gazed at the color and the brocaded collar. She was falling in love with the dress. She asked Sophia to help her put it on, leaving Cain at the table waiting.

She was surprised that Taska seemed so happy about the dress and so willing to wear it. But she didn't question that, nor did she mind her light-hearted manner. It warmed Sophia's own heart and made her happy to see Taska smile, and carry on as anyone should from time to time.

When they returned from Taska's bedroom, she stood before Cain and Sophia and looked down upon the sprawling dress. Sophia gleamed with satisfaction. She looked as Sophia always thought she should — refined and graceful, aristocratic like her mother.

Sophia was quickly reminded of Viviana Valimar, when she danced at the festivals, her flowing hair and her spirited personality. They were distant thoughts that, like many childhood memories, seem perfect, flawless.

"You look beautiful, Taska." She spoke a confession she had waited so long to express.

Philip walked quickly to the warehouse carrying the ledger and inventory under his arm. The villagers were standing at the end of the docks looking out to *Lucifer's Wing*. Philip didn't gaze at the ship, or even notice the villagers for fear that someone might speak to him. He shut the warehouse door and stared out the small windowpanes that looked out over the docks. Philip could see a few men walking on the deck of the great ship, scrubbing the decks and securing the rigging.

He put the ledger and the inventory down on the table and sat down, allowing his back to slouch down in the chair. He brought his eyes to the center of the table where the lantern stood next to Sophia's broken pen.

The Lieutenant and the Captain were going over the tax register on the ship, looking for discrepancies. They would do as they wished with the ledger and alter it to suit their own desires. He knew a great power, harnessed by anger and misery, was being unleashed every moment that the ship sat at anchor in the harbor.

Philip opened the ledger from the warehouse, and turned to a blank page in the back. He ripped out the paper and found a pen that he could write with. He placed the inkwell on the table and sat back down. He took the pen in his left hand and held it for a moment. It felt foreign and uncomfortable. He dipped the tip into the inkwell and let the excess drip off. He held the glimmering tip over the page for a moment and began writing, "I will be free tonight, and I will come for you."

He pulled back from the paper and looked at the shaky, almost unreadable script. No letter in the note seemed familiar to Philip's own writing, making him confident that the message would serve its purpose. It was a simple tool used by Philip to set his revenge into motion. By day break the next morning, Philip would be free to live in peace, without convictions of misery and frustration. He could live unabated by the council. Finally, Philip would be able to rest.

Philip knocked on Emmit's door and waited. Emmit came to the door. He looked at Philip with wide eyes as if something were about to strike out at him, tear him down, and drag him away.

"Emmit, they want to bury one of their men in the cemetery. They had a murder on the ship last night."

Emmit allowed him into the cottage and shut the door. Philip looked around the cottage and sat down. "Just let them do it," unsteady in the tone of his voice.

"Fine."

"Philip, are they leaving, I mean are they staying for a long time?"

It was a matter of the register. If it were in order they would be gone soon. He didn't mention Captain Urvon's warning of taking people away.

"They won't be here long. It is a matter of meeting their satisfaction," Philip said.

"I see..."

"I wouldn't worry, Emmit. They are not concerned with anything beyond the taxes. Your little secrets won't be revealed. But let me ask you this, how many people were in the register, that we collected taxes from?"

Emmit looked at him for a moment, knowing that something might be wrong, "I believe we had five hundred and sixty-four."

Philip felt a shock strike his backbone, but he concealed the sensation from his face. He waited for a moment and allowed the numb feeling to fall away.

"I see. You are sure of the number?"

"Of course. Is there a problem?"

Langston came to the door. He stepped in from the winter sun and into the dim cottage. He was angry and raising his voice, "They are bringing a dead body into the village! What is the meaning of this Lazarous?"

"They want to bury him. There was a murder on the ship last night," Philip said.

"You cannot allow this, Emmit. We cannot have him buried in the cemetery with the villagers, it is wrong."

Emmit was stern, "It is none of your business. You're not buried there, so don't concern yourself."

He shouted loudly, "My wife is buried there, our families... what is the matter with you!"

Emmit shook his head, "We buried the assassin there and you had no objection — so how is this different? Enough — leave us."

Philip turned his head up to Langston and glared at him, "We will fix it when they leave."

"That is easy for you to say, emissary. Are you going to dig him up?"

Finally, Emmit took Langston by the arm and walked him out the door, into the lane, slamming the door. Philip stood alone in the cottage, while Emmit and Langston finished outside.

He took the note from his pocket. He placed the little

piece of parchment down on Emmit's bed, by the pillow. He knew he was moving through the motions of a plan that came to him every night, wide-awake — determined. The details, the motions that he couldn't see clearly in his mind, seemed to become evident as though deceit were using Philip to deliver its end.

Later that afternoon, Sophia stood in her cottage being fussed over and pruned as she stood perfectly still. Her dress was a flush scarlet color with white lace trimming her elegant dress. It took more than four months for her mother to complete the dress. The winter festival was more than just dancing and drinking; it was a time for people to present an image of themselves never before seen by anyone, never considered, and never envisioned by the other villagers. That is not to say it was a masquerade of exotic costumes, but rather a refinement of one's elegance.

Sophia was done being put together, "That is fine mother, hurry and get yourself ready before they light the pyre. I don't want to miss that."

Mrs. Lazarous walked away and shouted over her shoulder, "Will Taska come tonight?"

Sophia swiping at her skirt to keep the dust and dirt off, walked by the door where her mother was dressing, "I don't know. She may come for a little bit. She seems so optimistic, perhaps she will surprise us, and stay the night."

Sophia went to the front door and stepped outside. She looked down the lane toward the center of the village. Daylight faded. Sophia watched a few people walk by in their best of clothes. She stood for a moment and watched a quick stepping parade of people pass by, some with musical instruments, and some with their families. The people who lived outside of the village on farms or in the woods came early to enjoy the company and festivities that alleviated their somber and dim winter days.

Sophia closed the door when she heard her mother come from the next room. Her mother was wearing the same dress she wore every year to the winter festival. It was a black dress that clung tight to her awkward curves. The front was embroidered with a mesmerizing pattern sewn in with black silk thread. Mrs. Lazarous would wear that dress to the festivals, to church and funerals. Sophia often pleaded with her mother to make a dress of her own, that she could wear to the festival, but Mrs. Lazarous didn't mind wearing the black dress, using her time to work on what she called "Sophia's masterpiece."

Cain stood near the hearth with his new clothes on. The new trousers and the shirt were stiff. He felt out of place and awkward. Taska told him that he looked fine. Taska finished his outfit with a long coat that was left by her father. It was black and hung down to the knees. When he put it on, Taska stepped back to look at him and saw an image of the things to come, and an image of the past — together.

Taska was dressing while Cain paced around the room, trying to get used to his stiff and starched clothes. He knew tonight would be awkward, misguiding and confusing. After tonight, his perceptions and feelings would change about his life, and the things around him. He remembered when he was attacked in the cottage, it brought about memories, things felt familiar — it was the gun blast, the smell of gunpowder. Did he know that smell? It was peculiar how change came about without want or desire, and without warning. Had he fired a weapon? Had he hunted or trapped in the woods before?

He slipped his hands into the pockets of his trousers and stood staring into the flames of the hearth. Memories, he thought, are slowly coming back. When the door unlatched and Taska stepped out of her bedroom, Cain pulled his hands out of his pockets, speechless.

She looked embarrassed, "Cain, how do I look?"

Cain put his hand on the back of a chair to steady himself. He was unsure of his sentiments to praise her, although he was overwhelmed, "You look... like..."

Taska walked to him slowly, lifting the hem of her skirt off the floor, "Bad?"

"Oh, no, no... you look, I don't know... like an angel."

Taska laughed and smiled, "The dress is beautiful."

Cain looked up, "What do you mean?"

She seemed surprised and spoke lightly, "The fabric, and the collar and the sleeves, they are very beautiful."

"It is more than the dress... it is your beauty."

She looked down at her shoes that stuck out from under the hem on her dress. Did Cain understand what he was saying — or was it something he pulled from his reading? Did he really comprehend beauty?

Taska rubbed the skirt of her dress with her fingers to make sure it was real. The texture of the royal blue shined in her eyes and made her feel impassioned, "It is very important to know beauty and seek it out — for you will find so many days that are lackluster — painful and tiresome. Heed your desire to find beauty. It will come to you and you should always rush to it. It is very important."

Lieutenant Thadium and Babble were the first off the boat. The five soldiers that came with them was Captain Urvon's idea. He thought that perhaps it would improve the celebration with some stiff, medal adorned military uniforms marching about. As the sky was becoming dim and the sun was extinguished they pulled up alongside the dock.

Philip greeted them as they climbed up the dock and spilled into the town square. He walked slowly with them down the pier. Around the dock, the festival was beginning. In front of the blacksmith's shop, round tables were set up. Already, food was beginning to appear. The smell of pork and beef filled the air. Everyone brought some food to contribute to the celebration. Some brought jars of relish and tomatoes, while others made pies and sweets. It was never a competition and no one spoke about the food that would be brought to the festival; villagers brought what they could spare. Next to the table stood cast iron barrels, covered with grates for cooking the five pigs and six ducks that hung behind the cooking barrels. The giant casket of wine was only half-full, left over from last year, but it didn't matter, it appeared full. As people walked by, they smiled at the seemingly excessive amount of wine. Under the table were baskets of candied apples, sugarplums and sweet candies for the children. The festival was about sharing so everyone in the village could indulge in ways they were not used to.

Up by the cobbler, a small riser was set up for the musicians. The large drums were positioned on the platform. Two men with wooden instruments sat tuning up. People would stop in front of the musicians and speak with them, all with a sparkle in their eyes, frolicsome about the night of dancing before them.

Across the way by the warehouse, some of the teenage girls prepared games and a puppet show for the children to play and to watch. It was very important for the festival to include everyone.

The crew from the *Lucifer's Wing* walked with Philip. They looked around at the last minute festival preparation and the streamers of colored cloth strung above them. They were impressed with how everyone looked, dressed in the finest clothing. It was a sight for the men from the warship, who had been at sea for so long. Although it was apparent that the clothing was old, patched and re-sewn, it was a sight for their sea-weary eyes.

Lieutenant Thadium threw an arm around Philip's shoulder, "We came to add some class to the festival. That is, if we are invited?"

Philip nodded, "Of course."

The soldiers were ordered to form a line by the warehouse steps. Philip, Babble and the Lieutenant walked inside. Philip ignited an oil lamp.

Lieutenant Thadium sat down at the table and Babble

lingered in the shadows. When Philip sat down, he gave his inventory list and the register to Thadium. He didn't seem to care what was on the pages of the ledger and the inventory sheet, but he looked them over. While he did so, the Lieutenant said, "We are still going over the tax register. It doesn't seem... correct according to the Captain's wishes. We will have to take people from this village."

"What do you mean? How many?" Philip asked.

"At least eight people will come with us when we leave. You remember - relocation."

Philip leaned forward and asked in a voice of panic, "How will it be decided, these people have lived here a lifetime? You can't just...."

"We can do what we wish," said the Lieutenant viciously. "But I wouldn't worry my friend. You have been very obliging to us; we won't take your family."

Philip shook his head, "You are just going to start taking people?"

Looking up from the book he said calmly, "I believe that is how it works."

Philip shook his head and waited a moment, "That is unlawful, just as kidnapping, and stealing might be considered...."

Babble laughed, "It is for us to decide the law, friend."

Lieutenant Thadium slammed the book shut, "Looks like everything is in order. You're not hiding anything in here are you? Weapons?"

Philip shook his head, "No."

Sophia walked into the office. The Lieutenant rose and smiled dimly. She ignored him and his first mate in the corner. She stopped by the door, "Father, we need to light the pyre soon. The entire council should be present for the Reverend's prayer."

Philip nodded and glanced at his daughter. She left quickly. When Sophia was gone, the Lieutenant remarked, "Your daughter is pretty. You should hide her from men like us."

Philip said nothing but escorted the two men out of the office, down the steps and back out to the festival. By now more people had come and the crowd had filled up the village square. He looked at the soldiers, "Lieutenant, I must find the other council members. Excuse me."

Lieutenant Thadium nodded, "Go and have your fun."

Philip walked through the growing crowd. Some of the villagers wanted to stop and speak with him, some with jovial smiles upon their faces, other inquiring about the Annual Visit.

Philip found two boys that he recognized and stopped them, "Wait! You two, come here."

They stood before Philip ready to obey. He pulled out two coins from his pocket, "A coin for each of you if you do me a little errand." The two boys, seven and eight years old agreed, "Go to Emmit's cottage and run around the outside, tapping on the windows, tap them all twice and then run back. But the trick is, don't let Emmit see you. Do you understand? It is a game!"

The boys smiled as they faced trickery and fun. Philip handed over a coin to each outstretched hand and they disappeared into the crowd.

Philip knew that Emmit was still in his cottage, still

deciding what to do about the mysterious note that was left on his bed. Emmit would be waiting for Cain to come and kill him. If the boys could pull off Philip's errand without being detected, Emmit would be waiting with his weapon for the assassin to come for him. Leading Thadium and his men to the cottage and the unlawful pistol would be a formality. Philip even hoped they would take him as part of their relocation plan.

Taska put on her white gloves and stretched them out by making a fist with her hands. She would have to wear them all night for warmth. She fastened the buttons along her arm. But they accented her dress very well. The only flaw in the way they looked was the chain that connected her to Cain. Taska knew she had to obey the law.

She put Cain's chain around his waist and gave him the end of the chain. She took the single key off the ring and put it in her waistband.

"I won't chain you until we get into the town. We might as well walk with comfort," said Taska.

He nodded, "You seem stunning tonight?"

"I feel different. After all, we look different, we should feel different."

Cain wanted to polish his shoes one more time. Taska told him they were fine, but he wanted to make a good impression. Taska watched him go to his bed and take off both shoes. While he buffed and polished his shoes, Taska spoke lightly to an ethereal audience, "I have been enshrouded by the wings of an angel, which shall conceal our flaws and our misgivings. We have felt the presence of a soft down, as we prefer to feel each feather, but we are warmed by the entire wing. This angel doesn't know of God, his archangels, saints, or sinners. This angel doesn't float overhead or carry a harp, but holds a small orchid in her narrow hand, and shows... royal blue silk, golden globes hanging in the sky, white gloves and the promise of a world so beautiful — a world of gold."

Cain came out with his shoes on, glaring with a new shine, "What did you say? I couldn't hear you."

Taska smiled and shook her head, "It doesn't matter...."

She straightened Cain's bow tie, making it perfect, although Cain thought it felt too tight around his neck. He looked at the parchments on the table, "Should we put the parchments away before we go?"

She looked quickly, "They will be fine... let's be off before they light the pyre. It is a grand sight to see. The flames fly so high."

Taska handed Cain a pair of gloves and asked him if he preferred a cap, but he declined. Taska stood for a moment looking around the cottage, making sure that everything was in order. She even noticed the red rose, pressed into the wooden frame. It was so dried out, that all that remained was its scarlet color.

Taska took Cain's arm and they walked out of the cottage. As they began walking through the woods, Taska looked up to the sky, "You can see all the stars tonight, so many of them."

Cain looked up. He stopped because he had never seen the sky so full and so alive with sparks and flickers, "You can almost see heaven. It is so clear."

Taska agreed, "Everything is so clear."

Philip finished a cup of brew that was handed to him from the cobbler. He drank it down and filled his cup once more. He spoke briefly with the men that were gathered around the barrel of brew, and then he mixed into the crowd. The sound of the musicians tuning their instruments began spilling out over the laughter and the conversation that seemed to give off a surging roar. The smell of roasting pig filled the cold air with a scent that was so luscious — it made his mouth water.

Philip walked through the crowd to the soldiers lined up by the warehouse. He looked at Babble who sat on the first step of the stairwell leading up to the warehouse.

"Where is the Lieutenant?"

"He is walking about, looking for you. He wants to get a death certificate for the buried deckhand," Babble said as his eyes scanned the crowd, mystified by some of the villagers, glaring at others. His mind was unstable and disconnected. It was in his eyes.

"Why does he need a certificate of death?"

"Family needs to know where the body is buried," Babble said.

"Will they come for the body?"

"Of course not. No one would come here. No one knows where this place is — or how to get here," Babble said.

"Then why proceed with a certificate of death...."

"It is a legal matter. No more questions!"

Philip sighed and looked over the crowd trying to distinguish the Lieutenant, but he couldn't find him. Yet, he saw his daughter. He walked through the crowd, watching her animated face and her jovial expressions.

As he wove through the crowd, the Reverend stopped him, "Let's begin Philip."

"I was looking for Emmit, but I suppose we can start without him."

Jarod and Langston stood next to the Reverend by the pyre. Philip followed them. Other members of the council gathered about and a hush fell over the crowd. The blacksmith came to the Reverend holding a bright torch.

The sky over the mountains glowed with what remained of the day.

Philip let his eyes fall upon the faces of the village. As he looked from one face to another he recalled the round face of Captain Urvon, and his relocation order. He felt a sudden shudder come over his body as he looked at the jumping boy, Mrs. Jarod and her daughter, and Taska, who had just arrived. He turned his head down as the Reverend began his prayer. While the sermon did not penetrate Philip's mind, the ghastly image of faces he knew for years and years, weeping, screaming, and pleading with the Lieutenant as they are taken out to the *Lucifer's Wing*, taken away forever, filled him with terror.

The Reverend finished with, "Amen," while Philip quietly said, "God, help us all."

Taska stood with Cain near the blacksmith's shop watching

the Reverend finish his prayer. The blacksmith walked to the wood pyre and threw the torch upon the pyramid of wood. It seemed to take a long time to catch and begin to brighten the village center, but once it sent a white column of smoke up into the sky, the fire was bright and warm. Everyone shouted and applauded the great flames. The villagers stood close to the fire to warm their frozen fingers and palms. Couples held one another close while others simply held hands. Langston and Jarod shook the Reverend's bony hand and mingled with the other villagers.

Sophia quickly found Taska and approached them. She embraced Taska and held her for a moment, then stood back to look at her. She smiled to Cain and shook his hand. He was somewhat embarrassed, so he didn't pay Sophia a compliment, as she did him.

"I am so delighted that you came," Sophia said.

"I must say I feel splendid," Taska said.

Sophia saw the chain that connected Cain to Taska and paused for a moment, recalling that no matter how different everyone looks and acts for this occasion, nothing changes under the superficial gloss, put on like veils over the eyes.

Sophia allowed her smile to fall, "I will find my mother and join you both for the remainder of the festival."

Taska said, "Don't bother with us, go and enjoy yourself, be with your father and your friends... don't let us ruin your evening."

Sophia smiled, "That is ridiculous. I shall return in a few minutes."

Taska looked down, somewhat honored and somewhat embarrassed by Sophia's kindness. Then Cain said quietly,

"She is very gracious."

Most of the villagers knew about the attack on Cain a few weeks ago and perceived a heroic image of Taska using the staff to fend off the attack. It was spoken in the cottages along the lanes, and in the farm sheds where men worked. Everyone listened, told or just imagined the scene that unfolded in the cottage. Some of the villagers looked upon Taska as courageous, but they would never speak of it aloud. Over the few weeks before the festival, a secret sect of people, men and women, had considered Taska as a brazen, courageous woman. This courageous sympathy slowly swelled from quiet talks in the somber cold of winter.

Taska slid her gloved hand down the smooth wood of the staff. It had been some time since she had carried the staff. After the attack, she had been avoiding the village and anyone who came to bother them. Hillmond Wenner was relentless. It felt comfortable within her hand. Every time someone would walk by and gaze at her, she shifted the staff slightly, drawing their eyes to the weapon, known for its honor; the menacing symbol seemed to absorb the village. For Taska, the staff was her deliverance into a new reality that she could not share with anyone.

Hillmond Wenner approached Taska and fawned over her dress.

"You are so beautiful. Your beauty is like that of your mother — refined and stunning."

Taska nodded, "It would be a wonderful festival if we could dismiss the Annual Visit."

"It is a shame that they have invaded our festivities.

Perhaps they will only stay for awhile. I will come and sit with you..."

"Please, Hillmond. Enjoy this time. We are content being here. I know we are outsiders — have fun with your family," Taska said.

"You are so resilient in your duty. It is a solemn and sad pride and honor that comes from you. It is greater than sacrifice or pity," Hillmond said. "It is impregnable courage."

Taska looked the other way, ignoring her. She waited until Hillmond wandered off.

Taska stood with the staff in her hand, while a few people, awestruck by her pose, her royal colored dress and the staff, spoke briefly to her. They spoke of trivial things, and the festival, but their eyes looked upon a fabricated fearlessness, and disregarded her compassion. One boy of nineteen even shook Cain's hand before passing by.

They took a seat upon a bench in front of the blacksmith's shop. Taska put the staff down next to her, leaning across the seat.

"If you are cold, we can stand closer to the fire," she said to Cain. He shook his head and watched the people passing by. The flames shot flickering light upon the dancing couples and the mingling crowd.

"So many people, so much food. There is a lot of sacrifice here. Most of the villagers can not afford to squander food and their supplies away for a festival," Taska said.

Cain looked over to the tables, "But they seem so happy, as if they want to sacrifice something."

Taska nodded, "Perhaps they do. Perhaps we all do."

Cain thought for a moment and reached into his pocket, allowing his fingers to caress the small triangle of glass. He watched people, arm in arm, laughing and speaking about this and about that. He never watched people carry on as they did. He wasn't sure if he was allowed to smile, allowed to enjoy the expressions and the motions of the shifting people. He didn't want to speak with them or even stand among them, but just watch.

The jumping boy, who seemed to be running about in a frenzy of people, food and warmth, went to Taska with a candied fig and held it out to her. She crossed her legs and put her elbow upon her knee. She took the fig from his grubby hand, and then she looked at it curiously, only to give it back to him.

The jumping boy smiled and tried to give it back to her again. But Taska said gently, "You eat it. You have it," and she pointed to the boy. The boy looked the fig over a final time and put it in his mouth. She laughed, "Good boy."

He jumped a few times and disappeared into the crowd. Cain watched him spin away. Something came to his mind. There was something about that jumping boy, but it was allusive, like a feel or a distant dream forgotten by morning.

Although the air was bitter, the warmth from the fire and the constant rush of people moving around from one person to another warmed everyone.

Philip found Sophia and his wife. He was awed when he saw them dressed for the celebration. His wife looked as she often did when she went to funerals and other festivals, but Philip found the modest dress elegant. It was a relic from a past life — from a different world. While they passed from one group of friends to the next, they smiled and laughed. From afar, it was wonderful to see them elated with the festival and the people around them.

Philip dashed through the crowd to gather up his wife into his arms. She let out a yelp at his childlike behavior. He kissed her on the cheek. He turned to Sophia, "I hope you will dance with your poor, old father tonight?"

She smiled, "Of course, I would be delighted"

"And may I say that I have never seen my family look so exquisite, and happy."

Sophia laughed with embarrassment at her father. Her mother said, "You must have had a little brew already."

Philip smiled, not pleading to his wives accusations. Then Sophia said, "Taska and Cain are by the blacksmith's shop. Why don't we see them? I want you to see how wonderful they look, father."

When Philip saw Taska and Cain standing together, he felt tamed of his overzealous emotions. Sophia smiled when she presented, all too formally, Taska and Cain to her parents. Taska shook Philip's hand and curtsied to Mrs. Lazarous.

Philip shook Cain's hand stiffly, "It is nice to see you tonight."

Cain looked up to him, "Thank you, sir...."

"Of course you are escorted by the prettiest woman in the village," Philip said. He looked over to Taska and then let his eyes fall away. It wasn't much, but they both needed to be welcomed, although it seemed awkward.

Mrs. Lazarous spoke in jest, "Forgive Philip, he has

been feeling good since they have opened the brew spicket."

Taska laughed outright, "With every reason to be...."

Philip felt a hand upon his shoulder. He thought it would surely be that of Lieutenant Thadium. He turned to the smiling face of Jarod and his wife. His mouth dropped somewhat in a sigh, "Jarod, good evening."

He shook Mrs. Jarod's hand and looked over to the soldiers near the warehouse. "It is a good night for the festival."

Mrs. Jarod smiled and questioned quietly, "Do you think they should be here?"

"The soldiers are here with the Lieutenant; there was nothing I could do," Philip said as he looked around him.

Mrs. Jarod whispered again, "No, the killer and Valimar."

Philip was struck with distress. He wanted to lash out in Taska's defense, but he stopped himself, "She is part of this village. She is also standing before us, so you should speak to her, not to me of your worries and your candor."

She looked to her husband appalled, but he didn't notice as he spoke with Mrs. Lazarous and Sophia.

Jarod then said in a deep voice, "And Philip has been fussing with the Annual Visit."

"Yes, it has been a long day, but I think they will be gone soon. They have a few more things to check over, then they will be gone," Philip said dismissing Mrs. Jarod.

"Everything is... all right isn't it?"

"I believe they will be gone by tomorrow morning, if not, sooner."

He shook Jarod's hand and dismissed himself. He didn't

want to lie to Jarod, but he didn't want to speak about the Lieutenant's plan either.

Philip walked through the crowd speaking with a few people enjoying the good spirits that prevailed. As he moved from one place to another, he caught a boy by the shoulder, a boy he had paid a coin.

"Did you do as you were told?"

The boy smiled, "We did it three times, around and around, tapping on all the windows."

Philip smiled a devilish smile, "Did he see you?"

"No sir. He screamed but he didn't see us at all."

Philip let the child go.

Philip walked back to the warehouse where Babble and the Lieutenant stood among the cluster of soldiers. He trotted up behind him. He knew now was the time to expend all he had in one burst. He had moved through the motions and fate had shadowed him step by step.

"Lieutenant Thadium, I understand you need a death certificate. We can fetch it now, if you wish. We just have to walk up to Emmit's house and ask him for it."

"Where is he? Is he not the council leader?"

"Yes...."

"Then why isn't he here, among his people... celebrating?"

Philip looked around, "Perhaps he is sick, or on his way. I don't know."

Lieutenant Thadium was annoyed by this distraction. He wanted to watch the dancing and hear the music. He agreed,

"Let us go and see what he is up to. I need that certificate in case we have to hang the man who killed him and prove to his kin that we buried the body. Things are a little different when you get back to the world."

"I would not know, sir."

With a sharp look to the first mate he ordered, "We are going up the lane. You men stay here. The first mate and I will be back in a moment."

The three men started up the lane with an odd, purposeful walk. They walked up past Dr. Keller's cottage, to Emmit's door. Everyone was at the festival, leaving all the cottages dark. Philip walked to the door and turned back to the Lieutenant, "He may be at the festival, but I have yet to see him there."

Babble asked, "Could he be up at his office?"

The noise and the ruckus from the festival could be heard as the musicians started another set of dance tunes.

"Perhaps, but why during the festival?" Philip suggested and said, "He probably fell asleep and doesn't realize the time."

They stood before the door of Emmit's cottage. A dim light came from within, most likely the light of the fireplace.

Lieutenant Thadium unbuttoned his overcoat and walked up the steps. He pounded three times upon the wooden door, "Emmit, we are here for you to give us the death certificate."

Philip heard something behind the door, then watched as Lieutenant Thadium pounded three more times on the door, shouting, "We've come for the death...."

The thunderous blast seemed to shake the ground.

Philip, not realizing, had instinctively fallen to the ground.
The bullet shattered a hole through the wooden door,
sending splinters in every direction. Philip thought the
Lieutenant was about to knock once more when he saw his
hand fall forward. Thadium fell forward, on to the door, and
down to the threshold. An odd gasp came from his mouth.

Philip was able to see the Lieutenant's face as he fell
back. The blood was flowing down, spilling over the pure
white uniform collar that came out above his overcoat. The
wound was a burnt hole just over his right eye. Philip peered
at the Lieutenant's face for a moment and turned away in
disgust. Babble fell backwards, then scrambled to his feet.
He ran down the lane calling for the soldiers.

Philip, fearing another shot from within the cottage,
scrambled back toward Dr. Keller's cottage. In the moments
before the soldiers arrived, Philip heard the music soaring
and the villagers laughing. Frozen, Philip looked at
Lieutenant Thadium and the pool of blood that was growing
around him, running over the threshold and down the stoop
of Emmit's cottage.

Philip stood upright when he saw the soldiers run up the
lane. Babble ordered them into a line in front of the cottage.
They seemed so formal and precise in their motions. Babble
stood next to the soldier on the end giving commands. His
face and shirt were splattered with the Lieutenant's blood.

"Load!"

He waited and watched each soldier methodically load
his musket.

"Aim!" It came so quick that Philip thought it was a
show. The wooden muskets were raised and checked.

Babble stood nervously waiting for all the soldiers to aim. Philip turned to the villagers coming up the lane. He tried to wave them off, but he couldn't shout.

Just before Babble was about to give the command to fire, another shot came through the door, striking a soldier in the belly. The soldier fell, allowing his weapon to fire off in a muzzle blaze of red and white smoke. As Philip crouched in the road, he watched the soldier fall and scream in pain.

"Fire!" Babble yelled as the four remaining muskets blasted the door. The tremendous sound felt like hammers coming down upon Philip's soul. He let out a yell that was hardly audible in the frantic actions of the men. The smoke and the smell of gunpowder hung heavy in the air. The door splintered and shattered into bits.

For the curious few that heard the shot fired at Emmit's cottage over the music, it appeared as if this firing squad had terminated the Lieutenant, still lying upon the threshold in front of the door. It was a mural of complete confusion and bewilderment.

The soldier lying in the lane didn't move. Philip crawled to him as the other soldiers reloaded their weapons. When he turned the soldier's head over, he saw that the soldier was gone. Dr. Keller came and examined the dead soldier in the midst of the reload. When the blood from the soldier's wound covered Philip's hands, he realized he was sitting in a growing puddle.

Commotion could be heard within Emmit's cottage. It sounded like glass breaking and things being tipped over. Philip slowly rose to his feet. One of the soldiers shouted,

"Someone is still in there!" He was barricading the door.

Babble looked around. As he walked away, he shouted, "Fire at will."

Philip crouched down next to the dead soldier as each of the muskets fired at the door again in sporadic chaos. By now more of the villagers had followed the noise up the lane to see what had happened. When Babble returned, he had a casket of oil used for oil lamps.

"Someone go to the back and be sure he doesn't escape," Babble shouted and dragged the flammable casket close to the door. He used a bayonet to punch a broken hole in the top of the container. Then he began soaking the front of the cottage.

Philip could smell the oil permeating the air. Philip watched Babble's motions, crazy and drastic like a madman opening the gates of hell. Philip was waiting for something else to erupt from the cottage. Babble soaked the front of the door, the walls and even the body of Lieutenant Thadium.

Babble, with a crazed look in his eye, took a match and set the liquid ablaze.

The fire quickly began to burn the front of the cottage. The windows quickly shattered. The fire seemed to hiss and turn the snow on the roof into white steam. Philip rose from the dead soldier, unaware of his tears and stumbled down the lane. He fell back on to his rear end.

Babble took a loaded musket and fired it into the flames.

Sophia came running through the crowd. She looked frantically for her father. Some of the villagers tried to restrain her, but she broke free and ran up to her father, covered in damp, red stains. She thought he was hurt because of all the blood. When she held him, he didn't react, he just continued to watch the fire grow and grow. The soldiers continued to shoot into the flames. Each bang of the muskets seemed more and more absurd as Philip allowed his daughter to cling to him.

Sophia continued to ask, "What is it? Are you hurt? What has happened?"

Philip just looked into the flames of Emmit's cottage. He watched the flames evaporate into smoke and twist up into the night sky obscuring the stars above. He expected Emmit to come out of the flames, unaltered, unharmed. Philip waited for Emmit to reveal his form in the middle of the brilliant yellow and orange flames.

"What have they done?" Sophia cried as she looked to the dead soldier up the lane. The Lieutenant was partially engulfed in the flames. Sophia looked to her father's eyes as he began to weep. She didn't know what to say. She sat with him in the lane, quietly saying, "It is over, it is over."

The center of the village was now deserted. Most of the villagers worked their way up the lane to find the source of the black smoke and the stream of glowing embers. Cain sat on the bench with Taska.

"It looks like a fire," Cain said as he watched the smoke rise into the sky higher and higher until the stars became eclipsed. He could hear people screaming and shouting, but couldn't make out what was being said. He watched the flames grow higher over the cobbler's shop. They seemed to grow bigger and bigger making the pyre for the festival seem insignificant.

"I wonder what happened," Cain said and looked over to Taska. He looked at her face that seemed somber. Looking down to her hands, he saw her blood. In Taska's hand was the staff blade separated from the pole. Her destiny was sealed in the thrusting motion of the dagger to her stomach, finally not aching anymore.

Cain watched her slip off the bench and down to the icy cobblestones. He looked at the blood coming from her chest, "But you loved this dress... you can't...."

She looked at Cain, her eyes sharp and clear, "When they come and find you still chained to me, they will accuse you of my murder. You won't be able to tell them otherwise. I have condemned you to this. I am sorry."

Cain took her hand and squeezed it tightly, "No, no, we must go, we can mend your wounds, we can go...."

"When they come, don't fight them. Let them carry out their procedures, sort through their laws, and when they ask you how do you plead, simply say — not guilty."

Cain's voice broke as he tried to speak through his panic, "You can't leave yet, you've got to tell me more.... How will I know of the world, how will I know of anything?"

Taska shut her eyes as a calm settled over her, "You will go to heaven, Cain. No matter what happens here, no matter what is said... you will be among the angels, you are worthy."

Cain looked down to her face as it became placid, "Why can't you take me with you? I won't make trouble, or embarrass you, I will be good...."

She spoke dimly, "In the moment it took to begin my

journey, with one thrust, I have found freedom. Nothing has really changed, just our perceptions."

Cain wept, "I don't even know what perceptions are —"

Taska put her hand to Cain's cheek, "Your perceptions are everything."

"But I have lived through your perceptions... you have created who I am. Yet I know so little of life, or freedom, I know so little of you."

Taska said quietly, "You must be free of what I am, then you will be free and pure. Don't fear what you don't know about yourself. Your perceptions are clear — and your perceptions are truth. Now begin recalling heaven, and see it clearly in your mind. Don't be angry, don't get confused, hold onto that vision and it will come to you."

She shut her eyes and said, "I never doubted you. You were always what you are."

Cain waited but her lips fell silent.

Cain held her hand tightly, pressing it against his cheek. He had to do as he was told. He shut his eyes and envisioned heaven. He tried to see all the images he contemplated as he read the bible. Although he heard voices overcome him, he did not fall away from his visions. The voices were dim and the feelings of touch were numbing. He peered down to his lap where Taska laid, motionless and peaceful. When the villagers carefully lifted Taska's body from Cain's lap, he gazed one last time upon her face, her flawless cheek, her round chin and the few strands of hair that escaped her white cap. Taska's face, without a flaw, was how Cain saw heaven.

Jarod unlocked Cain's binders and pulled him away.

Cain clutched his triangular glass shard in his hand and squeezed it tightly. The glass fragment was an icon for his altering religion based upon Taska's image alone. As he stood and looked into the many faces that surrounded him, he could hardly hear the profanities and bitter words. Each face was an empty space, spewing words. His mind's eye was focused on Taska's rich brown eyes and her fleeting smile that glowed with a superior radiance. Cain had finally met the expectation of deceit that the village expected. It was the only way out.

When Sophia arrived, she looked upon him with fierce pity. She touched his brow and asked, "What happened, Cain?" Her red hair escaped the perfect bun that she created earlier, her eyes unseen by Cain. Her lips quivered and her cheeks were flushed. He turned back to Taska. The only sound he could hear was the piercing sob of Sophia's voice. It was alone without any other sound to affect it.

When Cain looked back to Taska's body, it laid on the cold, icy cobblestone, her head turned slightly. The royal blue color of her dress mixed with the scarlet blood that blotched upon Sophia's skirt, as she knelt down to envelope Taska's body into her arms. She wept so hard that it sounded like thunder pounding.

As Cain was pushed and shoved through the crowd, Philip came up next to him, "What happened, tell me what happened?"

He couldn't speak. He focused on his image of heaven and the image of Taska etched into his mind. He clutched the piece of glass tightly, allowing it to cut into his flesh. His palm began to bleed.

Philip walked with Cain, keeping him close so he wouldn't be attacked. Some of the villagers didn't know what had happened. Philip, soaked in blood with Cain, and the great fire that burned Emmit's cottage, appeared like one great catastrophe. As word traveled through the crowd, Babble came and faced Philip.

"Bring him up to the old maples. I must fetch the Captain and bring him here. You are now the head council member. I will meet you up at the maples, with the rest of the council."

The crowd continued along with Cain in the center, and Philip guiding him up the lane. Langston and Jarod also walked with Cain. Philip's hands trembled as he tried to speak clearly, "Don't be afraid... the Reverend will come. Don't be afraid." But Cain couldn't hear him. Philip didn't realize what Babble said until he was gone. Then he absorbed the magnitude of what he meant, and what his new position held. He looked down for a moment, "Don't be afraid, Cain. It will be over soon."

Cain looked blankly ahead and thought of the parchments on the table, he recalled the abandoned cottage in the woods where they foraged for lumber, and the jumping boy that visited. Cain stopped for a moment and looked all about. He was searching for him. When he found the little jumping boy, he gazed at him. The jumping boy stood motionless, dazed by the confusion. He didn't know if the confusion was good or bad. He didn't know what was happening. Cain paused and saw what he was leaving behind in the image of the jumping boy. Cain shouted, "Jump! Jump!" The boy smiled, showing his teeth and a flash in his eye. The boy began jumping and jumping, laughing, and carrying on and on. And then he remembered, the face of his own son. His curly hair and the way he laughed and smiled. His son, he had a son.

When they reached the top of the lane, the Reverend said a brief prayer. His tone was morbid and somewhat out of breath from the turmoil that was all around him.

Captain Urvon came up the hill with Babble and reinforcements to witness the hanging of a murderer. Captain Urvon, enraged by the loss of his Lieutenant, approached Philip, "And where is the person responsible for the murderer of my officer?"

Philip turned from the other council members, "He was killed in the fire."

He pointed down the lane at the ever-growing fire that consumed Emmit's cottage and now was burning Old Lady Gertrude's cottage. The fire seemed to spread and stretch in the wind, pawing its way towards anything that stood in its path. Emmit's office was the next cottage to burn once Old Lady Gertrude was obliterated within her house. She would not be the last casualty of this enmity. The soldiers found a barrel and rolled it under the tree.

Captain Urvon walked up to Cain, "What do you have to say about this? Do you have anything to say?"

Cain looked beyond the eyes of the Captain. The Captain nodded and looked to Philip, "What religious endeavor must we... manifest, for this man — this killer?"

"He was consulted by the Reverend," Philip said.

"Then say something more for the ignorant bastard," he snapped. The Reverend walked over to Cain who stood next to the barrel. A soldier tied his hands behind his back, binding his wrist once again.

"To thee, O Lord, do we commend the soul of thy servant, Cain, that being dead to the world he may live unto thee; and whatsoever sins he has committed through the frailty of his mortal nature do thou, by pardon of thy most merciful love, wash away."

Philip looked to Cain, "Amen."

The soldiers lifted Cain over their shoulders and stood him on the barrel. He stood crooked, as he always did, like a scarecrow drenched with rain, falling from his makeshift crucifix. They took the slack out of the rope. Philip peered at Cain's eyes, looking for rationality, looking for truth in what he knew and what he did. Yet, Cain never changed or turned away from what was caught in his eyes.

After the Reverend stepped back, he made the sign of the cross. Cain looked out over the village. The fires in the village were burning brightly, sending an odd orange color into the sky.

The soldiers slipped the coarse rope around his neck and made him stand for a moment. His eyes could see way out over the ocean. He took a breath and said, "My son, my son, my son." It was all pouring back into him.

Philip gasped for air as he felt Cain's reproachment from all who judged him fall away. Cain could see his vision of heaven, still focused clearly in his eyes. Cain recalled the colors and the sweet smell of the earth and the brilliant faces of angels, a wife and his child. It was all so vivid. He recalled Taska, dressed for the festival. This was his vision of heaven, images from his past, seen in a dream or a sudden thought, but never completely lucid in his mind. He looked upon these visions with comfort. Were they all just dreams?

When Langston was told to kick the barrel out from under Cain's feet, he didn't hesitate. He knew what Cain was. He walked to the barrel with confidence and kicked it out with a hard blow of his foot. The rope pulled hard. It was silent, as Cain felt his hand open and the piece of glass tumble down, free of his possession, into the snow and leaves.

Cain rose through the branches of the old maples, higher and higher. He didn't look down for fear of what he might see. He rose up through the trees, intermingling with the smoke and the glowing embers of the fire. When he reached the treetops he could see for miles and miles. Beyond the mountains, he could see a glowing light that shined like a star nestled in the earth. He peered at the Golden World on the edge of the world, knowing that Taska was there. He felt elation and shudders of immense joy come over him as he ascended from hell.

"Look at the beauty... so far away."

He continued up and up.

Sophia sat at the table as dawn came. The embers in the fireplace were still glowing. It was a comfort to her. She gazed at the handwriting and the phrases she had spent the night reading. She realized what Taska became in this cottage, and how distorted Sophia's image of Taska really was. Although they were unknowingly different, they still shared a common thread, a sullen life alleviated from time to time by their companionship.

She had left the village when she saw Cain's body hanging in the tree. Her father tried to stop her from going up the lane, but she had to see him. She passed the brilliant flames of the engulfed cottages and could see his figure, swaying slightly, at the end of the rope. The Captain wanted him left on the rope until morning.

She knew, in her heart that he was innocent. She had watched Cain and his simple ways.

After seeing Cain in the tree, she disappeared from the village. She left nothing behind to suggest her whereabouts, she just disappeared.

She had spent the night at Taska's cottage. All night she was reading the parchments left on the table, recalling Taska's words, "They are for you." But Sophia never expected to find such an enlightened manuscript of ideas, so removed from the world, and so collective, all at once.

After reading the parchments, she felt as if she had escaped her complete immersion of the village, the council and the church. The more she reflected upon Taska's declarations, the more feelings of release welled up in her. Her soul had been reborn from last night's inferno. The parchments had healed her.

Sophia bundled some clothes into a sack. They were mostly blankets and an extra wool cape to keep her warm. She found a box of matches and a small lantern.

She rolled up the parchments carefully and tied them with a string. She knew this was her most important possession now. This was her future. It was her gift.

She walked around the cottage one last time. She looked at Cain's bed and his chaining post. The iron rings on the post would soon rust and fall away. She looked at Taska's bed, bigger in size. She looked at the dress that Taska hung on the door of the bedroom. The empty garment made Sophia grieve all over again. As she wept, she held one of Taska's work smocks. When her pain subsided, she found one of Taska's white bonnets. She packed it with some of her blankets.

It was Taska's beauty that made Sophia adore her. It was her freedom that beckoned Sophia's never-ending devotion to her, and now she would live her life as Taska had written upon the parchments.

Among Taska's words and phrases came her revelation of life. She asked for forgiveness for her escape, but explained how wonderful a life could be if it were free of deceit, lawlessness and fear, and filled with joy, comfort and truth. Taska's words would become Sophia new study — her new scriptures.

Sophia knew she had to leave. Soon, her father and the villagers would come looking for her. As she stood by the door, she looked at the old frame on the wall with the pressed red rose encased between the glass. It was so simple to the eye, the cup of the flower and the stem which hung down held a beautiful symmetry. The red color, slowly turning to brown with the years seemed to call to Sophia, leading her away from the center of her fear, anger and pain.

When she shut the door of the cottage, the dim light was illuminating the mountains. The sun still had not revealed itself to the world.

She passed the old, abandoned cottage in the woods. The air was bitter but somehow invigorating to her. As she past the church, she thought of the church bells that would ring for the congregation to meet, and bury what was left of the dead. Sophia looked up at the church spire. Never before had it seemed so odd and removed from her life. Instead of going into town, she went through the field behind the church and walked by Langston's cottage.

She looked around the cottage and saw no one inside. She walked around to the barn in the back and began her work. She bridled the old gray nag and tied her bundles to the saddle on the horse's back. She wouldn't ride until she couldn't bear to walk any further, giving the old beast a rest.

As the sun slowly came up, and the dim light began to illuminate the world, Sophia walked through the snowy field, toward the woods. The horse walked behind with an eager step. Behind her, the village still smoldered in white and gray smoke. She wept for her mother and father as she hurried away. Her father was now the head council member. He had admitted that Langston and Hillmond helped obtain illegal weapons to kill Lieutenant Thadium. They would hang for it. But she knew her father would never turn into a beast, as Emmit did over the years of his service. Her father would be fair and lawful.

When she reached the woods, she quickly found the first red marker hanging from a branch. Like the red rose pressed on the wall of Taska's cottage, this red marker was part of a family, part of a love and a bond that held more power than any council, any village or any religion.

Sophia didn't look back to the village. She kept her eyes

sharp and focused, looking for the next red marker. It would take her to a greater place.

Acknowledgement

All my life I've thinking, hearing and writing stories. I have been able to live by the words of one of my favorite writers Katherine Anne Porter who once said, "I will try to tell the truth, but the result will be fiction." And so it has been a big part of my life to live between the lines of fiction. As a dyslexic writer, it hasn't come easy, but it has come with grace, patience, and the kindness of so many people in my life.

I owe so much of my creative life to my family who has always supported my writing, creativity, and adventures. A special thanks to Ron and Ann for always being part of all things creative. It is with your confidence, vision, and trust that creativity and the heart to be an artist is made possible. For that I am eternally grateful. A special thanks to Cindy Samul for her kindness and patience. Her meticulous sense of art and compassion has been invaluable. A special thanks to Sanderson Tattersall for being there always for all these years like a brother.

There are a lot of teachers who inspired and pushed me as a writer. Tom Kelly for reading my pages in high school. Thanks for laughing at me when I didn't know I was being funny. It helped. Ted Hargrove and Doctor Medeiros deserve special thanks for seeing a writer, editor, and English major in an uncertain college student. Dr. Ducas and Hugh Blumenfeld for their patience and vision in terms of books and literature at Eastern. I still sit in silence with my students like Dr. Blumenfeld did with us. It is cathartic for me (worrisome for the students).

Coming out of college special thanks to Sean McKenna, Erin Sullivan, and Mary Cahill for their kindness and trust in me as a writer, as a person, and as an emerging teacher. To my extended family at Western Connecticut State University MFA in Creative and Professional Writing, I can't thank you all enough for your connections, time, and interconnected experience we shared as writers. A special thanks to Dr. Brian Clements who gave me every opportunity to be what I am now - a better writer and a better educator. Thank you to all the mentors that shared and gave so much of their writing life to shape mine. Don Snyder, Mark Sundeen, Paola Corso, Daniel Asa Rose, Tim Weed, and Cecilia Woloch. Andy Alexander for sharing your humble but important feedback. To my fellow writers who inspired me including Maeve Ewing, Fletcher Dean, Kirsten Genthner, and the imaginative David Hayes. Special to thank you to Melissa Shafner for her editorial acumen and her friendship.

And finally, to Jennifer for your love, dedication, and your belief in me. I am lost without you. Lana for your sense of humor and your awesome style, you remind me how important our gifts are every time you sing. And Emily, brave and thoughtful, I will always be there with you in your (saltwater) happy place.

Ron Samul is a writer and educator at Mitchell College in New London, Connecticut. He is a writing mentor in the Western Connecticut State University Masters in Creative and Professional Writing program.

Send your thoughts and feedback about the book using the email below. Feel free to write your good vibes and emotional atmosphere about the book on Amazon and Goodreads.

ronsamulwriter@gmail.com

Made in the USA
Las Vegas, NV
09 December 2023

82414596R00215